AT LAST COMES LOVE

This Large Print Book carries the
Seal of Approval of N.A.V.H.

AT LAST COMES LOVE

MARY BALOGH

THORNDIKE PRESS
A part of Gale, Cengage Learning

GALE
CENGAGE Learning

Detroit • New York • San Francisco • New Haven, Conn • Waterville, Maine • London

GALE
CENGAGE Learning

LIBRARY OF CONGRESS CATALOGING-IN-PUBLICATION DATA

Balogh, Mary.
   At last comes love / by Mary Balogh.
     p. cm.
   ISBN-13: 978-1-4104-1445-8 (hardcover : alk. paper)
   ISBN-10: 1-4104-1445-0 (hardcover : alk. paper)
   1. Large type books. I. Title.
PR6052.A465A92 2009
823'.914—dc22   2009004818

Published in 2009 by arrangement with The Bantam Dell Publishing Group, a division of Random House, Inc.

Printed in the United States of America
1 2 3 4 5 6 7 13 12 11 10 09

AT LAST COMES LOVE

1

When Duncan Pennethorne, Earl of Sheringford, returned to London after a five-year absence, he did not go immediately to Claverbrook House on Grosvenor Square, but instead took up a reluctant residence on Curzon Street with his mother, Lady Carling. Sir Graham, her second husband, was not delighted to see him, but he *was* fond of his wife so did not turn his stepson from his doors.

Claverbrook House was where Duncan must go sooner rather than later, though. His funds had been cut off, without warning and without explanation, at just a time when he was preparing to return home at last — home being Woodbine Park in Warwickshire, the house and estate where he had grown up and that had provided him with a comfortable income since his father's death fifteen years ago.

And he had not been going there alone.

The Harrises, who had been in his employ for the past five years in various capacities, were going with him — the position of head gardener had fallen vacant and Harris was to fill it. Most important of all, four-year-old Toby was going there too. He was to be known at Woodbine as the Harrises' orphaned grandson. Toby had been wildly excited when told that he would be living henceforward at the place about which Duncan had told him so many exciting stories — Duncan's memories of his boyhood there were almost exclusively happy ones.

But then, suddenly, all his plans had gone awry, and he had been forced to leave the child with the Harrises in Harrogate while he dashed off to London in the hope of averting disaster.

His only warning had come in a formal note written in the bold hand of his grandfather's secretary, though his grandfather's signature was scrawled at the foot of the page, unmistakable despite the fact that it had grown shaky and spidery with age. At the same time the steward at Woodbine Park had grown suddenly and ominously silent.

They had all known *where* to write to him, much of the need for secrecy having been lifted with Laura's death. Duncan had felt obliged to inform a number of people about that unhappy event.

It made little sense to Duncan that his grandfather would decide to cut him off just when a measure of respectability had been restored to his life. It made even less sense when he considered the fact that as the Marquess of Claverbrook's only grandson and only direct descendant, he was his heir.

But sense or nonsense, he was cut off, turned loose and penniless, with no means of supporting those who were dependent upon him — or himself for that matter. Not that he worried unduly about the Harrises. Good servants were always in demand. Or about himself. He was still young and able-bodied. But he *did* worry about Toby. How could he not?

Hence this desperate dash to London, which was perhaps the last place on earth he wanted to be — and in the middle of the Season, to boot. It had seemed the only course of action open to him. The letter he had written in reply to his grandfather's had been ignored, and already precious time had been lost. So he had been forced to come to demand an explanation in person. Or to *ask* for it, anyway. One did not demand anything of the Marquess of Claverbrook, who had never been known for the sweetness of his temper.

Duncan's mother did not have any re-assurance to offer. She had not even known he had been cut off until he told her so.

"I only wonder," she said when he went to her boudoir the morning after his arrival — or the early afternoon to be more precise, since mornings did not figure largely in her favorite times of the day — "that he did not cut you off five years ago, my love, if he was going to do it at all. We all *expected* that he would then. I was even toying with the idea of going to plead with him *not* to, but it struck me that by doing so I would quite possibly goad him into cutting you off even sooner than he planned. Perhaps he forgot until recently that you were still drawing on the rents of Woodbine. Not so harshly, Hetty — you will pull out every hair on my head and whatever will I do then?"

Her maid was vigorously brushing the tangles out of her hair.

But his grandfather was not renowned for a poor memory either, especially where money was concerned.

"Graham says he will not support your excesses for longer than a week at the outside," his mother added, returning her attention to her son as she arranged the flowing folds of her peignoir to show her figure to best advantage. "He told me so last evening after you arrived. But I would not worry about that, my love. I can wind Graham about my little finger whenever I choose."

"You need not do it on my account, Mama," Duncan assured her. "I will not be staying here for long, only until I have spoken with Grandpapa and settled something with him. He cannot intend to leave me quite out in the cold, can he?"

But he very much feared that it could indeed happen — that it already had, in fact. And it seemed his mother agreed with him.

"I would not wager more than ten guineas or so against it," she said, reaching for the rouge pot. "He is a stubborn, crotchety old man, and I am more than delighted that he is no longer my father-in-law and I do not have to pretend to dote upon him. Do hand me that rouge brush, if you please, my love. No, not that one — the other. Hetty, have I not told you repeatedly to set my things down so that they are within my reach while you are busy with my hair? You must believe that my arms are long enough to reach my ankles. How peculiar *that* would be."

Duncan left the room after handing his

11

mother the correct rouge brush. He could not decide between turning up unannounced at Claverbrook House on the one hand and writing to request an audience on the other — for that was what a familial visit to his grandfather amounted to. If he went in person, he might have to suffer the ignominy of being turned away by his grandfather's Friday-faced butler — if Forbes still held the post, that was. He must be nearly as ancient as his master. If he wrote, on the other hand, his letter might yellow with age before his grandfather's secretary deigned to give it any attention.

The pot or the kettle.

The devil or the deep blue sea.

Which was it to be?

And there was a degree of urgency to the situation that threatened to throw Duncan into a panic. He had settled the Harrises and Toby in a couple of cramped rooms in Harrogate and paid one month's rent. There was simply not enough money for another month. And one week of this one was gone already.

Even so, he procrastinated instead of making a decision and spent one whole day reacquainting himself with London — and London with him. Much as one set of instincts warned him to lie low, to avoid being seen if he possibly could, another part of him argued that since he could not avoid the company of his peers for all of the rest of his life without becoming a hermit, he might as well sally forth now with all the nonchalance he could muster.

He went to White's Club, where he still had a membership and where he did not find the doors barred against him. He met a number of former friends and acquaintances there, none of whom gave him the cut direct. On the contrary, a number of them hailed him with jovial familiarity, as if he had been there just last year or even last week and had never in his life dashed away from London and from society under a huge cloud of scandal. And if a few gentlemen ignored him, well, there was nothing so very unusual about that. One did not hail everyone one met, after all, at White's or anywhere else. Nobody made a scene and demanded that he be removed from the hallowed sanctum of the club.

He allowed himself to be borne off to Tattersall's with a group of equestrian enthusiasts to look over the horses, and then on to the races. He even acquired some modest winnings at the latter by the end of the afternoon, though they were far too modest to make any significant difference to his financial circumstances. In the evening he went to a card party, where he lost the afternoon's windfall before winning more than half of it back again.

He packaged up the money before going to bed and dispatched it the next morning to Harrogate. By now Toby was bound to have put his heel through a stocking or his knee through his breeches or his toe through his shoes or . . . Well, the possibilities were endless. Bringing up a child was a decidedly expensive undertaking.

On the second day the ticklish decision of how best to approach his grandfather was taken out of his hands. There was a note beside his plate at the breakfast table, written in the all-too-familiar hand of the secretary. It was a summons to appear before the Marquess of Claverbrook at one o'clock precisely. The old gentleman did not go out much these days, according to Duncan's mother, but obviously he did not miss much of what went on beyond his doors. He had heard that his grandson was back in town. He had even known where to find him.

And it was definitely a summons rather than an invitation — *at one o'clock precisely.*

Duncan dressed with care in a coat of blue superfine that was neat and elegant but not in the first stare of fashion. He had his valet tie his neckcloth in a smart yet simple knot. He wore a plain fob at his waist and pulled on well-polished Hessian boots over his gray pantaloons, but plain black ones rather than anything more flamboyant. He certainly did not want to give the impression that he lived extravagantly — which he did not.

"You do understand, Smith," he said to his man, "that I will be unable to pay you this week and perhaps will not be able to next week either — or the week after. You may wish to look about for other employment, and London is by far the best place to do it."

Smith, who had remained with him through thick and thin for eleven years — though never before in utter poverty — sniffed.

"I understand a great deal, m'lord," he said, "not having been born an imbecile. I will leave when I am good and ready to leave."

Which would not be immediately, Duncan gathered — a loyalty for which he was silently grateful.

He frowned at his image before leaving the room. He did not want to appear obsequious before his grandfather any more than he wished to look expensive, though of course he *was* desperate. He sighed inwardly, took his hat and cane from Smith's hands, and left the room and the house.

Forbes took Duncan's things when he arrived at Claverbrook House, scarcely sparing him a glance as he did so, and invited his lordship to follow him. Duncan followed, raising his eyebrows and pursing his lips at the butler's stiff back. It was probably a good thing he had not come yesterday, uninvited. He doubted he would have got past Forbes unless he had been prepared to wrestle him to the ground.

The Marquess of Claverbrook was in the drawing room, seated in a high-backed chair he had possessed forever, close to a roaring fire despite the fact that it was a warmish spring day. Heavy velvet curtains were half drawn across the windows to block most of the sunlight. The air was heavy with the smell of the ointment he used for his rheumatism.

Duncan made his bow.

"Sir," he said, "how do you do? I hope I find you well."

His grandfather, who had never been one to indulge in unnecessary chitchat, did not deign to deliver a health report. Neither did he greet his grandson or express any pleasure at seeing him again after so long. Nor

16

did he demand to know why he was back in London when he had fled from it five years ago under the blackest cloud of scandal and disgrace. He *knew* why, of course, as his opening words revealed.

"Give me one good reason," he said, his bushy white eyebrows almost meeting over the bridge of his nose, a sharply defined frown line between his brows the only feature that revealed where one ended and the other began, "just *one,* Sheringford, why I should continue to fund your excesses and debaucheries."

He held a silver-headed wooden cane in both gnarled hands and thumped it on the floor between his feet to give emphasis to his displeasure.

There was one perfectly good reason — even apart from the fact that really there had not been a great many of either excesses or debaucheries. But his grandfather knew nothing about Toby and never would, if Duncan had any say in the matter. Nor would anyone else.

"Because I am your only grandson, sir?" Duncan suggested. And lest that not be sufficient reason, as doubtless it was not, "And because I plan to live respectably for the rest of my life now that Laura is dead?"

She had been dead for four months. She

had taken a winter chill and just faded away — because, in Duncan's opinion, she had lost the will to live.

His grandfather's frown deepened, if that were possible, and he thumped the cane again.

"You dare mention *that name* in my hearing?" he asked rhetorically. "Mrs. Turner was dead to the world five years ago, Sheringford, when she chose to commit the unspeakable atrocity of running off with you, leaving her lawful husband behind."

It had happened on Duncan's twenty-fifth birthday — and, more to the point, on his wedding day. He had abandoned his bride, virtually at the altar, and run away with her sister-in-law, her brother's wife. Laura. The whole thing had been one of the most spectacular scandals London had seen in years, perhaps ever. At least, he assumed it had. He had not been here to experience it in person.

He said nothing since this was hardly the time or the place for a discussion on the meaning of the word *atrocity.*

"I ought to have turned you out then without a penny," his grandfather told him. He had not been invited to sit down, Duncan noticed. "But I allowed you to continue drawing on the rents and income of Woodbine Park so that you would have the where-withal to stay far away out of my sight — and out of the sight of all decent, respect-able people. But now the woman is gone, unmourned, and you may go to the devil for all I care. You promised solemnly on my seventieth birthday that you would marry by your thirtieth and have a son in your nursery before your thirty-first. You aban-doned Miss Turner at the altar five years ago, and you turned thirty six weeks ago."

Had he promised something so rash? Of course, he would have been a mere puppy at the time. Was *this* the explanation for the sudden cutting off of his funds? That his thirtieth birthday had come and gone and he was still a single man? He had been with Laura until four months ago, for the love of God. But not married to her, of course. Tur-ner had steadfastly refused to divorce her. His grandfather had expected him to find a bride within the past four months, then, and marry her just to honor a promise made many years ago — by a boy who knew noth-ing of life?

"There is still time to produce an heir before my thirty-first birthday," he pointed out — a rather asinine thing to say, as his grandfather's reaction demonstrated. He snorted. It was not a pleasant sound.

19

"Besides," Duncan continued, "I believe you must have misremembered the promise I made, sir. I seem to recall promising that I would marry before your eightieth birthday."

Which was . . . when? Next year? The year after?

"Which happens to be sixteen days from now," his grandfather said with brows of thunder again. "Where is your bride, Sheringford?"

Sixteen days? Damn it all!

Duncan strode across the room to the window in order to delay his answer, and stood looking down on the square, his hands clasped at his back. Could he pretend now that it was the eighty-*fifth* birthday he had named? He could not even remember the promise, for God's sake. And his grandfather might be making all this up just to discomfit him, just to give himself a valid excuse for cutting off his grandson from all funds. Woodbine Park, though a property belonging to the Marquess of Claverbrook, was traditionally granted to the heir as his home and main source of income. Duncan had always considered it his, by right of the fact that he was the heir after his father's death, even though he had not lived there for years. He had never taken Laura there.

"No answer," the marquess said after a lengthy silence, a nasty sneer in his voice. "I produced one son, who died at the age of forty-four when he had no more sense than to engage in a curricle race and try to overtake his opponent on a sharp bend in the road. And that one son produced one son of his own. *You.*"

It did not sound like a compliment.

"He did, sir," Duncan agreed. What else *was* there to say?

"Where did I go wrong?" his grandfather asked irritably and rhetorically. "My brother produced five lusty sons before he produced any of his daughters, and those five in their turn produced eleven lusty sons of their own, at least two each. And some of *them* have produced sons."

"And so, sir," Duncan said, seeing where this was leading, "there is no danger of the title falling into abeyance anytime soon, is there? There is no urgent hurry for me to get a son."

It was the wrong thing to say — though there probably *was* no right thing.

The cane thumped the floor again.

"I daresay the title will pass to Norman in the not-too-distant future," his grandfather said, "after my time and after yours, which will not last even as long as your father's if you continue with the low life you have chosen. I intend to treat him as though he were already my heir. I will grant him Woodbine Park on my eightieth birthday."

Duncan's back stiffened as if someone had delivered him a physical blow. He closed his eyes briefly. This was the final straw. It was bad enough — nothing short of a disaster, in fact — that Woodbine and its rents were being withheld from *him.* But to think of *Cousin Norman,* of all people, benefiting from his loss . . . Well, it was a viciously low blow.

"Norman has a wife and two sons," the marquess told him. "As well as a daughter. Now, *there* is a man who knows his duty."

Yes, indeed.

Both Norman's father and his grandfather were dead. He was the next heir after Duncan. He also had a shrewd head on his shoulders. He had married Caroline Turner six weeks after Duncan abandoned her on their wedding day, and he had apparently got three children off her, two of them sons. He had taken all the right steps to ingratiate himself with his great-uncle.

Duncan frowned down at the empty square beyond the window. Though it was not quite empty. A maid was down on her hands and knees scrubbing the steps of a

22

house on the opposite side.

Did Norman *know* that Woodbine was to all intents and purposes to be his in sixteen days' time?

"If I had written down that promise I made on your seventieth birthday, sir," Duncan said, "and if you had kept it, I believe you would discover now that my promise really was to marry by your eightieth birthday rather than my thirtieth, though they both fall in the same year, of course."

His grandfather snorted again — a sound that conveyed utter contempt.

"And what do you plan to do when you leave here in a few minutes' time, Sheringford?" he asked. "Grab the first female you meet on the street and drag her off in pursuit of a special license?"

Something like that. When one had been brought up to be a well-to-do gentleman, to administer land, to expect to inherit an illustrious title and fabulous wealth one day, one was not educated or trained to any other form of gainful employment. Not any that would give him sufficient income to support dependents, including a child, as well as keep his own body and soul together, anyway.

"Not at all." Duncan turned to look steadily at his grandfather. "I have a bride

23

picked out, sir. We are already unofficially betrothed, in fact, even though there has been no public announcement yet."

"Indeed?" There was a world of scorn in the one word. His grandfather raised his eyebrows and looked incredulous — as well he might. "And who *is* this lady, pray?"

"She has sworn me to secrecy," Duncan said, "until she is ready for the announcement to be made."

"Ha! Convenient indeed!" his grandfather exclaimed, his brows snapping together again. "It is a barefaced lie, Sheringford, just like everything else in your miserable life. There is no such person, no such betrothal, no such impending marriage. Take yourself out of my sight."

"But if there *is?*" Duncan asked him, standing his ground though he had the feeling he might as well be standing on quicksand. "What if there *is* such a lady, sir, and she has agreed to marry me on the assumption that I have security to offer her, that we will live at Woodbine Park and finance our marriage and our family on its rents and income?"

His grandfather glared at him with no diminution of either anger or scorn.

"If there *is* such a lady," he said, almost spitting out the words, "and *if* she is undisputedly an eligible bride for the Earl of Sheringford and future Marquess of Claverbrook, and *if* you present her to me here the day before the papers announce your betrothal, and *if* you marry her no later than one day before my birthday, then Woodbine Park will be yours again on that day. That is a formidable number of *ifs,* Sheringford. If you fail in any one of them, as I have no doubt you will, then Woodbine Park will be your cousin's on my birthday."

Duncan inclined his head.

"I believe," his grandfather said, "Norman and his lady may safely continue packing up their belongings ready for the move."

Continue? Norman *did* know, then?

"They would be well advised not to, sir," Duncan said.

"I will not invite you to stay for refreshments," his grandfather said, his eyes raking over his grandson with contempt. "You are going to need every hour of the next fifteen days in which to find a bride — a *respectable* bride — and persuade her to marry you."

Duncan made him another bow.

"I shall explain the necessity for haste to my betrothed without further delay, then," he said, and heard his grandfather snort one more time as he let himself out of the room and proceeded down the stairs to retrieve his hat and cane.

This was one devil of a nasty coil.

How the deuce was he to find a bride and marry her all within fifteen days? And a respectable lady of good *ton* to boot — his grandfather, he knew, would accept no less. No respectable lady would touch him with a twenty-foot oar — not once she knew his infamous story, anyway. And soon enough the fact that he was back would spread all over London — even if it had not already done so.

Besides all of which, he had no wish *whatsoever* to marry. He had only recently been freed from a lengthy connection that he had found tiresome, to say the least — though poor Laura had *not* gone unmourned. He wanted to enjoy his newfound freedom alone, at least for a few years. Besides, and far more important, there was a purely practical reason why a wife would be a severe encumbrance. No respectable lady would tolerate the presence of an illegitimate child in her home — or even a strong attachment between her husband and his gardener's presumably legitimate grandson. And how would he ever be able to mask that attachment?

It was unthinkable.

Besides, Toby, however well he had been coached, would not remember all the time to call him *sir* or *my lord* instead of *Papa*.

Damn it all!

But marry he must. He needed Woodbine. He needed his home and his roots. It was true, of course, that eventually he would inherit all his grandfather's properties and vast fortune, *including* Woodbine Park, which was entailed and could not be given as an outright gift to Norman or anyone else. His grandfather could do nothing to prevent any of that happening beyond outliving him. But the trouble was, Duncan could not afford to wait for his grandfather's demise, which might be many years in the future. Besides, he could not under any circumstances wish for the old man's death. Far from it.

He needed Woodbine *now*.

He had a sudden image of Norman as lord of the manor there — with Caroline as its lady. And their children roaring through the house and romping in the park instead of Toby. It was a painful image. Woodbine was *his home*.

Marriage really was the only option open to him, then. But there was no time in which to choose a bride with any care to make sure he had picked someone who would not drive him to distraction within a fortnight — or, to be fair, someone *he* would not drive to distraction. There was only time to grab whomever he could find. *If* there was time even for that. He could hardly walk up to the first lady he saw at the first ball he attended and ask her to marry him. Could he? And even *if* he did, and *if* for some strangely peculiar reason she said yes, he would still have her family to persuade.

It simply could not be done.

Except that failure was not an option.

She would have to be someone very young and biddable. Someone whose parents would be only too glad to bag a future marquess for their daughter, scandalous reputation be damned. Some cit's daughter, perhaps — no, she would not be acceptable to his grandfather. Some impoverished gentleman's daughter, then. Someone plain of face and figure.

Duncan felt himself break out in a cold sweat as he stepped out onto the square.

Or someone . . .

But of course, it *was* spring, was it not? The time of the Season in London? The time of the great marriage mart, when ladies came to town with the express purpose of finding themselves a husband? And notoriety aside, he was the Earl of Sheringford, even if it *was* just a courtesy title and essentially meaningless in itself. He was also the heir to a marquess's very real title and properties and fortune — and the incumbent was eighty years old, or would be in sixteen days' time.

His case was not hopeless at all. It was a little desperate, it was true — he had only fifteen days. But that ought to be sufficient time. It was getting close to the end of the Season. There must be a number of girls — and their parents — who were growing uneasy, even a little desperate, at the absence of a suitor.

As he strode out of the square, Duncan found himself feeling grimly optimistic. He would hold his grandfather to his promise and get Woodbine Park back. He *had* to. He would somehow have to fit marriage in with his other plans.

The thought brought out the cold sweat again.

There must be entertainments galore to choose among. His mother would get him invitations to any he wished to attend — *if* he needed an invitation. As he remembered it, most ladies were only too eager to entice enough guests to their homes that they could boast the next day of having hosted a squeeze. They were not going to turn away a titled gentleman, even if he *had* run off with a married lady five years ago — on his wedding day to someone else.

A ball would be his best choice. He would attend the very next one — this evening, if there happened to be one.

He had fifteen days in which to meet, court, betroth himself to, and marry a lady of *ton*. It was certainly not impossible. It was an interesting challenge, in fact.

He strode off in the direction of Curzon Street. With any luck his mother would still be at home. She would know what entertainments there were to choose among during the next few days.

2

Margaret Huxtable was thirty years old. It was not a comfortable age to be, especially since she was not married and never had been. She had been betrothed once upon a time — or, to be more accurate, she had had a secret understanding with a man who would have married her immediately, if she had not taken on the responsibility of holding together her family of two sisters and a brother after their father's death until they were all grown up and could take care of themselves. Crispin Dew, eldest son of Sir Humphrey Dew, had set his heart upon purchasing a military commission and taking Margaret with him to follow the drum. She would not give up her duty, though, and he would not give up his dream, so he had gone off to war without her, promising to return for her when she was free.

They had been very deeply in love.

Before that time came, though, he had

married a Spanish lady while he was fighting in Spain with his regiment in the Peninsular Wars against the forces of Napoleon Bonaparte. Margaret had fought quietly for several years afterward to put back the pieces of her heart and find some new meaning in life. Her family was not enough, she had found, much as she loved them. Besides, they did not need her any longer. Vanessa — Nessie — was now married to the Duke of Moreland, Katherine — Kate — to Baron Montford, and both were love matches. Stephen, the youngest, was now twenty-two years old and was very much in command of his life. At the age of seventeen he had unexpectedly inherited the title of Earl of Merton, and in the intervening years he had grown comfortably into his new role as an aristocrat in possession of several properties and a large fortune. He was handsome and good-natured. He was popular with other gentleman and a great favorite with the ladies. Within the next few years he would almost certainly turn his thoughts to matrimony.

When that time came, when he married, Margaret would be displaced as lady of the manor at Warren Hall, Stephen's principal country seat. His wife would take her place. She would become simply a dependent spinster sister. It was a prospect that filled her with dread — and it was one of the things that had led her to the decision she had made over the winter.

She was going to marry.

There *were* other reasons. The arrival of her thirtieth birthday had been a dreaded milestone in her life. No one could even pretend now that she was not a spinster. Her chances of marrying would grow slimmer with every passing year. So would her chances of being a mother.

She wanted to marry. And she wanted to have children. She had always wanted both, but all her youth had been devoted to the upbringing of her brother and sisters, and all her youthful ardor had been expended upon Crispin Dew. He had been her first, and only, love.

He was back in England — as a widower. He was at Rundle Park in Shropshire with his parents. So was his young daughter. And Lady Dew, who had never known of the secret understanding between Margaret and her son, had written to Margaret with the news, and gone on to say that Crispin had asked about her and about her marital status. Lady Dew had reminded Margaret of how exceedingly fond of each other they had been as children. Perhaps, she had suggested in her letter, Margaret would consider coming to stay at Rundle Park for a while. Perhaps the two former childhood friends would discover deeper feelings for each other now that they were both grown up and free of other obligations. Crispin, she added, very much hoped Margaret would accept the invitation.

The letter had upset Margaret. She was very fond of Lady Dew, their former neighbor, who was unfailingly good-natured. But the lady did have a tendency to embellish the stories she told. Had Crispin *really* asked about her — *and her marital status?* Had he *really* expressed a hope that she would come to Rundle Park? Did he *really* expect to rekindle the feelings they had shared in the past? Because his wife was now dead? Because he had a daughter to raise and needed a mother for the girl?

She *hoped* the story was embellished. Crispin had hurt and disappointed her enough when he had betrayed her and married someone else. She would think even worse of him if she discovered now that he believed he could come back home and crook a finger her way and she would run right back into his arms.

She would marry, she decided — but not Crispin Dew, even if he was prepared to court her again. She would show him that she had not been pining for him and waiting around all these years in the hope that he would come back to her.

The very idea!

She knew whom she *would* marry.

The Marquess of Allingham had proposed marriage to her three times over the past five years. She had refused each time, but the connection between them had never been broken, since it was based upon friendship. Margaret liked him and knew that he liked her. They were comfortable together. Neither of them ever had to search for a topic of conversation. Sometimes they could even be silent together without feeling discomfort. The marquess, a distinguished-looking gentleman, was perhaps eight or nine years older than she and had been married before.

Only one thing had held her back from accepting him. She was not in love with him. She had never felt for him that surge of exhilaration and magic she had once felt for Crispin, and he did not fulfill any of the secret dreams of romance and passion she had clung to over the years. But she was being very foolish, she had decided over the winter. Romantic love had brought her nothing but heartache. It would be far more sensible to marry a friend.

She had said no each time the marquess had asked. However, on the third occasion — at the end of the Season last year — she had hesitated first and he had seen it. He had taken her hand in his, raised it to his lips, and told her he would not press the issue this year and cause her any distress. They would meet again next year, he had promised, and they would still be friends, he hoped.

He had all but promised to ask her again. By her hesitation, she had all but promised to say yes next time.

And she *would* say yes.

She was going to be married before she turned thirty-one. She felt comfortable, even happy, with her decision. She no longer loved Crispin Dew and had not for a number of years. But being married to the Marquess of Allingham would finally close the book on any lingering attachment to that youthful fancy. She was only sorry she had not accepted him before now. But perhaps it was as well she had not. She had needed to feel quite ready, and now she did.

So Margaret went to London at the end of May, rather later in the Season than she had intended, as certain local commitments had kept her busy at Warren Hall. Stephen was already in town. So were Vanessa and Elliott and their two children, and Katherine and Jasper and their one. Just the thought of seeing all her family again, including the children, buoyed her spirits. But beneath it all, she felt a glow of happy anticipation in knowing that at last she would begin her own independent life by marrying and starting a family.

She could scarcely wait to see the marquess again.

She spent the first few days after her arrival visiting her family and going shopping and walking with her sisters. The first entertainment she planned to attend was Lady Tindell's ball, always a well-attended event. She felt rather like a girl anticipating her very first ball. Every hour she changed her mind about what she would wear and how she would have her maid dress her hair.

She wanted to look her very best.

The day before the ball she went walking in Hyde Park with her sisters. It was the fashionable hour of the afternoon, and it was a fine day after three days of almost steady drizzle. The carriage paths were packed almost axle to axle with fashionable carriages of various descriptions. Riders on horseback wove their way among them whenever they could find passage. Pedestrians ambled in a dense, slow-moving crowd along the footpaths. No one was in a hurry. This was not the route one would take if one wished to get anywhere fast. One came into the park during the afternoon in order to observe the beau monde and exchange greetings and gossip with friends and acquaintances. One came to see and be seen.

"After all," Vanessa said gaily as they strolled among the throng, "I did not spend half of Elliott's fortune on this bonnet in order to hurry along a deserted back street."

"And very fetching it is too," Katherine said. "Meg and I must be content to bask in your reflected glory, Nessie."

They all laughed.

And then Margaret felt her own smile drain away, and with it half the blood in her head. One horseman, a military officer who was riding with a group of others, all looking very dashing in their scarlet regimentals, had stopped a few yards ahead of them and was looking intently at them, first in astonishment and then in open delight. A smile lit his face as he swept off his shako and made them a bow.

Crispin Dew!

"Meg!" he exclaimed. "And Nessie. And *little Kate?* Is it possible?"

Margaret curled her gloved fingers very

tightly into her palms at her sides and concentrated hard upon not fainting, while her sisters exclaimed at the sight of him. He swung down from the saddle and came striding toward them, parting the crowd, one of his hands holding the bridle of his horse.

Oh, *why* had she not been warned of this? Why had no one *told* her?

"Crispin!" Vanessa cried, and she stepped forward to hug him. She had once been married to Hedley Dew, his brother, until Hedley died of consumption.

Katherine inclined her head and curtsied. "Crispin," she said, her voice cool and polite.

His eyes came to rest again on Margaret, and he held out both hands for hers.

"Meg," he said, his smile softening. "Oh, Meg, how have you contrived to grow even more beautiful over the years? How many years has it been anyway?"

She kept her hands at her sides.

"Twelve," she said, and then wished she had not shown such an exact awareness of how long it had been since that afternoon when they had said good-bye. When she had promised to wait and he had promised to come back. When the very air had throbbed with their passion and grief. When she had thought her heart would surely break.

He was even more handsome now. His reddish hair had darkened a shade or two, and his fair complexion had weathered. He looked broader and more rugged. There was a white scar just above his right eyebrow that slanted across his forehead to disappear into his hairline. It made him look curiously attractive.

"Can it possibly be that long?" he asked, returning his arms to his sides.

He looked back at his fellow officers, who had also stopped though they were being jostled by the crowds.

"These three lovely ladies were neighbors and dear friends when I was growing up," Crispin called to them. "I will walk with them for a while if they will permit it. You fellows go on without me."

These three lovely ladies. What foolishly flattering words.

They were given no choice since he did not actually ask their permission. Vanessa looked slightly uncomfortable now, and Katherine looked almost morose. They knew, of course, about the secret betrothal and Crispin's betrayal of it, though Margaret had never talked of it.

Margaret's mind was in turmoil as Crispin turned to walk and make polite conversation with them. He had heard of Nessie's second marriage, of course, and told her he was delighted by it. She had been a wonderful wife to Hedley and deserved to be happy again, he said. His mother had told him about Kate's marriage to Lord Montford. He was delighted by that too and hoped to meet the gentleman soon.

But it was impossible to walk for long in a group of four. Soon Vanessa and Katherine were detained by a mutual acquaintance, and Margaret found herself walking alone at his side.

She was finding it difficult to breathe — and she was alarmed and annoyed by her own discomposure. This was *Crispin Dew,* who had married a Spanish lady and fathered a daughter after promising to return to *her.* Crispin, whom she had loved with her whole heart — and trusted with her love and her future.

"Well, Meg," he said, his eyes warm with admiration, "you are greatly to be commended. You remained faithful to your promise to your father. You stayed with your sisters and Stephen until they grew up, and did a very good job of raising them all. But you never did marry, did you?"

As if marriage were no longer possible for her.

She did not answer him. She pretended to be distracted by the crowd.

"I am *glad* you did not marry," he said, lowering his voice. "Why would you not come to Rundle Park when I joined my voice to Mama's to invite you there?"

Ah. So he *had* known what Lady Dew had written to her. He *had* endorsed it. She thought the less of him — if there were less to think.

"I had other commitments," she said.

"And they were too important," he said, "to postpone in order to visit an old friend who longed to see you again? But no matter. I have come to town and have met you here instead. I expect to be here for a month or two. I will give you my company whenever I have the time while I am here, Meg. It will be a pleasure. You are still amazingly lovely."

Would it *not* be a pleasure if her looks had faded?

I will give you my company whenever I have the time . . .

What exactly did he mean by that? He was not asking for her company. He was not even offering her his. He was *granting* it to her as if it were some precious gift. As if she might be all alone and lonely without it. As if she were past the age when she might expect any but her family members or an old friend to take any notice of her. As if she ought to be grateful that he would find time for her in his busy life.

. . . whenever I have the time.

As if he were prepared to fit her in whenever he had nothing better to do.

She was suddenly angry.

She hated him with a passion.

All the pent-up fury of years pulsed through her.

You are still amazingly lovely.

How . . . oh, how *condescending!*

"That is remarkably kind of you, Crispin," she said, trying to keep the edge out of her voice, "but it will be quite unnecessary."

"Oh, it will be no trouble," he assured her. "I would never have it said that I would not show all the gallantry that is in my power to a lady who was once such a dear friend of mine. And still is, I hope. And always will be?"

. . . a dear friend . . .

He looked down at her, his eyebrows raised in inquiry.

She was unaccustomed to feeling raw fury. She had no idea how to deal with it, how to remain prudent until she could bring it under control. So she spoke very unwisely.

"You misunderstand, Crispin," she said.

"It is quite unnecessary to extend a hand of charity my way. My fiancé might not like it."

She heard the words come from her mouth as if someone else was speaking them. And suddenly she wished that someone else *was.* Whatever had she been goaded into saying so prematurely?

"Your *fiancé?*" he asked her, all astonishment. "You are *betrothed,* Margaret?"

"Yes," she said with fierce satisfaction, "though no announcement has yet been made."

"But who is the fortunate gentleman?" he asked her. "Would he be someone I know?"

"Almost certainly not," she said, evading his first question.

He had stopped walking. "When will I meet him?" he asked her.

"I do not know," she said.

"At Lady Tindell's ball tonight?" he asked.

"Perhaps," she said, feeling horribly trapped.

"I was not at all sure I would attend that particular ball," he said. "But now nothing could stop me. I shall come and meet this gentleman, Margaret, and see if he is worthy of you. If he is not, I shall challenge him to pistols at dawn and then throw you across my saddle bow and ride off into the sunset

44

with you — or perhaps into the darkness of midnight."

He grinned at her, and she was smitten by a sense of familiarity. It was the sort of thing he would have said to her when they were very young — and she would have responded in kind until they were both helpless with laughter.

She bit her lip.

If the Marquess of Allingham was at the ball tonight — and she had counted upon his being there — would Crispin demand an introduction and say something about their engagement?

She would positively die of embarrassment.

She did not know for certain, of course, that the marquess would be at the ball. Indeed, she was not even quite certain he was in town, though he surely would be since he took seriously his role as a member of the House of Lords, and Parliament was in session. Perhaps she should stay away from the ball herself. But she had been so looking forward to going and seeing the marquess again.

Besides, why should she stay at home and postpone seeing him just because Crispin was going to be there — and because anger had goaded her into telling a lie, or a very premature truth, anyway?

"You must say nothing about my betrothal, Crispin," she said. "I ought not to have mentioned it. Even my sisters do not know of it yet."

"Then I am privileged indeed." He took her right hand in his and turned it in order to set his lips briefly against the pulse at her wrist. "My lips are sealed. Ah, Meg, it is so very good to see you again. It has been far too long. And I have come too late as well, alas."

"Twelve years too late," she said, and swallowed awkwardly. She could feel the imprint of his lips like a brand across her wrist.

It *was* too late. She could feel only a pained hostility toward him. Surely he could have shown some embarrassment, some shame, some sign that he remembered how dishonorably he had treated her. He had not even *written* to her. She had found out about his marriage quite by chance.

Vanessa and Katherine had finished their conversation and caught up with them at last. Vanessa asked Crispin about his daughter, who was still living at Rundle Park with her grandparents.

"They are coming to town," he said, "since I cannot do without my little Maria for too long. They should be here any day."

46

Katherine took Margaret's arm and squeezed it in silent sympathy.

Margaret smiled at her.

Her head was throbbing. If she had known that he was coming to London, she would have stayed at Warren Hall. She would not even have hesitated. It was too late now, though.

Would the Marquess of Allingham propose marriage to her tonight, when it would be their first meeting since last year — *if* he attended the ball, that was? It seemed highly unlikely that he would declare himself so soon. Surely he would wait until their third or fourth meeting, and even then he might be cautious since she had already refused him three times.

Oh, everything felt ruined. She would feel somehow manipulative if she encouraged his suit — although she had intended to do so even before this afternoon. She would feel as if she were trying to force him to propose marriage to her simply so that she would not lose face with a former faithless lover.

It was not that way at all!

What did she care for Crispin Dew? She cared for the kindly, courtly man she had decided to marry.

"Oh, Meg," Katherine said. "How very

distressing this must be for you. I wish we had known he was in town so that we could at least have warned you."

"I am not distressed at all," Margaret said. "I have been walking quietly at your side because I am having an inner debate with myself about which gown I will wear tonight for my first ball since last year. It is a very serious decision, you must understand. I wish to cut the very best possible dash. The gold, do you think?"

Katherine sighed theatrically.

"Nessie's new bonnet this afternoon and your gold gown tonight," she said. "I shall be quite overshadowed by the splendor of my sisters."

They looked at each other and laughed.

Katherine was the loveliest of them all with her tall, slender figure and golden brown hair. If she wore a sack to the ball tonight, she would turn more than her fair share of appreciative heads.

Crispin was turning to take his leave of them. Margaret smiled and nodded to him and felt a queasiness in her stomach again.

He was going to be at the ball tonight — with the express purpose of meeting her betrothed.

Lies were never worth telling, were they? And that was a massive understatement.

3

Margaret wore her gold gown to Lady Tindell's ball. She had bought it at the end of last Season, a foolish extravagance, she had thought at the time, as she had had no opportunity to wear it before returning to Warren Hall for the summer. But she had loved it from the moment she saw it, ready-made and ready to purchase and her exact size — though she had been a little afraid it was too revealing at the bosom. Both Vanessa and Katherine, who had been with her at the time, had assured her that it was not, that since she *had* a bosom she might as well show it to best advantage. It was an argument that was not necessarily reassuring, but Margaret had bought the gown anyway.

She felt young and attractive in it now. She was not really young, of course. But was she still a little attractive? Modesty said no, but her glass assured her that what beauty she had been blessed with had not altogether faded yet. And she had never lacked for partners at any of the balls she had attended during the past few years.

She had attracted the Marquess of Allingham, had she not? And he was without a doubt one of the most eligible matrimonial catches in England.

Oh, she *hoped* he would be at the ball tonight.

And she hoped Crispin would change his mind and stay away. She really did not want to see him again.

The underdress of fine ivory-colored silk clung to her every curve, and the transparent gold overdress shimmered in the candlelight. It was a high-waisted gown cut daringly low at the bosom, its sleeves short and puffed above her long gold gloves, which matched her dancing slippers.

She almost lost her courage before leaving her dressing room. At her age she should surely be wearing far more sober and decorous gowns. But before she could give serious thought to changing into something else, there was a tap on the door, and when her maid opened it, Stephen poked his head inside.

"Oh, I say, Meg!" he exclaimed, his eyes moving over her with open appreciation.

"You look quite stunning, if I may say so. People will think I am escorting my younger sister. I am going to be the envy of every gentleman in the ballroom when I enter it with you on my arm."

"Thank you, sir." She laughed at his absurdity and made him an elaborate curtsy. "And I am going to be the envy of every lady. Perhaps we ought to remain at home and save everyone all the heartache."

Stephen had been extraordinarily good-looking even as a boy, with his tall, slender frame, unruly blond curls, blue eyes, and open, good-humored face. But now, at the age of twenty-two, he had grown into his height with a careless sort of grace, his curls had been tamed somewhat by an expert barber, and his features had taken on maturity and a vivid handsomeness. Margaret was biased, of course, but she saw the way he turned female heads wherever he went. And it was not just his title and wealth that did it, though she supposed they did not hurt.

"Better not." He pushed the door wider, made her an elegant bow to match her curtsy, grinned at her, and offered his arm. "Are you ready to go? I would not deprive the male world of your company."

"Well, there *is* that." She smiled at her

maid, wrapped her silk shawl about her shoulders, picked up her fan, and took his arm.

They arrived at the Tindell mansion half an hour later and had to wait only five minutes before their carriage took its place at the end of the red carpet and Stephen handed Margaret out. She gave her shawl to a footman inside the hall and ascended the stairs toward the receiving line and the ballroom on Stephen's arm. And if they were attracting admiring glances — and they surely were — she was free to believe that some were intended for her, even though most were undoubtedly for Stephen.

She felt as excited as if she were attending her first London ball. Excited — and apprehensive too.

She fanned her cheeks after they had passed along the receiving line. A quick glance about the ballroom revealed the fact that neither the Marquess of Allingham nor Crispin Dew had arrived yet. It was early of course. But her sisters were both there. They were standing together at the far side of the ballroom with Elliott and Jasper.

She and Stephen crossed the room, nodding to acquaintances as they went and stopping a few times to exchange verbal greetings.

They both hugged their sisters, and Stephen shook hands with their brothers-in-law.

"Stephen," Katherine said, "I absolutely insist that you dance the Roger de Coverley with me later in the evening. No one dances the steps better, which I am delighted to say, since I was the one who taught them to you when you were fifteen. Besides, you are looking quite deliciously gorgeous, and I have a strict rule that I will dance only with the most handsome gentlemen."

"That is a relief to hear," Jasper said, "since you have already promised to dance every waltz with me, Katherine. But poor Elliott will be afraid to ask to dance with you now lest you say no."

"My knees are already knocking," Elliott said.

They all laughed.

"I must beg you to grant me the opening set, Meg," Jasper said, "Con having already solicited Katherine's hand for it."

"*Constantine* is here?" Margaret asked, looking about eagerly. And there he was some distance away with a group of gentlemen. She caught his eye, and they both smiled and raised a hand in greeting. "He has not called on me at Merton House yet. I shall scold him for gross neglect as soon as we come face to face."

Constantine Huxtable was their second cousin. He would have inherited the Merton title instead of Stephen if his mother and father had married even one day before his birth instead of two days after. Those two days had cost Constantine his birthright, and Margaret had often marveled over the fact that he did not appear to hate Stephen — or Stephen's sisters either, though there *was* a coolness between him and Vanessa. He and Elliott — the Duke of Moreland — were estranged by a long-standing quarrel over something Margaret knew nothing about, and Vanessa, naturally enough, had taken her husband's side. It was a pity. Constantine and Elliott looked more like brothers than cousins, with the dark Greek good looks they had inherited from their mothers. Families ought not to quarrel.

When the lines began to form for the opening set, Jasper — Baron Montford — led Margaret out to join them. She loved the country and often told herself that she would be perfectly happy if she never had to leave it for the busy frivolity of life in town. But there was something undeniably alluring about the London Season. It felt wonderful to be in a London ballroom once more, surrounded by the flower of the *ton,* their jewels sparkling and glittering in the light of the hundreds of candles fixed in two great chandeliers overhead and in dozens of wall sconces. The wooden floor gleamed beneath her feet, and large pots of flowers and greenery provided a feast for the eyes and filled the air with their fragrances.

There was still no sign of the Marquess of Allingham.

Nor, to her relief, of Crispin Dew.

The music began, and Margaret curtsied with the line of ladies to a bowing Jasper in the line of gentlemen and gave herself up to the enjoyment of the intricate figures of the dance. She always loved the sound of the violins and the rhythmic thumping of the dancers' feet.

But halfway through the set she was distracted by the sight of a swath of scarlet at the ballroom doors and saw that it was Crispin arriving with two of the officers with whom he had been riding yesterday. Her heart fluttered uncomfortably and sank in the direction of her slippers.

There went her peace.

The three of them were causing a noticeable stir among those who were not dancing.

He looked about until his eyes found Margaret, and then he smiled. She might have pretended that she had not seen him, she supposed, but that would be silly. She smiled in return and was very glad she was looking her best as she danced beneath one of the chandeliers and her gold gown sparkled. And then she felt annoyance at such a vain thought.

I will give you my company whenever I have the time . . .

There was *still* no sign of the marquess. He might not even be in London, of course. And even if he were, and even if he came later this evening . . .

"Oh!" she exclaimed suddenly, returning her attention to Jasper with a start as she trod heavily on his shoe. "I am so sorry. Do forgive me."

She had stumbled awkwardly too, and he had to grasp her arm until she had righted herself and picked up the steps of the dance again. It was very humiliating. A few of the dancers around them looked at her with concern.

"My fault entirely," Jasper assured her. "I only hope Katherine did not notice that I almost toppled her sister. But if you need someone to plant him a facer or worse, Meg, do feel free to call upon me at any time. It would give me the greatest pleasure.

I have not been embroiled in any good brawls lately. Marriage does that to a man, alas."

Margaret looked at him, startled. And it was no use pretending that she did not know what he meant. He had obviously seen Crispin too, and guessed from his uniform who he was. That meant that Katherine had told him the story. How embarrassing! She was thirty years old and a spinster because the only love of her life had abandoned her and married someone else. And all she had to do was see him again and she went stumbling over the feet of her dancing partner.

The pattern of the dance separated them for a while, but Margaret replied as soon as they came together again between the lines to circle each other back to back.

"That all happened *years* ago," she told him. "I have quite forgotten it."

Which was a remarkably ridiculous thing to say. *What* all happened years ago? he might well ask. And how would she even be able to refer to it if she had forgotten it? She had only made herself look more abject in her brother-in-law's eyes.

Oh, how she *hated* this! Where had the years gone? And how had she somehow been left behind? And *where* was the Marquess of Allingham when she most needed him? Whatever would she say to Crispin if he talked to her later and asked where her betrothed was? She was just going to have to tell the truth, that was all — that there was no such man, that there was no such betrothal. And she must not even add the face-saving words *not yet, anyway.* She would thereby risk humiliating herself further if for some reason the marquess was not in town this year.

And let her learn her lesson from this. She would *never* allow herself to be goaded into telling a lie again — even the smallest of white lies. Lies could only bring one grief.

And then suddenly, just before the set came to an end, there he was at last — the Marquess of Allingham, strolling through the ballroom doors, looking dearly familiar. He stopped to look about. He had not seen *her* yet, Margaret realized as she circled about Jasper again and returned to her line. But that did not matter. The important thing was that he was here — and looking very distinguished indeed in his black and white evening clothes. There was a natural stateliness of manner about him. He must have seen someone else he knew and moved purposefully in that direction.

The set came to an end and she rested

her hand on Jasper's sleeve.

"Thank you," she said, laughing. "I must be quite out of practice. I am all out of breath. But it was a delightful way to begin the evening."

"It was," he agreed. "For a few minutes I was assailed by the uncomfortable suspicion that all the other gentlemen in the ballroom were watching me. I thought perhaps I had put my dancing shoes on the wrong feet or that my neckcloth was askew. It was an enormous relief to discover that it was, in fact, *you* they were all watching. You look outstandingly lovely tonight, Meg, as I am sure your glass informed you before you left home."

Margaret laughed again. "But it is far more satisfying to hear it from a gentleman," she said, "even if he *is* prone to exaggeration."

Before they reached the place where Vanessa and Elliott were standing with Katherine, Margaret saw that they were about to pass close to the Marquess of Allingham. At the same moment he spotted her, and his face lit up with a warm smile as he stepped away from the group he had just joined.

"Miss Huxtable," he said, bowing to her. "What an unexpected pleasure. Montford?"

"My lord." She curtsied and stayed where she was while Jasper continued on his way after returning the greeting.

"You have come to town after all, then," the marquess said. "I concluded when I did not see you anywhere that perhaps you had decided to remain in the country this year."

"I was detained at Warren Hall until just a week ago," she explained. "But here I am at last to enjoy what is left of the Season. Lady Tindell must be very pleased. Her ball is extremely well attended, is it not?"

"It is a veritable squeeze," he said, "and therefore must be deemed a great success. May I compliment you on your appearance? You look lovelier than ever."

"Thank you," she said.

"I hope," he said, "you have a set of dances left to grant me. I arrived rather later than I would have liked, I am afraid."

"I do indeed," she told him.

"Shall we agree to the set after this next one, then?" he suggested.

"Yes." She smiled at him. "I shall look forward to it."

And perhaps another set later in the evening — a waltz, she hoped. He waltzed well.

It amazed her now that she had not accepted his offer last year. Even then she had known that she must marry, if she was not to remain a spinster for the rest of her life and be a burden upon Stephen and her sisters. And even then she had known that she could not possibly do better than marry the Marquess of Allingham, whom she liked exceedingly well.

"The next set has not even begun to form yet," he said, glancing beyond her. "There is plenty of time. Do come and meet her."

He took her by the elbow and turned her toward the group of people with whom he had been standing.

Her?

"My dear," he said to a pretty auburn-haired lady in green, "do you have an acquaintance with Miss Huxtable, sister of the Earl of Merton? She has been a friend of mine for a number of years. This is Miss Milfort, my affianced bride, Miss Huxtable, and her sister, Mrs. Yendle, and . . ."

Margaret did not hear the rest of the introductions.

. . . my affianced bride . . .

He was betrothed. To someone else.

For the moment the realization bounced off the outer layer of her consciousness and did not really penetrate — which was per-haps fortunate.

Margaret smiled — brightly and warmly

— and held out her right hand to Miss Milfort.

"Oh, this *is* a pleasure," she said. "I do wish you happy, though I daresay my wishes are unnecessary."

She smiled — very brightly and warmly — at Mrs. Yendle and the other members of the group and inclined her head affably to them.

"Miss Milfort and I met at the home of mutual friends at Christmas," the marquess was explaining. "And she made me the happiest of men just before Easter by accepting my hand. But you must have seen the notice of our engagement in the *Morning Post,* Miss Huxtable."

"I did not," she said, her smile still firmly in place. "I have been in the country until very recently. But I *heard* of it, of course, and I was delighted for you."

Another lie. Untruths had come easily to her tongue recently.

"The next set is forming," remarked a lady whose name Margaret had entirely missed, and the marquess extended a hand toward Miss Milfort.

With her peripheral vision Margaret became aware of a flash of scarlet off to her right. Without even turning her head to look she knew it was Crispin and that he was making his way toward her, perhaps to ask her to dance with him, perhaps to seek an introduction to the Marquess of Allingham, *who was betrothed to someone else.*

The ghastly truth rushed at her.

She was not engaged.

She was not about to be engaged.

She was thirty years old and horribly, irreparably single and unattached.

And she was going to have to admit it all to Crispin, who had believed that she *needed* his gallantry since no other man could possibly want to offer her his company. Her stomach clenched with distress and incipient queasiness.

She could not bear to face him just yet. She really could not. She might well cast herself, weeping, into his arms.

She needed time to compose herself.

She needed to be alone.

She needed . . .

She turned blindly in the direction of the ballroom doors and the relative privacy of the ladies' withdrawing room beyond. She did not even take the time to skirt the perimeter of the room but hurried across it, thankful that enough dancers had gathered there to prevent her from looking too conspicuous.

She felt horribly conspicuous anyway. She

remembered to smile.

As she approached the doors, she glanced back over her shoulder to see if Crispin was coming after her. She was in a ridiculous panic. Even *she* knew it was ridiculous, but the trouble with panic was that it was beyond one's power to control.

She turned her head to face the front again, but she did so too late to stop herself from plowing into a gentleman who was standing before the doors, blocking the way.

She felt for a moment as if all the breath had been knocked from her body. And then she felt a horrible embarrassment to add to her confusion and panic. She was pressed against a very solid male body from shoulders to knees, and she was being held in place there by two hands that gripped her upper arms like a vise.

"I am so sorry," she said, tipping back her head and pushing her hands against his broad chest in a vain effort to put some distance between them so that she could step around him and hurry on her way.

She found herself gazing up into very black eyes set in a harsh, narrow, angular, dark-hued face — an almost ugly face framed by hair as dark as his eyes.

"Excuse me," she said when his grip on her arms did not loosen.

"Why?" he asked her, his eyes roaming boldly over her face. "What is your hurry? Why not stay and dance with me? And then marry me and live happily ever after with me?"

Margaret was startled out of her panic.

His breath smelled of liquor.

There had been no ball the evening after Duncan's interview with his grandfather. Not one single one. London positively teemed with lavish entertainments every day and night of the Season, but for that one infernal evening there had been nothing to choose among except a soiree that was being hosted by a lady who was a notable bluestocking and that would doubtless be attended by politicians and scholars and poets and intelligent ladies, and a concert with a program clearly designed for the musically discerning and not for anyone who happened to be shopping in a hurry at the marriage mart.

Duncan had not attended either but had been forced to waste one of his precious fifteen days. He had gone to Jackson's Boxing Salon yesterday afternoon when he might, he thought too late, have joined the afternoon promenade in Hyde Park to look over the crop of prospective brides. And today, when he *had* thought of going there, rain had been spitting intermittently from low gray clouds, and all he met were a few hardy fellow riders — all male — and one closed carriage filled with dowagers.

He had been reminded of those dreams in which one tried to run but found it impossible to move even as fast as a crawl.

But tonight there was Lady Tindell's ball to attend, and it was a promising event. According to his mother, who planned to be there, it was always one of the grand squeezes of the Season since Lady Tindell was renowned for her lavish suppers. Everyone who was anyone would be there, including, Duncan fervently hoped, armies of young, marriageable hopefuls who were running out of time in the Season to find husbands.

It was enough to make him feel positively ill.

He had not told his mother about his grandfather's ultimatum though he might have to enlist her help if he found himself unable to come up with a bride on his own within the next few days. His mother knew everybody. She would be sure to know which girls — and, more important, which parents — were desperate enough to take a man of such notorious reputation in such indecent haste.

He arrived late. It was perhaps not a wise thing to do when time was of the very essence, but earlier in the evening he had acquired cold feet — the almost inevitable consequence of having been forced to wait more than twenty-four hours to begin implementing his search — and had stayed at White's long after he had finished his dinner and his companions had left to go about their evening business, some of them to attend this very ball. He might have come with them and hoped to enter the ballroom almost unnoticed. Instead he had stayed to fortify himself with another glass of port — only to discover that fortification had demanded several more glasses of port than just one.

He did not have an invitation to the ball, but he did not fear being turned away — not after a few glasses of port, anyway. He was, after all, the Earl of Sheringford. And if anyone remembered the rather spectacular scandal of five years ago, as everyone surely would — well, they would undoubtedly be avid with curiosity to discover what had become of him in the intervening years and how he would behave now that he was back.

Duncan wondered suddenly if any of the Turners were in town this year, and fervently hoped not. It would not be a comfortable thing to come face to face with Randolph Turner in particular — the man he had cuckolded.

He was *not* turned away from the ball. But of course he had arrived late enough that there was no longer any sign of a receiving line or even of a majordomo to announce him. He stepped into the ballroom, having left his hat and cloak downstairs in the care of a footman, and looked about him.

He felt very much on display and half expected that after all there would be a rush of outraged persons, led by ladies, to expel him into outer darkness. It did not happen, though undoubtedly he *was* attracting some attention. He could hear a slightly heightened buzz of sound off to his right.

He ignored it.

It was indeed a squeeze of a ball. If everyone decided to dance, they would have to push out the walls. And if everyone decided to rush him . . . Well, he would be squashed as flat as a pancake.

He had arrived between sets, but couples were gathering on the floor for the next one. Good! He would be able to view the matrimonial prospects at his leisure provided that buzz of interest to his right did not develop into a swell of outrage to fill the ballroom.

He could see Con Huxtable and a few other male acquaintances some distance away, but he made no move to join them. He would become too involved in conversation if he did and perhaps allow himself to be borne off to the card room. He would be willing enough, by God. He could feel his mood turn bleaker and blacker with every passing second. This ought not to be happening.

He had *not* planned to go wife hunting yet — or perhaps ever. He had *certainly* not planned to come to London any year soon.

How the devil was he to begin?

There were pretty women and plain ones, young ones and old ones, animated ones and listless ones — that last group being the wallflowers, he suspected. Most of them, indeed, were still standing on the sidelines, nary a partner in sight though the dancing was about to resume. He should probably concentrate his attention upon them.

It was one devil of a way to choose a bride! Pick the most bored-looking wallflower and offer to brighten her life. Offer her marriage with a man who had abandoned his last bride almost literally at the altar in order to run off with her married sister-in-law and live in sin with her for almost five years. A man who had no wish whatsoever to marry but was being forced into it by the threat of penury. A man who no longer believed in romantic love and had never practiced fidelity. A man with an illegitimate child he refused to hide away in some dark corner of the country.

He had fixed his narrowed gaze upon a mousy-haired young girl who, if his eyes did not deceive him from this distance, had a flat chest and a bad case of facial spots, and who was beginning to notice his scrutiny and look decidedly frightened by it, when he was distracted.

A missile almost bowled him off his feet — something hurled his way in order to expel him after all, perhaps?

He clamped his hands about the two arms of the missile in order to save himself from landing flat on his back — what a spectacular reentry into society *that* would be! — and realized that it was a human missile.

A female human, to be exact.

Very female.

She was all generously sized breasts and delicious curves and subtly fragrant dark hair. And when she tipped back her head to apologize, she revealed a face that did the body full justice, by thunder. She had wide eyes and a porcelain complexion and features that had been arranged on her face

70

for maximum effect. She was loveliness personified from head to toe.

He held her against him longer than was necessary — and far longer than was wise in such a public setting, when his sudden appearance was already provoking attention. But she would surely fall over if he released her too soon, he reasoned.

She had long legs — he could feel them against his own.

She was beautiful and voluptuous — and pressed by some happy chance to his body. Could any warm-blooded male ask for more? Privacy and nakedness and a soft bed, perhaps?

The only negative thing that could be said about her — on the spur of the moment anyway — was that she was not young. She was probably his own age, give or take a couple of years. That was not at all young for a woman. She was undoubtedly married, then. She must have been snaffled up off the marriage mart ten or twelve years ago. She probably had half a dozen children. A pity that. But fate was ever a joker. He must not expect his search to be *this* easily or happily concluded.

There was no ring on the left hand that was splayed over his chest, though, he noticed.

All of which thoughts and observations flashed through his head in a matter of moments.

"Excuse me," she said, flushing and looking even more beautiful, if that were possible.

She was pushing at his chest. Trying to get away.

There was no harm in being hopeful, was there?

"Why?" he asked her. "What is your hurry? Why not stay and dance with me? And then marry me and live happily ever after with me?"

He felt her body grow still and watched the arrested look on her face. Then her eyebrows arched above her eyes — and even *they* were lovely. It was no wonder some poets wrote poems to their ladies' eyebrows.

"Does it *have* to be in that order?" she asked him.

Ah. An intriguing answer indeed. An answer in the form of a question.

Duncan pursed his lips.

She had bowled him over after all — and rendered him temporarily speechless.

4

Margaret almost laughed, though more with hysteria than with amusement.

What had he said?

And *what* had she answered?

Gracious heaven, he was a total stranger, and not a very reputable-looking one at that. Was anyone observing them? Whatever would they *think*?

His hands had loosened their hold on her arms though they still remained there. She could have broken away quite easily and hurried on her way out of the ballroom. Instead she looked up at him and waited to see what he would say next.

He had pursed his lips, and his very dark eyes — surely they could not be literally black? — gazed steadily and boldly back at her.

He appeared to be quite alone. Some instinct told Margaret that he was not the sort of man with whom she ought to be talking, especially without a formal introduction. But here she was standing very close to him, her hands splayed on his chest, his clasping the bare flesh of her upper arms between her sleeves and her gloves. And they had been standing thus for more seconds than any ordinary collision ought to have occasioned. They ought to have sprung apart, both embarrassed and both apologizing profusely.

Oh, goodness.

She pushed at his chest again and, when he still did not release his hold on her arms, she dropped her own to her sides. Her back prickled. Half the *ton* was somewhere behind her. Including her family. And including Crispin Dew. And the Marquess of Allingham.

"I am afraid it does," the stranger said at last in answer to her question. "If I dash off immediately in pursuit of a special license, you see, and then someone to perform the ceremony, this particular set will surely be over by the time I return. And someone else will have discovered you and eloped to Scotland with you and left me clutching a useless document. If we are to both dance and marry, it must be done in that order, I am afraid — much as I am flattered by your eagerness to proceed to the nuptials without further delay."

How very outrageous he was, whoever he might be. Margaret ought not to have laughed — she ought to have been offended by the levity of his words, absurd and quick-witted though they were.

But she laughed.

He did not. He gazed intently at her and dropped his hands to his sides at last.

"Dance with me now," he said, "and tomorrow morning I will procure that special license. It is a promise."

It was a strange joke. Yet he showed no sign of finding it amusing. Margaret found herself shivering slightly despite the fact that the smile lingered on her face.

She really ought to run from him as fast as her feet would carry her and keep the whole width or length of the ballroom between them for the rest of the evening. Her own words had been very indiscreet. *Does it have to be in that order?* Had she really spoken them aloud? But his answer, alas, proved that she had.

Who on earth *was* he? She had never set eyes on him before tonight. She was sure of that.

She did not run.

"Thank you, sir," she said instead. "I *will* dance with you."

It would be better to do that than run away simply because the Marquess of Allingham, whose hand she had refused three separate times, had chosen to betroth himself to someone else. And because Crispin was at the ball, and she had told him she was betrothed.

The stranger inclined his head and offered his arm to lead her out to join the other dancers. It surprised Margaret to discover that the dancing had still not begun. That collision and the bizarre exchange of words that had followed it must all have happened within a minute or two at the longest.

The arm beneath her hand was very solid indeed, she noticed. She also noticed as she walked beside him that her initial impression of his physique had not been mistaken. His black evening coat molded a powerful frame like a second skin. His long legs looked equally well muscled. He was taller than she by several inches, though she was a tall woman. And then there was that harsh, dark, almost ugly face.

It struck her that he might be a frightening adversary.

"It occurs to me," he said, "that if I am to be granted a special license tomorrow, I ought to know the name of my bride. And her place of residence. It would be mildly irritating to pry myself away from my bed at some ungodly hour of the morning only to have my application denied on account of my inability to name my bride or explain where she lives."

Oh, the absurd man. He was going to continue with the joke, though his grim face had not relaxed into even the suggestion of a smile.

"I suppose it would," she agreed.

The orchestra struck up with a lively country dance tune at that moment, and after a short spell of dancing together they moved away from each other in order to perform a series of steps with the couple adjacent to them. When they came together again, it was with the same couple, and there was no chance for private conversation, absurd or otherwise.

This was really very improper, Margaret thought. As he had just reminded her, he did not know her and she did not know him. Yet they were dancing with each other. How on earth would she explain the lapse to Vanessa and Katherine? Or to Stephen? She had always been a stickler for the social niceties.

But she discovered that she did not much care. She was almost enjoying herself. The marquess's announcement — and his assumption that she already knew — had seriously discomposed her. So had the appearance of Crispin. But here she was dancing and smiling anyway. And there was something definitely amusing about the joke the stranger had set in motion.

How many ladies could boast of meeting a total stranger and being asked to dance with him and marry him — all in one breath?

Her smile widened.

"*Might* I be permitted," the stranger asked her when they were dancing exclusively with each other again, "to know the name of my prospective bride?"

She was tempted to withhold it. But that would be pointless. He could quite easily discover it for himself after they had finished dancing.

"I am Margaret Huxtable," she told him, "sister of the Earl of Merton."

"Ah, excellent," he said. "It is important to marry someone of impeccable lineage — important to one's family anyway."

"Absolutely, sir," she agreed. "And you are . . . ?"

But she had to wait another couple of minutes while the pattern of the dance drew other couples within earshot again.

"Duncan Pennethorne, Earl of Sheringford," he said without preamble when they were alone again. "The title, I must warn you before you get too excited about marrying it, is a courtesy one and therefore of no real value whatsoever except that it sounds good — and except that it is an indicator that a more real and illustrious title is to follow if and when the incumbent should predecease me. The Marquess of Claverbrook, my grandfather, may well not do so even though he is eighty — or will be in two weeks' time — and fifty years my senior."

He had offered a great deal more information than she had asked for. But it was surprising she had not met him before. And yet . . . *the Earl of Sheringford.* Something tugged at the corners of her memory, but she could not pull it into focus. She had the impression that it was something not too pleasant. Something scandalous.

"And where," he asked, "may I come to claim you tomorrow, Miss Huxtable, marriage license in hand?"

She hesitated again. But it would take him only a moment after he had left her to discover it for himself.

"At Merton House on Berkeley Square," she said.

But the joke had continued long enough.

As soon as the set was at an end, she decided, she must put as much distance between herself and the Earl of Sheringford as she possibly could. She did not want to encourage him to continue to be as bold and familiar with her as he had been thus far.

She must make some discreet inquiries about him. There was *something* there in her memory.

Crispin, she could see, was talking with Vanessa and Elliott. It still seemed unreal, seeing him again like this after so many unhappy years. She had not expected ever to see him again after his marriage. She had expected him, she supposed, to settle in Spain with his wife after the wars were over. Or at Rundle Park.

"Miss Huxtable," the Earl of Sheringford asked her, bringing her attention back to him, "why were you fleeing the ballroom in a panic?"

It was a thoroughly impertinent question. Did he know nothing of good manners?

"I was not *fleeing,*" she told him. "And I was not in a panic."

"Two bouncers in a single sentence," he said.

She looked at him with all the hauteur she could muster. "You are impertinent, my

80

lord," she said.

"Oh, always," he agreed. "Why waste time on tedious courtesies? Was he worth the panic?"

She opened her mouth to deliver a sharp retort. But then she closed it and simply shook her head instead.

"Was that a *no?*" he asked her. "Or a *you-are-impossible* gesture?"

"The latter," she said curtly before they were separated again.

A short while later the orchestra paused before beginning another tune in the same set. But Lord Sheringford appeared to have had enough. He took Margaret's hand from her side without a by-your-leave, set it on his sleeve, and led her off the floor and into a small, semicircular alcove close to the doors, where a comfortable-looking sofa was temporarily unoccupied.

"It is impossible," he said as Margaret seated herself hesitantly and he took the seat beside her, "to hold a sustained conversation while dancing. Dancing has to be the most ridiculous social activity ever invented."

"It is something I particularly enjoy," she said. "And one is not *expected* to hold a lengthy conversation while dancing. There is a time and place for that."

"What did he do," he asked her, "to throw you into such a panic?"

"I have not admitted," she said, "that there even *is* any such gentleman or that there *was* any such incident." She picked up her fan from her wrist, flicked it open, and plied it to her overheated face.

He watched her movements. He was seated slightly sideways, his elbow resting on the top of the sofa not far from her shoulder. She could feel the heat from his arm against the side of her neck.

"Of course there were both," he said. "If the cause had been a burst seam, it would have revealed itself rather shockingly when you collided with me."

She ought to just get up and walk away, Margaret thought. There was nothing to stop her, was there? But his persistent questions had revived the memory of her misery and panic, and some of the former returned. She had really had no chance to digest the fact that she would never be married to the Marquess of Allingham.

Lord Sheringford was a stranger. Sometimes it was easier to talk to strangers than to loved ones. She doubted she would ever pour out her heart to Stephen or either of her sisters. It had never been her way to burden them with her woes. Instead, she had always bottled up her emotions deep inside — at least all the negative ones. She had always been the eldest sister, the substitute parent. She had always had to be the strong one, the one upon whom they could all depend.

Talking to strangers was dangerous. But there was something quite unreal and bizarre about this whole evening so far. Margaret's normal caution and reticence deserted her.

"I told a gentleman of my acquaintance yesterday," she said, "that I was betrothed. I expected that it would be true by tonight. But this evening I have discovered that the gentleman concerned is betrothed to someone else, and the first gentleman is here and will be expecting to meet my fiancé. Oh, dear, this all makes no sense whatsoever, does it?"

"Strangely it does," he said. "The gentleman to whom you made this claim once hurt you?"

She looked at him, rather startled. How could he possibly have discerned that?

"What gives you that idea?" she asked him.

His eyes bored into hers as if they could lay bare all her secrets.

"Why else would you be rash enough to tell him such a thing so prematurely?"

he said with a shrug. "It was a boast. Why boast to him if you did not wish to thumb your nose at him? And why wish to thumb your nose at him if he had not hurt you at some time in the past? What did he do to you?"

"He went away to war," she said, "while I stayed at home to raise my younger sisters and brother after our father died. We had an understanding before he left, though, and that sustained me through years that were often difficult, even bleak. And then word came through a letter to his mother that he had married in Spain."

"Ah," he said. "This paragon of devotion is one of the scarlet-clad officers who are dazzling all the ladies, is he?"

"Yes," she said.

"And the man to whom you expected to be betrothed?" he asked. "He also has behaved toward you in a dastardly manner?"

"I cannot in all conscience accuse him of that," she said. "He offered for me three times over the past five years. I refused all three times, though we were still friends and told each other at the end of last Season that we looked forward to meeting again this year. I arrived in town very recently and therefore neither saw the announcement of his engagement nor heard of it. I came here this evening, expecting . . . Well, never mind."

She was beginning to feel very uneasy, not to mention ridiculous. What she had intended to be a very vague explanation of her earlier panic had turned into a rather detailed and very humiliating confession.

"You waited too long in both instances," he said. "With both gentlemen. Let it be a lesson to you."

She fanned her cheeks more vigorously. She deserved that harsh and unsympathetic judgment. Though it was very typical of a man to take the part of other men. It must be *her* fault that she had lost both Crispin and the Marquess of Allingham.

But he was perfectly right to think so, of course. She need not feel so indignant or so abject. She had not been abandoned by either man. She had made them wait too long.

It was humbling to see oneself through the eyes of a man.

"And does the dashing, faithless officer know the identity of the gentleman to whom you expected to be betrothed this evening?" Lord Sheringford asked.

"Oh, no," she said. "I was not *that* indiscreet. Thank heaven."

One must be thankful for small mercies,

she thought. How truly dreadful it would have been if . . .

"Then there is a simple solution to all your woes," the earl said. "You may introduce *me* to your officer as your betrothed, and at the same time demonstrate to the other man that you were not waiting for him to offer for you yet again."

Oh, he really was quite outrageous. Yet there was still no glimmer of humor in his eyes, as she saw when she turned her head sharply to look into them.

"And what would you do tomorrow," she asked, "when you discovered my brother and brothers-in-law on your doorstep, demanding to know your true intentions? And what would *I* do when I came face-to-face with Crispin tomorrow or the day after? Tell him that I had had a change of heart?"

He shrugged.

"I would inform your fierce relatives that my intentions are entirely honorable," he said. "And you could continue to thumb your nose at the officer."

"I do thank you for the gallant offer," she said, laughing and wondering how he would react if she chose to take him seriously, poor man. "And I thank you for your company during this set. It has been amusing. But I must go now and —"

She was given no chance to finish. The hand belonging to the arm that was propped against the back of the sofa moved to rest firmly on her shoulder, and his face dipped a little closer to hers.

"One of the scarlet uniforms is approaching," he said, "draped about the person of a large red-haired officer. Doubtless your erstwhile lover."

She did not turn her head to look. She closed her eyes briefly instead.

"You had better do as I have suggested," Lord Sheringford said, "and present me as your betrothed. It will be far more satisfying for you than admitting the abject truth would be."

"But you are not —" she said.

"I can be," he said, interrupting, "if you wish and if you are prepared to marry me within the next fourteen days. But we can discuss the details at our leisure later."

Was he *serious?* It was not possible. This was all quite bizarre. But there was no opportunity to question him. There was no time to think or consider. There was no time at all. His eyes had moved beyond her, and he was raising his eyebrows and looking like a man who was none too delighted at having his tête-à-tête interrupted. It was a haughty, cold look.

Margaret turned her head.

"Crispin," she said.

"Meg." He made her a bow. "I trust I am not interrupting anything important?"

"Not at all." Her heart was thumping so hard in her chest that it deafened her despite the loudness of the music and of voices raised to converse above it. "My lord, do you have an acquaintance with Major Dew? May I present the Earl of Sheringford, Crispin?"

Crispin bowed again, and Lord Sheringford regarded him with raised eyebrows.

"And this is the same Major Dew," he said, "with whom you once had an acquaintance, Maggie?"

Maggie?

Oh, goodness! Margaret's vision was beginning to darken about the edges. At the other extreme, she felt a quite inappropriate urge to burst into laughter. She must be on the verge of hysteria again.

"We were neighbors," she said. "We grew up together."

"Ah, yes," Lord Sheringford said. "That was it. I knew I had heard the name before. A pleasure, Major. I hope you have not come to solicit Maggie's hand for the next dance, though. I am not finished with that hand myself yet, and the present set, you will observe, is not quite over."

"Meg?" Crispin said, virtually ignoring the earl apart from the fact that his nostrils flared slightly. "Are you ready to be escorted back to your *family?* I shall certainly claim a dance later in the evening if I may."

There were certain moments upon which the whole of the future course of one's life might turn. And almost inevitably they popped out at one without any warning at all, leaving one with no time to consider or engage in a reasoned debate with oneself. One had to make a split-second decision, and much depended upon it. Perhaps everything.

This was such a moment, and Margaret knew it with agonized clarity as she closed her fan. She could get to her feet now and go with Crispin, or she could stay and tell Crispin the truth, or she could stay and do what the earl had suggested — and deal with the consequences tomorrow.

Margaret was *never* rash, even when forced to act upon the spur of the moment. But this was a different type of moment altogether.

"Thank you, Crispin," she said. "I will be delighted to dance with you later. For now, though, I will remain with Lord Sheringford. The Marquess of Allingham will be along soon, I daresay, to claim me for the next set." And then a deep breath and the rest of the decision was made. "Lord Sheringford is my betrothed."

The ballroom suddenly seemed unnaturally hot and airless. But she doubted she had enough control over her hands to open her fan again.

Crispin looked from her to the earl, poker-faced, and it seemed to Margaret that he knew the man or at least knew *of* him, and did not like what he knew. He had offered to escort her back to her *family,* with emphasis upon the one word.

"Your *betrothed,* Meg?" he said. "But Nessie and the Duke of Moreland do not know anything of it."

He had just been talking with them. They had all seen her with the Earl of Sheringford. Perhaps Crispin had volunteered to come and wrest her away from him and escort her to safety. What did they all know of the earl that she did not? It must be something quite unsavory.

"I told you yesterday, Crispin, that the betrothal has not yet been made public," she said.

"It will be very soon, however," the earl said, squeezing her shoulder. "We have decided to wed within the next fortnight.

When one has discovered the partner with whom one wishes to spend the rest of one's life, why wait, after all? Many a prospective match comes to grief because the couple — or one member of it — waits too long."

It occurred to Margaret that he really might be serious.

But how could he *possibly* be? They had just met.

He could *surely* not intend to marry her within two weeks.

She did not even know who the Earl of Sheringford *was.* Apart from being heir to the Marquess of Claverbrook, that was.

She felt one of the earl's knuckles brushing against her cheek and turned her head to look at him. His eyes, she could see now, were a very dark brown. Was it the color, almost indistinguishable from black, that gave the extraordinary impression that he could look inside her and see her very soul?

"I must offer my felicitations, then," Crispin said, executing another bow. "I will seek you out for a dance later, Meg."

"I shall look forward to it," she said.

He turned without another glance at the earl and strode away with stiff military bearing.

"He is not pleased," the earl said. "Is the Spanish wife still alive?"

"No," Margaret said. "He is a widower."

"He was hoping, then," he said, "to re-kindle an old flame with you. You have had a fortunate escape, however. He looks very dashing in his uniform, I daresay, but he has a weak chin."

"He does not!" Margaret protested.

"He does," the earl insisted. "If you are still in love with him, Maggie, you had bet-ter be careful not to allow yourself to be lured back to him. You would be wasting your sensibilities upon a weak man."

"I do *not* still love him," she said firmly. "His actions persuaded me long ago of the weakness of his character. And I do not recall granting you permission to use my given name, my lord. Especially a shortened form that no one has ever used before."

"A new name for a new life," he said. "To me you will always be Maggie. Who is the man to whom you expected to be betrothed tonight?"

"The Marquess of Allingham," she said, and frowned. That information, at least, she might have withheld.

"Allingham?" He raised his eyebrows. "Your next dancing partner? That is interest-ing. But you have had another fortunate escape. If he is as I remember him, he is a dull dog."

"He is *not,*" she protested. "He is charming and amiable and a polished conversationalist."

"My point exactly," he said. "A dull dog. You will be far better off with me."

She looked steadily at him, and he looked as steadily back.

Oh, dear God, she thought, he really *was* serious.

The edges of her vision darkened again. But this was not the moment to faint. She picked up her fan and somehow found her hand steady enough to open it and waft it before her face once more. She drew in lungfuls of warm, heavily fragrant air.

"Why?" she asked him. "Even if you can meet a complete stranger and be convinced after one glance that she is the one lady above all others whom you wish to marry, *why* must you marry her within two weeks?"

For the first time there was a slight curve to his lips that might almost be described as a smile.

"If I am not wed within the next fourteen days," he told her, "I am going to be utterly penniless until my grandfather shuffles off this mortal coil, which may well not be for another twenty or thirty years. Apart from some rheumatism, he appears to be in excellent health. He will be eighty in two weeks' time, and yesterday he summoned me into his presence and issued an ultimatum — marry before his birthday or be cut off from the rents and profits of the home where I grew up and from which the heirs traditionally draw their income. I was raised as a gentleman with expectations of wealth and therefore never expected to have to seek employment. I do believe I would make an abysmally inept coal miner even if I felt inclined to try my hand at it. I must marry, you see. And in almost indecent haste. My grandfather, I feel compelled to add, believes it will be impossible. He plans to turn Woodbine Park over to my cousin, his next heir after me, on his birthday unless I am respectably married before then."

Margaret stared at him, speechless. He *was* serious.

"What have you done," she asked him, "to incur such wrath? The punishment seems unusually cruel if it is just that you have procrastinated in choosing a bride."

"I chose a bride five years ago," he told her. "I was happy with my choice. I was head over ears in love with her. But the night before our wedding I eloped with her brother's wife and lived in sin with her — since the husband would not divorce her — until her death four months ago."

Margaret stared at him, transfixed. Yes. Oh, yes, *that* was it. Five years ago. It had happened just before she came to London for the first time with Stephen and her sisters, all of them new to Stephen's title and their life in the heart of the *ton*. The scandal was still being talked of. She had thought that the Earl of Sheringford must be the devil himself.

This was *him?*

His eyes were fixed on hers. His dark, angular face was filled with mockery.

"My grandfather doubtless wishes," he said, "that he could simply make my cousin his heir and cut me out of everything that is his. It cannot be done, of course, but he *can* make me very uncomfortable and very miserable indeed for the rest of his life."

"Are you not *ashamed?*" she asked him, and then felt the color flood her face. It was an impertinent question. What had happened was none of her business. Except that he wanted *her* to marry him in fourteen days or fewer just so that he could keep his income.

"Not at all," he said. "Things happen, Maggie. One adjusts one's life accordingly."

She could think of nothing to say in response. She could ask a thousand questions, but she had no wish whatsoever to hear the answers. But why had he done it? How could he *not* be ashamed?

She was saved from the necessity of saying anything at all.

"Your newly betrothed swain is approaching to claim his dance," the earl said, looking beyond her again. "It is as well, Maggie, is it not? I have shocked you to the core. I shall take the liberty of calling upon you tomorrow and hope I will not find the door barred against me. I have so very little time in which to find someone else, you see."

She had not even noticed the one set of dances ending and the next beginning to form. But when she turned her head, she could see that indeed the Marquess of Allingham was approaching.

"This is my set, I believe, Miss Huxtable," he said, smiling genially at her and acknowledging the Earl of Sheringford with the merest nod of the head.

"Oh, yes, indeed."

The Earl of Sheringford stood up when she did. He took her right hand in his even as the marquess was extending one arm, and raised it briefly to his lips.

"I shall see you tomorrow, then, my love," he murmured before nodding to the marquess and walking away — and out through the ballroom doors.

My love?

The marquess raised his eyebrows as she set her hand on his sleeve.

Margaret smiled at him. There was no point in trying to explain, was there? She owed him no explanation, anyway.

But really . . .

My love.

He had eloped with a married lady the night before his planned wedding to her sister-in-law.

Could any gentleman be further beyond the pale of respectability?

And he wanted her to marry him.

He would indeed find the door barred against him if he should have the effrontery to come calling tomorrow.

Could any day — any evening — be stranger than this one?

5

Margaret felt very embarrassed as she danced with the Marquess of Allingham. She would have felt self-conscious anyway under the circumstances — though fortunately he had no way of knowing what her expectations had been when she set out for the ball this evening.

But he had heard the Earl of Sheringford calling her *my love,* and though she had told herself that it was none of his business what anyone else called her, nevertheless the words seemed to hover in the air about them as they danced. It did not help that they danced in silence for the first ten minutes or so.

She smiled until her lips felt stiff.

Did he know who the Earl of Sheringford *was?*

But *of course* he must know.

He was the one who spoke first.

"Miss Huxtable," he said gravely, "forgive

me if I am speaking out of turn now and forgive me if I did not speak when perhaps I ought. I *ought* to have taken that fellow to task for the familiarity with which he addressed you, when I daresay you have never met him before this evening."

That fellow? Yes, indeed he knew.

"Lord Sheringford?" she said lightly. "Oh, I did not take offense, my lord. He was joking. I am relieved you did not take any more notice of his words than they merited."

"But as your friend," he said after hesitating a few moments, "I feel that I ought to warn you to keep your distance from the Earl of Sheringford, Miss Huxtable. It would pain me to see your reputation tarnished by any connection with his. I daresay you do not know who he is or why he is justifiably shunned by all respectable people. I would wager he did not receive an invitation to the ball tonight but came quite brazenly without one. And I do not know who thought it appropriate to introduce you to him."

"You are wrong about one thing," she said. "I *do* know about him. I even remember the scandal, which was still quite fresh when I made my first appearance at a London Season five years ago, just after Stephen inherited his title. You must not concern yourself, my lord. I am quite capable of looking after myself and choosing my own acquaintances."

Like the gentleman he was, he said no more on the subject, and Margaret thought that was surely the end of the matter — beyond having to deny admittance to Lord Sheringford if he did indeed put in an appearance at Merton House tomorrow, of course, and beyond having to tell Crispin the truth when she saw him next.

Oh, dear, she *had* behaved foolishly this evening.

She was not proud of herself. She had always been the soul of propriety and discretion. She would remember this evening for a long time and with considerable discomfort. She turned hot and cold again when she remembered all that she had poured out to the Earl of Sheringford — all her most embarrassing and humiliating secrets. That was surely the worst thing she had done all evening.

Whatever had possessed her!

Vanessa and Katherine were both waiting for her when the marquess returned her to their sides. Elliott and Jasper were conversing with a group of gentlemen nearby.

"Meg." Vanessa linked an arm firmly and possessively through hers. "I was never more happy in my life than to see you dancing with the Marquess of Allingham. Whoever presented you to the Earl of Sheringford? If it was Lady Tindell, she really ought to have known better and I will not scruple to tell her so. The earl is absolutely beyond the pale."

"He even *looks* disreputable," Katherine added. "And downright dangerous. Meg, do you know that —"

"Yes," Margaret said, interrupting. "I *do* know that he eloped with his bride's sister-in-law five years ago. I cannot see that that makes him an utter pariah today. Perhaps people ought to be entitled to a second chance."

"That is true," Vanessa said, patting her hand. "It is very true, indeed. I daresay he is a very sad and contrite gentleman. She died recently, I have heard — the lady with whom he eloped, I mean, though he never married her. Her husband would not divorce her. It is just like you to refuse to give him the cut direct, Meg, though it was a little alarming to watch him lead you off the dance floor in the middle of a set in order to sit with you in that alcove."

"Which is in full public view," Margaret pointed out. "I was in no danger whatsoever of being kidnapped or otherwise assaulted."

"True." Vanessa laughed. "But I had visions of him whispering all sorts of improper suggestions in your ear. I might have stridden over there to rescue you myself, but Kate was dancing at the time and could not accompany me, and Elliott thought it unnecessary to risk making a public scene, since he trusts your good sense. Crispin went to see if you needed rescuing, though. I was glad of that even though I know you are not entirely delighted that he is in London."

And a mistaken sense of pride had goaded her into introducing the Earl of Sheringford to him as her betrothed. The enormity of what she had done swept over Margaret again. Thank *heaven* she had at least sworn Crispin to secrecy — or as good as sworn him, anyway. She had told him the betrothal had not yet been publicly announced. She must find him without further delay and tell him the truth. But he had asked to dance with her later, had he not? She would tell him then, humiliating as it would be. And there — finally — would be an end of the matter.

It was already too late, though.

Stephen was striding toward them across the ballroom, looking uncharacteristically grim, his eyes fixed upon Margaret.

"Stephen," Katherine said as he came up to them. "Whatever is the matter?"

He spoke directly to Margaret.

"Meg," he said, "I do not know who on earth introduced you to that fellow. Whoever it was deserves to be shot. But that is the least of our worries. The most ridiculous rumor is spreading and we are going to have to move quickly to quash it. It is being said that you and Sheringford are *betrothed*."

"Oh, Stephen, no!" Vanessa exclaimed.

"But how very ridiculous!" Katherine said, laughing. "No one will take it seriously, Stephen."

Margaret stared at him, speechless.

Elliott and Jasper must have heard what Stephen had said. They both turned away from their group.

"I'll draw his cork for this," Elliott said. "What does he think he is up to?"

"It would be more to the point," Jasper said, "to draw the cork of the joker who began the story. It was hardly Sherry himself, as he left the ball half an hour ago. Do you know who *did*, Stephen?"

It was Margaret who answered him.

"I fear it must have been Crispin Dew," she said, and not for the first time that evening she felt on the verge of fainting.

There was that quite unmistakable buzz

in the ballroom that always accompanied the spreading of the newest salacious rumor. And a quick glance about the room confirmed Margaret in her fear that it was indeed she who was the subject of that rumor. Far too many eyes were turned in the direction of her group to be normal.

"Dew?" Stephen's voice was like thunder. "Why the devil would he start any such rumor?"

He did not even apologize for his language — and no one in the group thought to demand an apology.

"I fear it was something I said," Margaret said. But that was clearly not explanation enough. She drew a deep, somewhat ragged breath. "I introduced the Earl of Sheringford to him as my betrothed."

"You *what?*" Elliott asked very quietly.

The others stared at her as if she had suddenly sprouted a second head.

"I also told him no one else knew yet," she said. "It was a *joke.* It was . . . Well, it was something I said impulsively and would have corrected later when I dance with him."

To say she felt foolish — as well as a number of other uncomfortable things — would be a massive understatement.

The buzz of excited conversation about

them had not abated.

"But what," Katherine asked, "did Lord *Sheringford* have to say about such an extraordinary announcement, Meg?"

Margaret licked lips that were suddenly dry. "It was he who suggested it," she said. "And he wants to make it real. He wants to marry me. But it is really all nonsense and best forgotten."

This whole evening seemed like a ghastly nightmare. She would be fortunate if they did not haul her off to Bedlam before the night was out.

"Which may be easier said than done," Jasper said, bowing to her and extending a hand for hers. "You are attracting a great deal of attention, Meg, especially as Sherry has absconded and cannot take his half share. Come and dance with me again. And smile. Katherine and I will escort you home afterward, and the others may remain to dispel the rumors as best they can."

Margaret set her hand in his.

"This is so very ridiculous," she said.

"Most gossip is," he said. "It can also be very tenacious."

"Where is Dew?" Stephen asked grimly, looking around the room. "I'll break his damned neck for him."

"Tomorrow will be time enough for that,"

Elliott said. "We do not need you confronting him here to add to the general delight, Stephen. Dance with Vanessa, if you will. And do watch your language in the presence of my wife and sisters-in-law. Katherine, may I have the pleasure?"

And Margaret danced with Jasper for a second time and smiled at the light, amusing banter he kept up throughout. It was truly awful to be the main focus of attention in the room, especially when she knew she had brought it on herself.

But how *could* Crispin have done this to her? She had never known him to be openly spiteful.

She was going to have to wait out the gossip with all the patience she could muster, she decided later as she rode home beside Katherine in Jasper's carriage. It ought not to take too long once the *ton* realized there was no basis to the rumor. And then she was going to settle back to her old respectable life even if it meant being a spinster and Stephen's dependent for as long as she lived.

Margaret went to bed that night before Stephen returned home. She even managed to sleep fitfully between spells of agonized wakefulness in which she remembered every secret she had poured out to that black-eyed, grim-faced stranger who had once abandoned his bride and eloped with a married lady and lived in sin with her until her death. And there were the wakeful spells in which she remembered introducing him to Crispin as her betrothed.

And Crispin had gone and told the whole world!

She even slept later than usual in the morning. Stephen was up before her. He had already breakfasted and left the house, the butler informed her when she asked.

He had left his place at the breakfast table untidy. The dishes had been cleared away, but the morning paper had been left open and bunched in a heap beside where his plate had been. Margaret went to fold it up neatly but first let her eyes rove over the topmost page. It was the one always devoted to society gossip.

And there was her own name, leaping off the page at her as if it had legs and wings.

She bent closer to read, her eyes widening in horror.

Miss Margaret Huxtable, the journalist had written, eldest sister of the Earl of Merton, had been seen sitting in scandalous seclusion in a remote alcove of Lady Tindell's ballroom the previous evening tête-à-tête with that very notorious jilt and wife-stealer, the Earl of Sheringford, whom the writer had reported seeing skulking about town a few days ago. And when confronted by a friend, who had approached in order to rescue her from scandal or even worse harm, Miss Huxtable had boldly presented the earl as her *betrothed.* The beau monde might well be asking itself if the lady was quite as respectable as she had always appeared to be. The reporter might humbly remind his readers of what had befallen her younger sister two years ago . . .

Margaret did not read any further. She closed the paper with trembling hands, as if she could thereby obliterate what it said. A bad dream had just turned into the worst of nightmares.

She sat down shivering and remembering how the spreading of vicious and almost entirely untrue gossip had forced Kate into marrying Jasper two years ago.

History was not about to repeat itself with her, was it?

Oh, surely not! Such catastrophes did not happen twice within the same family.

Whatever was she going to *do?*

Duncan very much doubted that Miss Margaret Huxtable was a gossip — especially at her own expense and on the topic of her meeting with him. It must have been the military officer with the peculiar wet-sounding name and the red hair, then.

For gossip there was.

It was his mother who alerted him. She actually appeared at breakfast the morning after the Tindell ball, albeit well after Sir Graham had left for his club and just as Duncan himself was about to rise from the table. He knew she had been at the ball, though he had not been there long enough himself to see her.

"Duncan," she said as she swept into the breakfast parlor, still clad in a dressing gown of a pale blue diaphanous material that billowed and wafted about her, though her hair had been immaculately styled and he suspected that her cheeks were rouged, "you are up already. I scarcely slept a wink all night. I feel quite haggard. But you were not in your room when we arrived home last night, you provoking man, and so there was no talking with you then. I did not hear you come home. It must have been at some unearthly hour. *Do* tell me if it is true. Can it *possibly* be? *Are* you betrothed to the Earl of Merton's eldest sister? Without a word to your own mother? It would be a splendid match for you, my love. Your grandfather will be quite reconciled to you if it *is* true. And that will be a very good thing as Graham has been grumbling and complaining, the silly man, that you will be living under his roof for the rest of our lives. Not that he does not love you in his own way, but . . . But speak up, do, Duncan, instead of sitting there silently as though there were nothing to tell. *Are* you betrothed?"

"In one word, Mama," he said, hiding his surprise and signaling the butler to fill his coffee cup again, "no. Not yet, anyway, and perhaps never. I danced with the lady once last evening, that is all."

"That is *not* all," his mother protested. "Miss Huxtable presented you to someone — I cannot for the life of me remember who — as her betrothed. Prue Talbot told me, and she never spreads stories unless they are accurate. Besides, *everyone* was saying so."

"Then, Mama," he said, getting to his feet after taking one sip of the fresh coffee, "you had no need to ask me, did you? You will excuse me? I ought to have been at Jackson's Boxing Salon twenty minutes ago."

"It is *not* true, then?" she asked, looking crestfallen.

"Miss Huxtable was provoked into saying what she did," he said, "at my suggestion. I will be calling on her later today to discuss the matter."

She looked befuddled but hopeful as she gazed at him and ignored the food on the plate before her.

"But when did you *meet* her, Duncan?" she asked. "That is what has been puzzling me all night, and I daresay it is puzzling Graham too, as he could suggest no answer when I asked him that very question. He would only grunt in that odious way of his. You have been in town only a few days. Now that I think of it, I do not believe Miss Huxtable has been here much longer. I do not remember seeing her before last evening, though I have seen her sisters everywhere and that very handsome brother of hers. Oh, *now* I see! You met elsewhere and arranged to meet again here. You —"

He took her hand in his and raised it to his lips.

"Keep all this to yourself for a while, will you, Mama?" he asked.

Though it was surely a pointless thing to ask, if the ballroom had been buzzing with the rumor last evening after he left.

"But of course," she said. "You know that I am the soul of discretion, Duncan. I shall tell Graham what you have told me, of course, but we hold no secrets from each other."

He went off to Jackson's. The first man he encountered there was Constantine Huxtable, and his initial suspicion that Con had been waiting there for him was soon confirmed.

"Come and spar with me, Sherry," he said, but it was more an ultimatum than an affable invitation.

"It will be my pleasure," Duncan said. "You look as if you are ready to punch my head in, though. Which, I must confess, is preferable to sparring with one of those fellows who like to prance about striking poses that they think make them look manly."

Con did not laugh or even grin. He went on looking grim and a little white about the mouth.

Con was Merton's cousin, Duncan remembered suddenly. He was Constantine *Huxtable.* One would not expect there to be much love lost between the two branches of the family, though, since Con had been the eldest son of the late earl and ought by rights to have inherited the title himself. But there was that asinine law to the effect that a man — or woman — was forever illegitimate if born out of wedlock, even if his mother and father later married. A couple of days or so later in Con's case. And so when the old earl had died, it was Con's sickly young brother who had inherited and then — after *his* death — a second or third cousin. The present Merton.

Miss Margaret Huxtable's brother, in fact.

Now, why should Con care about Margaret Huxtable?

He apparently did, though.

He spoke again after they had stripped down to the waist and were in the ring, circling each other warily and taking preliminary jabs, testing the land, watching for weaknesses, looking for openings.

"I cannot believe, Sherry," he said, "that you can be serious in your intention to marry Margaret. Why did you allow that story to spread last evening?"

Duncan saw a clear path to his opponent's chin and headed through it with a right jab. But Con neatly deflected the blow and buried one of his own in Duncan's unprotected stomach.

It hurt like the devil, and for a moment Duncan was winded. He would not show it, though. He was a little ashamed at finding himself so out of practice, if the truth were told. He hooked his left arm wide and dealt Con a blow to the side of his head.

Con winced.

"One does not either permit a story to

spread or stop it from doing so once it has started," Duncan said. "Stories quickly develop a life of their own when there are people to begin them and people to believe them. This particular story did not even start up until after I had left the ball."

They concentrated upon throwing punches at each other for several minutes. It became quickly obvious to Duncan that it was no friendly bout.

"You are saying, then, that the story is untrue?" Con asked somewhat later, when the ferocity of their attack had abated and they were catching their breath before going back at it.

"That I am betrothed to Miss Huxtable?" Duncan said. "Yes, it is. That she introduced me to a popinjay in a scarlet coat as her betrothed? No, it is not. That I offered her marriage? No, it is not. I was not there to hear the details of the story myself and so am not sure what it is exactly I am being called upon to confirm or deny."

He spotted that same path to Con's chin again — there was a definite weakness in his defenses there — and this time he successfully planted a right upper cut, snapping Con's head back. But, as before, he had left his own defenses weak, and Con buried a fist in his midriff again. Duncan received it with a woof of expelled air and stepped in closer with both fists flying. Two fists flew back at him with equal ferocity.

They pummeled each other for several more minutes without talking, until they were both sore and breathless and sweating and the strength was going from their arms. Eventually they backed off by unspoken assent, neither of them having succeeded in putting the other down.

"I like you, Sherry," Con said, reaching for his towel. "I always did. It did not bother me that you ran off with Mrs. Turner instead of marrying *Miss* Turner. A fellow's business is his own, and I assumed that you had your reasons for doing what you did. But this time your business is mine too."

Duncan flexed his knuckles, though not with any intention of renewing their fight. They were looking red and even raw.

"Miss Huxtable is your business?" he asked.

"She is when someone is about to hurt her," Con said, "even if only her reputation. She has had a raw deal of a life, Sherry, as women all too often do. She was not quite eighteen when she promised her father on his deathbed that she would make a home for her brother and sisters until they were all grown up and settled in life. That was long before my own father and then Jon died and her brother inherited the title. They were poor. But she kept her promise anyway. Merton reached his majority and the youngest sister married just two years ago. She is free of the obligation, but she is no longer young. She has probably realized that if she does not marry soon she will have the unenviable life of a spinster for the rest of her days, and be rewarded for all she has done for her family by being eternally dependent upon them. I can see that she would be an easy prey to such as you."

He spoke heatedly despite the fact that he was still half out of breath.

"Such as me?" Duncan raised his eyebrows.

"Mrs. Turner is dead," Con said. "So is your father, Sherry, and your grandfather is an old man. You have come to town, I presume, in order to choose a bride."

"And if I have chosen Miss Huxtable," Duncan said, wrapping his towel about his shoulders and wiping his face with it, "it must be because I intend to *hurt* her?"

"Your notoriety itself will hurt her," Con said. "Leave her alone, Sherry. Choose someone less vulnerable."

"But if the story of how she presented me to Frost — or was it Fog or Dew? *Dew!* That was it. If the story has spread, Con, and obviously it has," Duncan said, "will I not hurt her quite irreparably by withdrawing my offer now?"

Con gazed stormily at him. "Damn you, Sherry." He scrubbed at his face and arms and chest with his towel and stalked off to retrieve his clothes. "Why did you have to choose Margaret of all people? If you marry her and hurt so much as a hair on her head, you will have me to answer to. *This* was nothing." He jerked his head back in the direction of the ring. "This was mere sparring."

"Are you going to White's by any chance?" Duncan asked. "If you are, I will walk with you."

But going to White's brought him face-to-face with the Duke of Moreland, who had still been just Viscount Lyngate when Duncan had last frequented town.

"Moreland." Duncan nodded affably to him and the blond young man who was with him, and would have proceeded on his way to the reading room to look at the morning papers if the duke had not stood quite deliberately in his way.

"Sheringford," he said, frowning ferociously. "I will have a word with you. My wife, if you did not know it, was the former

Mrs. Hedley Dew and before that Miss Vanessa Huxtable. This is the Earl of Merton."

Ah. So Moreland had a connection with both the Dews and the Huxtables, did he? Duncan sighed inwardly. He had not realized that.

Merton inclined his head and looked grim. He was a handsome lad and a slender one, but Duncan's practiced eye registered the fact that it would be a mistake to assume that he was therefore a weakling. That youthful physique looked very well honed indeed, and the face had character.

"Ah, Merton, well met," Duncan said. "You are just the man I would have been seeking out later today."

He had not thought of doing so until this very moment actually. It was a while since he had made any formal marriage offer. But though Margaret Huxtable must be several years older than this brother she had brought up almost single-handed, it was surely the decent thing to do to meet formally with him to discuss marriage settlements and all the other business surrounding an impending marriage offer.

"Later today is a little *too* late, is it not," Merton asked him curtly, "when the question has already been asked and answered and word spread among half the *ton?* And announced in the morning paper?"

"Announced in the paper?" Duncan asked in astonishment.

"More or less," Merton said. "On the gossip page, anyway."

Extraordinary. And it *must* have been the military officer with the weak chin. No one else could have seen him and Miss Huxtable talking with each other and thought of spreading the rumor that they were *betrothed.* Duncan would not mind having a word or two with Major Dew.

How was Miss Huxtable holding up this morning? he wondered. Were circumstances playing into his hands and almost forcing her into accepting him? If the *ton* believed that she was betrothed to him — and clearly it did, or *would* once it had read the papers this morning — she would cause herself some embarrassment if she cried off. On the other hand, marrying him was going to bring her scandal. He was not the *ton*'s favorite son.

Miss Margaret Huxtable, it seemed, had trapped herself somewhere between the devil and the deep blue sea.

"I would have said no a thousand times over," Merton said while Moreland loomed, silent and menacing, "if you had done all this properly and spoken with me privately first. I would *still* say no if the answer were mine to give. Unfortunately, Meg is not subject to my will. She is her own person and can answer for herself. I do not like you, Sheringford."

Duncan raised his eyebrows.

"As far as I remember," he said, "we met for the first time a few moments ago, Merton. You form impressions with great haste."

"I do not like men," Merton said, "who abandon their brides to private heartache and public scorn and run off with lawfully married ladies instead. I do not like such men at all especially when they are contemplating marriage to one of my sisters. And I do not need any prolonged acquaintance to form such an opinion."

Duncan inclined his head.

"We are beginning to attract attention," Moreland said.

The hall was large enough and wide enough that they were in no danger of blocking the progress of other gentlemen as they arrived or left. But heads were indeed turning their way — and no wonder if the Tindell ballroom had been as abuzz with gossip as Duncan imagined it must have been — and if the gossip writer had made as juicy a morsel of the story as gossip writers usually did. And now here was he, the notorious Lord Sheringford, in company with Miss Huxtable's brother and brother-in-law, all of them looking as solemn as if they were attending a funeral. Yes, of course they were attracting attention.

"I promised Miss Huxtable last evening," Duncan said, "that I would call upon her at Merton House this afternoon. If I may, Merton, I will speak with you there first."

Merton nodded stiffly, and Duncan bowed to the two gentlemen and went on his way.

He would have left White's without having gone farther than the reception hall, but sheer pride prevented him from crawling away now. Besides, he wanted to read what had been written about him in the papers. He proceeded upstairs, where he was greeted by a number of gentlemen. Indeed some of the greetings were jovial and even raucous and accompanied by much back-slapping. Among a certain crowd, it seemed, he had established himself as one devil of a fine fellow.

And then he read the description of himself as a jilt and a wife-stealer.

Both perfectly true.

And he read that he had been presented to the friend who had come to the rescue of Miss Huxtable as her betrothed.

It was indeed Dew who had betrayed her, then.

Again.

Duncan would definitely want a word with that particular military officer.

There was, he learned before leaving the club after an early luncheon, a wager written into the betting book on whether or not he would abandon *this* bride at the altar. The odds were heavily in favor of his doing so.

And this afternoon he would be making Miss Margaret Huxtable a formal marriage offer, which she might well feel compelled to accept now. He would be left with thirteen days in which to present her to his grandfather and arrange a wedding by special license.

His freedom was going to be bought — *if* she accepted him, that was — at a high price.

Though freedom was not the issue, was it?

Toby was.

6

Margaret's first instinct after seeing the paper was to retreat to her room, crawl back into bed, and pull the covers up over her head. Perhaps by the time she emerged the whole sorry episode would be ancient news and someone would have murdered his grandmother or married his scullery maid or ridden naked along Rotten Row or done something equally startling with which to distract the fickle attention of the *ton.*

The *ton* could not be seriously interested, surely, in the fact that a dull, aging spinster had lied to a man who had once spurned her love by telling him she was betrothed to a villainous, wife-stealing rake?

But, oh, dear, when put that way, the facts really did sound intriguing, even to her.

Creeping off back to bed would solve nothing, she decided. She would go out instead. She would call on Vanessa, and perhaps together they would go to

Katherine's, and the three of them would share a good laugh over last evening and the silly story in the paper this morning.

It was a good thing they all had a good sense of humor.

But was any of this *funny?*

She would dearly like to have a word with Crispin Dew, Margaret thought. More than a word. She would like to give him a good tongue-lashing about now. It was true that it was she who had told the lie, but why had he spread the story about when she had *told* him no one else knew yet, even her family? Had it been done out of sheer spite? But *why?*

It was as if her wish conjured him. A footman came into the breakfast parlor at that moment to inform the butler, who informed Margaret, that a Major Dew had asked to see Miss Huxtable and had been shown into the visitors' parlor.

Margaret followed the butler there and swept past him after he had opened the door for her.

Crispin, in uniform, was standing before the empty fireplace, looking smart and imposing and decidedly uncomfortable — as well he might. He bowed to her.

"Meg —" he began.

"I want an explanation," she demanded,

glaring at him. "Do you hate me so much, Crispin? But *why* do you hate me? What have I ever done to deserve it?"

"My God, Meg," he said, taking a step toward her and looking at her, aghast, "I do not hate you. I have always adored you. You must know that."

Her head snapped back as if he had struck her.

"*Adored* me?" she said with scorn. "*Have* you?"

"You are thinking of Teresa," he said. "I can explain that, Meg."

"So can I," she said. "An imbecile could explain it. But I am not interested in hearing your explanation. Why did you betray me last evening?"

"Betray?" he said. "That is a harsh judgment, Meg. You *are* betrothed to Sheringford, are you not? You told me so yourself — both in Hyde Park and at the ball."

"And on *both* occasions," she said, "I told you that no announcement had yet been made, that even my family had not been told. It did not occur to me to swear you to secrecy. I trusted to your discretion and your honor."

He winced visibly.

"I was concerned about you, Meg," he said. "I was talking with Vanessa and Moreland when you left the dance floor to sit in that alcove with Sheringford. Moreland explained who he was and wondered who had dared introduce him to you. You could not possibly know that he was not a suitable acquaintance, he said. That worried your sister, and she would have gone to you herself if Moreland had not advised against it. I went instead. I hoped to draw you away from him without creating any sort of scene — I thought perhaps you would welcome a chance to escape if you already knew about him or would be grateful once you learned the truth. But instead you told me you were betrothed to him. What was I to do then?"

"Obviously," she said, "there was only one thing *to* do, and you did it. You told everyone in the ballroom."

"I confided in two of my fellow officers," he admitted. "They are my friends and I trust them. I asked their opinion on whether a man who had known you all his life as a neighbor and friend had the right to interfere in your life to the extent of trying to persuade you to break your engagement."

"You have *not* known me all my life," she said. "You have not known me *at all* for the last twelve years, Crispin."

. . . *as a neighbor and friend* . . . Those words had stung. Had there been nothing else between them as far as he was concerned?

"Meg," he said, "Sheringford is a scoundrel of the first order. He ought not even to have been there last night. I doubt he had been sent an invitation. You cannot possibly be serious about marrying him. Break off the engagement and marry me instead."

"What?" Her eyes widened.

"No one will blame you," he said. "Indeed, everyone will applaud your good sense."

"In choosing to marry *you?*" she said.

He flushed.

"You would have married me once upon a time," he said. "If your father had lived, we probably *would* have married long ago. Nothing much has changed since then except that we are both a little older. And except that you are lovelier now than you were then." He smiled.

"And that you have been married in the meanwhile," she said. "And that you have a daughter."

"Who needs a mother," he said softly. "Meg —"

But she held up a hand and he stopped.

He was asking her to marry him. After all this time, after all that had happened, he expected her to *marry* him? After the terrible embarrassment he had caused her last evening?

But she would not allow her attention to be diverted from the main issue.

"It was one of the other officers who spread the news of my betrothal last evening, then?" she asked. "Is that what you are saying, Crispin?"

"It was not intentional, and it was certainly not malicious," he said. "I was ready to rip him apart this morning after hearing all the gossip last evening and reading the papers this morning. But he was as concerned as I. He merely mentioned what I had told him to his cousin when he spoke with her after leaving me — in strictest confidence, of course. He had wanted her opinion."

And so stories, rumors, gossip spread as surely as a wildfire did after a single spark had caught alight. The cousin had told someone else in confidence, and that someone else . . .

Well.

"I am so very, very sorry, Meg," he said. "I realize it must be distressing to you to have your betrothal made public before you had even had a chance to break the news to your family — and presumably before Sheringford could apply formally to Stephen for your hand. But there would have been gossip sooner or later, you know, if your brother and sisters had been unable to talk you out of such an ineligible connection. It was not to be avoided. Sheringford is a social pariah, and justifiably so. I really do not understand how you can have listened to an offer from him, let alone accepted one. Meg —"

"Your apology has been made," she said, interrupting him. "I assume that was your reason for coming here this morning, Crispin. You will excuse me now. I was on my way to call upon Nessie when you arrived."

"Meg," he said, taking another step toward her, "don't marry him. I beg you. You will be miserable. Marry me instead."

"And live happily ever after?" she asked him.

He had the grace to flush again.

"Sometimes," he said, "we need time in which to gain wisdom and make up for past mistakes."

"I do hope," she said, "you are not calling your late wife a mistake, Crispin. Or your daughter. And perhaps Lord Sheringford ought to be granted the same opportunity to demonstrate that he is wiser now than he was five years ago and is willing and able to recover from past mistakes."

He sighed audibly and then made her another bow.

"Your family will all have something to say about this betrothal, I promise you," he said. "Listen to them, Meg. Don't go against them just out of stubbornness. You always were the most stubborn person I knew, I remember. If you will not listen to me, then listen to them. Promise me?"

She merely raised her eyebrows and stared at him, and he was obliged to bid her an abrupt good morning and stride past her to let himself out of the room.

Margaret stood where she was, listening to his boot heels ringing on the marble floor of the hall and to the sounds of the outer door opening for him and then closing behind him.

He had asked her to marry him.

The last time he asked she had wanted quite literally to die because she had loved him so very dearly but had been unable to accept his proposal, because he was going away to war and she had to stay home to bring up her brother and sisters.

And now?

Could a love of that magnitude die? If it was true love, could it ever die? Was there such a thing as true love? Life was very sad if there were not — and unbearably so if one's experience with romantic love turned one into an incurable cynic.

She did not love Crispin any longer. She did not *want* to love him again. Things could never be the same between them. Was love conditional, then? Was she determined not to love him because he had been faithless once and caused her years of heartache?

Whoever could possibly deserve love if it was conditional upon perfect behavior?

Did *he* love *her?* He had said he adored her. But did he also *love* her? Had he *ever?* But if he had, how could he have married someone else?

Had he loved his wife — Teresa?

Oh, she was horribly upset again. She had thought Crispin could never again have this power over her.

Margaret sighed and shook her head and turned determinedly to the door. She would go and make that call on Vanessa. She would see the children and restore her spirits. Never mind that silly gossip last evening or the even sillier paragraph in this morning's paper. And never mind Crispin Dew. Or the Earl of Sheringford, who had to marry within the next two weeks or lose everything until after his grandfather died. Why should she care about that? And never mind the Marquess of Allingham and his pretty Miss Milfort.

Life could be unutterably depressing at

times, but it went on. There was no point in giving in to depression.

There was a tap on the door and it opened before she could reach it.

"There is a Mrs. Pennethorne to see you, Miss Huxtable," the butler informed her. "Will you receive her?"

Mrs. Pennethorne? Margaret frowned, trying to think who the lady could be. The name sounded familiar. But why would she be calling in the morning when most social calls were made in the afternoon?

Mrs. *Pennethorne.* Her eyes widened slightly. Had not the Earl of Sheringford introduced himself as Duncan Pennethorne? Who *was* this lady? His *mother?*

Was this whole foolish business *never* to end?

"Show her in, by all means," she said.

Mrs. Pennethorne was probably younger than she was, Margaret decided as soon as the lady stepped into the room. She was fashionably clad in a pale green carriage dress with a poke bonnet to match, and she was small and slender and blond and exquisitely lovely in a fragile sort of way.

Not his mother, then, Margaret thought. His sister? But she was *Mrs.* Pennethorne.

"Miss Huxtable?" The lady curtsied and regarded Margaret with slightly slanted eyes, which were as green as her dress.

Margaret inclined her head.

"We have not met," the lady said, her voice sweet and breathless, "but I felt compelled to call upon you as soon as I heard. You *must* not marry Lord Sheringford, Miss Huxtable. You *really* must not. He is the very devil and will bring you nothing but misery and ostracism from society. Do please forgive this impertinence from a complete stranger, but I had to take the risk of coming and warning you."

Margaret rejected her first impulse, which was to offer the lady a seat. She clasped her hands at her waist and raised her eyebrows. Yes, this *was* an impertinence.

"Mrs. Pennethorne?" she said. "You are a relative of the Earl of Sheringford?"

"It pains me to have to admit it," the lady said, flushing, "though fortunately he is a relative only by marriage. He is my dear husband's second cousin."

Margaret kept her eyebrows raised. She did not know what to say.

"You may know *of* me," Mrs. Pennethorne said. "My maiden name was Turner. I came within a few hours of making the most dreadful mistake of my life. I almost married the Earl of Sheringford myself five years ago. Instead, I married my dear Mr.

Pennethorne shortly after and have been blissfully happy with him ever since."

Oh, goodness. This was the abandoned bride, the sister-in-law of the infamous Mrs. Turner, who had run off with the earl.

"Yes," Margaret said, "I *have* heard of you, of course. But —"

But this was none of her business. She had no wish to listen to the whole sordid story — or any part of it, for that matter.

"I do not have an acquaintance with you," Mrs. Pennethorne said. Clearly she had come to talk, not to listen. "But I *do* know you by reputation. You are very well respected as the eldest sister of the Earl of Merton and the Duchess of Moreland and Baroness Montford. I daresay it is irksome to you still to be unmarried when your younger sisters have made such brilliant matches, but believe me, Miss Huxtable, the answer does not lie in marrying Lord Sheringford. My brother was the happiest of men before Laura was seduced away by that *monster.* He would have taken her back and forgiven her at any time after she left. He would not divorce her, as everyone who knew him advised. He never lost hope that she would return home and beg his forgiveness — which he would freely have given. He was devastated by the news of her death.

That man, Miss Huxtable, has ruined my brother's life for all time, and he would have ruined mine too if my dear Mr. Pennethorne had not been kind and honorable enough to marry me himself."

Margaret gazed at her in pure astonishment.

"I must thank you for your visit and your concern," she said. "Will you forgive me if I do not offer you refreshments? I am about to go out. My sister is expecting me."

She had decided very recently, she remembered, that she would never tell a lie again.

"Of course," the lady said. "I will not delay you. And I do beg you to forgive me, Miss Huxtable. It has been almost unbearably painful, you must understand, to know that *that man* has had the effrontery to return to London. My brother suffers dreadfully from the knowledge, as do I. My dear Mr. Pennethorne is chagrined beyond words, since he must bear the shame of sharing a name with Lord Sheringford. It has been our fervent hope that we would neither see nor hear from him until we leave town at the end of the Season. We certainly had no wish to be embroiled in his business. But when I learned this morning that he had snared yet another innocent, respectable lady into his net, I found the knowledge *truly* unbearable. I knew I had no choice but to come to warn you, to *beg* you to break off the betrothal before it is too late. Promise me that you will, Miss Huxtable."

"I appreciate your concern for my happiness," Margaret said, crossing the room with firm steps to open the door. "And I thank you for coming. You will excuse me now?"

"Of course," Mrs. Pennethorne said, waiting until Margaret held the door open for her. "I felt it my duty to come."

Margaret inclined her head and stood in the doorway to watch her visitor leave.

She was still all astonishment. What had *that* been all about? It was perfectly understandable, of course, that the lady would hate the Earl of Sheringford, both on her own account and on that of her brother. But why would she feel it necessary to call upon the woman who was supposedly betrothed to the earl? It could not possibly be *jealousy,* could it? Did she secretly still *love* Lord Sheringford?

That was surely impossible.

This, Margaret thought, was all very bewildering indeed. For the sake of a moment's triumphant satisfaction in telling Crispin that she was betrothed to someone else, she had set in motion all these ridiculous consequences.

Perhaps instead of going to call upon Vanessa, she should remain here and give orders for her bags to be packed. She suddenly longed for the peace and sanity of Warren Hall.

That was what she would do, in fact.

But before she could leave the doorway of the visitors' parlor, there was yet another knock at the outer door, and a footman opened it to admit Vanessa and Katherine, come together to call upon her.

"Oh, well," Margaret said without even trying to disguise the irritability from her voice, "you had better come in here, the both of you, and join your voices to the choir."

"The choir?" Vanessa said after they had stepped into the parlor and the footman had closed the door from the outside.

"Of those urging me to put an end to a nonexistent betrothal," Margaret said. "First Crispin, then Mrs. Pennethorne, and now presumably you. Whoever will be next, I wonder?"

It was a rhetorical question. But it was answered almost immediately. There was a tap at the parlor door even before they had all sat down, and it opened to admit Constantine.

"Ah," Margaret said, throwing both hands

in the air.

"I will not ask if that gesture demonstrates delight at seeing me or displeasure," he said cheerfully as he crossed the room toward her and took one of her hands in both his own before releasing it again. "But I hope it is the former. I have just come from a vigorous sparring bout at Jackson's and am hoping you will offer me tea or coffee."

Stephen and Elliott arrived together before the tea tray was brought in.

Jasper followed them in before Margaret had finished pouring the tea.

Margaret wondered if she had ever felt more foolish in her life and decided that it was not possible.

And talk about storms in teacups!

She was also angry but had not decided with whom she was most annoyed. Herself, perhaps?

Crispin had told her she was stubborn and always had been. The accusation had irritated her. But he must have been right, she concluded after a few minutes.

The choir sang in perfect unison. There was not one dissenting voice. Vanessa and Katherine were incredulous and aghast that she would even *think* of marrying a man she had met for the first time last evening — without even a formal introduction. Nor-

138

mally their reason would have been that she could not possibly know a thing about him on such short acquaintance. But on this occasion just the opposite was the case. She knew *everything* about him — he had even admitted it all himself — and none of it was good. And *that* was a massive understatement.

Stephen, with Elliott's concurrence, had agreed to allow the Earl of Sheringford to pay a formal call at the house during the afternoon. He could hardly have refused when Margaret had introduced him to Crispin Dew last evening as her betrothed. Both men agreed, though, that he should be allowed to proceed no farther into the house than the library and to see no one there but Stephen. Meg must give him leave to inform the earl that she would not receive him, today or any other day.

"After all," Stephen said, "you are not embroiled in any real *scandal,* Meg, only a great deal of silly gossip. If you are never seen with the man again, and if nothing more is said about any betrothal between you, it will be concluded soon enough that there never was any truth in the story — as is the case with most rumors."

"Very true, Stephen," Katherine said.

"And very sensible," Vanessa agreed.

"And everyone knows you as the soul of propriety, Margaret," Elliott added.

Which was perhaps a bit of a mistake on his part. Being the soul of propriety sounded to Margaret like a very dull thing to be. Did she want *that* written on her epitaph?

"Sherry was a friend of mine at one time," Constantine said. "He still is, I suppose. We sparred with each other at Jackson's this morning and then walked to White's together. But it would be extremely unwise to ally yourself to him, Margaret. He has an undeniably wicked past, and you would not want a deservedly spotless reputation sullied by association with him."

A deservedly spotless reputation. That would look good too on her headstone. Future generations would yawn as they read.

"Rakes would be doomed to eternal infamy if some decent lady did not fall in love with them and take a chance on them," Jasper said, grinning at Margaret and threatening the choir's harmony for the moment. He ought to know the truth of what he said. He had been one of London's most infamous rakes when Kate had taken a chance on him — nudged on her way, it was true, by the eruption of scandal. "However, Sherry is not exactly a rake, is he? Justly or otherwise, he is seen as the blackest-hearted of villains. Certainly no one can deny that he did something pretty villainous five years ago — two things, actually. You would not be able to handle him, Meg — or he you, for that matter. You have lived a righteous life and deserve better."

"Oh, that is *exactly* what we have all been trying to say," Katherine said, laying a hand on his sleeve. "We want someone perfect for you, Meg. We want you to be *happy.* You deserve the very best life has to offer."

You would not be able to handle him . . .

You have lived a righteous life . . .

These were the people who loved her most in the world. The people who loved her so dearly that they wanted only the very best for her that life had to offer. To them she was the soul of propriety, a woman with a spotless reputation who had lived a virtuous, righteous life. They wanted someone perfect for her — someone equally proper, blameless, virtuous, righteous . . . A very dull man, in fact.

He sounded a little like the Marquess of Allingham. Was *that* why she had hesitated so long about accepting his marriage offers? It seemed disloyal. He was all those things, and she had always liked him. She had always considered him a friend.

Friend, not lover.

The Earl of Sheringford had called him a dull dog.

She had been horribly disconcerted by the marquess's announcement last evening. But had she also been *upset?* Did she feel heartbroken today? In light of everything else that had happened, she had spared him scarcely a thought.

These people wanted her to be happy. But how did they know what would make her happy?

Did *she* know?

Once she had thought happiness and Crispin Dew were synonymous terms. But today he had offered her marriage again, and she had refused because . . . Oh, there was a host of reasons.

But she realized something as her family all looked at her in love and concern and waited for her to say something.

She was ripe for rebellion.

Or else she was just stubborn.

She had such a short acquaintance with the Earl of Sheringford that she could not even remember clearly what he looked like. She knew he was tall, well built, dark-haired and dark-complexioned, with angular features and almost black eyes. She knew that her first impression of him was that he was almost ugly. She remembered too that her eyes had nevertheless been drawn to that face while they talked. There had been an intensity there, in his eyes, in the tautness of his almost morose features, that had somehow fascinated her.

He had fascinated her.

She had never held a conversation with any other man that even remotely resembled her conversation with him. His honesty had fairly taken her breath away. He had urged her to marry him in almost the same breath as he had admitted to being a wife-stealer and a man who had abandoned his bride on their wedding day. And he had not pretended to any sudden infatuation for her, Margaret. He had told her exactly why he wished her to marry him. He needed a wife before two more weeks had passed.

Surely any other man in the same circumstances would have gone out of his way to charm her with sweet talk and lies, and to keep the truth about himself from her for as long as possible — until after their marriage if he could.

He was — *different.* She was quite sure that if she met him again in the cold light of day and listened to his marriage proposal, she would reject him in a heartbeat. Today she would see him for the unattractive, ill-tempered villain that he was. She would see the desperation in him and be repulsed by it. What man, after all, would be prepared to marry a stranger — *any* stranger — merely in order to keep the house and property from which he drew an income until his grandfather died and left him a fortune?

And she was the stranger he had chosen.

It was really quite insulting.

But he had fascinated her and still did.

And she *was* stubborn. Her family was united in urging her against even seeing the Earl of Sheringford again. Crispin had urged her to change her mind and marry *him* instead. Mrs. Pennethorne had urged her to put an end to her betrothal.

The silence had become quite lengthy — and very tense.

"The Earl of Sheringford is coming here this afternoon," she said, "to speak with *me* — after he has spoken with you, Stephen. It would be uncivil of me to refuse to receive him, especially when I was the one who caused all the gossip by introducing him to Crispin as my betrothed last evening. It was not *he* who said it, remember."

"You were upset," Vanessa said, "at seeing Crispin again so unexpectedly, Meg. It is understandable that —"

But Margaret held up a hand to stop her

144

from continuing.

"It is neither understandable nor excusable," she said, "that I would use one gentleman merely to spite another. Which, if I am to be perfectly honest with you and myself, is exactly what I did. I will speak with the earl this afternoon. I will apologize for involving him in all this foolish gossip when I daresay he hoped to slip quietly back into society after so many years as a castaway. What has happened was all my fault, and I owe it to Lord Sheringford to tell him so in person."

"It is just like you to take all the burden of blame on your own shoulders, Meg," Stephen said, looking troubled. "It is something you always did. Let me do something for you now in return. Let me send the fellow on his way."

"He is not *the fellow,* Stephen," she said, getting to her feet. "He is the Earl of Sheringford. And I will speak with him myself."

"Bravo, Meg," Jasper said.

"Oh, Meg," Vanessa said, hurrying toward her to hug her, "you are always so noble. But I am just afraid that you will see him to apologize to him and end up betrothing yourself to him."

"Trust me," Margaret said as they all got up.

Trust her to do *what,* though?

Would she really be seeing Lord Sheringford only to express her regrets over the consequences of her impulsive words last evening? Which he had urged upon her, by the way.

Or would she be seeing him because she wanted to bring his face into focus again?

Or because she was fascinated by her memories of him?

Or because she was thirty years old and had just come face to face with a faithless lover from her past and with the fiancée of the man she had expected to marry herself this year?

Or because she had just been called righteous and the soul of propriety and a woman of spotless virtue?

"Oh, we *do* trust you, Meg," Katherine said, hugging her after Vanessa had stepped back. "Of course we do."

Yes, of course they did. She had always been eminently trustworthy and dependable and predictable, had she not?

And dull.

7

Almost precisely fifty hours after his grandfather had issued his ultimatum, Duncan was standing alone in the library at Merton House, staring out through the window, waiting to make a formal marriage offer to Miss Margaret Huxtable.

It was all disorienting, to say the least. Good Lord, he did not know the woman at all. She did not know *him*. He could scarcely even remember what she looked like. He remembered well enough what she had *felt* like, pressed against his body, but the more he tried to bring her face into focus in his mind, the more he saw a blank surrounded by dark hair. He could remember only that he had thought her beautiful.

Which was *some* consolation, he supposed.

It had been something of a relief to find Merton alone in the library when he had been admitted more than half an hour ago.

He had fully expected Moreland to be there too — and the duke was a formidable figure of a man. He had Greek blood in him, and it showed.

But Merton was no soft touch either, young as he was. Duncan would guess his age to be no more than twenty-two or three. He had made no bones about the fact that that he disliked and despised Duncan and opposed any match with his sister. He had offered a more than generous dowry with her but had insisted that every penny of it be put at her disposal and that of any children of the marriage. He had probed meticulously into Duncan's present means and future prospects and had declared that he would call upon the Marquess of Claverbrook to confirm what he had heard — since he did not trust the word of a known villain.

It had taken all of Duncan's self-control to stop himself from stalking out of the room and out of the house. It could not be done. He had made Miss Huxtable an offer of sorts last evening, the morning paper had made much of it this morning, and honor dictated that the offer be made official today. If she refused him, so be it. He would resume the hunt with thirteen days to spare.

He had taken a huge bouquet of flowers,

he remembered, when he had called to propose marriage to Caroline Turner. A footman had whisked it away at the door and he had not seen it again. He had been welcomed with smiles and bows and a hearty handshake by her father. He had gone down on one knee when alone with Caroline and delivered a rehearsed speech that was more floral than the vanished bouquet. He had covered the back of her hand with kisses when she had said yes and called himself the happiest of men. He had assured her that he loved her and would until he drew his final breath — and beyond that through all eternity. And he had meant every word, God help him.

He had come empty-handed today, and there was no rehearsed speech rattling around in his brain. And no ardor accelerating his heartbeat.

The door opened behind him and closed again even as he turned. He was relieved to recognize her, though she looked somewhat different. She was dressed in dark blue today. Her hair was styled more simply and looked thicker and glossier. Candlelight had not unduly flattered her. She must be one of the most beautiful women he had ever seen. Not to mention voluptuous — he had not exaggerated *that* fact in his memory.

She also looked calm and self-possessed. And . . . intelligent. Her eyes looked him over steadily and unhurriedly. Perhaps, like him, she had been afraid that she might not even recognize him today.

He bowed formally. She did not curtsy in return. She inclined her head instead.

"Miss Huxtable," he said.

"Lord Sheringford."

"I do apologize," he said, "for the very public reaction to our encounter last evening."

"On the contrary," she said, "it is I who must apologize to you, my lord. If I had been looking where I was going, I would not have run into you. And if I had not told Major Dew in the park the day before yesterday that I was betrothed and then been embarrassed last evening to discover that the Marquess of Allingham was already engaged to marry someone else, I would not have presented *you* as my betrothed. It was all very foolish and very out of character for me. But that latter fact is beside the point. I have caused you embarrassment and I am sorry."

He had been surprised last evening by her candor. He was surprised again today. He had expected that she would heap blame upon him.

"There will be no further embarrassment for either of us," he said, "when a formal announcement of our engagement appears in tomorrow's papers."

She moved farther into the room and seated herself on a chair by the fireplace. She indicated one on the other side.

"Do sit down," she said. "You are under no moral obligation whatsoever to offer for me today, you know. It would be absurd for either of us to feel forced into marrying by a little idle gossip. We have done nothing wrong or even indiscreet. We danced and talked in a crowded ballroom, as did everyone else who was there. Both activities are the very point of a ball. There really has been nothing resembling scandal, has there? Gossip is simply that — empty talk that is quickly replaced by some other. Everyone will forget within a week."

"But Miss Huxtable —"

She held up a hand to stop him from continuing.

"However," she said, "I do remember your telling me that your need to marry without delay is a rather desperate one. It is this fact, I suppose, that has brought you here this afternoon."

"I hope," he said, "I would have come anyway."

"I would have had Stephen assure you that your gallantry was appreciated but quite unnecessary," she said. "I would have had him send you on your way to freedom with my thanks. But freedom is not what you will face if I send you away, is it?"

"There is always freedom," he said, "unless, I suppose, one is actually incarcerated. I could seek employment."

"But you would prefer to marry," she said. "Why is that?"

She was actually *interviewing* him. This encounter was not proceeding at all as he had expected.

"I suppose," he said, "because I would prefer to live the life of a landed gentleman to which I am accustomed."

"Poverty is not a pleasant thing," she said. "We were always poor until Stephen inherited the earldom. We were not unhappy. Indeed, we were often very happy indeed. But we had never known wealth or the security of a large home and farms and a sizable income. Now that we *do* know it, I do not doubt we would find it extremely difficult to go back. You have never known poverty, I suppose. Are you afraid of it?"

He leaned back in his chair and cocked one eyebrow.

"I am not really afraid of anything, Miss

Huxtable," he said.

There was indeed very little left to fear. The worst had happened to him already. And somehow he would manage no matter what happened — or did not happen — during the next two weeks. All sorts of little boys, after all, were raised quite adequately by men who had to work for a living.

"You would be a foolish man if that were the truth," she said. "But I do not believe it is. I believe you are simply a liar. You are in good company, however. Men will admit to almost any shortcoming before they will admit to feeling fear. It is considered weak and unmanly."

"Miss Huxtable," he said, "I have Woodbine Park in Warwickshire to offer you if you marry me. It is a sizable home in spacious, well-kept grounds. And its income, though no vast fortune, is more than comfortable. I have future prospects of far greater splendor. I am the Marquess of Claverbrook's heir, and he has properties dotted all over England. He is vastly wealthy."

"And is this *all* you have to offer, Lord Sheringford?" she asked after regarding him in silence for several moments.

He opened his mouth to speak and then shut it again. What else *was* there? She was not imagining, was she, that he had fallen

153

violently in love with her last evening and had his heart to lay at her feet?

"I cannot offer an unsullied name," he said. "I am afraid I earned a notoriety that will not quickly die — if it ever does."

"That is true," she agreed. "But the past cannot be changed. Only the future is at least partially in our control. Are you sorry for what you did?"

He felt a spurt of anger. Was she about to read him a sermon?

"No," he said curtly.

"You would do it again, then?" she asked.

"Yes," he said. "Without hesitation."

"It must be good," she said so quietly that he almost did not hear the words, "to be loved that dearly."

He opened his mouth to reply and closed it yet again.

"What will you do," she asked him, "if I reject you today?"

He almost hoped she would. He did not find her . . . comfortable.

He shrugged.

"Resume the hunt," he said. "I still have almost two weeks."

"Thirteen days, to be exact," she said. "An eternity."

"Yes."

"But this time," she said, "you will carry

154

the unpleasantness of today's gossip with you into the courtship, as well as your notoriety. Your chosen bride and her family will believe that you have jilted me too."

"Perhaps." He would not glare. It would suggest that she was getting under his skin. He fixed her with a stare that many people found intimidating.

When trying to recall her face earlier, he had assumed that with her dark hair she must have brown eyes. They were actually a startling blue — and they did not waver from his.

"Why should I marry you?" she asked him. "Give me reasons, Lord Sheringford. Not the financial details. I knew of those even before stepping in here. I am not swayed by such considerations. I no longer have to fear poverty even if I never marry and live to be a hundred. Why should I marry you? With what persuasions did you arm yourself before you came here?"

If he had arrived in that ballroom two minutes before or after he actually had, he thought, there would have been no collision and no dance and no conversation in an alcove. He would have picked out some pathetic-looking girl who would have been only too delighted to marry him. Indeed, he had already picked out such a girl a moment before the collision, had he not? He would not be sitting here now being interrogated by a woman he suspected he might easily come to dislike quite intensely.

He stopped himself from drumming his fingertips on the arm of his chair.

"You are not a young woman," he said. "How old *are* you?"

"Thirty," she said. "You think I am desperate for a husband, then? You did not expect that any great persuasion would be necessary?"

He stared at her for a few moments.

"You would have to be blind to be desperate," he said. "Since you are not, you must know how beautiful you are. You must also realize how sexually appealing you are, though I do not suppose you use just those words in your genteel mind. We both know that I do not represent your last chance, Miss Huxtable. But you have been shaken during the past few days by the reappearance of a former lover. *Was* he a lover, by the way? Or was he merely a man you loved?"

For the first time she flushed. She did not look away from him, though.

"He was —" she said before stopping abruptly. "You are impertinent."

Ah — interesting!

"You went to last evening's ball," he said, "expecting that Allingham would offer you marriage. You were ready to accept him even though you do not love him."

"How do you know I do not?" she asked him.

"You were not distraught," he said.

She raised her eyebrows.

"I was not? Yet I collided with you when attempting to dash from the ballroom in ungainly haste," she reminded him.

"Because you were chagrined, even humiliated," he said, "and because you had spotted your faithless lover and remembered that you would not after all have a fiancé to dangle before him. When Allingham came to claim his dance with you, you showed no symptoms of a woman whose heart he had just shattered."

"I am relieved to hear that," she said. "Major Dew came here this morning to beg me not to marry you. He offered to marry me instead."

"And?" He raised his eyebrows.

"And I said no," she told him.

"And yet," he said, "you still love him."

She looked consideringly at him.

"Do I?" she said. "You seem to know me better than I know myself, Lord Sheringford. But you would marry a woman you

157

believe to be in love with someone else?"

"You would not be happy with him," he said.

"Because he has a weak chin?" She raised her eyebrows again.

"Because he loves *himself* more than he loves anyone else," he said. "Such men do not make good husbands."

"But you would?" she asked him.

"I am not in love with myself," he said. "Or with you."

The corners of her mouth lifted in a slight smile.

"Are you always so honest?" she asked him.

"We lie," he told her, "in order to persuade the world and ourselves that we are something we are not — usually something far better and more flattering than what we really are. I have no wish to deceive myself, and others already believe they know me very well indeed."

"And *do* they?" she asked him. "Are you defined by what you did five years ago?"

"You must confess," he said, "that there is nothing much worse a man can do than abandon his bride on her wedding day — except perhaps to run off with her married sister-in-law instead."

"Why did you do it?" she asked him.

"I suppose," he said, "because I liked the one woman better than the other and was willing to take what I wanted and be damned to the consequences."

"And yet," she said, "you told me last evening that you were head over ears in love with your bride. Are your feelings so fickle? And do you always take what you want?"

He ignored the first question and thought about his answer to the second.

"What I want is not always available for the taking," he said.

"Do you want *me?*" she asked.

But she held up a hand again before he could answer.

"You claim always to tell the truth," she said. "Tell it now, Lord Sheringford. As you said a short while ago, there is still time for you to find a different bride. Despite everything, there is bound to be someone out there who will be only too happy to marry an earl and future marquess. Do you want *me?*"

He scorned to look away from her, and she would not look away from him, it seemed.

Would he prefer someone younger, someone quietly biddable, someone who would be pathetically grateful to him for marrying her, someone who would be content to be bedded and impregnated and otherwise ignored? Someone too timid to protest the presence of an illegitimate child in her home — and one her husband doted upon?

With such a woman he could be almost free.

Except that he would always suspect that he had broken her spirit — about the worst thing any man could do to any woman.

Margaret Huxtable, he suspected, would be a constant challenge. A woman of unquenchable spirit. A constant thorn in the flesh. A constant . . .

"Yes," he said abruptly, "I do."

"I am going to ask a difficult thing of you, then," she said. "You must feel free to refuse my request. You owe me nothing, you see, since what happened last evening was entirely my fault. I cannot marry a stranger. I know that we must marry — if we *do* marry — within the next thirteen days. However, a marriage by special license can be performed at a moment's notice, can it not? It does not call for a great deal of planning. I will marry you on the last possible day, Lord Sheringford, provided we both wish to marry when the time comes. The difficult thing for you, of course, is that if you agree with this demand, you will be wagering everything upon my ultimately saying yes. And I may well not do so. I certainly will not marry you only to rescue you from having to earn your own living until your grandfather passes away."

"And in the meantime?" he said. "In the next twelve days?"

"Privately, we will get to know each other," she said, "as well as any two people *can* become acquainted in such a short time. And publicly you will court me. If you walk away today after refusing to agree to this condition, I shall not feel a moment's embarrassment. I shall live down the gossip with the greatest ease. But if I were to rush into a marriage with you during the next day or two, then I would be more than embarrassed. I would be humiliated. The *ton* would dream up a dozen reasons for my ungainly haste, none of them flattering. If you wish to marry me, Lord Sheringford, then you will pay determined, even ardent, court to me, and you will risk everything for me — including your beloved home and income."

He pursed his lips. He might very well grow to dislike this woman, he thought again — indeed, he was almost sure he already did — but he could not stop himself from respecting her.

She was a power to be reckoned with.

It was indeed a great risk — far more than she realized. She might reject him at the last moment. It was even possible that she was deliberately leading him into a trap on behalf of all abandoned women. She looked as if she might well be the crusading sort.

"I must warn you," she said, "that everyone who knows me — and even someone who does not — is horrified to find that I would even *consider* marrying you. They will keep on trying to persuade me against you — and they will be barely civil to you."

"Who is the someone who does not know you?" he asked.

"Mrs. Pennethorne," she said. "The lady you abandoned."

Ah.

"She came here this morning," she said, "and begged me not to court misery by marrying you. She is very lovely. I am not surprised that you once loved her — though not more than her brother's wife as it turned out. You *are* fickle."

"So it would seem," he said. "Do you still wish me to court you now that I have admitted that damning fact?"

"Yes," she said, "since you have not made the mistake of pretending to have fallen in love with *me*. I believe it would be an interesting experience to be wooed by

London's most notorious villain. And I have little to lose. If I decide at the end of it all that I cannot marry you, I will be hailed as something of a heroine."

Her lips curved slightly at the corners again, and he could not decide if she was a woman with a sense of humor or a woman whose heart was as cold as steel. He rather suspected the latter.

"I shall woo you, then, with persistence and ardor," he said, "on the assumption that you are giving serious consideration to marrying me in thirteen days' time."

"I will be attending the theater this evening," she said. "I will be sitting in the Duke of Moreland's box with the members of my family. Shall I inform them that you will be joining us there, my lord?"

Daniel into the lions' den. Or into the fiery furnace.

She stood, and he got to his feet too. Presumably he was dismissed. He bowed to her.

"I shall see you this evening, then," he said. "It is a pleasure to which I shall look forward with some eagerness . . . Maggie."

This time that suggestion of a smile lurked in her eyes as well as at the corners of her mouth.

Perhaps she *did* have a sense of humor.

8

Margaret did not invite the Earl of Sheringford to stay for tea even though all her family was assembled in the drawing room above, anxiously awaiting the outcome of her meeting with him.

She was far more breathless than she ought to have been by the time she had climbed the stairs. Even so, she would gladly have climbed another flight to take refuge in her room. It could not be done, however. She squared her shoulders and opened the door.

Stephen was standing at the window, facing into the room, his hands clasped behind his back, his booted feet slightly apart, an unusually grim expression on his face.

Elliott was standing behind Vanessa's chair beside the fireplace, one hand on her shoulder. She was looking agitated; he was looking like a dark, brooding Greek god. Jasper was sitting on a love seat beside Katherine,

Baby Hal asleep in the crook of his arm. Katherine was perched on the edge of her seat, her hands clasped so tightly in her lap that her knuckles showed white.

All of them, with the exception of Hal, turned toward the door, glanced beyond Margaret's shoulder, and almost visibly relaxed when they saw that Lord Sheringford was not with her.

"Well, Meg?" Stephen asked tensely, and it occurred to her that at some time during the past couple of years, when she had not been paying particular attention, he had grown fully and admirably into his role as head of the family. He was no longer simply the carefree, sometimes careless, always charming youth she remembered.

"Well," she said cheerfully, "here I am, and I have given directions for the tea tray to be brought up without further delay. You must all be as parched as I am. There will be an additional guest in your box at the theater this evening, Elliott. I hope you do not mind. I have invited the Earl of Sheringford to join us there."

Of course he minded. It showed in the further darkening of his expression.

They *all* minded.

She would have minded, very much indeed, if she had been sitting there and one of her sisters had been standing here. She would have wondered if the sister concerned had windmills in her head instead of a functioning brain.

"Oh, Meg," Kate said, "you have accepted him."

"I am *not* betrothed to the earl," Margaret said. "If I had been, I would have brought him up here with me to present to you all."

Stephen's shoulders sagged with relief.

"I *knew* you would not accept him in a million years, Meg," Vanessa said, smiling warmly at her. "You have always been by far the most sensible of us all, and it would be decidedly *un*-sensible to marry a man like the Earl of Sheringford merely because of a little silly gossip."

Vanessa was right, Margaret thought. She *was* sensible. She was all sorts of very proper, very reasonable, very *dull* things. But since last evening, and more especially since this morning, she had conceived the startlingly irrational urge to do something that was not sensible at all. She wanted to . . . Well, she wanted to *live.*

"But you have nonetheless invited Sherry to join you at the theater this evening, Meg?" Jasper said. "A consolation prize for the poor man, perhaps?"

The tea tray must have been all ready to

bring when she had given the word. It was carried into the room almost on Margaret's heels, and they all fell silent while it was set on a low table that had been placed before her usual chair, which everyone had left empty.

It was a chair that would probably be left empty for her use all her life if she did not marry, Margaret thought. No one must sit in it because it was Aunt Margaret's chair — or *Great*-Aunt Margaret's — and she needed to be close to the fire to keep the chill out of her aged bones and close enough to the mantel to prop her cane against it.

It was a horrifying glimpse into the future.

She seated herself and picked up the teapot.

"I have not accepted the Earl of Sheringford's marriage offer," she said as the door closed behind the footman and Vanessa came to distribute the teacups. "Neither have I rejected it."

She set the teapot down and looked up. They were all waiting for an explanation. The atmosphere was tense again.

"He must be married before the Marquess of Claverbrook's eightieth birthday, which is in a little less than two weeks' time," she said. "If he is not, he will lose his childhood home and the income he has always derived from it. He will be forced to seek employment until his grandfather dies, which may be shortly in the future or a long time away — it is impossible to know. He will *not* lose his home if he marries even one day before the birthday. With a special license it can be done almost at a moment's notice."

"But you are not —" Katherine began.

"I have told Lord Sheringford," Margaret said, "that it is possible I will marry him in two weeks' time, but that it is equally possible I will *not.* I informed him that it is up to him in the meanwhile to woo me, to convince me that marriage to him is what I want for the rest of my life. It was extremely risky for him to accept the challenge, but he did. If I say no, it will be too late for him to find someone else."

"No one would have him, anyway," Stephen said, lowering himself into the nearest chair, "especially after last night and this morning."

"I am not so sure of that, Stephen," Elliott said. "His future prospects are dazzling enough to tempt any father with some ambition, few scruples, and a marriageable daughter. And Woodbine Park itself is a not inconsiderable property."

"But *why?*" Katherine asked, gazing at Margaret. "Why would you even *consider* such a marriage, Meg? You must realize as well as we do that apart from a little embarrassment, your reputation will not suffer any real damage if you simply say no. Why did you even *see* him today when Stephen was very willing to turn him away on your behalf?"

They were questions they all wanted answered, though she had answered some of them this morning. Not one of them had touched their tea. Vanessa had not even handed around the plate of cakes.

"I behaved badly last evening," Margaret said. "I wanted Crispin to know that I was not eagerly waiting for him to pay attention to me and perhaps even pay court to me. And I was annoyed — no, *angered* — when he came to rescue me from the earl's wicked clutches after talking with Nessie and Elliott. As if he were my keeper. As if I needed his protection. As if I had not been forced to protect myself *and* my brother and sisters in all the years after he went off to join his regiment. And so I said something very rash and very foolish. I told him that the Earl of Sheringford was my betrothed. None of what happened for the rest of the evening or today has been his fault. Indeed, he has been the soul of honor."

"Except that by your own admission he is

desperate for a bride," Stephen said. "And you also told us last evening that he *suggested* what you said to Dew. You appear to have played right into his hands, Meg."

She felt humiliated at the confession she had just made about Crispin. She had never spoken to anyone of her relationship with him or her terrible heartache and resentment after his betrayal. She had kept it all strictly to herself.

Had she really just come perilously close to admitting to the Earl of Sheringford that they had been lovers before Crispin went off to join his regiment?

"I believe," she said, "I owed Lord Sheringford the courtesy of receiving him this afternoon."

"And the courtesy of marrying him?" Elliott asked. "He will be very persuasive during the next two weeks, Margaret. You may depend upon that. His livelihood hangs upon your saying yes. And he must be extraordinarily good at persuasion. Not so very long ago he talked a married lady into ruining herself and running off with him."

"Though to be fair, Elliott," Katherine said, "it ought to be said that no one has ever accused him of taking Mrs. Turner against her will. I daresay she was at least partly to blame."

"If he can be persuasive enough," Margaret said quietly, picking up her own saucer and carrying her cup to her lips with hands that were almost steady, "I will marry him. If he cannot, then I will not. It is as simple as that. The decision will be mine."

There was an uncomfortable silence.

"Perhaps," Stephen said, "we should all take the man to our collective bosom and encourage the match with all the enthusiasm we can muster. Otherwise Meg will marry him to spite us — and will end up spiting herself in the process. You were always the most stubborn person I knew, Meg. If any of us ever wanted to do something and you said no, then no it was no matter how much we might beg and plead."

The accusation stung.

"I was *responsible* for you all," she said. "I stood in place of both parents to you even though I was ridiculously young myself. You will never know the burden that was, Stephen — to do the job as well as I was able and even better than that. Failure was out of the question. And none of you have turned out so very badly."

"Take Hal, love," Jasper said to Katherine, and he handed over the baby's limp sleeping form before getting to his feet and coming to sit on the arm of Margaret's chair and take one of her hands in both his own. "You did a superlative job, Meg. You proved dependable in that monumental task, and I for one would trust you with my life. More than that, I would trust you with my son's life if the need ever arose. Sherry was a friend of mine before he ran off with Mrs. Turner. He was no wilder than any of the rest of us — which is not saying a great deal, it is true. He did what he did for reasons of his own. Perhaps he will tell you what they were one of these days. But you must make your own decision concerning him, and I for one will trust you to make the right decision. Right for *you,* that is, and not just for your family. It is time you took your life back into your own hands and lived it for yourself."

He handed her a large linen handkerchief, and only then did she realize that she had been crying even before he left his place. She took it and spread it over her eyes, mortified. She had never been a watering pot. She had perfected the art long ago of repressing all her deepest feelings so that other people would be able to rely upon her as steady and dependable.

"Oh, Meg," Vanessa said, "*of course* we all trust you. It is just that we all love you so very dearly and want your happiness more than we could possibly want almost anything else in the world."

"Meg." Stephen's voice was filled with misery. "I did not mean a word. I am so sorry. Forgive me. It is just that you are more than a sister to me. I was the youngest. I hardly remember our mother. My memories even of our father are dim. *You* were my mother, and a wonderful one you were too. You were the Rock of Gibraltar. I will never forget what I owe you. I *certainly* do not owe you spite and bad temper."

Elliott cleared his throat.

"Sheringford will be treated with the proper courtesy this evening, Margaret," he said. "You may be assured of that."

She dried her eyes and blew her nose and felt very foolish.

"Thank you," she said. "Cook will be mortally offended if we send back the cake plate untouched."

"I thought," Jasper said, "no one would ever think of offering it and that I was doomed to return home hungry."

He picked up the plate and handed it around himself.

He had called her sexually appealing, Margaret remembered suddenly — the Earl of Sheringford, that was.

What shockingly outrageous words!

Sexually appealing.

A treacherous part of her mind told her that it was perhaps the most delicious compliment anyone had ever paid her.

What a shocking admission!

And there was something about him. He was not handsome. He was not even good-looking. But he was . . .

Interesting.

Fascinating.

Totally inadequate words. But properly brought up ladies did not have the vocabulary to describe such men.

Doubtless it was the fascination of the forbidden. He was a self-confessed jilt and wife-stealer. He scorned to use either lies or wiles or charm despite his desperate need to attract a bride. Perhaps she was simply curious to know how such a man could have persuaded a respectably married lady to give up everything — including her character and reputation — in order to elope with him.

He was very much *not* the sort of man she would have expected to find fascinating. And that was a fascination in itself.

Sherry.

It was a name suited to a happy, active, carefree young man.

What had he been like *before?* What had

he been like *during?* What was he like *now* — apart from a man who looked neither happy nor carefree?

She had two weeks in which to satisfy her curiosity and get to know him. Two weeks during which to understand her fascination with him and get over it — or convert it into a lifetime commitment.

Margaret shivered, but fortunately no one noticed. They were all taking cakes so that the cook would not be offended, and talking with determined cheerfulness.

Duncan arrived slightly late at the theater so that he would not have to hover outside Moreland's box looking conspicuous while he waited for the duke's party to arrive. It was a ruse that accomplished nothing, though, for being late meant that he had to make an entrance into a box where everyone else was already seated. And it had to be done in full view of an audience that was also seated and assuaging its boredom before the play began by observing and commenting upon each new last-minute arrival.

He might as well have been the lead actor making his entrance upon the stage. He did not doubt that every eye in the theater was fixed upon him. He did not look to see, but he did not need to. There was a changed quality to the sound of voices that told him he was the focus of all attention.

It was unnerving, to say the least.

This, he thought, had been deliberate, not to mention sadistic. Margaret Huxtable was testing his mettle. Perhaps she was testing her own as well, for she was going to be as much on public display this evening as he was. Of course, to be fair, she had not invited him to arrive late. But he saw immediately that she had taken a seat at the front of the box and had kept one chair empty beside her. She could not have chosen a chair at the back so that she — and he — could duck down behind her relatives if she chose?

Every head in the box turned his way. Moreland looked haughty, Merton looked grim — nothing new there — Monty was grinning, his lady opened her fan and merely looked, the duchess smiled broadly with what appeared to be a genuine attempt at warmth, and Miss Huxtable coolly raised her eyebrows.

"Ah, Lord Sheringford," she said, and, like her sister, she opened her fan.

He bowed, and she proceeded to introduce him to her sisters, both of whom were beauties, though the duchess perhaps possessed more warm charm than actual good looks.

"Do come and sit beside me," Miss Huxtable said, and he made his way to her side and seated himself. He could hardly feel more conspicuous, he thought, if he had decided to come here without a stitch of clothing.

He took Miss Huxtable's free hand as he seated himself and raised it to his lips.

"Bravo," he said softly, for her ears only. "This was quite deliberate, was it not?"

She did not pretend ignorance of his meaning. She smiled at him as she recovered her hand.

"Let us see how much you want me, Lord Sheringford," she said. "And let the *ton* see it."

She leaned a little toward him as she spoke, still smiling. No one else heard the words.

At this precise moment — or any other moment for that matter — he wanted her only because the alternative was unthinkable.

"You are looking astonishingly lovely," he said quite honestly. "But since you always do, I will not belabor the point. You are fortunate enough to have the sort of beauty that will survive into middle age and even into old age and only very gradually mutate into handsomeness."

"You certainly know how to turn a woman's head, my lord," she said, fanning her face vigorously. "I am quite in love with you already. Is that your intent?"

The words were not spoken with either venom or sarcasm. They were spoken with *humor.* She was laughing at him, but not with any apparent spite. Maybe she was not just a cold fish, after all. He must be thankful for small mercies.

He almost smiled back, but scores of eyes were boring into him from all directions, near and far, and if he did not look back into those eyes soon, he would not do it at all, and some infernal gossip writer would take note of the fact and discern his discomfort and interpret it as shame.

He would not enjoy that — chiefly because he did not *feel* ashamed. Never had and never would.

He had had the forethought to arm himself with a quizzing glass before leaving the house — a fashion accessory he did not normally affect. Indeed, Smith had had to go searching around in numerous drawers before finding one. He lifted it to his eye now and looked slowly about the theater — up at the tiered boxes, down to the pit, which was occupied almost exclusively by gentlemen, one or two of whom waved cheerfully up at him.

A few people looked boldly back at him from the boxes. Far more, though, turned away and pretended to be quite unaware of his very existence.

"You ought to be warned," Miss Huxtable said at just the moment when the warning became unnecessary, "that Mrs. Pennethorne is seated in a box almost directly opposite and above us. Elliott has identified the gentleman beside her as Mr. Pennethorne and the gentleman directly behind her as Mr. Turner, her brother."

Laura's husband, no less.

They were all looking back at him, Duncan saw as he lowered his glass and made a slight inclination of the head in their direction. Good God, no wonder there had been such a buzz when he stepped into Moreland's box. Caroline had not changed in any noticeable way in five years. She was looking as sweetly pretty and delicate as ever. Norman was surely larger in girth, but he looked as prosy a bore as he had ever looked. And he still liked to risk the health of his eyeballs with the height and sharpness of the points of his starched shirt collar. Randolph Turner was looking as if someone had drained all the blood from his handsome blond head.

Was he wondering, perhaps, if the *ton* would expect him to slap a glove in Lord Sheringford's face and proceed to put a bullet between his eyes from twenty paces on some chilly dawn heath? *That* would be enough to send all his blood pooling in his feet.

None of the three of them acknowledged his nod.

Then the buzz of conversation changed subtly. The play was about to begin.

"One might almost believe, Miss Huxtable," Duncan said, dropping his quizzing glass on its black ribbon and taking her hand to set on his shirt cuff, then holding it there with his other hand, "that you had orchestrated the whole thing. It is a marvelous piece of theater in itself, is it not?"

She laughed. "That would have been very clever of me," she said. "Do you admire Mr. Goldsmith's plays?"

"I shall answer the question after viewing the performance," he said.

But he could not concentrate upon it. He was very aware of the warmth of her hand, the slim length of her fingers, the perfect oval of her short-cut nails. And he was aware that she was a woman of great physical attractions, and that he was definitely attracted — physically, that was. Bedding her would be no hardship at all, if they ever married.

He was aware of her family sitting very close and watching in silence — though whether it was him or the play that they watched, he did not know since they were all behind him.

And he was fully aware that those who were in attendance tonight would have far more interesting things to discuss tomorrow than the caliber of the performance that was proceeding on the stage.

Would Randolph Turner finally defend his honor and challenge him to a duel now that he had dared show his face in London?

Even though duels were *illegal?*

Sound swelled as the first act came to an end and the intermission began.

"Is the performance better than you expected, Meg?" the duchess asked, leaning forward in her chair. "She believes, Lord Sheringford, that she prefers to *read* plays rather than watch them performed."

"It is because we grew up in the country," Lady Montford explained, "where there were far more opportunities to read than to watch a performance."

"The characters on stage almost never

look quite as I imagined them," Miss Huxtable said. "And the dialogue is never quite as sprightly. On the whole I prefer to bring my imagination to bear upon literature rather than my eyes and ears."

"But this is an unusually fine performance," Merton said.

"Tell me, Meg," Monty said, winking at Duncan. "Would you rather read a musical score than listen to a symphony?"

"That is a different matter altogether," she told him with a smile.

"Not really," Moreland said. "A play is written to be seen and heard, not read, Margaret."

"But I would say," Duncan said, "that anything that is written in any form for the purpose of entertaining an audience may be enjoyed in any manner each individual finds most entertaining."

"Oh, what a very diplomatic answer," Lady Montford said, clapping her hands. "I must remember that the next time you decide to tease Meg about her preferences, Jasper."

"Shall we go for a stroll outside the box?" he suggested, getting to his feet and offering an arm to his wife. "Would anyone care to join us?"

He looked deliberately at Duncan.

Merton and Moreland and his duchess were already on their feet.

"We will remain here," Miss Huxtable said, and a few moments later they were alone together in the box.

"You are showing a small degree of mercy on me, are you, Miss Huxtable?" Duncan asked. "Or on yourself? Do you enjoy the notoriety you have courted by inviting me here this evening?"

"It is a notoriety I brought upon myself the moment I gave in to temptation and introduced you to Crispin Dew as my betrothed," she said. "Though the word *notoriety* suggests the existence of some wrongdoing. I have done nothing wrong — except to tell that lie."

"Which," he said, "will soon turn out not to be a lie after all."

"*Will?*" she said. "You are very confident, my lord."

"What will happen to you," he asked her, "if you do not marry me?"

She was the sort of woman, he thought, who could wear any color and look as if that was the color she ought always to wear. Tonight it was a netted silver tunic over turquoise silk. She was the sort of woman who would look beautiful even when her dark hair began to turn gray.

She shrugged and fanned her face slowly.

"Nothing whatsoever will change," she said. "The gossip will soon die down for lack of fuel to feed it, and I shall go home to Warren Hall, where I am always happy and where I can always keep myself busily occupied."

"And as time goes on?" he said. "Will your life always remain the same? How old is Merton?"

"Twenty-two," she said.

"In five or six years' time, then," he said, "if not sooner, he will undoubtedly turn his mind toward marriage and the begetting of heirs. What will happen to your life at Warren Hall then?"

"It is a large house," she said. "There will still be room for me."

He gazed deeply into her eyes and said nothing.

"I will find *something* to do," she said.

"With your brother's children, no doubt," he said.

"Yes," she agreed. "That will be pleasant."

"Would it not be more pleasant," he asked, "if they were your own?"

She fanned her face a little more briskly.

"We are talking about what I will do if I do not marry *you*," she said. "Perhaps I will marry someone else."

"Who?" he asked her. "Major Dew?"

She folded her fan, laid it very carefully across her lap, and looked down at it.

"No," she said. "The time for that was ten years or more ago. What I felt for him then cannot be recaptured now, and I could not settle for less."

"And yet," he said, "if you marry me, you will be settling for considerably less, will you not? You have never loved me, and I have never loved you."

She looked up at him, a smile tugging at the corners of her mouth.

"Lord Sheringford," she said, "you are supposed to be *wooing* me. Do you expect to succeed if you tell me so baldly that you do not love me?"

"I suspect I would stand far less chance of success," he said, "if I were to sit here pouring ardent platitudes into your ear and sighing piteously like a lover who fears that his love will be scorned and his heart trampled underfoot."

"I believe you would," she admitted, laughing.

He held her eyes with his own.

"You are not a virgin," he said, "by your own near admission. Are you content to go through the rest of your life without any more sexual experiences?"

She flushed but did not look away from him.

"As you believe I will," she said, "if I do not marry you?"

"As you probably will," he said, "if you do not marry me or someone else. I do not judge you to be promiscuous. But why *not* me? I could give you that experience. I believe I could make it very enjoyable indeed for you. Unless, that is, you prefer the passive pleasure of simply reading about it."

"Assuming," she said, "that there were somewhere I could read about such a thing. Are there any such books? I daresay there are in the male world. But is this how you would woo me, Lord Sheringford? By telling me how skilled and satisfying you would be in the marriage bed?"

"It is not a slight consideration," he said, "even though properly nurtured ladies are doubtless taught to believe that a marriage bed is a place for duty, not pleasure — and that there is no other type of bed in which the pleasures of sex can be indulged and enjoyed."

"*You,* Lord Sheringford," she said, "are quite outrageous. Is this how you planned to woo a frightened young girl with impoverished parents?"

"Good God, no," he said. "I would not have needed to woo her at all. I would have wooed her father with statistics detailing the prosperity of Woodbine Park and a listing of my grandfather's holdings. Though it would have been unnecessary to do either. My title and the one to which I am heir would have been inducement enough."

"I believe God *is* good," she said. "But I would prefer not to have the fact blurted out as an exclamation in my hearing, Lord Sheringford."

"I beg your pardon." He felt his first real amusement of the evening.

"But you believe your present wealth — provided you marry within the next two weeks — and your future prospects will not weigh sufficiently with me?" she said. "But of course you do. I told you so this afternoon. And so I must be enticed with the promise of — of —"

She seemed unable to complete the thought.

"A good time in bed?" he suggested.

"I must be enticed by *that?*" she said.

"I believe it might weigh with you more than you will admit," he said. "You are beautiful and attractive, Miss Huxtable — and thirty years old. And single. And it is presumably ten years or more since you last lay with a man. I believe the prospect of being able to do so again, not just once but nightly — and even daily too, perhaps — must be very appealing indeed to you."

"Nightly and daily with *you?*" she said.

"Do you find me repulsive?" he asked her.

"You are not handsome," she said. "You are not even particularly good-looking."

Well, he *had* asked!

He raised his eyebrows.

Her flush returned with a rush.

"But you are not ugly either," she said. "You are certainly not repulsive. Indeed, you are —"

At which interesting point in their conversation they were interrupted when someone tapped on the door of the box and opened it without waiting for an invitation. His mother stepped inside, followed by Sir Graham.

"Duncan," she said. "Oh, how brave of you to come to the theater this evening, though Graham calls it foolhardy, just as he did last evening when you attended the Tindell ball. I ought to have waited for you to bring your betrothed on a formal visit, I know, but you did not come this afternoon when I remained at home in the expectation that you would, you provoking man. Introduce us now, if you please."

"Mama," he said, "may I have the honor of presenting Miss Huxtable, who is *not* my betrothed, though she was kind enough to invite me to join her family in the Duke of Moreland's box this evening? May I present my mother, Miss Huxtable? And Sir Graham Carling, her husband?"

"Not *betrothed?*" His mother stepped forward and took both of Miss Huxtable's hands in her own, preventing her from curtsying. "But of course you are or will be soon. The whole world believes it, and what the whole world believes inevitably come to pass later if not sooner. And did you not, Miss Huxtable, admit last evening to some military officer whose name escapes me that you are betrothed to my son?"

"I did, ma'am," Miss Huxtable said. "But I was vexed with Major Dew over a private matter and lied, I am afraid."

"At my suggestion," Duncan added, noticing the pained expression on Sir Graham's face.

"And so you have found yourselves in a very public scrape today," his mother said with a laugh. "But it need not continue to embarrass either of you when the solution is so easy. You must make the lie into the truth and announce your betrothal. You make a very handsome couple. Do they not,

Graham?"

"I believe, Ethel," he said after growling out something that might have been agreement and might not, "the play is about to resume. We had better return to our box."

"Yes, we must," she agreed, squeezing Miss Huxtable's hands before releasing them. "My son must bring you for tea tomorrow, Miss Huxtable. We will talk about the wedding, which must be arranged quickly because Duncan's grandfather, who has always been an old grump, is being even more odious than usual and has cut off his funds. He is bound to restore them if Duncan marries someone so very eligible. He will really have no choice, will he? But even a hasty wedding need not be a clandestine or dreary affair. I shall have some ideas to suggest by tomorrow. Do promise to come."

Miss Huxtable looked at Duncan — and then smiled.

"I will be delighted, ma'am," she said. "Though I must warn you that there may not *be* a wedding."

"Of course there will," his mother said. "All men develop icy feet when marriage looms large on their horizon. I shall work upon Duncan before tomorrow afternoon and bring him to heel. You must not lose a wink of sleep over the matter."

"I shall not, ma'am," Miss Huxtable promised, and her eyes were actually twinkling as Sir Graham ushered Duncan's mother from the box and they resumed their seats.

"Oh," she said, "I *do* like your mother. I like people with character."

"Do you also like the infamous sons of such mothers?" he asked.

But she merely laughed as her family returned to the box.

Perhaps, he thought as the play resumed, his mother would talk her into the marriage. He hoped so.

There was so little time left to begin all over again.

The box that had been occupied by Turner and Norman and Caroline was empty, he noticed.

9

Sir Humphrey and Lady Dew had arrived from Shropshire on a rare visit to London. They had brought their granddaughter with them and were staying at Grillon's Hotel.

They had come primarily to spend some time with their son and bring his daughter closer to him. However, they were delighted to find that their old neighbors, the Huxtables, were in town and lost no time in sending invitations to them all to come for dinner in their private dining room at the hotel the evening after the theater visit.

Stephen was obliged to send a reluctant refusal, though he did promise to call upon the Dews another day. He had another engagement for that evening. But the others were free to go.

Margaret wished she were not. She had loved the Dews as neighbors and was quite eager to see them. But she also feared that Crispin would be at dinner too. Indeed, it was almost inevitable that he would be. She really did not want to see him again. She was still angry with him and upset and confused. She did *not* still love him, and she did *not* want to marry him. But even so . . .

Well, she wished his wife had lived and he had stayed with her and their child in Spain. She had put that painful part of her life behind her, and it was disturbing to have it all resurrected again.

Lord Sheringford had told her she still loved Crispin.

He was *wrong.*

Nevertheless, she did send off an acceptance to her invitation.

In the meantime, though, she had agreed to take tea with Lady Carling in the afternoon. She could have walked or taken the carriage to Curzon Street, as she had pointed out to the earl last evening. But he had insisted that he would come and escort her there himself. He arrived earlier than she expected.

"I am under orders to woo you in public, Miss Huxtable," he said after they had stepped out of the house, leaving Stephen standing in the hallway like a concerned and brooding parent. "We will walk to my mother's house by a circuitous route, then, and go through the park. It is a lovely day and there are bound to be crowds there even this early in the afternoon."

"I daresay there will," she agreed, taking his offered arm.

"I would have brought a curricle in which to convey you," he said, "except that I do not have a curricle, I am afraid. I really am quite impoverished, you see."

"Walking is better exercise anyway," she said. "But am I now intended to feel so sorry for you, Lord Sheringford, that I will agree to marry you tomorrow if not sooner in order to restore your funds?"

"*Do* you?" he asked. "And *will* you?"

"No," she said.

"Then I did not intend any such thing," he said.

Margaret smiled.

"Had you seen Mr. Turner before last evening?" she asked as they walked in the direction of Hyde Park. "Since your elopement with his wife, I mean?"

"No," he said. "Nor his sister either, since the evening before my planned wedding with her. The morning papers made the most of the almost-encounter, did they not?"

"They did," Margaret said. It had been somewhat disconcerting to see her name in print for the second morning in a row. "It was noted that Mr. Turner and Mr. and Mrs. Pennethorne did not return to their box for the conclusion of the play, that a perfectly well justified outrage drove them away from having to share a roof with a notorious villain. Are you sorry that you spoiled their evening?"

"Not at all," he said. "If it *was* spoiled, that is. Which I very much doubt. They probably enjoyed an hour or two of righteous and thoroughly pleasurable indignation over their supper."

He handed a coin to the crossing sweeper as they crossed the road and then entered the park.

"Is your heart so very hard, then?" she asked him.

"I daresay it is," he said. "Life's experiences do that to a person, Miss Huxtable."

"Harden the heart?" she said. "I hope not. I would hate to become a cynic merely because I could not take responsibility for my wicked actions."

"Am I wicked, then?" he asked, looking down at her.

"*You* tell *me*," she said. "You are the one doing the wooing."

The paths and carriageway were busy enough even though it was not yet the fashionable hour. Their appearance attracted noticeable attention, as though the *ton* could not get its fill of looking at them. What did they expect to see, exactly?

What they saw was the Earl of Sheringford leaning his head closer to hers and looking very directly into her eyes as his free hand came up to cover hers on his arm. A deliberately intimate gesture? Well, she had asked for it.

"Things are not always what they seem, Miss Huxtable," the earl said.

No, indeed. She half smiled.

"Meaning that you are not wicked after all?" she said. "You did not really abandon the bride you professed to love? You did not really run off with another man's wife and live in sin with her for five years? We all know that gossip can err, but can it err to quite such a degree?"

"I did not love Caroline by the time I abandoned her," he said, "though that fact in itself did not excuse me for doing so. I daresay nothing did. And Laura Turner was very willing to run away with me, a fact that did not at all excuse me for taking her, I suppose. I daresay nothing did. Yes, Miss Huxtable, I must concede that by your definition of wickedness I am doubtless very evil indeed."

He curled his fingers about hers as an

open barouche of ladies bowled past, and moved his head a fraction closer.

"By *anyone's* definition," she said.

"If you will."

Constantine was cantering toward them with a few other gentlemen, all of whom Margaret knew. They reined in and stopped for a few moments to exchange greetings. All of them called the earl *Sherry.* Gentlemen, it occurred to Margaret, forgave far more easily than ladies did. Perhaps they envied a man who did as he pleased and thumbed his nose at society — and hurt other people in the process.

"Margaret," Constantine said, fixing her with a very direct look. "Your fame grows with every morning paper. May I join you and Sherry on your walk?"

"Thank you, Constantine," she said, "but we are on our way to take tea with Lady Carling."

"And I promise most faithfully, Con," Lord Sheringford said, "to chase away any wolves who take it into their heads to try to devour Miss Huxtable on the way."

Constantine gave him a hard look before riding off with the other gentlemen.

"It must be gratifying," the earl said, "to have so many people willing to champion your person against any and all villains."

"It is," she agreed. "But I warned you it would happen."

"Is it," he asked her, "why you decided to receive me yesterday instead of having Merton send me packing? Is it why you did not dismiss my offer out of hand when you *did* see me? And why you invited me to the theater last evening and agreed to take tea with my mother this afternoon? Is it simply *because* all your champions are set against your allying yourself with me? Are you a secret rebel, Miss Huxtable?"

She was beginning to believe that she really must be. The notoriety she had garnered during the past two days should have horrified her sufficiently to send her into full retreat. Instead . . . Well, here she was, *almost* enjoying herself.

"I find myself unwilling to reject you only because the world and all the evidence tell me that I ought," she said.

"I must be grateful to the world and all the evidence, then," he said, "and a secret rebel who insists upon forming her own opinions. But what more evidence do you need to convince you that you would be better off being a spinster for the rest of your life than allied with me?"

"I am not even sure," she said. "But you have faced the hostility of the *ton* — you are facing it now — with a certain dignity. Does that mean anything in your favor? I do not know."

"Perhaps it means that I am without conscience," he said, "or desperate enough to grovel at any cost."

"Yes," she agreed. "Or perhaps it means that there is more to know of you than just a few bare facts from five years ago. I know two things that you once did. That is all. I really do not know *you* at all, do I? And that is the whole point of these two weeks of courtship — getting to know who you really are, that is."

"I believe," he said, "you are attracted to me, Miss Huxtable, and are looking for a way to rationalize a desire to marry me."

"You may believe what you choose, Lord Sheringford," she said sharply. "But neither a reluctance to take unsolicited advice from the rest of the world nor any personal attraction I may or may not feel toward your person would impel me into doing something against my character or principles. Marrying you would seem an extremely . . . *unprincipled* thing to do. And you have said nothing so far that would make it seem less so. You have made no attempt to excuse your past behavior, and you have made no effort to show me how . . . reformed you are now."

He had turned them while she spoke onto a narrower path, one that led toward a grove of ancient oak trees. It was less crowded than the main path they had just left.

"Enough public wooing for now," he said, dropping his free hand to his side again and lifting his head to the vertical. "The past cannot be changed, Miss Huxtable. Or excused. And if it can be excused, or at least partially explained, then I choose not to offer excuses or explanations to a virtual stranger, which is what you are to me. If you become my wife, then I will perhaps attempt to put before you facts that the world will never know and would neither believe nor care about if it did. But you are not my wife yet, or even my betrothed. If you choose to marry me, you must choose me as I am."

"That is not fair at all," she said. "How can I make a judgment about you if I do not know all the facts?"

He drew her off the path when they were among the trees, and they wound their way among tall, thick trunks until they could see down onto the wide lawns of the park stretched below them. He released her arm and propped one shoulder against a tree, crossing his arms over his chest as he did so.

"Tell me," he said, "about your relationship with Major Dew. Everything. Including the physical details. How many times? Where? When? How satisfactory?"

She felt the color rise in her cheeks and her nostrils flare. She glared at him.

"*That,* Lord Sheringford," she said, "is absolutely none of your business."

"It is," he said, "if I am to marry you. Is a man not entitled to a virgin bride? Or to an explanation if she is not virgin?"

"The details of my relationship with Crispin Dew," she said, still glaring, "which happened twelve years ago, are absolutely *none* of your business."

"Precisely," he said and looked steadily back at her with eyes that seemed to see to the core of her skull. "Touché."

"But your case is different," she said. "You are the one wooing *me,* not the other way around. You are the one who has to convince *me* that you are worthy to be my husband. I do not have to prove anything."

"But if you marry me, Miss Huxtable," he said, "you will be as much my wife as I will be your husband. What if you loved Dew so much that you can never forget him? What if you still love him, despite your denials two evenings ago? What if your sexual experiences with him were so earth-shatteringly wonderful that you can never find satisfaction with me? Or so shudderingly awful that they rendered you frigid for the rest of your life? What if your past really does make you an undesirable bride?"

"I will *not* discuss my relationship with Crispin," she said.

"And I will not discuss mine with either Caroline or Laura," he said, raising his eyebrows.

She felt a grudging respect for him even though their situations really were quite different. Most men under the circumstances would make as many excuses as might seem credible in order to get their way.

"And as to being reformed," he said, "I am as I am, Miss Huxtable. I am as you see me. Many a marriage comes to grief, I believe, because the courting couple will show only their best side to each other — and often an artificial side — until after the marriage, only to discover when it is too late that they are strangers who can never even like each other particularly well. You wish me to charm you and fawn over you and whisper sweet words and sweeter lies in your ear at every turn? You will not find me like that after we marry."

He had a point. But it still surprised her that he would not say anything to entice her — except last evening's promise to . . .

"Come here," he said, holding out a hand for hers.

"Why?" She looked at his hand, frowning, but did not take it.

"You want me to woo you," he said. "I suppose you want more than just a public wooing. This is a very private place even though we can see a wide vista of the park. We are well off the path, which is not much used anyway, and we are in the shade here on a day that is brilliantly sunny out there. We are virtually invisible, then. Let me try a little private wooing."

"What *sort* of private wooing?" she asked, frowning. She felt somewhat breathless.

"I am going to kiss you," he said. "You need not worry that I intend to ravish you, Miss Huxtable. This may be a private place, and we might be virtually invisible, but it is not nearly private enough for more than kisses."

"I am not sure," she said, "I *want* you to kiss me."

Which was a horrible lie. To her shame she wanted it very much indeed.

"You had better come and find out, then,"

he said. "If you are giving serious consideration to marrying me, you are also considering facing nuptials with me within the next two weeks. And nuptials are invariably a prelude to a wedding night. If you do not wish to kiss me now, you will probably not wish to bed with me then. And that would be a severe annoyance to me."

"I suppose," she said, "you would force me."

There was a rather lengthy silence during which they stared at each other and for some reason she felt frightened. His eyes looked very black.

"If you wish to know something about me that you apparently do not already know, Miss Huxtable," he said, "then this is it. I would never force you into saying or believing or doing anything against your will. And if I could obliterate that distastefully asinine moment in the marriage service at which brides vow before God and human witnesses to obey their husbands, I would gladly do so."

He spoke with a soft menace that was quite at variance with his words.

"We had better be on our way," he said before Margaret could think of a reply. He pushed his shoulder away from the tree trunk. "Or we will be late for tea."

"I thought," she said, "you wanted to kiss me."

"And *I* thought," he said, "you did not want to be kissed."

"You were wrong," she said.

The words hung in the air between them for a few moments. Then he leaned his back against the tree again and reached out both hands toward her.

And oh, she thought as she closed the distance between them and set her hands in his, oh, she longed to be kissed. There had been a vast, dark emptiness in her life . . .

He clasped her hands firmly, twisted her arms behind her back, and brought her body against his from breasts to knees.

His eyes gazed into hers from a mere few inches away.

"Don't cry," he murmured.

"I am not —" But she was. "Yes I am."

"You do not want to do this?" he asked her.

"I do," she said.

And then his mouth was on hers, and her lips were trembling and her knees were buckling, and she was grasping his hands behind her back with enough force to leave bruises, and her breasts pressed to his chest felt swollen and sore, and she forgot to breathe.

Then she was gazing into his eyes again.

"I am sorry," she said, humiliated. "It has been a long time."

His body was as solidly muscled as she remembered it from the night before last.

Oh, goodness, was it really only the night before last?

He released her hands and raised his own to cup her face, pushing his fingers beneath the brim of her bonnet. He touched the pads of his thumbs to the center of her lips and moved them outward to the corners, leaving a trail of sensation behind them. He dipped his head and set his lips where his thumbs had been. She rested her hands on his shoulders.

His lips were closed. But then she could feel the tip of his tongue tracing a path across her lips and then prodding at the center and sliding through into her mouth until she was filled with the warm taste of him and reacted to the invasion with every part of her body.

His hands moved from her face, and one arm came about her shoulders and the other about her waist, and she slid one arm about his neck, the other behind his back while he drew her hard against him again.

It occurred to her later that it was probably not a terribly lascivious embrace. His hands did not wander at all, and his kisses were confined to her face and her throat. But she felt ravished nonetheless — or, if that was too violent a word, then she felt . . . Oh, she felt more alive, more feminine, more exhilarated, than she had felt in a long, long while.

Perhaps ever.

She felt very thoroughly kissed.

His hands were on either side of her waist, and hers were resting on his shoulders when she realized it was over. He was looking into her face again, his own as inscrutable as ever.

"I am not very good at it, am I?" she said.

"I am not complaining," he told her. "And indeed, I give you fair warning, Miss Huxtable — *Maggie.* If you marry me, you had better have a good night's sleep before the nuptials. I can promise you a very sleepless wedding night."

She swallowed and noticed that he swallowed at almost the same moment.

But she would not marry him only because he had made a wedding night sound like the most desirable thing life had to offer, she thought, moving firmly away from him and turning slightly in order to shake the creases from the muslin dress she wore beneath her spencer. Or because she had enjoyed his kiss more than . . . Well, more than anything she could think of at the moment. Or because she wanted more and knew she would dream of more for a long time to come.

She was playing with fire, and she was getting burned.

What would it be like — a wedding night with the Earl of Sheringford?

And a lifetime as the wife of a confessed rogue?

"We will almost certainly be late for tea," she said briskly, "if we do not leave immediately."

"If your cheeks stay that rosy," he said, "my mother will be charmed even if we are very late."

He offered his arm and she took it.

Miss Margaret Huxtable was prim and straitlaced and judgmental. Last evening she had even taken him to task for saying *good God* as an exclamation. And she kissed like a novice. She had not held anything back, it was true, but then he had not demanded much. She had initiated nothing. Whatever her experience was, it was either so old that she had forgotten it or so minimal that there was nothing much to forget.

If he had to wager on it, he would bet that

Miss Margaret Huxtable and Dew-of-the-weak-chin — with whom he had exchanged a few words in the park this morning — had rolled in the hay together once only, probably just before he marched off to war. She was very fortunate there had been no awkward consequences.

As they approached Curzon Street, not talking a great deal, Duncan asked himself if this really was the woman he wished to marry. It was a redundant question. *Of course* she was not — but then neither was anyone else.

He had received a letter from Mrs. Harris this morning — she could read and write though Harris could not. Toby had fallen out of a tree last week and sprained an ankle and given himself a goose-egg of a lump on his forehead. Although he had made an almost miraculous recovery, Mrs. Harris assured his lordship, they had nevertheless felt it wise to summon a physician, and the doctor had felt it wise to prescribe some medicine — all of which had cost money. And, of course, the fall had torn out the knees of his breeches so that they were quite beyond repair.

Old Tobe! He was as accident-prone as any other normal little boy. As accident-prone as he himself had been as a child.

There had been the time when Toby had insisted upon climbing over a stile unassisted though he had been warned that the wood was old and rough and the maneuver must be done very carefully. He had, of course, yelled out excitedly, "Watch me!" from his sitting position on the topmost bar and jumped. He had taken part of the bar with him in the form of a large splinter that had torn his breeches at the seat — not at the knee that time — and embedded itself in one tender buttock cheek. If Duncan had not caught him on the way down, he would also have smothered his entire person with the mud that lay in wait at the bottom. And there had been the time when he had sloshed into a late winter puddle of water after being told not to, only to discover that there was a layer of ice beneath the water. And the time when . . .

Well, the reminiscences could go on forever. But there were other things to think about at the moment than a sore little bottom after the splinter had been pulled free and a wobbly lower lip and a valiant effort not to cry and a wheedling little voice saying they must not upset Mama by telling her. Or a wet, miserable little body huddled against him for warmth and comfort during the walk home from the ice puddle, his little arms about Duncan's neck, his child's voice suggesting that Duncan not tell Mama. Which, of course, was the last thing Duncan would have done anyway.

"My mother," Duncan warned Miss Huxtable as they approached the house, "will wish to talk about our wedding."

"I know," she said. "I will make it clear to her again that there may well *be* no wedding."

"Making things clear to my mother," he said, "is no easy task when she has once made up her mind on a point. She dreams of a happily-ever-after for me."

"All mothers do it," she said. "So do all sisters who have acted as mothers to their siblings. I understand your mother's feelings perfectly. You must have caused her almost unbearable suffering during the past five years."

He doubted it. His mother was vain and flighty and affectionate, but he did not believe her feelings ran deep.

"You raise your eyebrows," she said, "as if to say that of course I am wrong. I do not suppose I am."

"In which case," he said, "you had better not cause her more suffering, Miss Huxtable. You had better marry me."

She opened her mouth to answer, but they

had arrived. And someone must have been watching their approach. The front door swung open before Duncan had climbed the steps, to reveal first Sir Graham's butler and then Duncan's mother, who was smiling warmly at Miss Huxtable and holding out her arms to draw her into a hug.

He might as well have been invisible.

10

Margaret found herself enveloped in soft warmth and the floral scent of some obviously expensive perfume.

"Miss Huxtable — may I call you Margaret?" Lady Carling said, releasing Margaret and linking an arm through hers before drawing her in the direction of the staircase. "I cannot tell you how happy you have made me. I had scarce a wink of sleep last night. Ask Graham. Though he is not here, provoking man. He says I am making a cake of myself since you said quite clearly last evening that you are *not* betrothed to Duncan, and why should you be since you are a sister of the Earl of Merton and everyone knows you to be a sensible and virtuous lady. It is only surprising that you would invite my son to sit in your brother-in-law's box with you, he said, but I pointed out that that is merely proof that in reality you are engaged to Duncan but have chosen to withhold the official announcement until you are ready to make it. But you can tell me. I am to be your mother."

By the time she paused for breath they were outside the doors of what was presumably the drawing room, and a footman who had been waiting there opened them.

The Earl of Sheringford was coming behind them.

It was indeed the drawing room, and the tea had already been brought up. A smartly dressed maid poured three cups as soon as she saw them enter and then left the room.

"Indeed, ma'am," Margaret said, "I have not yet said that I will marry Lord Sheringford, and perhaps never will."

"It is always wise," Lady Carling said, "not to appear too eager. I refused Duncan's father twice before I finally accepted him even though I was head-over-ears in love with him. And I refused Graham once, though that did not really count, as he *told* me the first time that we would marry instead of asking me. Can you imagine such a thing, Margaret? There are those who consider him a cold man, and no wonder when he talks and behaves in such a way. But of course he is not, as I know very well. Oh, do sit down on that love seat, and do sit beside her, Duncan. I have loved you dearly and steadfastly throughout your life, but I did not realize quite how sensible you can be until now. Tell me why you chose Margaret."

They did as they were bidden, and Margaret found her shoulder only inches from his. She could feel his body heat.

"Because, Mama," he said, "I went to the Tindell ball to look for a bride and collided with Miss Huxtable in the doorway and decided to look no farther."

His mother's cup paused halfway to her lips, and she looked suspiciously at her son.

"Oh, very well," she said, "*don't* tell me. It is sometimes very difficult, Margaret, to get sense out of Duncan. Why have you delayed the announcement of your betrothal? Is it because of his reputation, which is admittedly quite shocking? But it cannot be entirely that. Certainly you have a great deal of courage, appearing with him in Hilda Tindell's ballroom and then at the theater. Not many ladies would risk their reputations in such a way."

"I have been told, ma'am, by members of my own family," Margaret said, "that I am more than usually stubborn. I suppose that when I hear that other people would not do a certain thing, I feel an irresistible urge to do it myself."

"I like you," Lady Carling announced. "Duncan, have you finished your tea? It would be a wonder if you have not, since you always drink it in great gulps instead of taking delicate sips as any civilized being does."

"I have finished it, Mama," he said.

"Then go and amuse yourself elsewhere," she said, waving one hand in the direction of the door, "and come back in half an hour to escort Margaret home. We have matters to discuss that would doubtless bore you."

He got to his feet and bowed, the usual dark, inscrutable look on his face.

"You will excuse me . . . Maggie?" he asked.

"Of course." She inclined her head, though she did frown slightly too. Was he trying to influence her by implying to his mother that there was a greater intimacy between them than there was?

But she had just allowed him to kiss her in Hyde Park, had she not? And it had not been just an innocent peck on the cheek or lips. Oh, goodness, his tongue had been inside her mouth.

Margaret lifted her cup to her lips and realized too late that her hand was shaking ever so slightly.

"Margaret," Lady Carling said when they

were alone. She sat with her hands clasped in her lap. She looked instantly different — more serious, less frivolous. "Tell me why you are spending time with my son. Tell me why you hesitate to marry him."

Margaret drew a slow breath and set down her cup and saucer on the small table at her elbow.

"I suppose that like most people," she said, "I rush to judgment when I meet a stranger. And there are many judgments to rush to in Lord Sheringford's case. He does not even deny that he did dreadful things five years ago. But I am also aware that no one is defined by one set of actions — especially when those actions are well in the past. I suppose I am curious. I want to know more about him. I want to know if I would be misjudging him by spurning his acquaintance. And we really did collide with each other at the ball, you know. And I really did — very rashly — introduce him to another gentleman as my betrothed simply because that gentleman was a suitor of mine many years ago and was being patronizing when he discovered me this year still unmarried at thirty years old. Because Lord Sheringford was in active search of a bride, he encouraged the lie and offered to make it the truth. Neither of us expected that Major

Dew would mention what I had told him to a few of his friends, and that they would tell it to a few of theirs. I had told him that no one knew of the betrothal yet, including my own family."

Lady Carling had listened to her without even trying to interrupt.

"I daresay," she said, "Duncan hopes that if he marries well his grandfather will relent and restore Woodbine Park to him."

Margaret looked sharply at her. She did not *know?*

"The Marquess of Claverbrook has promised to do just that," she said, "provided Lord Sheringford is married to a lady of whom he approves before the Marquess's eightieth birthday. Otherwise he will grant possession of Woodbine Park to the next heir."

"To Norman?" Lady Carling said. "Oh, dear. He is a very worthy young man. I was always fond of him. But he is the sort of man who has never put a foot wrong his whole life — just the sort of man who is despised and even hated by his less virtuous brothers and cousins. Duncan could never abide him. And yet he was good enough to marry Caroline Turner."

"Yes," Margaret said.

"But how like that cantankerous old man

to play such games," Lady Carling said, bridling. "And when is his eightieth birthday, pray? I take it it must be soon."

"In less than two weeks," Margaret said.

Lady Carling raised her eyebrows.

"Poor Duncan," she said. "It would not be only the money, you know, though he must be desperate even for that. His funds have been completely cut, and he has refused to take anything from me. Men and their silly pride! But Woodbine Park was his childhood home. All his memories are there. It is true that he did not spend much time there from the age of eighteen or nineteen until he ran off with Mrs. Turner, but one does not expect a healthy, energetic young man to incarcerate himself in the country. He was busy sowing his wild oats, though I never heard that they were so very wild — merely normal for a man his age. He planned to settle in the country after he married Caroline Turner. And then he did something very impulsive and very foolish and is like to suffer for it the rest of his life."

"When Lord Sheringford came to make me a formal offer yesterday afternoon," Margaret said, "I explained to him that I needed time to get to know him better, even if two weeks was all the time I could have in which to decide. I pointed out to him that it was unfair of me to ask for that time, since he would have no chance to find a different bride if my final answer is no. He has taken the risk and given me the time."

Lady Carling looked at her silently for such a long while that Margaret began to feel uncomfortable. But she spoke at last.

"I know something of you, Margaret," she said. "I know you lost your mother early and your father when you were still only a girl. I know that you took it upon yourself to hold your home together and raise your younger sisters and brother — even though at the time you did not know that your brother would inherit the Merton title and fortune and eventually make all your lives considerably easier. I daresay you feel for your siblings as a mother as well as a sister."

"In some ways, yes, ma'am," Margaret agreed.

"Most people see me as a careless, empty-headed creature," Lady Carling said. "And it is as I wish. Other people, especially men, are more easily manipulated that way. It might appear that I am incapable of deep feeling. But I have suffered during the past five years. I tell myself that I have suffered less than if Duncan had died, but sometimes it has been hard to convince myself. If he had died, he would be at peace even if I was not. He has lost everything, Margaret, for a foolish whim that could not be reversed even before Mrs. Turner died. He has lost his youth, his character and reputation, his home, his livelihood, his happiness, his peace. And I am his mother. I do not ask you to try to put yourself in my place. It is too painful a place to be."

Margaret did not attempt a reply.

"He was a happy, mischievous, active, very normal boy," Lady Carling continued. "He loved animals and championed every one he felt was being mistreated — as well as every servant and child in the village too. He suffered dreadfully when his father died so suddenly — we both did. But suffering is part of life for everyone and of course he recovered. He was carefree and wild and active and very normal as a young man. And then, as you yourself just put it, his life was defined for all time by one utterly foolish act. Why he did it I suppose I will never know, but he did it. And so in a sense his life ended. I doubt the past five years have been happy ones for him. His face is not that of a man who has been happy. He has aged at least ten years in the past five. He was a handsome boy. But perhaps, Margaret, his life can resume after all. Perhaps it can be normal again, perhaps even happy.

I like you. You are better than I could possibly have hoped."

"But I may not marry him," Margaret protested.

Lady Carling smiled, though her eyes were suspiciously bright.

"And you will go away from here," she said, "convinced that I have behaved unscrupulously and used emotional blackmail on you when I ought to have been entertaining you as any good hostess would do. And you would be quite right."

Margaret smiled at the admission.

"He has not spent every day of his life abandoning innocent young ladies and running off with married ones," Lady Carling said. "He did those things once, both on the same occasion. I make no excuse for him, Margaret — as you have observed, he makes none for himself. But he is thirty years old. Multiply those years by three hundred and sixty-five, and even if you ignore the leap years, that is a large number of days in which he has *not* behaved in a dastardly manner. Find out about those days, Margaret. Find my son. Marry him if you can. Love him if you will. And now, let me offer you another cup of tea and compliment you on the bonnet you were wearing when you stepped into the house. Where did you find such a pretty thing? I look and look and never see anything I really like — except on the heads of other ladies. Graham would be horrified to hear me say so as he complains loudly about all the bills for bonnets he is obliged to pay, but if I could just find one or two really pretty ones I would not have to keep buying plain or even downright ugly ones, would I?"

"I bought a plain bonnet," Margaret explained, "and trimmed it myself."

"Well, then, that does it," Lady Carling said. "I absolutely must have you for a daughter-in-law, Margaret, and will hear no argument to the contrary."

They both laughed — just at the moment when the drawing room door opened to admit Lord Sheringford.

"I have been pleading your case, Duncan," his mother said. "I have discovered that Margaret trims her own bonnets and that I simply must therefore have her for a daughter-in-law."

"And I suppose, Mama," he said as Margaret got to her feet to take her leave, "that argument has weighed heavily with her. I suppose she is ready to permit me to place an announcement of our betrothal in tomorrow's papers."

"Not at all, you foolish man," she said.

"She will permit it when you have convinced her that marriage to you is the only thing that can possibly bring her real happiness for the rest of her life. Why else would a woman marry and become the possession of any male — just as if she were a thing? It is the reason why I married your papa and lived happily with him for almost twenty years. And it is the reason why I married Graham even if he *does* appear to be Sir Gruff and Grim half the time."

"Ah," he said as his mother got to her feet to hug Margaret again, "so I have your blessing to continue wooing her, do I, Mama?

"Not my blessing, Duncan," she said, "but my maternal *command.* Margaret, we will deal famously together. I feel it in my bones. We are both interested in bonnets."

Margaret doubted as she stepped out of the house on Lord Sheringford's arm that he even suspected how deeply his mother loved him or how passionately she had pleaded his case.

"That visit," he said dryly, confirming her suspicion, "was doubtless enlightening."

"I *like* your mother," she said. "If I marry you, it will be at least partly because I wish to have her for a mother-in-law."

He looked at her sidelong without really

turning his head.

Margaret smiled.

But she was thinking of him as a boy and young man — before the great folly of his life. His mother had not given much detail, but it was easy to picture a boy who frolicked with animals and stood up for them when they were being treated badly, and a young man who was happy and carefree and a little wild. A perfectly normal young man, in fact. Like Stephen.

Would everything that was Stephen be negated if he did anything as shockingly distasteful as what Lord Sheringford had done? The answer was, of course, yes. But would he not still be Stephen? But Stephen without the light and the joy? And the honor?

Had there once been light and joy in Lord Sheringford?

And honor?

"You are looking very serious," he said. "Are you realizing with regret that it is me you would be marrying, not my mother?"

"A shame, is it not?" she said. "Who *are* you, Lord Sheringford? And who *were* you?"

"And then," he said, "there is the crucial in-between time."

"Which you have refused to discuss," she said.

"Yes."

"Then I will have to content myself with the before and after," she said.

But they did not talk more during the walk home. Was it because there was too much to say? she wondered. Or too little?

He stepped inside Merton House with her but would come no farther than the hall.

"Are you to attend the Johnston concert this evening?" he asked her.

"I have a dinner invitation to honor," she said. "Sir Humphrey and Lady Dew, our former neighbors at Throckbridge, are in town for a short while and have invited my whole family."

"Ah." He raised his eyebrows. "And the gallant major will be in attendance too, I assume?"

"I suppose so," she said.

"My competition?" he asked her.

"Not at all," she told him. "I play no games, my lord. I have told you quite truthfully that I may or may not marry you in . . . What is it now? Twelve days' time? I am not interested at all in Crispin. I have not been for years."

"Except," he said, "that the lady doth protest too much."

"You are impertinent," she told him.

"I am," he agreed. "What about Mrs.

Henry's soiree tomorrow evening? You will be there?"

"I am sure that by tomorrow I will be thankful for an evening at home," she said. "I always find the constantly busy pace of a London Season somewhat overwhelming."

More than ever this year, though she had not been here many days yet.

"Let me escort you there," he said. "Mrs. Henry is my mother's sister and will not turn me away. She will certainly be delighted to meet you."

"I don't know," she said.

"Be fair, Maggie," he said. "You have commanded me to woo you publicly and become better acquainted with you privately. Give me an opportunity to do both. As it is, another whole day will have been lost. I will be down to eleven days."

"Oh, very well," she said with a sigh.

A soiree sounded like a quiet, decorous event. And surely by tomorrow evening the *ton* would have gawked its fill and exhausted all that could be said on the topic of her and the Earl of Sheringford.

He bowed over her hand and took his leave.

Was there such a thing as coincidence? Margaret wondered, standing in the hall looking at the door after it had closed behind him. If he had arrived in the ball-room one minute later than he had, if she had arrived at the doorway one minute sooner than *she* had, if they had both arrived there exactly when they had but she had been looking where she was going — if any of those things had happened, they would not have collided. And if he had not been desperate for a wife, and if she had not been desperate for a betrothed to introduce to Crispin, or if she had heard about the Marquess of Allingham's engagement even one day before she had, or one hour later — then they would have collided, been embarrassed, made each other a hasty apology, and gone on their way into very separate lives.

But all those *ifs* had converged on one moment as surely as their persons had in the ballroom doorway.

Which left the question — had it all been coincidence?

Or not?

And if it had not, what did it all mean?

She shook her head and turned away in the direction of the stairs and her room.

11

The evening at Grillon's Hotel was really a very enjoyable one. Sir Humphrey greeted them with his usual hearty affability, and Lady Dew hugged them all tightly — even Elliott and Jasper — and exclaimed in delight over the elegance and good looks of the ladies.

She hugged Vanessa with an extra warmth, of course, because Vanessa had been married to Hedley, her younger son, for a year until he died of consumption. She still considered Vanessa to be her daughter-in-law — so did Sir Humphrey. And they thought of her children with Elliott as their grandchildren. They were full of plans for calling upon the children the next day, acquainting them with little Maria, and taking them all to the Tower to see the animals and to Gunter's for ices.

"Can you imagine," Lady Dew said, smiling about at all of them, "that I have never in my life tasted an ice? I shall be as excited as the children. I hear they are a delicacy not to be missed."

"One's life is not complete, ma'am," Jasper said, a twinkle in his eye, "until one has tasted one of Gunter's ices."

The ladies were taken upstairs to the room where a nurse was reading a story to Maria. She was a dark-eyed, dark-haired little beauty, very Spanish in coloring, though she resembled Crispin in features. She must be all of four years old, Margaret thought.

Under other circumstances she might have been *her* child.

Dinner stretched over much of the evening since the conversation was lively. Crispin recounted some of his experiences in the wars, at the prompting mainly of Elliott, though his father was obviously proud of his exploits and wanted them known. And Lady Dew turned to beam at Margaret several times while her son spoke.

"Can you believe, Margaret," she asked, "that this is the same boy with whom you used to romp as a girl? Has he not grown into a handsome man? Despite the nasty scar, which gave me quite a turn when I first saw it, as you may imagine."

"I can certainly imagine it," Margaret agreed, evading the other questions.

Most of the conversation was a mingling of news from home and reminiscences of the old days, when they had all lived in Throckbridge and its neighborhood — all except Elliott and Jasper, that was. But they appeared as interested as any of the rest of them.

Margaret soon relaxed, despite the presence of Crispin. It seemed that the Dews knew nothing of the rumors and gossip that had so disturbed her during the past couple of days. Crispin had not told *them,* at least.

She had come with Vanessa and Elliott. She expected to return with them, but Sir Humphrey was eager to offer their own carriage for her use, and Lady Dew joined her voice to his. They simply would not take no for an answer, she declared. It was the least they could do for one of the most admirable neighbors they had ever known. *She* would never forget how dear Margaret had devoted half her youth to her sisters and brother, giving them as loving and secure a home as any children with both parents could ever desire.

"And Crispin will escort you," she said, dabbing at the tears in her eyes.

"Oh, no, indeed, ma'am," Margaret said in some alarm. "That would be quite —"

"The streets of London are said to be

teeming with footpads and cutthroats and other dastardly villains," Sir Humphrey said. "Crispin will certainly go with you, Miss Huxtable. Any scoundrel would take one look at *him* and run as fast as his legs would carry him in the opposite direction."

"It would be my pleasure, Meg," Crispin said.

So Sir Humphrey ordered the carriage brought up to the hotel doors, and Lady Dew beamed happily from her son to Margaret and back again.

"This is *just* like old times," she said. "I would be rich if someone were to give me a sovereign or even a shilling for each time Crispin walked you home from Rundle Park, Margaret, very often after *you* had walked *him* home from the village. And many times Vanessa and our dearest Hedley were with the two of you, and sometimes Katherine and our girls. Oh, they were *good* times. How I wish they could be recaptured — or renewed, at least in part. Though we can never have Hedley back."

She shed a few more tears while Sir Humphrey withdrew a large handkerchief from his pocket and blew his nose, and Vanessa set an arm about Lady Dew's shoulders and rested a cheek against the top of her head.

A short while later Margaret was returning home in the Dews' large, old-fashioned carriage, Crispin on the seat beside her.

"Meg," he said when the carriage was on its way, "I ran into Sheringford in the park this morning. Did he tell you? Have you seen him today? He told me he would give me a poke in the nose if he were not already quite notorious enough, and he proceeded to lecture me on the etiquette of holding my tongue when a lady had requested it of me and of doing all in my power to see that she and her words and actions were never held up to public scrutiny and public judgment. The nerve of the man! After what he did to Miss Turner and Mrs. Turner! Tell me you are not really betrothed to him, despite what you said at the ball and despite the fact that he was at the theater with you and your family last evening. There has still been no announcement in the papers. Don't let it happen, *please.* Marry me instead."

Lord Sheringford had said nothing this afternoon about the meeting in the park. He had scolded Crispin — on her behalf. And yes, it did seem a little like the case of the pot and the kettle, but all that business with the Turner ladies had happened five years ago. She was growing mortally sick of hearing about it. Five years ago Crispin had married his Spanish lady — Teresa.

"Why did you do it?" she asked. "Why did you marry her, Crispin?"

He leaned back away from her, into the corner of the seat.

"You must understand, Meg," he said. "I had been away from you a long time. I was lonely. A man has needs that a woman is fortunate enough not to feel. I would have come back to you. I *loved* you. But Teresa discovered that she was with child, and she was of a respectable family. I could not simply pay her off or abandon her. I had no choice but to marry her. I never loved her. I loved *you.* I never wavered in that devotion. I still love you. But you must understand that you had set me an impossible task. You asked me to wait too long. You did not need to stay with your family. Vanessa was not much younger than you were."

"Why did you not write to me?" she asked.

The Earl of Sheringford, she was thinking, made no excuses for what he had done. He admitted everything even though he needed her to think well enough of him to marry him and rescue him from penury and the loss of his home.

"I wrote a hundred letters," he said, "and crumpled them all up and threw them in the fire. I knew I would be breaking your heart. I wrote to my mother. I thought she was more likely to break it to you gently."

Margaret said nothing.

"*Was* your heart broken?" he asked. "*Mine* was, Meg. Having to marry Teresa was cruel punishment for a few stolen moments to alleviate my loneliness."

"Was she the only woman with whom you soothed your loneliness?" she asked.

"Meg!" he exclaimed. "How am I expected to answer *that?*"

"With a yes or a no," she said. "*Was* she?"

"Well, of course not," he said. "I am a *man,* Meg. But it would not have happened if you had been there. It *will* not happen if you marry me now. Do it. Send that scoundrel on his way and marry me. Don't punish me any longer. Don't continue to punish yourself."

The carriage had stopped moving. They must be outside Merton House already. The coachman did not open the door.

"That is what you are doing, you know," he said, sitting forward again and taking one of her hands in his. "Punishing yourself. If you marry Sheringford, it will be to spite me. But then you will find yourself in a marriage that may last for the rest of your life. I was fortunate to be set free of mine after only four years. You may not be so fortunate. Don't do it, Meg. Don't."

He squeezed her hand tightly and bent his head to kiss her hard on the lips. His free hand came behind her head and held it while he kissed her harder still.

Oh, she had forgotten. He had always kissed her with almost bruising urgency. He had made love to her the same way in a secluded corner of Rundle Park the day before he left to join his regiment. It had been swift and hard and painful and had left bruises. But her need for him on that occasion had been just as desperate.

Oh, it was all a lifetime ago. Except that he kissed the same way now — or tonight, at least.

She set a hand against his shoulder and pressed firmly until he lifted his head and loosened his hold on her hand.

"After you married, Crispin," she said, "my heart *was* broken. I will not deny it. But I did not slip into a sort of suspended life, a life that would be forever gray and meaningless if you did not somehow come back to me. I put back the pieces of my heart and kept on living. I am not the woman I was when I was in love with you and expecting to marry you. I am not the woman I was when I heard that you were married. I am the woman I have become in the five years since then, and she is a totally different person. I like her. I wish to continue living her life."

It was true too. Though there was a terrible ache in her throat.

"Let that life open to include me again, then," he said. "I need you, Meg. I am lonely without you. And I *know* you still love me. You knew I was back in England. That was why you betrothed yourself to Sheringford, was it not? You picked the very worst man you could find. Perhaps you did not even understand why. But I do. You did it so that I would come and rescue you. You did it because you were angry with me and wanted to punish me and bring me back to you. Ah, you did not have to do that, Meg. I was coming anyway."

"Crispin," she asked him, "when was the last time you had a woman? I mean lay with one?"

The new Margaret — the *very* new one — was far bolder than the old. But even the new Margaret was horribly shocked by the question she had just asked. Anger was deep in her, though. And grief.

"I am *not* going to answer that," he said, sounding as shocked as she was. "That is *not* the sort of question a lady asks, Meg. I can't *believe* —"

"*This* lady just asked it," she said. "*When,*

Crispin? Some time during the past week?"

"That need not concern you at all," he said. "Good Lord, Meg, that —"

"Then you can not be very lonely," she said.

"I am lonely for *you*," he told her. "There will be no one else once I have you, Meg."

"Or no one else I would ever know about, anyway," she said. "Crispin, this has been a lovely evening. Your parents are as warm and hospitable as they have ever been. Let us not spoil it. I am tired. Will you give the coachman the signal to open the door and set down the steps?"

He sighed and released her hand before rapping on the front panel.

"Think about what I have said," he told her after he had handed her down from the carriage and Stephen's butler was holding the door of the house open. "Don't marry Sheringford to spite me, Meg. You will end up spiting only yourself."

"Crispin," she said, "you flatter yourself. Good night."

He jumped back into the carriage and sat looking straight ahead while the coachman put the steps up again and closed the door.

Margaret went into the house before the carriage drew away from the steps.

She was very agitated. Quite upset really.

He still had the power to stir her emotions.

But the emotion she felt most was anger — and that terrible grief.

Lord Sheringford had been quite right about him. He *was* weak. She could not like anything he had said tonight about himself.

But he was still Crispin. She had loved him.

Ah, *how* she had loved him.

She trudged up to bed though she did not believe she would be able to sleep.

After twelve dry years, she had been kissed twice today — by different men.

Both of whom wished to marry her.

Neither of whom was a particularly desirable mate.

But only one of them would admit it.

Mrs. Henry, Duncan's Aunt Agatha, had not sent him an invitation to her soiree, but she surely would have done, he reasoned, if he had been in London when she sent out the cards. He had always been a great favorite with her, perhaps because she had had six daughters of her own but no sons.

Her greeting was not particularly effusive, though, when he arrived in the middle of the evening with Margaret Huxtable on his arm.

"Oh, goodness me," she said as soon as she saw him, looking more dismayed than delighted, "Duncan! How very —" She did not complete the thought, but raised her eyebrows before taking his offered hand in both her own and laying her cheek against his. "Well, never mind. My soiree is certain to be talked about tomorrow and perhaps for the next week or two, and no hostess could possibly ask for more, could she? Besides, you are my nephew."

She turned to smile warmly at his companion.

"Miss Huxtable," she said, "what a lovely shade of rose red your gown is. Of course, you have the coloring for it. And so you have taken on my scamp of a nephew, have you? I do commend your courage."

"Thank you, ma'am," Miss Huxtable said. "I was delighted by my invitation to your soiree."

She *had* received an invitation, it seemed. And yet, Duncan thought, she had not been in London much longer than he, had she? Had his aunt really not wanted him here, then? It was a humbling thought.

But she was turning away to greet another group of new arrivals.

"I suppose," he said, offering his arm to Miss Huxtable and covering her hand with his own when she set it on his sleeve, "we had better proceed to make the evening memorable for my aunt. All eyes appear to be upon us already, as you may have observed. One grows almost accustomed to it. Do you enjoy being notorious?"

"Not at all," she said. "But I am not. Why should I be? I have merely accepted the escort of a gentleman to a soiree for which I received an invitation."

Her chin was up, he noticed. There was a slight martial gleam in her eye.

"A gentleman who is actively wooing you," he said, dipping his head closer to hers and looking directly into her eyes. "And I see two of my cousins over there. I really ought to go and make myself agreeable before Susan's eyes pop right out of her head."

They crossed the room, and Duncan introduced Miss Huxtable to Susan Middleton and Andrea Henry, two of Aunt Agatha's daughters.

"Oh, not *Miss Henry* any longer, Duncan," Andrea protested. "I am Lady Bodsworth now. Did you not hear? I married Nathan two years ago."

"Did you indeed?" he said. "Fortunate Nathan. But you did not invite me to the wedding? How unkind of you. I must have

241

been off doing something else at the time."

She bit her lip, her eyes dancing, and Susan laughed outright. He had always been as great a favorite with his girl cousins as he had with his aunt — a partiality he had always returned. They had been jolly girls, always up for a lark.

"I cannot *believe*," Susan said, "that you have come back to London, Duncan. Though I am *very* glad you have, I must say. I never could abide Caroline Turner, as you may remember my telling you before you betrothed yourself to her."

"You really ought not to have come to Mama's soiree tonight, though, Duncan," Andrea said. "Not without consulting her or one of us first, anyway. Any one of us would have advised against it. If I were you, I would not stay longer than a few minutes. Miss Huxtable, I *do* admire your gown. The color is divine. It would not suit me, alas — I would fade into pale nothingness inside it. But it suits you to perfection."

"Thank you," Miss Huxtable said.

Duncan turned to look about him.

His aunt's home was admirably suited to a party of this nature, consisting as it did of a line of connecting rooms spanning the whole length of the house — drawing room, music room, library, and dining room. The doors of each room had been folded back tonight so that guests could move from one room to another as if they were all one.

The drawing room was already almost uncomfortably crowded with guests. Someone was playing the pianoforte in the next room.

"Shall we go and listen?" he suggested to Miss Huxtable, indicating the door into the music room.

"Oh, I would not if I were you," Andrea said, but Miss Huxtable had already set a hand on his sleeve. "Oh, dear, this *is* awkward."

They passed through the first door to find a group of people standing about the pianoforte, which was being played with more than usual competence by a very young lady in pale pink. Merton was standing behind the bench, turning the pages of music for her.

"Miss Weeding," Miss Huxtable explained. "She has real talent. She is also very modest. I am delighted that she has been persuaded to play tonight."

They stood with everyone else to watch and listen, and attracted somewhat less attention than they had in the drawing room.

Except from Merton himself.

He spotted them after a minute or two

and looked noticeably restless and uncomfortable until the music came to an end. He bent his head then to say something to Miss Weeding and came striding across the room toward his sister.

"Meg," he said, "I have been waiting for you to arrive. I was afraid to come back home for fear I would pass you on the way and not realize it. You must allow me to escort you home again without delay." He looked at Duncan for the first time, his expression tight and hostile. "You ought not to be here, Sheringford. I'll wager Mrs. Henry did not invite you."

Duncan merely raised his eyebrows.

"But she *did* invite *me*, Stephen," Miss Huxtable said, "and so it is quite unexceptionable for me to be here, and Lord Sheringford too, I daresay. Mrs. Henry is his aunt."

"*Turner* is here," Stephen said, his voice low but urgent. "So are the Pennethornes."

Ah.

Well, it was inevitable, Duncan supposed. They were in London for the Season, as was he, alas. They were bound to come face-to-face sooner or later. It had almost happened the evening before last, though the whole width of a theater had separated them, and Turner had made no move to force a confrontation. Instead he had run during the first intermission, which had seemed entirely in character. Tonight perhaps he would have no choice in the matter, unless Miss Huxtable wished to turn tail and run now before it was too late.

She was looking at him.

"I suppose," she said, "that is what Mrs. Henry meant when she said her soiree would be talked about for some weeks to come. And what your cousins meant when they said you should not stay long or venture farther than the drawing room."

"Will *you* take her home, Sheringford, or shall I?" Stephen asked.

"Do you *wish* to leave, my lord?" Miss Huxtable asked, virtually ignoring her brother. She was looking closely at him.

He did actually. This was a very public place. And he was escorting the lady he hoped to marry, the lady who could rescue him from penury and the inability to give Toby the country home he had promised him after Laura's death. He was in company with dozens of people who thought the very worst of him and would spare him no sympathy whatsoever in any confrontation with Laura's husband — or with Caroline Pennethorne.

It really was not a pleasant thing to be

hated. One might be blasé about it on the outside, but inside . . .

Yes, he wished to leave. But there were certain moments in life that forever defined one as a person — in one's own estimation, anyway. And one's own self-esteem, when all was said and done, was of far more importance than the fickle esteem of one's peers. He would not turn away from this particular moment any more than he had turned away from the painful decision he had made five years ago.

Not, at least, unless Miss Huxtable wished to leave. His primary responsibility at the moment was to her.

But she had asked him a question.

"No," he replied. "But I will certainly escort you home if you wish to go."

"There is no need for you to put yourself out," Merton said curtly. "It will give me the greatest pleasure to remove my sister from harm's way and myself from a potentially ugly scene. If I were you, Meg, I would say a permanent good-bye to the Earl of Sheringford."

Her eyes had not left Duncan's.

"Thank you both," she said, "but I intend to stay. It would be ill-mannered to leave so early."

"Allow me at least, then," her brother said

with a sigh, "to escort you back to the drawing room, Meg. There are —"

She turned her head to look at him at last.

"Stephen," she said, her voice soft and warm, "thank you. But I have my own life to lead, you know, and I am quite capable of doing it without assistance. Go and enjoy yourself. Miss Weeding has been looking quite forlorn since you abandoned her."

"Meg," he said softly and pleadingly. He glanced at Duncan and turned back to join the young lady, who had relinquished her seat at the pianoforte to someone else with a far more heavy hand.

"Miss Huxtable," Duncan said, "you have been placed in an awkward position, to say the least. I really ought to insist upon escorting you home."

"I put *myself* in an awkward position," she said, "when I lied to Crispin at Lady Tindell's ball. I compounded it when I received you at home the day before yesterday — oh goodness, was it really so recent? — and commanded you to woo me. You have done nothing yet to convince me that I *ought* to marry you — and nothing to convince me that I ought *not*. If I run now, I will forever wonder if I might have married you and achieved something like happiness with you. I am going to stay. It is beyond your power to insist upon taking me home."

. . . something like happiness . . .

He stared grimly at her. Was happiness —
or even *something like* happiness — a possibility if he married? All he wanted — all
he had wanted for years, in fact — was
peace. And his own familiar home. And a
secure, happy environment for Toby to grow
up in. The presence of a *wife* at Woodbine
would be a severe complication. But without
a wife there would be no home at all either
for himself or for the child — the one
person in life whom he loved totally and
unconditionally.

Margaret Huxtable was a brave woman.
Perhaps a formidable woman, as he had
suspected before tonight. She was prepared
to stay and face whatever might happen.
Randolph Turner was here. So was Caroline.

"You did not discover last evening," he
asked her, "that Major Dew can make you
happier than I?"

Her lips tightened. He ought not to have
asked. She might think he was jealous. But
though he did not like Dew, he did suspect
that she still harbored tender feelings for
the man. He certainly did not want her married to him and pining for another man for
the rest of her life.

"I am not making a choice between the two of you," she said. "This is not a competition, my lord. Crispin Dew offered me marriage again last evening, and again I said no. I have not said no to you — yet. When I know the answer to be no, I will say it. And if I ever know the answer to be yes, I will say that too."

He half smiled at her.

"Shall we move into the next room, then?" he suggested. "My uncle has an impressive collection of old maps, which he has always kept in the library, though I doubt they are on display tonight."

"Let us go and see," she said, and she gripped his arm a little more tightly and smiled.

12

The sudden hush in the crowded library, followed by a renewed rush of conversation, informed Duncan that at least one of the three people he least wished to meet must be in this very room. He looked unhurriedly about him. And sure enough, there was Caroline seated on the padded window seat, Norman standing beside her.

Duncan inclined his head affably in their direction. Miss Huxtable was greeting Con, who was with a red-headed beauty.

"Margaret? Sherry?" Con said with an unnecessary degree of heartiness. "Have you met Mrs. Hunter? Do come into the music room with us and add your voices to mine. I am attempting to persuade her to sing for the company. Miss Huxtable and the Earl of Sheringford, Ingrid."

"I remember you as having a lovely contralto voice, Mrs. Hunter," Miss Huxtable said. "I do hope you *will* agree to sing.

However, Lord Sheringford and I have just come from half an hour spent in the music room. We are on our way to find refreshments."

Mrs. Hunter was looking at Duncan with pursed lips and eyes that were somewhat amused.

"I remember you from long ago, Lord Sheringford," she said. "All the young girls making their debuts with me — including myself, I must confess — were ready to swoon at a single glance from you. Alas, you did not know we existed."

She spoke with a low, musical voice.

"I daresay," he said, "I was more foolish in those days than I am now, Mrs. Hunter. Mr. Hunter was obviously far wiser."

"Poor Oliver," she said. "He survived our nuptials by less than a year, though I hasten to add that there was no connection between the two events. Shall we continue on our way into the music room, Constantine?"

Con hesitated and gave his cousin a hard, meaningful look, but he offered his arm to the widow, and the two of them proceeded on their way.

Norman was making his way toward them with purposeful strides. Duncan had been right in the impression he had had of him the night before last. He had not changed, except in girth and the amount of hair that remained on his head. There was nothing new about the height of his shirt points or the look of pomposity he wore. He was also looking righteously outraged.

And at some time during the past five years he had acquired a second chin.

"Sheringford," he said when he was close enough to make himself heard, and though there was no noticeable abatement in the volume of conversation in the library, Duncan would be willing to bet a fortune, if he had one to bet, that everyone in the room would be able to report the conversation verbatim tomorrow morning to anyone unfortunate enough not to be here in person.

"Norm," Duncan said pleasantly. "May I have the pleasure of presenting Miss Huxtable? Norman Pennethorne, my love. My cousin — on my father's side, as his name would imply. *Second* cousin, to be precise."

Norman nodded curtly to Miss Huxtable.

"I understand, ma'am," he said, "that my dear wife called upon you two mornings ago, though I did not know of her plan until after it had been executed and would have forbidden it if I *had* known. But I must applaud her courage in doing something so distressing to her entirely out of a concern for your happiness and good name. I see, alas, that her effort was in vain. You have ignored her warning."

Duncan would have spoken, but Miss Huxtable spoke first.

"Indeed I have not, Mr. Pennethorne," she said. "I was honored by your wife's call and listened very carefully to what she had to say. But there are two sides to most stories, you see, and it would have been quite unfair of me to listen only to hers in this particular case and not also to Lord Sheringford's, especially when he has done me the honor of offering me marriage."

She spoke quietly. Even so, Duncan did not doubt there were those who heard every word — or their own version of every word, anyway.

"And you have accepted the offer?" Norman said sharply.

"If I have," she said, "or if I do at some time in the future, you will be able to read the announcement in the morning papers the following day, sir."

Caroline, Duncan noticed, had remained where she was. She looked pale and interesting and had attracted a small cluster of ladies, who were patting her back and her knees and waving handkerchiefs and vials of hartshorn in the vicinity of her nose.

Norman turned his attention away from Miss Huxtable, his chest swelling visibly as he did so.

"And *you,* Sheringford," he said, "have not improved with time. You are as contemptuous of the proprieties as you ever were. You do not even have the decency to keep far away from my dear wife and my brother-in-law. You do not have the decency to keep far away from entertainments such as this, where decent folk have the expectation of being kept safe from scoundrels. I would wager Mrs. Henry did not invite you here this evening."

Unlike Miss Huxtable, Norman was making no attempt to pitch his voice below the general level of conversation. He spoke as if he were addressing one of the chambers in the Houses of Parliament, with clear enunciation and eloquent passion.

"It has been a pleasure to see you again too, Norm," Duncan said amiably. "Now, if you will excuse us, we will continue on our way to the dining room. Miss Huxtable is in need of refreshments."

By a process of elimination, he thought, Turner must be in the dining room. But he would not turn back now and have the morning papers expose him as a coward.

"I must demand," Norman said, "that you leave a home that also shelters my wife."

Oh, good Lord, the man really ought to be on the stage.

"I shall be happy to leave the house, Norm," Duncan said, "when Miss Huxtable informs me that she is ready to return home. Or when my aunt asks me to leave."

He looked down at Miss Huxtable and wished he had insisted that she go home earlier. It was unfair to embroil her in this nastiness. The gossip of the last few days would surely be nothing compared to tomorrow's. And here she was, trapped in the middle of it.

Except that, as she had informed him a few minutes ago, he did not have the power to compel her to do anything she did not wish to do.

"If you are attempting to attract attention and embarrass your wife, sir," she said quietly to Norman, "you are succeeding admirably. You will excuse us, if you please."

And she linked her arm through Duncan's again and drew him in the direction of the dining room — at the exact moment when Randolph Turner, a young lady on each arm, was exiting it.

It was an exquisitely timed moment, Duncan was forced to admit. Excellent theater.

Very few people in the library even pretended any longer not to be eavesdropping.

"Turner," Duncan said, and inclined his head.

Turner stopped walking abruptly and blanched.

He looked like the quintessential romantic hero, Duncan thought, looking critically at him while he awaited some reply to his slight greeting. He was tall and well formed, with smooth blond hair, pale blue eyes, a finely chiseled nose, and a sensitive mouth. They had made an extraordinarily handsome couple, he and Laura, who had shared his coloring.

Norman did not wait for his brother-in-law to reply. Instead, he came striding up to stand between Turner and Duncan.

"Randolph," he said, "I tried to persuade Sheringford to leave quietly before you were forced to come face-to-face with him. I understand how unspeakably painful this encounter must be to you — and in such a public place too. But he has refused to leave, and so on his own head must be the consequences. There are numerous witnesses, all of whom no doubt share your outrage and mine. No one will blame you for speaking your mind here and now and demanding satisfaction. All will attest to the fact that you were given no alternative."

Duncan regarded Turner with raised eyebrows. The man's already pasty complexion acquired the color and consistency of chalk. He stared back at Duncan, his jaw set hard, his eyes inscrutable.

What *did* one say to the man one had allowed to run off with one's wife without making any attempt to pursue him and run him to earth and throttle the life out of him on the one hand, or to spurn and divorce the faithless wife on the other?

What did one say to the man one must suspect knew all one's deepest, darkest, nastiest secrets?

"I loved my wife," Turner said, "more than life itself."

The two young ladies drew closer to his sides. One of them gazed worshipfully up at him. The other twined both arms about his.

Duncan nodded.

"Yes, she told me all about that," he said.

"You had *no right,*" Turner said, "to interfere between a man and his lawful wife."

Duncan did not turn his head to look, but he would wager a sizable amount that more than one lace-edged handkerchief was being raised to more than one feminine eye in the room behind him.

"No *lawful* right at all," Duncan agreed.

"Randolph," Norman said sternly.

Turner glanced at him uneasily and licked his lips.

"You will wish to demand satisfaction from the scoundrel," Norman said.

There was a collective feminine gasp from the room.

Miss Huxtable's hand tightened on Duncan's arm.

"A duel?" Duncan said. "Have duels been made legal since I was last in London, then, Norm? That is an interesting development. Do you *wish* to challenge me, Turner? With so many witnesses? Even ladies?"

"I —" Turner began.

"Of course you do, Randolph," Norman said briskly and firmly. "I will be your second. There is surely not a person here present who would not applaud you for taking such a firm stand with the villain who exposed your sister to public humiliation and destroyed your happy marriage."

Someone really ought to find Norman a seat in the House of Commons if he did not wish to be an actor. He would sweep all before him with his oratory.

"There is at least one person present who would *certainly* not applaud such a childish way of settling an old quarrel," Miss Huxtable said. "What on earth will be

258

settled if one of you blows out the brains of the other? I would suggest a rational discussion of your differences — in private."

The pervading silence suggested that hers was a minority view. It was not an entirely unilateral one, though.

"Miss Huxtable," Turner said, fixing his eyes on her. "I presume that is who you are, ma'am, though I regret never having been introduced to you. You are quite right. Mrs. Henry's home is *not* the place for such a distasteful confrontation. And it has never been my belief that violence settles anything. Besides — forgive me, ma'am — I do not believe the Earl of Sheringford worthy of the honor of a duel. He has chosen his path to hell and will be allowed to tread it to the end as far as I am concerned. I feel no compulsion to speed him on his way."

Now *both* young ladies were gazing worshipfully at him. Someone in the library stifled a sob. Someone else sniffed quite audibly.

Duncan smiled, his eyes fixed on Turner's. "It has never been your belief that violence settles anything," he said softly. "One can only admire and respect such pacifist views. If you should change your mind, you know where to find me, I do not doubt, though I must caution you that Sir Graham Carling may not be overly delighted to have his home invaded by two belligerent gentlemen — an aggrieved husband and a man who is his relative, though not his brother."

Turner's eyes bored back into his own.

Yes, of course I know, Duncan told him silently. *Did you comfort yourself for one moment in the last five years with the possibility that I did not?*

"Randolph," Norman said sharply, "think of your poor late wife if you will. Think of your sister."

Duncan looked down at Margaret Huxtable.

"Shall we go in pursuit of that lemonade?" he suggested.

"A drink would be very welcome indeed," she said, and they proceeded into the dining room after Turner and his entourage had stepped smartly out of the way.

It was clear that the occupants of the dining room had been following the encounter as avidly as those in the library. There was a loud silence as everyone gawked at them, and then everyone turned away and rushed back into merry conversation with one another.

"Well," Duncan said, "I hope you are enjoying your public wooing, Miss

Huxtable."

"If a duel is ever fought," she said, her voice trembling with emotion, "and if one drop of blood is shed on either side, I shall personally kill you."

"That," he said, "is mildly illogical, is it not? But I did not realize you cared so deeply."

She looked into his eyes and kept her voice low, though it still throbbed with feeling.

"That poor man," she said. "Tomorrow, Lord Sheringford, you must call upon him — *if* he will receive you — and apologize. Most humbly and most sincerely. You wronged him, and while you cannot change the past or expect forgiveness for it, you can at least acknowledge that what you did was very wrong, that the suffering you caused was inexcusable. You will apologize, Lord Sheringford."

He raised his eyebrows. "Or else?"

"Oh," she said, "do there have to be ultimatums before you will do what is right? You *must* apologize."

"You advocate lies, Maggie?" he asked her.

"Lies?" She frowned. "No, I do not, though I have told some of my own in the past few days — none of which has done me a great deal of good."

"And yet," he said, "you would have *me* lie?"

She continued to frown.

"I am not sorry," he said. "If I apologize, I will be lying."

She closed her eyes for a moment and her shoulders slumped.

"Oh, you foolish man," she said. "You must have loved her a great deal. But love ought not to cause dishonor. Or pain."

"Can you have lived to the age of thirty and still be so naive?" he asked her.

Her eyes snapped open.

"Let me fetch you some lemonade," he suggested.

The Earl of Sheringford was taking an empty plate from her hand and returning it to one of the tables before Margaret realized that she must have eaten something — she could not remember what. And her glass was empty. Lemonade? Yes, she could still taste it.

She was smiling. Lady Carling was coming toward her like a ship in full sail, both hands outstretched in front of her.

"The Deans invited us to dinner ages ago," she said, kissing Margaret's cheek, "*long* before Agatha set the date for her soiree. We have only now been able to get away and come here. And thus we have missed all the excitement. Margaret, my dear, you must be a saint to have borne it all and still be standing at Duncan's side. I understand Randolph Turner declined to challenge him to a duel, which is surprising really and even slightly shameful, though I am vastly glad he did. My nerves would never have recovered from the strain. Duncan, my love, you have no choice now but to eat a great deal of humble pie and apologize. You ought to have done it long ago."

"He says he will not," Margaret told her. "He says he is not sorry."

His mother clucked her tongue.

"Laura Turner was a very fortunate woman, then," she said. "Duncan, you may fetch me some ratafia."

Another half hour or so passed, most of it in company with Lady Carling and some of her friends, before Lord Sheringford suggested again that he escort Margaret home. She had never been more glad of anything in her life, though she would have died rather than ask to be taken. She felt exhausted.

Whatever had she got herself into? But whatever it was, she had no one to blame but herself.

Ought she to inform him when he took her back to Merton House that she had made a definite decision not to marry him, that she did not wish to see him again? He would still have time to find someone else. And really and realistically — how could she ever agree to marry a man who apparently had no conscience?

But who else would have him if she did not?

That was *definitely* not her concern.

Stephen was in the drawing room, part of a large group of young people who seemed all to be talking and laughing at once. He detached himself from the group when he saw them come in from the music room.

"You are leaving, Meg?" he said. "May I escort you?"

"No, thank you, Stephen," she said. "Lord Sheringford will do that."

"Let me at least call the carriage, then," he said.

"No." She smiled at him. "It is a lovely evening — or was the last time I looked out a window."

The earl did not own a carriage, and she had rejected his offer to hire one for the occasion. They had walked the short distance to the soiree.

They took their leave of Mrs. Henry, who

shook her head at her nephew, kissed his cheek, and told him that he had made her so famous that simply everyone would clamor to attend her next entertainment.

"Everyone who refused an invitation to this one will bitterly regret it," she said.

13

A few minutes later they were out on the pavement, Margaret shivering slightly beneath her shawl. The air seemed loud with the silence.

Lord Sheringford offered his arm and she took it.

"What are your thoughts?" he asked her after they had walked for a little while without talking.

"I scarcely know," she said. "I feel as if my whole life has been turned upside down."

"Would you rather," he said, "that I ceased courting you? Your reputation would recover very quickly and leave you quite unscathed. Gossip soon dies when there is nothing to feed it."

"I think," she said, "that what I *would* rather, Lord Sheringford, is an explanation of why you are not sorry, or why you refuse to apologize to that poor man. Is it just stubbornness? Or is it really love? Was Mrs.

Turner the great passion of your life, worth everything you gave up, including your character and honor? And worth your refusal to do the right thing and admit that you caused irreparable suffering to her husband?"

She shivered again. Her shawl had slipped off her shoulders and exposed them to the cool air of late evening.

He stopped walking and lifted her shawl, wrapping it more closely about her and keeping one arm about her shoulders to hold it in place. He was looking very directly into her eyes, though she could scarcely see him in the darkness. She could smell the wine he had been drinking.

"The great passion of my life?" he said. "It would be a terrible insult to you if I were to continue to woo you and allow you to believe that to be a possibility. I did not love Laura at all, Maggie — not in any romantic sense, anyway."

She gazed at him, baffled. They were beneath a straight row of trees that had been planted along the edge of the pavement, she realized suddenly. That was why it was so dark despite the fact that the sky was bright with moon and stars. The street was deserted. There was not even a night watchman in sight.

"Then it is only stubbornness?" she said. "An unwillingness to admit that a fleeting passion ruined lives, including your own? And you think other people, including me, will respect you for your steadfast stubbornness? You believe it to be unmanly to admit that you did something so dreadfully wrong, its effects quite irreversible? Admitting you were wrong, asking pardon, is the only decent, manly course of action remaining to you — surely?"

He sighed.

"I ought to have apologized profusely to you when we collided in Lady Tindell's ballroom," he said, "and allowed you to hurry on your way to wherever it was you were going. I ought to have chosen someone with far less firm opinions to save me from penury. Maggie, there are many kinds of decency. Snatching a married lady from her husband and running off with her is sometimes the most decent thing a man can think of to do. Even when he is forced to leave behind a bride of his own, almost literally waiting at the altar for him — though Caroline Turner was not treated quite as shabbily as that."

"Then tell me what." She turned to face him fully and was forced to spread her hands across his chest when he did not take a step back. His one arm was still about her shoulders. "How can such a sin be *decent?*"

She gazed up into his face, barely visible even at this distance.

And then she had a sudden inkling of the truth and wondered that it had not occurred to her before.

"Randolph Turner is a coward," he said. "You may have noticed it a short while ago. Any other man in his position would have felt that he had no option but to slap a glove in my face, even if only a figurative one. He found a way of wriggling out of doing so and appearing rather heroic into the bargain — to the ladies, at least."

"Perhaps," she said, "he abhors violence and understands that it is no solution to any problem."

"And perhaps," he said, "any normal husband whose wife had run off with another man would scour heaven and earth to find her and punish her abductor — or else would publicly spurn and divorce her. He would at the very least take firm exception to her abductor's returning to society after her death and attending the same social functions as he, just as if he had every right to the forgiveness and respect of society."

"Perhaps," she said again very distinctly, "he abhors violence and understands that it is no solution to any problem."

He sighed.

"And perhaps," he said, "he possesses that quality that so often goes hand in hand with cowardice."

She searched his eyes in the darkness. She did not wait for him to explain. Her inkling had been right, then.

"He was a bully?" She was whispering.

He released his hold on her and took a few steps away to lean back against a tree trunk. He folded his arms over his chest, and Margaret grasped the ends of her shawl and drew it more closely about her.

"I promised her that I would never tell a soul," he said, "and indeed the necessity for secrecy was dire. Her main reason, though, was that she felt guilty. She felt that she had failed as a wife, that she had drawn every bit of censure and violence upon herself. She thought people would blame her if they knew the truth and seemed to prefer being known simply as a faithless wife."

"He beat her?" Margaret was gripping the ends of her shawl as if her life depended upon her hanging on.

"Among other things," he said. "She really was in the wrong for running away from him, of course. A man has a right to beat his wife or to administer any form of correction he deems necessary to make her obedient and submissive. She is, after all, his possession. A man has a right to beat his dog too."

"Oh, poor Mrs. Turner," Margaret said, looking quickly about. But there was still no one in sight. She had always thought that violence within a family was one of the worst afflictions that could be visited upon any person. One's family ought to be one's safest haven. "How did you come to know?"

"Quite by accident, I suppose," he said. "I was newly betrothed to Caroline and so was a part of the family. I cannot for the life of me remember why Laura and I were so far separated from the rest of the company one evening that we were able to talk privately with each other for a few minutes. Turner kept her on a very short leash — especially after a beating. Which meant that she was almost always on a short leash. It looked like marital devotion to anyone who did not know differently. *I* thought it was marital devotion at first — until that evening, in fact."

Margaret stared at him in the near darkness. She forgot about the chilliness of the air, though she shivered anyway. Hooves clopped along the street to her left, but the horse and its rider must have turned into another street. The sound grew fainter and then disappeared altogether.

"However it happened, we *were* separated from the group," he said, "and she let her guard down sufficiently to afford me a glimpse of a dark bruise on her upper arm. The sleeves of her gown were somewhat longer than was fashionable, I remember. She appeared frightened when I mentioned it and then turned her head in such a way that her silk shawl fell away from her neck for a moment before she yanked it back in place. The bruise on her jaw was fading but still unmistakable. It was, I realized, the 'indisposition' that had kept her in seclusion at home for the past week. There had been numerous such indispositions since I had known Caroline. Laura was known as a woman of delicate health. I can remember being shocked enough to speak bluntly. I believe I can even recall my exact words. 'Turner is a wife-beater,' I said, and with one darted glance in the direction of the rest of the company, all of whom were comfortably out of earshot, she settled a smile on her face and told me hurriedly all about it. It had been going on for two out of the three years of her marriage and was becoming both more frequent and more severe."

"Oh," Margaret said. She could think of nothing else to say at the moment. She had always thought wife-beaters surely the most despicable of mortals. "And so you took her away?"

"Not immediately," he said. "It was obvious that she had never told anyone before me and that she was extremely frightened as soon as she had unburdened herself. She blamed herself for everything — basically for being a bad wife who could not please her husband. When I offered to speak sternly to Turner on her behalf, I thought she would swoon quite away with terror. She would not speak to me for several weeks afterward — but then she did on the night before my wedding. She came to see me privately, an extremely indiscreet and dangerous thing to do, as you must know. But she was distraught and had no one else to turn to. She spoke of taking her own life, and I believed her. I still believe she would have done it. And if she had not, sooner or later Turner would have done it for her. And so I did the only thing that seemed possible to do. I ran off with her — after promising that I would never disclose any part of her story to another soul. It is a promise that I am breaking tonight. You may never marry me, Maggie. Indeed, you would be well advised not to. I will have to trust to your discretion concerning what I have told you."

Margaret was biting hard into her bottom lip, she realized.

"People ought to know," she said. "They ought to be told that you are not the villain you are depicted as being."

"But I am," he said. "A man has the power of life and death over his wife, Maggie. He has the right — some would say even the obligation — to correct and discipline her in any way he sees fit. No man who is *not* her husband, even her father or brother, has any right to interfere. Both church and state will tell you that. I am exactly the villain everyone thinks me — just a slightly different sort of villain, perhaps."

Margaret drew a deep breath.

"Why," she asked him, "did he not pursue you?"

"Because he is a coward," he said, "as bullies usually are. And also perhaps because we hid very carefully indeed — for almost five years, until her death. He could have taken her back if he had found her. Both the law and the church would have been on his side. I could have done nothing to prevent it. He would have killed her, Maggie. I feel no doubt about that. Sadly, she did it for him. She did not literally take her own life, but she put up no fight for it either. He had taken away her belief in her own inherent goodness. And when one does not believe oneself in any way good, there is very little for which to live — and one feels unworthy of even what little there is. I will not apologize to a man who effectively murdered a woman whose only fault was a certain mental and emotional inability to fight back against cruelty and injustice."

Margaret sighed and took a couple of steps forward until she stood against him. He uncrossed his arms, and she laid her forehead against one of his shoulders. She felt instant warmth.

And she had acted purely from instinct, she realized too late to act with greater propriety. She had felt the overwhelming need to seek out his human warmth and had acted upon that need — just as Laura Turner had done five years ago.

"Now I understand," she said, "why I could not spurn you even when all the evidence and the opinion of everyone I know said that I ought. Sometimes one's intuition is to be trusted above all else. I could not convince myself that you were an evil man."

"But I am," he told her. "There is no law, either temporal or ecclesiastical — or moral

— that would support what I did, Maggie. A woman is her husband's property, to be dealt with as he sees fit."

"That is utter nonsense," she said, still without lifting her head.

"The law often is," he said. "But it is the only glue that holds society together and prevents utter chaos. We can only hope, I suppose, to reform the law gradually until it represents true morality and the rights of all — including women and the poor and even animals. I will not hold my breath waiting for that day, though. It could be a long time coming — if it ever does. What I did was wrong, Maggie. Evil."

"Then thank heaven," she said, lifting her head, "for a little bit of evil in the world. Morality is not a black-and-white thing, is it? And what a profound statement *that* is. As if no one had ever noticed before."

He could not be totally absolved of *all* he had done, though, she remembered suddenly.

"But what about Miss Turner?" she said. "She was left behind on her wedding day, an innocent victim of both humiliation and heartbreak."

"She was the only one to whom I confided some of what I had been told," he said, "before I promised not to do so, that was. I can remember feeling afraid that perhaps Caroline had suffered similar treatment at her brother's hands. I was quite prepared to pummel him within an inch of his life if she had. But she had not. She knew about Laura, though, and defended Turner quite vigorously. If Laura did not push him to it, she told me, he would not be forced to punish her. It was all Laura's fault. The day after that Laura went into seclusion again and remained out of public sight for well over a week, even longer than usual. I believe I caused her one of the worst beatings of her life by speaking with Caroline. She had good reason to swear me to secrecy."

"Miss Turner *told* him?" Margaret asked unnecessarily.

"Do you wonder," he asked in return, "that I fell rather hastily out of love with her, Maggie?"

No, she did not.

She kept her forehead against his shoulder and closed her eyes as a carriage drawn by four horses made its rather noisy way past them and continued on.

"I think," she said when they were alone again, "I had better marry you."

His hands came to rest lightly on her hips.

"Because you find me pathetic?" he asked.

"Because I find you anything *but,*" she

said. "You need some peace in your life, Lord Sheringford. So do I."

"*Peace,*" he said. "That is a word from a long-ago past. And you think marriage to you will bring me that, Maggie?"

"Life at Woodbine Park will," she said. "And unfortunately for you, that can be achieved only at the expense of marriage to me — or to someone else you may be able to find in the next week or so. I would be better for you than anyone else, though. I know the truth about you and can respect you, even admire you."

His arms circled her waist as he sighed.

"Don't make the mistake of believing that you know me now any more fully than you did before," he said. "You merely know a few more facts."

"Oh, there you are wrong," she told him, sliding her own arms as far about him as the tree at his back would allow. "I know more than facts now. I know *you*. Or at least I am on the way to knowing you."

"And you believe I can bring you *peace?*" For a moment she felt his cheek against the top of her head. "Or that Woodbine can?"

"I have no real way of knowing," she said. "We can never know the future. We can only take calculated risks."

She lifted her forehead from his shoulder

and looked into his eyes.

"*Very* risky," he said. "The world will always despise me, Maggie — and you too if you marry me."

She smiled at him.

"You have been desperate to persuade me to marry you," she said. "Are you now trying to persuade me *not* to?"

He set his head back against the tree and closed his eyes.

"Reality creeps up on one, does it not?" he said. "For a few days — is it two or three or more? I have lost count already. For a few days, anyway, I have been desperate to do whatever I must do to prevent the loss of Woodbine. And yet now, when it seems that what I want is within my grasp, the reality comes home to me that I can do it only at the expense of the happiness of another innocent."

"You believe," she said, "that I will be unhappy as your wife, then?"

"How can you not be?" he said without opening his eyes. "We have known each other for two or three or four days — which *is* it? For a very brief time, anyway. I have only mercenary reasons for wishing to marry you. I believe I like you, though it is only this evening that I have come to that opinion. I do not love you. How could I? I do not *know* you and I have become an incurable cynic where romantic love is concerned. And you do not know me. You have lived an ordered, decorous life with a close, affectionate family. You have always been very well respected. It is possible that you still love a man who has angered you. You would be stepping into a yawning unknown with a social pariah if you married me."

He was right about everything — except Crispin. So very right. She did not know quite why retaining possession of Woodbine Park *now* was so important to him since it would be his eventually anyway, along with a great deal more, and in the meanwhile he was young and fit and surely capable of earning a perfectly decent living. But however it was — perhaps it was just his reaction to a long exile, now over — Woodbine *was* important. Yet she sensed that if she said no now, he would walk away from it. If he could not bring himself in all conscience to marry her purely for his own convenience, then he would not be able to do it with anyone else.

It was a pleasant surprise to discover that he was after all a man of tender conscience. Perhaps more than usually so. He had pitted his conscience against the whole of his world five years ago.

"I will marry you if you still wish to marry," she said. "But only *if*. You must not now feel that you are obliged to wed me only because you made me an offer which I have accepted. *If* you wish to marry, then I will marry you. I will take a chance on the future."

He had opened his eyes though he had not moved his head. He was looking steadily back into her own eyes. His looked very black. His face looked very severe and angular in the darkness. A few days ago she might have been frightened.

"I wish to marry you," he said.

"I would ask only one thing," she said, "and this I beg of you as a great favor. Allow me to tell my family what you have told me tonight — Stephen, Vanessa and Elliott, Katherine and Jasper. I would stake my life on their honor and discretion, on the fact that not one of them will say a word to anyone else without your express permission. But I really cannot bear to have them believe that I am marrying an unconscionable villain. I cannot bear their puzzlement and pity. And I cannot bear that they will dislike and despise and avoid you for the rest of our lives."

He sighed.

"They will think just as badly of me, Maggie," he said. "Moreland will, at least. And Merton. Probably your sisters too."

"No, they will not," she said. "No, *they will not.*"

He lifted one hand and set his knuckles lightly against one of her cheeks.

"It must be wonderful," he said, "to be so innocent, still to have such faith in the world."

She leaned her cheek into his hand.

"If I were to lose faith in my own family," she said, "I might as well be dead."

He dipped his head toward hers and kissed her. His lips were warm, soft, moist, and moved over her own, parting and deepening the pressure as one arm came about her shoulders and the other tightened about her waist.

Oh, she liked kisses without ferocity, she thought — just as he raised his head.

"You wish to marry me, then, Maggie?" he asked. "And by the same token bed with me nightly?"

He was, she realized, waiting for an answer. It was a good thing he could not see the color of her cheeks.

"Yes," she said. And an aching weakness between her thighs assured her that she was not lying. Yes, she wanted to bed with him.

Nightly. She did not love him any more than he loved her, but . . . Oh, but she wanted to be *married* to him. She found him strangely attractive. She wanted to go to bed with him.

She verbalized the admission in her mind and felt breathlessly wicked. But it was not wicked. She was going to be his wife.

"Kiss me, then," he said.

"I just *was* kissing you," she protested.

"No, you were not," he said. "You were holding your mouth relaxed for my pleasure, just as you did yesterday afternoon in the park. I do not want a passive, submissive woman. There are too many of those in the world, forced to it by the demands of their menfolk. *My* wife will not be one of them. If you wish to marry me, if you wish to bed with me on our wedding night and every night thereafter when we are both in the mood for sex, then kiss me now as if you mean it."

And the thing was that he was neither joking nor teasing. His face and his voice both attested to that fact. Just as he had not been joking or teasing at the Tindell ball when he had offered her marriage within a minute or two of colliding with her.

He was not someone, then, who took kisses as if it were his right to do so.

"Kiss me," he said softly.

"We are on the *street*," she reminded him.

"And everyone in the neighborhood is either asleep or still out carousing," he said. "There is not a single light in a single window. And if there is a Peeping Tom behind one of the darkened ones, he is having lean pickings tonight. We must be almost totally invisible beneath this tree. Maggie, you are either a coward or you do not wish to kiss me. And if it is the latter, then you do not wish to bed with me either and therefore do not wish to marry me."

She laughed.

"Which is it?" he asked.

She gripped his upper arms, leaned forward, and set her lips firmly to his. She was instantly more fully aware of the hardness of his thighs against her own, of his broad chest pressed to her bosom, of the wine flavor of his mouth and the warmth of his breath.

His lips remained still and passive against hers, and after a few moments she was at a loss. She drew back her head.

"Oh, dear," she said, "I suppose you are demonstrating the way *I* was kissing *you*. I am so sorry. It is just, you see —"

His mouth covered hers again, and she leaned deliberately into him and burrowed

284

the fingers of one hand into the back of his hair beneath his tall silk hat, angling her head slightly as she did so and parting her lips, moving them over his, touching his lips with her tongue and then venturing within them until his arms tightened about her and he sucked her tongue into his mouth while his hands slid downward to spread over her buttocks and half lift her against him.

He was ready for her. Oh, dear God, he was . . .

She drew firmly away from him.

"Frightened?" he murmured.

"Yes," she said. "And also aware that we are on the street even if we *are* invisible to Peeping Toms."

"The voice of reason," he said, brushing his hands over his clothes and stepping away from the tree trunk. "But you need not be afraid, Maggie. We may be marrying for all the wrong reasons — though I am no longer sure what *right* reasons there can be for matrimony — but we can still expect pleasure from our union. It is obvious that pleasure is within our grasp."

"Yes," she said, and she saw the flash of his teeth in the darkness. "Are we going to remain here forever? Soon we will be sending down roots to join the trees."

He offered his arm, and they resumed

their walk home to Berkeley Square.

"Tomorrow," he said, "I shall take you to meet my grandfather, if I may. It may be rather like ushering Daniel into the lions' den, I am afraid, though he will have no reason to turn his wrath upon *you.* The day after I will have an announcement of our betrothal appear in the morning papers."

It was all very real indeed now.

"Yes," she said. "That will be satisfactory."

"And then," he said as they came to a stop outside the doors of Merton House, "I shall purchase a special license and we will decide upon a suitable day for the nuptials. I believe there will be ten or so among which to choose."

"Yes," she said. "I am not sure you answered my question. *May* I tell my family what you told me tonight?"

He hesitated.

"Yes," he said, and leaned forward to kiss her briefly on the lips before raising the door knocker and allowing it to fall back against the brass plate. "At least after the announcement is made you will be able to thumb your nose at the likes of Dew and Allingham."

"A marvelously mature thing to do," she said.

"And marvelously satisfying too," he said.

"*If*, that is, you wish to do so. Be very sure."

"I am," she said. "I *did* love him, you know, and there is still pain where he once occupied my heart. But the pain is caused by the realization that he was never the man I thought him to be and that he has not grown into the man with whom I could be happy spending the rest of my life."

"But I am?" he said softly.

"With you I have no illusions," she said. "You will not allow me to have any. You do not pretend to be what you are not, and you do not pretend to tender feelings you do not feel. On that foundation we can build a friendship, even an affection. That is my hope, anyway. It is what I will attempt to make of our marriage."

The door opened before he could reply, and under the eagle gaze of Stephen's butler he raised her hand to his lips and bade her a good night.

And so she was betrothed, Margaret thought as she stepped inside the house and made her way toward the staircase with a firm stride quite at variance with her feelings. To a man for whom conscience and personal honor meant more than reputation or law or church or peace of mind.

She could love such a man.

Certainly she admired him — perhaps

more than she had admired anyone else in her life.

Was *that* why she had made the abrupt decision to marry him when she had promised herself to take all the time she was allowed?

Or was it as she had said to him outside a couple of minutes ago? Was it that with no promises, no illusions, no veil of romance, she could dream of an honest relationship that could be shaped into something meaningful and satisfying?

She felt rather like weeping by the time she reached her room. She dismissed her maid and threw herself across her bed fully clothed and did just that.

For no reason that she could fathom.

14

"Do you suppose, Smith," Duncan asked while his valet was helping him into his coat the following morning and ensuring that his shirt and waistcoat beneath it did not suffer so much as one crease as a consequence, "that when one has lived a lie for a number of years one is incapable of telling the truth ever again?"

Smith, not satisfied with his handiwork, hauled the coat higher on the right shoulder and stood back to take a critical look.

"When one has lived the truth most of one's life," he said, brushing the coat vigorously to remove the last stubborn spot of lint, "one is still capable of telling lies. I suppose the matter works both ways, m'lord."

"Hmm," Duncan said. "Reassuring. You have finished with me?"

"I have," Smith said. "She will take one look at you and swoon with delight."

"Really?" Duncan said. "That would be a miracle. She has already informed me that I am neither handsome nor particularly good-looking."

Smith looked at him sidelong as he put away the clothes Duncan had recently discarded.

"It is no wonder you are worried about telling lies, then, m'lord," he said, "if you have found such an honest woman."

Duncan was still chuckling as he closed the dressing room door behind him and made his way downstairs.

He was going to take Miss Huxtable to call upon his grandfather this afternoon. He had gone to bed with the intention of spending an hour at Jackson's Boxing Salon again this morning and another hour or two at White's. But sleep had refused to come to him all night until he had made a certain decision at dawn.

He had lain on his back staring at the canopy over his bed when he was not curled up on his left side, his forehead almost touching his knees, or on his right side, one arm burrowed beneath his pillow, or when he was not flat on his stomach trying to find a way to position his head that would allow him to breathe. It was no good. There was no such thing as a comfortable position.

It was a ghastly fate, he had thought eventually, on his back again, his fingers laced behind his head, his eyes on the rosebud at the center of the canopy, to have been born with a conscience. It played havoc with a man's chances of living comfortably in the real world and of enjoying a good night's sleep.

And here he was this morning, all dressed up as if he were on his way to make another marriage offer — which, in a sense he was. To the same lady and in the same place. He was on his way to Merton House to speak with Miss Huxtable. He hoped fervently that she was not at home. Did not ladies use their mornings for shopping and visiting and exchanging their books at the library and walking in the park and . . .

She was at home.

Merton's butler did not even make any pretense of going to see if she was. Instead, he took Duncan's hat and gloves, preceded him up to the drawing room, which was empty, and told him that he would inform Miss Huxtable of his arrival.

Too late Duncan realized that the butler must have assumed this was a planned visit. A good butler ought not to make such an assumption.

There had been another letter from Mrs.

Harris this morning, reminding Lord Sheringford that the rent was going to be due again soon.

As if he needed reminding.

She had enclosed a picture that Toby had made for him. They were all in it, spread across the bottom of the paper — Toby with a mop of curly hair and the Harrises, all modestly small, himself a great hulking giant filling the right half of the page, a round sun with beaming rays above his head.

The protector.

The one who filled a child's world and brought him the sun.

Duncan could almost see Toby drawing the picture, his little body hunched over the paper, the charcoal clutched in his left hand despite all Mrs. Harris's efforts to make him use the right, a frown of concentration on his brow, the tip of his tongue protruding from the right side of his mouth.

He could almost smell the baby smell of the child.

He felt such a swell of yearning that for a moment he closed his eyes and reminded himself of what he was about to do. The right thing?

How could one know what was right and what was wrong?

There was conscience — and then there

was a child.

Miss Huxtable was obviously neither going out nor expecting visitors. She came to the drawing room a mere two minutes after he arrived there, dressed in an off-white cotton morning dress that looked as if it must be an old favorite, her hair styled in a simple knot at her neck. It must not have occurred to her that she might have kept him waiting while she changed and did something with her hair.

Strangely, she looked even more lovely than usual.

She also looked flushed and bright-eyed. Like a young innocent who had been kissed the night before and had rather enjoyed the experience.

"Lord Sheringford?" She came well into the room before stopping a few feet from him. She was smiling. "This is a pleasant surprise."

She offered him her hand, which he took in his and squeezed. Belatedly, he realized that she had probably expected him to raise it to his lips. He released it.

"Perhaps not so pleasant," he said. "I have come to give you the chance to rescind your acceptance of my marriage offer before our betrothal has been made public."

The color deepened in her cheeks. Her

smile remained, but it became more guarded.

"Mr. Turner has challenged you to a duel," she said.

"No."

"If it is what was written in the morning papers," she said, "you must not concern yourself. I have grown quite accustomed to such silliness being written about me — and about you. And Stephen was much affected by what I told him at breakfast. He was hoping to meet you at White's this morning and make his peace with you. I am sure my sisters and brothers-in-law will feel the same way. I have sent letters to them. I would have gone in person, but I feared that I would be exhausted by the time I returned home and not quite up to facing the Marquess of Claverbrook."

"Miss Huxtable," he said, "I have not been quite frank with you. There is something I have not told you that will almost certainly cause you to reconsider your decision to marry me."

Not that he could be perfectly frank even now. Certain details were not his to divulge.

Her smile had faded entirely, and she looked away from him.

"We had better sit down," she said, and she took a chair beside the fireplace.

He sat on a love seat adjacent to it.

"I would not be attempting to contract such a hasty marriage," he said, "just for the sake of retaining Woodbine Park, much as I love it. It will, in the normal course of things, be mine eventually anyway. Neither would the simple prospect of losing all my funds propel me into marriage with a virtual stranger. I will be wealthy enough eventually, I daresay, and in the meanwhile I am perfectly capable of earning enough money to keep body and soul together, unaccustomed though I am to earning my living. To be honest, I would not even be *thinking* of marriage yet — or perhaps ever."

He paused long enough for her to speak.

"You have realized since last evening," she said, "that you really do not wish to marry me or anyone else, Lord Sheringford, that you would prefer to take employment until such time as you inherit from the Marquess of Claverbrook. I can understand why the reality of being betrothed has awoken you to what you really want to do with your life until then. I can even respect you for it — and for coming here this morning to be honest with me before any announcement has been made. Better that than be abandoned at the altar." She smiled fleetingly. "You must not feel badly. I am not in love with you, and I do not *need* to marry. After a few days I do not doubt I will realize that I have had a fortunate escape. It is *not* comfortable to be notorious."

Perhaps he should leave it at that. Perhaps she really would be thankful in a few days' time to have been released from all this madness. Perhaps he should simply get to his feet, make her a heartfelt apology, and take his leave.

"Miss Huxtable," he said instead, "there is a *child.* Toby — Tobias. I love him, and I have promised him a home at Woodbine Park. A safe haven after all he has known in his life so far. Laura was constantly terrified of being found. We were constantly on the move, settling into one home only to be uprooted and having to start all over again — with new names, new identities each time. I have promised Toby Woodbine as a home."

She was staring at him, her face expressionless.

"A child," she said. "You and Mrs. Turner had a child."

She bit her upper lip.

"There is a couple looking after him," he said. "The Harrises. In Harrogate. They at least have been a constant in his life. Woodbine needs a new head gardener, and I offered the position to Harris before I heard from my grandfather and understood that the position was not mine to offer. Mrs. Harris has always been Toby's nurse. He was to pass as their orphaned grandson so that the neighborhood need not be scandalized and outraged at the presence of an illegitimate child in the nursery. Since learning that I must marry in order to retain Woodbine, I have toyed with the idea of putting the three of them in one of the cottages on the estate, but I could not push Toby out of the house merely so that my wife could live there. I hoped somehow to keep you all under the one roof and hide the truth from you. But Toby has been accustomed to calling me *Papa* even though we have been trying to train him to address me as *sir* before the move to Woodbine. You would have found out soon enough, I do not doubt, but it would be too late then for you to refuse to marry me. And even if the secret could be kept from you forever, I realized last night, I could not do it. I cannot put you in the position of having to share your home with a — with a bastard child."

Good Lord, he had never *ever* used that word of Toby before now.

"Thousands of fathers," he said, "*most* fathers, in fact, house and feed and clothe their children on their earnings. I will do it too for as long as I must. Forgive me, Miss Huxtable. I ought not even to have come to London to plead with my grandfather. I certainly ought not to have been tempted by his ultimatum, which I goaded him into making. I ought to have apologized to you at the Tindell ball for colliding with you and let you go on your way. I ought not even to have *been* at the ball."

"You did not collide with me, Lord Sheringford," she said. "It was the other way around."

He laughed — totally without humor.

"How old is he?" she asked.

"Four."

"Does he look like you?" she asked.

"Like Laura." He closed his eyes and then opened them to look down at his hands draped over his knees. "Blond and blue-eyed and delicately built — and the very devil. He suffers from anxiety and insecurities, but he has all the makings of a happy, mischievous hellion. He will be a perfectly normal little boy, given the chance. I have promised myself that he will have that chance. I am sorry, Miss Huxtable. He must come first in my life. He did not ask to be born. He did not ask for the difficulties of the first four years of his life. For better or worse, he is in my care, and care for him I will. I hope I have not caused undue embarrassment to you with your family. Though dash it, of course I have."

"Lord Sheringford," she said softly, "will you marry me? Please?"

He looked up at her, startled.

"I understand," she said, "that you do not really want to marry at all. I understand too that if you did want to and had the time to look about you at some leisure, you would very probably not choose me. But your child does need the home and the life you have promised him. He needs a father who is always close by to soothe his insecurities and anxieties. And I daresay he needs a mother, though no one will ever be able to replace his real mother, of course."

"Laura," he was startled enough to say, "had very little to do with him. She was depressed after his birth. She never got over her depression. Or her fears. She spent most of her time alone."

In a darkened room. Usually in bed. She could not bear to look at Toby.

"Poor lady." She frowned. "And poor little boy. Then he needs a mother, Lord Sheringford. Let me be a mother to him."

"You cannot mean it," he said. "Just think, Maggie. The very thought of it should scandalize you. You would be sharing your home with m-my bastard."

She looked steadily at him.

"I notice your hesitation," she said. "Is that a word with which you are accustomed to describe your son, Lord Sheringford?"

"No," he said. "I have never used it before today."

"Then never use it again," she said, "either in my hearing or out of it. As you said a short while ago, your son did not choose to be born of a married lady and her rescuer and lover. He is a child, as valuable as a king's child. In the future when you refer to him, call him your son."

He was surprised into smiling at her.

"The neighbors would be scandalized," he said. "It would have to be our secret."

She clucked her tongue.

"Will you never learn your lesson?" she asked him. "Your neighbors doubtless know of the scandal. And so they will be very suspicious of you when you return, perhaps even hostile for a while. You might as well be hung for a sheep as a lamb, then. We will make open reference to the fact that the child who is coming to Woodbine Park to live with us is your son. We will both show without any artifice at all that we love him as if he were ours. Your neighbors may react as they wish, but if I know anything about neighbors in a country setting — and I *do* — I can feel perfectly confident that almost everyone will soon forgive you and accept your son and get on with their lives."

He sat back in his seat and regarded her in silence for a while.

She was formidable indeed. He wondered if after all he would come to dislike her intensely after he had lived with her for a while. Or if he would come to love her.

If the latter were the case, he suspected that he might love her with a passion to end passions.

Though where *that* thought had come from he did not know.

"Are you quite sure?" he asked.

She stared back at him.

"I think," she said, "I must believe in fate. I have never thought much about it before now, but I think I must believe in it. The last few days have been bizarre. Ten days ago I was still at Warren Hall — I left there late in the morning to come to town. Four days ago I was planning to attend Lady Tindell's ball and hoping to meet the Marquess of Allingham there and rekindle our friendship. Four days ago I had not even met you. And then a whole series of strange things happened at the ball that led up to my colliding with you — and a string of events had happened to you that had brought you there in search of a bride. So much has happened since then that sometimes I think I have crammed a whole year's worth of living into a few days. All this cannot possibly have happened just by chance or for nothing. If I send you on your way this morning and return to my former life, I will forever suspect that I missed the whole point of my life. This *has* to be the point, or why has it all happened? There have been so many coincidences that I cannot escape the conclusion that it has not been coincidence at all. Perhaps fate intends that I be a mother to your little boy, Lord Sheringford."

"And a wife to me?" he said.

She hesitated and then nodded.

"Yes," she said. "Strange, is it not? I hope I am not wrong. I hope we do not all end up living unhappily ever after."

He got to his feet and extended a hand for hers. She set her own in it and rose to stand before him.

"I will do my very best," he said, "to see that you do not regret your decision but that rather you will rejoice in it. I said that Toby must come first in my life. But you will not be second, Maggie. I do not believe life and relationships work that way."

He raised her hand to his lips and turned it to kiss her palm.

His heart was aching. She had persuaded him to bring the secret out into the open when they returned to Woodbine — and he had capitulated because he knew she was right. Toby had been hidden in the shadows for too long. But he was well aware that what he had really agreed to was the opening of a Pandora's box. It had started last evening, in fact, when he had told her about some of the events surrounding his elopement with Laura Turner. It would not end at Woodbine, though. Woodbine was not a world unto itself. Word of its doings sometimes spread beyond its boundaries — especially if they were unusual and interesting doings.

Toby needed freedom. But what might be the cost of that freedom?

"I had better take my leave," he said. "I may return this afternoon as planned, then, may I, and we will go to face the lion in his den?"

"We will," she said. "I look forward to meeting the Marquess of Claverbrook. No one ought to be allowed to inspire as much fear as he appears to do."

"I worshipped him as a child," he said. "He used to frown and harrumph and look ferocious whenever I saw him, and then he would invariably feel around in his pockets until he came out with a shilling. He would always look surprised and comment that *that* was what had been digging into him before tossing it my way and telling me to spend it wisely on sweets."

She laughed.

He bowed to her and took his leave.

And wondered if she was right.

Was this all fate?

Had the whole of his life been leading him to that strange meeting with Maggie Huxtable?

It was a dizzying thought.

He had a *son.* Margaret did not know why she had been taken so much by surprise. He and Mrs. Turner had been together for almost five years before her death, after all. In a sense, it was surprising there had not been more than one child.

He had told her on a previous occasion that he had never loved Mrs. Turner — not in any romantic sense. All this was very reminiscent of Crispin. Was love impossible for men? Or *romantic* love, anyway? It was a depressing thought.

It was a good thing she was no longer looking for romantic love.

Vanessa arrived soon after Lord Shering-ford had left. She had come to rejoice with her sister over the fact that he was not after all the villain everyone thought him to be. But she did not stay long. She had promised the children an outing — indeed they were outside with their nurse in the carriage wait-ing for her — and would not disappoint them.

Half an hour after Margaret had waved them on their way, Katherine came. She had been at the library when Margaret's note had been delivered, but she had read it with such delight even before taking off her bon-net that she had come without delay to hug her sister and even shed a few tears over her. But Jasper was expected home at any moment, and she wanted to be there to share the good news with him.

"Oh, Meg," she said when she was leav-ing, her eyes shining with tears, "your mar-riage is going to turn into a love match. Just wait and see."

Margaret did not say a word to either of them about the child. Tobias — Toby. She wondered what last name he bore.

They would know soon enough, though, she supposed. She was determined that the little boy would not be hidden away in some dark corner with an assumed identity, as if there were something shameful about him. Everyone in the neighborhood of Woodbine Park would know who he was. There were scores of gentlemen, she was well aware, who had illegitimate children, most of them hidden discreetly from the view of wives and polite society with their mothers or at some private orphanage or school.

It was not going to happen with the Earl of Sheringford's son. And let anyone try to sympathize with her at having to endure such an indignity. She would give that person an earful!

Margaret dressed with care for the visit to the Marquess of Claverbrook. It was important that he approve of her, though he would surely have no reason *not* to unless he was playing games with his grandson and intended to disapprove of anyone who was presented to him. Well, she would give *him* an earful too if that were the case.

She left her room as soon as she heard the door knocker. She was feeling quite martial, perhaps because inside she was quaking with nervousness. She paused at the top of the stairs when she saw that Stephen was in the hall with her betrothed. He was shaking his hand.

"I will not apologize," he was saying, "for the manner in which I have received you during the past few days, Sheringford. My primary responsibility is to my sisters, especially Meg, who lives under my roof and to whom I owe more than I can ever repay. I would do anything in my power to protect her from harm or lasting unhappiness — and all the available evidence suggested that you might well bring her both. But she told me something this morning, in strictest confidence, that has convinced me I have misjudged you. I do hope that if I were ever called upon to make a decision as excruciatingly difficult as the one you faced five years ago, I would have the courage to make the same choice you made — and to keep it a secret too, according to the lady's wishes. Indeed, I honor you."

"Nothing has changed, you know," the earl said. "Miss Huxtable will still be marrying a social pariah. I am still guilty of jilting one woman and stealing another from her lawful husband. I take it your sister also informed you that she has accepted my offer?"

"She has," Stephen said, "and I must confess that I still felt it my duty to caution her, as marriage to you will *not* be easy. I respect her decision, though. Meg is nothing if not courageous."

"I will do my utmost —" the earl began,

but Margaret cleared her throat at that point and made her descent.

Lord Sheringford bowed to her.

"Maggie," he said.

"Lord Sheringford."

"Maggie?" Stephen said with a laugh. "That is a new one."

"A new name for a new life," she said, "as Lord Sheringford pointed out a few evenings ago. I believe I rather like it. It makes me seem less dull and staid. I am ready."

"Dull?" Stephen said, laughing. *"Staid?* You, Meg?"

He kissed her cheek and waited to see them on their way. It still seemed strange to realize that he was all grown up, that he was the one now who felt responsible for *her.*

She felt a rush of love for him.

15

"Stephen wishes to host a wedding breakfast for us," she said as they walked. "Will it be appropriate, do you think? More to the point, will anyone come?"

"Appropriate?" he said, glancing uneasily up at the sky. It was surely going to rain in the not-too-distant future, and she was wearing a pale blue walking dress and spencer and a straw bonnet trimmed with cornflowers. He had had the forethought to bring an umbrella with him, but even so it was infernally inconvenient to be without a carriage. "There is to be a wedding, is there not? Why not a wedding *breakfast*, then?"

He had not actually thought of their nuptials as a *wedding*. Which, of course, had been extremely shortsighted of him. There were still ten days left before his grandfather's birthday, plenty of time in which to organize something that resembled, well, a wedding. It was a ghastly thought, but he supposed he owed her that. All ladies liked to have a proper wedding, did they not? Of course, her misgivings might prove to be justified. The *ton* might well decide overwhelmingly that such a wedding in London itself was in the very poorest taste. Though perhaps not.

"And I would wager," he said, "that the whole of the fashionable world will come if it is invited. How could anyone resist going to the church to discover at first hand whether I will turn up for my wedding this time? There is a wager in at least one of the club betting books that I will not."

"Oh, dear," she said. "I would have been just as happy if you had not mentioned that."

"They will lose their bets," he said.

"I know," she agreed.

"My mother will be ecstatic," he said, "at the prospect of a wedding. She will wish to help plan it."

He winced inwardly.

"So will Nessie and Kate," she said. "I believe I might safely leave all the details to the three of them. Though I fear it is not in my nature to be passive."

"As long as you do not expect *me* to help," he said, "I will be entirely happy."

She laughed, and two unknown gentlemen who were passing on the pavement turned their heads and regarded her with identical looks of admiration.

They arrived at Grosvenor Square a few minutes later, and Duncan rapped on the door of Claverbrook House with the knob of his umbrella.

Forbes opened the door.

"Good afternoon," Duncan said briskly, ushering Miss Huxtable inside and following her in. "Lord Sheringford and Miss Huxtable to see the Marquess of Claverbrook. Inform him we are here, Forbes, if you would be so good."

Forbes looked from one to the other of them as if to assure himself that they were not impostors.

"I will see if his lordship is at home," he said.

Duncan raised his eyebrows and looked down at Miss Huxtable as the butler made his unhurried way up the staircase.

"He has been at home for the past twenty years at the very least," he said.

She smiled. "But in all that time," she said, "he has reserved the right to refuse admittance to unwanted guests — as every man and woman is at liberty to do in their own homes. Has he ever refused to admit you?"

"No," he said. "He has always been glad of yet another chance to give me a thorough scold on some subject or other."

"Then I daresay," she said, "he will admit you today. I suppose he reads the morning papers."

She was quite right, of course. No sooner had Forbes disappeared from the head of the stairs than he reappeared there to make his way back down.

"Follow me, my lord, miss," he said when he reached the bottom instead of simply hailing them from the top. And he turned to trudge upward again. Perhaps it was his way of keeping reasonably fit, Duncan thought.

Nothing in the drawing room had changed in five days. It would not surprise Duncan to learn that his grandfather had not moved from his chair in all that time. And he was looking in no better a temper. His eyebrows almost met over the bridge of his nose again.

"The Earl of Sheringford, m'lord," Forbes announced, "and Miss Huxtable."

"You will forgive me, Miss Huxtable," the marquess said, both hands on the head of his cane, which was braced between his legs, "for not getting to my feet. The getting is a slow and rather painful business these days."

He ignored Duncan.

"But of course, my lord," she said. "Please do not even think of it."

"Step forward, young lady," he said.

She stepped forward.

"Another step," he commanded, "so that you are in the light from the window. It is infernally dark in here. I suppose it is raining outside. It usually is. Sheringford, open the curtains a little wider."

While Duncan went to do so, his grandfather studied Miss Huxtable in silence.

"There has been no official announcement yet," he said at last, addressing himself solely to her, "but the *ton* has believed such an announcement to be imminent for the past several days. And I suppose it *is* imminent if Sheringford has brought you here this afternoon. This is no mere social call, I daresay. He has brought you here for my inspection and approval before sending off the announcement to the papers."

"Yes, my lord," she said. "That is correct."

"Are you a fool, woman?" he asked.

Duncan took one firm step away from the window, but she did not look as if she were about to collapse in a quivering heap of vapors or hysterics.

"I do not believe so," she said, her voice quite calm.

"Then why are you marrying Sheringford?" he asked her. "Eh? You are not poor. You are not without looks. And your family disapproves — at least that young puppy of a brother of yours does. He told me so in no uncertain terms when he came to pry into my financial worth. He disapproves very strongly."

"No longer," she said. "But the important thing is, my lord, that I have agreed to marry the Earl of Sheringford and have come here with him in accordance with your command so that he may keep Woodbine Park as his home and its rents and farm profits as his income after we marry. I have freely agreed to marry him. He has used no coercion whatsoever. My *reasons* for agreeing concern no one but me — and Lord Sheringford himself."

Duncan took another step forward. Good Lord! Had she really just told his grandfather in so many words to mind his own damned business?

There was a pregnant pause.

"I daresay," his grandfather said, "it is because of your age. The shelf you are on must have been gathering dust for a number of years. How old are you?"

"That also is my own concern, my lord," she said. "As is my practice of always returning courtesy for courtesy and courtesy for *discourtesy.* May I have a seat? It will be more restful for you to look across at me rather than up."

Duncan resisted the powerful urge to laugh. Though he might be laughing on the other side of his face in a moment, after his grandfather had dismissed her in his wrath and refused to endorse Duncan's marriage to her. But really, what a priceless setdown — *my practice of always returning courtesy for . . . discourtesy.*

"Sit down," his grandfather commanded gruffly. "You have a saucy tongue, Miss Huxtable."

"I beg to disagree, my lord," she said, gathering her skirts about her and seating herself on the edge of a large sofa that looked as if it had not been sat upon for a decade or more. "It is merely that I do not allow myself to be browbeaten."

"I daresay," he said, "you have had some practice during the past few days."

"They have not been easy days," she admitted. "I am not accustomed to attracting a great deal of attention and I do not enjoy it. But I do not cower away from it either, when I have done no wrong and in no way regret anything I have done to draw that attention. The *ton,* I am sure, will recover its equilibrium after Lord Sheringford and I are married and living quietly and respectably at Woodbine Park. Gossip becomes tedious when there is no fresh scandal to feed it."

Except that Toby would be there too and the plan to pass him off as the Harrises' orphaned grandson was to be abandoned. He had been mad to agree to that, Duncan thought. There was going to be no way of confining word of it to the neighborhood.

"I understand," the marquess said, "that you are the daughter of a country parson, Miss Huxtable."

"I am," she said.

There was a slight pause.

"You are not about to rush in to remind me that he was also a descendant of a former Earl of Merton?" he asked her.

"Since you knew about the country parson part of my heritage, my lord," she said, "I assume that you know the rest. And since you doubtless know that my brother is the Earl of Merton, I would assume you did not even have to dig very deep to uncover the information. The village was Throckbridge in Shropshire, but I suppose you know that too. If there is anything you do *not* know and wish to be informed of, I will be pleased to answer your questions."

"Except the one concerning your age," he said.

"Except," she agreed, "any personal details that cannot concern you at all."

"Your age *does* concern me," he said, thumping his cane on the floor and looking irritable. "Sheringford is my heir, Miss Huxtable, and it is high time he produced an heir of his own. How am I to know that you are still in your breeding years?"

Lord! Duncan felt stranded somewhere between the window and the sofa. He was rooted to the spot, if the truth were known — with a horrified sort of embarrassment. It took a great deal to embarrass him, but his grandfather had just succeeded in doing it. He had asked Miss Margaret Huxtable, sister of the Earl of Merton, if she was a breeder. Specifically if she was still *young* enough to breed.

He could see only half of her face around the brim of her straw hat. But if he was not much mistaken, she was actually *smiling.* Her voice confirmed the fact when she spoke — there was laughter in it.

"You are not to know any such thing, my lord," she said.

The marquess made a show of setting his cane against the side of his chair and moving until his spine was resting against the back and his hands were gripping the arms.

"Sheringford," he said without taking his eyes off Miss Huxtable, "I believe you have just done the wisest thing you have done in your entire life — or the most foolish."

Duncan rescued his feet and moved the short distance to the side of the sofa in order to set a reassuring hand on Margaret Huxtable's shoulder, though she seemed to be doing very well without his support.

"Nothing in between?" he said.

"She will not crumble under adversity," his grandfather said. "And there may be much adversity to test her mettle. On the other hand, you will find it impossible to ignore her or to rule her. I will expect to read an announcement of your betrothal in tomorrow's papers — unless, that is, Miss Huxtable returns to her senses before then."

"And Woodbine Park?" Duncan gripped the shoulder beneath his hand.

"It will be yours on your wedding day," his grandfather said. "Which will be . . . ?" He raised his shaggy eyebrows.

"The day before your birthday, my lord," Miss Huxtable replied without hesitation, though it was something they had not decided upon together. "My brother and sisters and Lady Carling are to organize a grand wedding breakfast at Merton House, which you must, of course, attend. We will be able to drink an early toast to your birthday on the same occasion."

"I do not leave this house under any circumstance, Miss Huxtable," the marquess said, "having discovered long ago that there is nothing but foolishness beyond my own walls. And, lest you suddenly dream up some wild scheme, I do not entertain here either. Neither do I celebrate birthdays — least of all eightieth birthdays. Anyone who chooses to celebrate an eightieth birthday must have windmills in his head, and a few moths too."

"Nevertheless," she said, "you *will* attend our wedding breakfast, my lord. The Earl of Sheringford is your only grandson, and I will be your only granddaughter-in-law. And this birthday will be celebrated as the one on which you were reconciled to your grandson and gained a granddaughter who just might still have a few breeding years left before she withers into her dotage. You would not knowingly spoil my wedding day. I am sure of it. You *would* spoil it by remaining here in self-imposed isolation."

"Hmmph," his grandfather said. "I have just realized who you have been reminding me of ever since you stepped through that door and opened your infernal mouth, Miss

Huxtable. You are just like my late wife, God rest her soul. She was a pest, to put it mildly."

"But did you love her, my lord?" Miss Huxtable asked softly.

Good God! Duncan could remember his grandmother, a small, smiling, gentle, mild-mannered lady upon whom his gruff grandfather had doted.

"None of your business, missy," he said. "Two can play at *that* game, you see."

She was smiling warmly when Duncan looked down at her.

"I liked Merton," the marquess said, changing the subject abruptly and looking at Duncan for the first time. "He is a mere puppy, though I daresay he must have reached his majority if he has donned the mantle of head of the family. But he was no groveler, by Jove. He asked his questions, and he made sure that he got his answers."

"I will bring him here again," Miss Huxtable said, "and perhaps my sisters too, my lord, once all the arrangements have been made for the wedding and the break-fast. We will come in a body together and tell you all about it, and you will discover that we Huxtables do not take no for an answer when we have set our minds on something."

She got to her feet, and that was the end of it. Two minutes later, she and Duncan were out on the street, where a light drizzle was falling.

"Well," he said, "that was remarkable."

He could not for the moment think of any other words to describe the visit. He would be almost willing to swear that his grandfather actually *liked* Maggie Huxtable, though it was doubtful anyone had spoken to him as bluntly as she had for years.

"I like him," she said, proving that the feeling had been mutual. "He loves you, Lord Sheringford."

He almost laughed. That might have been true when he was a boy, though his grandfather had never given much indication of it beyond those endless shillings. But now? He very much doubted it. He struggled with his umbrella and hoisted it over her head and his own.

"He has a strange way of showing it," he said.

"Not at all," she said. "He has been hurt and angry and puzzled for five years. He must have been dreadfully disappointed in you since you did not offer him any explanation of your behavior. But instead of cutting you off, as he surely would have done if he had truly not loved you, he waited until it was possible for you to fight back, in the hope that you would do just that, that you would give him a good enough reason to continue to love you. Which you have done."

"By finding you," he said, "and persuading you to marry me."

"He is a little afraid," she said, "that I may be too old to present him with a great-grandson before his death, which is, of course, absurd. But yes, he is happy that you are to marry and return home. He will come to our wedding."

"Hell might freeze over too," he said.

They were almost out of the square. The drizzle was already turning into a steady rain, which was drumming on the umbrella. But instead of hurrying onward, Duncan stopped walking abruptly.

"He *adored* my grandmother," he said.

She turned her head to look at him. How foolish she had been, choosing to wear pale blue on such a day, and a straw bonnet, when she had known they would be walking. Was she an eternal optimist? And was he up to the challenge?

He bent his head and kissed her on the lips — and her own pressed firmly back against them and clung for a totally indecorous stretch of time.

He felt slightly dizzy when he thought of

the changes six days had wrought in his life.

16

Margaret had ten days in which to prepare for her wedding and for married life. Ten days in which to have second and third and thirty-third thoughts about the wisdom of her decision to marry a stranger — who had lived with a married lady for almost five years and had had a son with her. Ten days to shop for bride clothes — sometimes with her sisters, sometimes with Lady Carling, sometimes with all three. Ten days in which to draw up a guest list and send out invitations and wait for replies and try to resist the temptation to insist upon involving herself with the planning of the wedding breakfast. That last point was one of the hardest.

She would have been content to keep the guest list short, to have no one at her wedding, in fact, except her family and Sir Graham and Lady Carling and the Marquess of Claverbrook.

Her sisters had other ideas. Of course.

So did Lady Carling. Of course.

"You must invite everyone with whom you and Lord Sheringford have even a passing acquaintance," Vanessa told her.

"I do agree, Meg," Katherine said. "It is what we decided to do for *my* wedding, you will recall, and while it was something of an ordeal at the time, I have been so very glad since. A big wedding provides wonderful memories."

"But no one will *come*," Margaret protested.

Her sisters looked at each other and laughed.

"Meg!" Katherine exclaimed. "*Everyone* will come. How could they possibly resist? It will be the wedding of the Season."

"With only nine days' notice?" Margaret asked doubtfully.

"Even if it was tomorrow," Vanessa said. "Of course everyone will come, you silly goose."

It was an opinion with which Lady Carling concurred when she called at Merton House the same day.

"And even if we were to invite only family," she said, "the numbers would be quite vast, Margaret. There are your brother and sisters and Mr. Constantine Huxtable. And there are Agatha, my sister, and Wilfred, and all my nieces — there are six of them, did you know? All of them are married. And on his father's side Duncan has four uncles and their wives and two aunts and their husbands. Not that they are actually uncles and aunts, since they were my late husband's cousins, but that is what Duncan always called them. And *they* have so many children all told that I lost count years ago. There are even grandchildren who are old enough to attend a wedding without any fear that they will dash about whooping and getting under everyone's feet. If you give me paper and pen and ink, I will write down the names and addresses of all I can remember. Most of them are in London and will certainly expect invitations. Duncan was always very close to his cousins and second cousins as a boy. Except Norman, that is. He was a dear enough boy, but he was always very good and very ready to disapprove of any brothers and cousins who were *not* good. That did not endear him to any of them, as you may imagine. And I suppose we cannot invite him to the wedding anyway, can we? Not when he is married to poor Caroline."

Margaret capitulated and invited the whole world — or so it seemed. Certainly her hand was severely cramped by the time she had finished writing all the cards.

The whole world replied within two days, and at least nine tenths of it was coming to the wedding at St. George's on Hanover Square and to the breakfast at Merton House.

The Marquess of Claverbrook was coming too. Margaret had carried through on her promise to visit him again with Stephen and her sisters, and none of them gave him any chance to say no. Of course, he did save face by declaring that he would attend only to see with his own eyes that his rogue of a grandson really did put in an appearance at his own wedding this time.

The days passed in a blur of activity. Before Margaret knew it, her wedding day had dawned and it really was too late to change her mind even if she wanted to.

She did not.

Crispin caused her more than one restless night, it was true, but she knew that she would never marry him even if she were free to do so. There were too many things about him that disturbed her, and the leftover dregs of an old attachment were simply not enough.

He was coming to the wedding, though she suspected it was only because Sir Humphrey and Lady Dew were still in London and he did not wish to arouse their curiosity by staying away. Lady Dew was delighted by the approaching nuptials, though she did admit to a little disappointment that her small attempt at matchmaking between Margaret and Crispin had been unsuccessful. She had finally heard of the scandal concerning Lord Sheringford, but she gave it as her opinion that if a lady was foolhardy enough to leave her husband in order to run off with another man, then she must have had a very good reason to do so. For her part, she would not hold it against the earl, especially as he now had the good sense to ally himself to Margaret.

Margaret stood barefoot at the window of her bedchamber early on the morning of her wedding, gazing up at a sky that was deep blue and cloudless — a rarity so far this summer. She was not particularly enjoying the sight, though. She was fighting panic by telling herself that it was surely what every bride faced on her wedding day.

She did not turn to look at the rumpled bed behind her. The linens would be changed after she had left for her wedding. Tonight it was to be her wedding bed. They were to leave in the morning for Warwickshire, she and Lord Sheringford, but tonight

Stephen had insisted they stay at Merton House while he went to Vanessa and Elliott's.

Margaret set her forehead against the cool glass of the window and closed her eyes.

How strange it would be to be married!

And how she ached for it. And for tonight. Was that a shameful, unladylike admission? But she did not really care. She had waited long enough for this. *Too* long. Her youth was already gone. And since it *was* gone, and with it all her youthful dreams of romance, then it was as well to turn her mind to the future with a positive wish for it to come as soon as possible.

Today and tonight she would be a bride — and she was going to enjoy every moment. Tomorrow and for the rest of her life she would be a wife. She was going to enjoy that too. It was what she had always wanted, after all, and what she had decided over the winter that she would *be.* It really did not matter that her bridegroom was neither Crispin, whom she had loved, nor the Marquess of Allingham, with whom she had enjoyed a comfortable friendship. She had made her decision to marry the Earl of Sheringford, and somehow she would make something good out of their marriage.

There would be a child to bring up.

Again.

She smiled fleetingly.

Even before she gave birth to any of her own.

Oh, *let* it be the right thing she was doing, she prayed to no one in particular as she lifted her forehead away from the window and moved into her dressing room to ring for her maid. *Please,* let it be the right thing.

It was fourteen days since she had collided with the Earl of Sheringford in the doorway of the Tindell ballroom. Fourteen days since he had asked her to dance and to marry him — all in one sentence. His first words to her.

Only fourteen days.

Weddings by special license, Duncan discovered during the ten days preceding his marriage to Margaret Huxtable, did not differ significantly from weddings by banns except that one did not have to wait the obligatory month for those banns to be read.

They were going to be married at St. George's in Hanover Square, for the love of God. It was the scene of most *ton* weddings during the Season, it being the parish church of most of the beau monde. It was where legend had it he had left Caroline waiting tragically and in vain at the altar for his arrival five years ago. Legend erred on the side of good theater, of course, as legend often did, but even so . . .

How foolish of him to have imagined a mere two weeks ago that he would procure a special license, bear Miss Huxtable off to the nearest church, marry her there with only the clergyman and a witness or two for company, and then make off into Warwickshire with her to live obscurely ever after.

He could do nothing but kick his heels while his wedding crept up on him with the speed and inevitability of a tortoise.

The only thing of any real significance he did during those days was to call upon Norman and Caroline. It went severely against the grain to do so. Norman had never been his favorite person. Indeed, he had probably occupied the place of very least favorite for as far back into their childhood as Duncan had conscious memories. He was a pompous ass who had behaved in typical Norm fashion at Aunt Agatha's soiree. And Caroline was no better in all essential ways than her brother. Which meant that she was a pretty rotten human being.

Nevertheless, Duncan had wronged her. Even though he had written to her before he ran off with Laura and had made sure she would receive the letter as soon as she woke up on their wedding day, abandoning her had been an admittedly dastardly thing to do.

He owed her an apology.

And perhaps he needed to hold out some sort of olive branch to Norman. Losing Woodbine Park, when he had fully expected that it would be his in a few days' time, must be a severe disappointment to him. Though Duncan was not the one who had played cruel games with him, nevertheless he felt bad for his cousin. He had never wished Norm any real harm, even if he *had* bloodied his nose on one occasion when they were both boys, and blackened one of his eyes on another.

So he called upon the two of them one afternoon and hoped ignominiously that they would be from home — or that they would pretend to be.

He was no more fortunate on that account than he had been when he had gone to tell Margaret Huxtable about Toby.

He was admitted to a small visitors' parlor on the ground floor and left to kick his heels there and otherwise amuse himself for almost half an hour.

Caroline arrived first, looking not a day older than eighteen and as fragile and lovely as ever, though she had had three children during the past five years, had she not?

Duncan bowed.

She did not curtsy.

"Caroline," he said, "I must thank you for receiving me."

"I do not believe, Lord Sheringford," she said, "I have given you permission to make free with my given name."

She spoke with the light, sweet voice that had once so enchanted him.

"Mrs. Pennethorne," he said, "apologies are cheap, as I am well aware. They cannot set right what has been done wrong. Nevertheless, sometimes an apology is all that is available. I beg you to accept mine for all the humiliation and suffering I caused you five years ago."

"You flatter yourself, Lord Sheringford," she said. "What you did was release me from a connection that had grown distasteful to me, though of course good breeding would have forced me to honor it. I am grateful that you felt no such compunction. I am far happier with my dear Mr. Pennethorne than I could ever have been with you."

If she spoke the truth, he was vastly relieved. And why would it not be the truth? She must have grown as unhappy with him as he had with her when he had started trying to enlist her support to plead with her brother to put an end to Laura's sufferings.

"I am happy for you," he said. "You will forgive me, then?"

Delicate eyebrows arched above large hazel eyes.

"Oh, you must never expect *that* of me, Lord Sheringford," she said as the door opened again to admit Norman. "Certain actions are quite unforgivable. I can certainly be very glad that you left me free to engage in the happiest marriage in the world, but I cannot forgive your behavior. Neither could I *ever* forgive you for tearing Randolph and Laura asunder and thus destroying a marriage that was made in heaven and that rivaled my own in happiness. Indeed, you might almost be called a murderer. She would very probably still be alive now if you had not dragged her off with you to satisfy your wicked desires."

"My love," Norman said, hurrying toward her, taking her by the shoulders, and leading her to a love seat. "You ought to have remained abovestairs and left this unpleasantness to me. But you are always so foolishly brave."

"I have never been a moral coward," she said, seating herself. "I even called upon Miss Huxtable at Merton House when I believed her to be the innocent dupe of a scoundrel. It seems I was mistaken in her. She will be sorry she did not listen to me one day soon, but my conscience is clear at least. And she will be getting only what she deserves."

The visit went downhill from there.

"Norm," Duncan said, "I am sorry about Woodbine. It was just Grandpapa being fiendish, I am afraid. He used you in order to bring me to heel. But he ought not to have promised you something he was prepared to withdraw at a moment's notice if he succeeded. Will you feel free to visit my wife and me at Woodbine? And to bring Car — Mrs. Pennethorne and your children with you, of course."

Norman fixed him with a stern stare — something he had perfected at the age of eight or so. His shirt points waited hopefully a scant inch from his eyeballs.

"I am only sorry, Sheringford," he said, "that I felt compelled to admit you today under the same roof that shelters Mrs. Pennethorne and my children. I did it because I have something to say that I will say once only. I wish it were possible to slap a glove in your face and proceed to put a bullet between your eyes. It would give me the greatest satisfaction. It would, however, expose Mrs. Pennethorne to gossip again and cause her unnecessary distress. I deeply regret that my brother-in-law is too mild-mannered and peace-loving a man to challenge you himself. He is a gentleman with a conscience, and I must honor him for that even if I do not like it. I spurn your acquaintance, Sheringford. If you come here again, you will be refused admittance. If we come face-to-face, you will be ignored. If you should try speaking with Mrs. Pennethorne again, I shall punish you like the cur you are. I hesitated about moving my family to Woodbine Park because *you* once lived there. You are mistaken if you believe I am now disappointed."

Dash it all, but the man was a born orator — if one liked bombast and pomposity, that was.

"And now," Norman said, "get out, Sheringford."

Duncan nodded, bowed to Caroline, and took his leave.

He wondered as he did so if Caroline had ever told Norman any part of the truth of what had happened five years ago — any significant part, that was. He somehow doubted it. And that meant, of course, that Norman's righteous indignation was justified. He had every right to his anger and his fervent desire to put a period to Duncan's existence.

Caroline certainly knew the truth — the *whole* of it. He had told her himself, and it had not come as a surprise to her. If only Laura would show more wifely loyalty to Randolph and his family, she had said plaintively, blows and bruises would be quite unnecessary. On the contrary, Randolph would love her for the rest of his life — as he already did, of course — and see to it that she had everything that could possibly make her happy. She deserved whatever she was getting instead.

Just as Margaret Huxtable did in marrying him.

Duncan did *not* call upon Randolph Turner or hold out any sort of olive branch to him. Caroline had been right about one thing. Certain actions *were* unforgivable. Or if that was not strictly true, then it *was* true of a man who had never shown any remorse for his unspeakably wicked and cruel actions.

Apart from that one visit, Duncan spent the nine days before his wedding simply avoiding the madness associated with it as much as he was able. A grand wedding was necessary, his mother explained to him at great length the day she arrived home from

337

Merton House with the news that Margaret Huxtable was sending out more than two hundred invitations — or perhaps not quite as many as that since some people were in couples and only one invitation was necessary, it being a foolish waste of paper and ink and time and energy to send two.

He did not argue the point with her in the hope that she would not feel the necessity to share any more of the details with him.

Vain hope!

"A grand wedding is very necessary, my love," she went on to explain with her own particular form of logic. "Anyone who attends it can hardly give you the cut direct afterward, as you will realize very clearly for yourself if you stop to think about it. You may still not be society's favorite son, but you will be firmly back in the fold, and that is what really matters."

"Society," he said, "can go hang for all I care, Mama."

"Oh, men can be so foolish," she said. "But even if you do not care for its regard on your own account, Duncan, you must remember that you are going to be a married man. You are going to have a *wife* to consider, and if society snubs you, it will snub her too. You owe it to Margaret to do all in your power to ingratiate yourself with the *ton* again."

He sighed audibly. She was quite right, of course.

Dash it all!

"Anyway," he said, "I daresay no one will accept the invitation — except a few of the uncles and cousins, perhaps."

Another vain hope — as he had explained to Maggie a few days before.

His mother clucked her tongue.

"Men!" she said with the utmost scorn and a glance tossed at the ceiling. "They have *no idea* how people think. *Of course* everyone will accept the invitation. *Everyone!* No one would miss it for any consideration."

It was an opinion that was corroborated on the gossip page in the next morning's paper. The upcoming event was heralded there as the wedding of the Season — *if,* that was, the Earl of Sheringford did not run off on the day and leave Miss Huxtable standing at the altar alone.

He was in for a grand wedding, then, Duncan realized, as surely as a condemned man was in for an appointment with the gallows.

He dressed on the fateful morning with the full awareness that he was going to be on display more than he had yet been since his return to London.

Which was saying something!

"Not so tight," he half growled at Smith as his valet tied his neckcloth in a knot that was not too simple, not too elaborate. It was perfect in all ways but one, in fact. "Are you trying to throttle me?"

"I think it is the occasion that is doing that, m'lord," Smith said without tampering further with the neckcloth. "You don't want it swinging about from one shoulder to the other, now, do you? And even if you do, I will not have it. I would never be able to hold up my head again among my fellow valets. Stand up and let me give that coat a final brush. You have a positive gift for picking up bits of lint, though for the life of me I don't know where you find them."

Duncan finally escaped the clutches of tyranny and went downstairs, where a small group awaited him in the hall. Carling looked resigned to a day of boredom that would, nevertheless, release him of the charge of housing and feeding his stepson. His mother declared that she would not hug him lest she crush her new dress and crease his coat, and that she would not weep lest she ruin her face — she would not mention cosmetics, but they were there in full, colorful evidence. But she did blow him kisses before leaving for the church, and she did dart at him at the last moment for a quick hug, and she did dab at a stray tear with a large white handkerchief she pulled from one of Carling's pockets before she preceded him from the house.

Duncan turned to Con Huxtable, who had agreed to be his best man. They both raised their eyebrows.

"Sherry," Con said, "I have no idea what happened five years ago. But if you should take it into your head to bolt between here and St. George's, you are going to have to bolt through me."

"I am not going to run," Duncan assured him irritably.

Con nodded.

"I do not understand how all this came about either," he said. "Margaret has always seemed to me like a sensible lady. However, it *has* happened, or will have when I have dragged you to the church and prevented you from bolting. You will treat her right, Sherry."

It was not a question.

"There are many things we do not understand," Duncan said. "I don't understand, for example, why Miss Huxtable's happiness is important to you, when her family moved into Warren Hall five years ago and pushed you out."

Con's dark eyes were immediately hooded.

"*Circumstances* pushed me out," he said. "My father's death, and then Jon's. It is easy to rush into hatred, Sherry, and to wallow in it for a lifetime. I *did* so rush. I *did* hate them — or Merton, anyway. But sometimes one needs to stop to ask oneself if a certain person really deserves to be hated. Merton and his sisters were innocent — and they are pretty hard to hate. And one needs to ask who is most hurt by hatred. Do we need to be having this talk at this precise moment?"

"We do not," Duncan said, resisting the urge to pull at his neckcloth. "We need to get to the church. Under the circumstances, it would be more than usually calamitous if I were late."

"Off we go, then," Con said cheerfully.

Because it was a lovely day and society weddings always attracted a large crowd anyway, Stephen's coachman had to maneuver the carriage carefully before St. George's in order not to run over some of the people who had spilled over from the pavement onto the roadway.

There was a noticeable "Oooh" from the crowd as Stephen descended and turned to hand Margaret out — almost as if they thought *he* was the bridegroom. But of course, Stephen always looked remarkably handsome even when he was not dressed in formal black and white attire as he was this morning.

Margaret set a gloved hand in his and stepped down to join him, smiling at him as he smiled back. He had actually shed tears back at the house after Vanessa and Katherine had left with Elliott and Jasper — and had turned his back hastily in the obvious hope that she had not noticed. But he had turned to her again without drying his eyes.

"Meg," he had said. "Oh, Meg, you have always been the most wonderful sister any boy or man could ever ask for. I had no idea today would be so painful — or so happy at the same time. He is a good man. I am convinced of that. And I think you are fond of him, even though you have known him for such a short time."

He had taken both her hands in his and squeezed them tightly.

"*Are* you fond of him?"

But she had been on the edge of tears herself and had merely nodded.

"And he is of you too," he had said. "I am sure he is. He will love you, Meg. I can safely promise that. How can anyone know you and not love you?"

"You are not biased by any chance, are you?" she had asked, smiling. "Ah, Stephen, I have loved you all dearly. I still do and always will. But forgive me if I want to go to my wedding now and not be late."

He had chuckled, turned to pick up his hat, and offered his arm.

The crowd outside the church let out a collective "Aahh!" as she stepped down from the carriage. And indeed she did believe she was looking her best. She had resisted all the brightly colored garments Lady Carling had thought appropriate for the occasion and had chosen a cream-colored dress of satin and lace, which was high-waisted and simple in design but that had been expertly cut so that it molded her figure to perfection. She wore a new straw hat trimmed with white rosebuds.

Jasper had told her it was a good thing she was the bride or no one would even spare a glance for the poor woman. And then he had turned and grinned and winked at Kate.

Stephen offered his arm now, and they made their way into the church.

Margaret was assailed suddenly by the panic that had grabbed her earlier. What if he was not here? What if he was not even late? What if he was not coming at all?

But it was an ignominious fear. She trusted him better than to believe he would abandon her now. She pushed the terror aside even before they stepped inside the church doors and she realized that the church was full to capacity and that no one looked worried or unduly agitated. What seemed like scores of heads turned in her direction, and at the end of the nave the clergyman gave a signal with one hand and two gentlemen stood. They both turned to see her.

One of them was Constantine. The other was the Earl of Sheringford.

Her bridegroom.

Margaret swallowed and fixed her eyes on him as Stephen bent to straighten the hem of her dress at the back and then gave her his arm.

She saw no one else. All the trappings of the wedding were quite unimportant despite Kate's protestations about the importance of memories. It did not matter if there were a dozen people here or two hundred. She was getting married and her bridegroom was here, at the front of the church, turned toward her and watching her as she approached.

And he was the bridegroom she wanted,

she realized with great clarity. She felt an upsurge of happiness and smiled at him.

He smiled back, and for the first time it struck her that he was really quite handsome after all — tall and dark and lean with intense eyes and features that were rugged rather than classically sculpted.

He did not smile often, did he? The expression imparted kindness to his face. He must *be* a kind man. A poor abused lady had confided in him when she had confided in no one else. It was to him she had run when she was in real trouble. He loved his young son first of anyone else in his life because the child needed him and the affection and security he had to offer.

It was a strange moment for such a revelation.

She was marrying a kind man, Margaret realized.

And it was enough. She moved toward him with hope.

A short while later Stephen placed her hand in Lord Sheringford's, and together they turned to face the clergyman.

The church was hushed.

Half the *ton* was in the pews behind them, Margaret realized. More important, so were their families. But it did not really matter. She was where she chose to be, and she was with the bridegroom she wished to marry. He might be a near stranger, she might have known him for only two weeks, but it did not matter.

Somehow this felt right.

Please, please let it *be* right.

"Dearly beloved," the clergyman began.

It was all so terribly public. Although they stood with their backs to the congregation through most of the nuptial service, Duncan could *feel* them there — avidly curious about this strange wedding of their most notorious member to one of the most respectable.

They would all wait as avidly afterward for something to go wrong.

Margaret Huxtable believed this was fate, and he had had the strange thought himself that perhaps the whole course of his life had been directed to that moment when they had collided in a ballroom doorway.

But he did not know her.

He had no idea how he would make her happy.

He was marrying her for Toby's sake. He would not be doing this if it were not for the child, would he? He would be out somewhere far from London, searching for employment. He would not have set foot in

London to beg for Woodbine to be restored to him if he had had only himself to consider.

"I pronounce that they be man and wife together, in the name of the Father, and of the Son, and of the Holy Ghost. Amen," the clergyman was saying, and it was all over.

Somehow he had missed his own nuptial service. But it did not matter. He was a married man anyway. He was married to Margaret Huxtable — Margaret Pennethorne, Countess of Sheringford.

Ah, Tobe.

And a few minutes later, having signed the register, they were walking back up the nave of the church together, acknowledging the smiles — and tears — of their relatives and the more curious stares of other guests. The only persons Duncan really saw were his mother, her eyes shining with tears, and his grandfather in the second pew, frowning ferociously at him, but in just the way he had always used to frown as he searched his pockets for a shilling.

And then they were stepping out into sunshine and a cheering crowd and church bells just beginning a joyful peal.

As if a wedding had taken place. As indeed one had.

His own.

He looked down at his bride on his arm. It seemed that every time he saw her she looked more beautiful than the time before, but on this occasion she definitely did.

"Well, Maggie," he said.

"Well, Lord Sheringford."

"We are going to have to correct that," he said. "You cannot be forever Lord Shering-fording me now that we are married."

"Duncan," she said.

"Come," he said, and led her toward an open barouche his grandfather had sent for the occasion.

It was only as they approached it that he saw it had been decorated with gaily colored ribbons and bows — and with a couple of old boots to drag behind. And there were the perpetrators, mingling, grinning, with the crowd and clutching handfuls of flower petals, which they hurled with great glee as the bride and groom passed.

A horde of his cousins — partners in crime and other mayhem from his child-hood and youth.

He was really back in the fold, then, was he?

Strangely and ignominiously, his throat ached is if he were about to weep.

His bride was laughing as he handed her

into the barouche and she settled among the garish ribbons and turned her face to him as he settled beside her. Her hat and dress were dotted with petals. He reached for the pouch of coins tucked into the side of his seat and tossed them by handfuls into the crowd.

The carriage rocked on its springs and drew away from the curb — with a great clattering from the boots — as the congregation was spilling into the outdoors.

Maggie tucked a hand into his without any apparent self-consciousness.

"Duncan," she said. "Oh, Duncan, was it not all *wonderful?*"

He squeezed her hand.

If it had been wonderful for her, then wonderful it was. He owed her that. He owed her a great deal.

"It was indeed," he said as the cousins and other members of the crowd whistled and cheered and there was no abatement in the noise the boots were making — someone must have hammered nails all over them. "I suppose we had better give them all back there something to *really* talk about. Something juicy for tomorrow's gossip column."

And he leaned toward her and kissed her on the lips — a lingering kiss that she made no attempt either to avoid or to end. Her lips clung to his and pressed warmly back against them.

The whistles behind them grew more piercing.

17

The whole of her wedding day was wonderful, Margaret found as the hours rushed by. Finding it so took her somewhat by surprise. She had looked forward to it with determined optimism, it was true, once her decision to marry the Earl of Sheringford had been made, but — *wonderful?*

The nuptials themselves had been perfect, surely every woman's dream wedding. She had concentrated upon every moment of the service, every word that had been spoken, every vow they had made. She had concentrated upon the warm strength of her bridegroom's hand as it had held hers, upon the contrasting coldness of the ring as he slid it onto her finger, upon the faint musky smell of his cologne. She had even become fully aware, after the first minute or two, of the congregation behind them, an integral part of this solemn occasion. Her family was there and his. Half the *ton* was there.

And when they had been leaving the church, although they had not moved along the nave at a crawl, she had seen *everyone* — Stephen beaming at her, Elliott smiling, Nessie dabbing at her eyes with his handkerchief, Katherine smiling through eyes bright with tears, Jasper winking, Lady Carling clasping her hands to her bosom and sinking her teeth into her lower lip, the Marquess of Claverbrook with eyes that did not quite match the ferocity of the rest of his expression . . . Oh, and everyone else. She saw them all individually, it seemed, and almost everyone was smiling back at her. People were not spiteful at heart, she thought. Everyone was prepared to give her new husband a second chance.

And there had been the crowd outside the church, the colorful shower of flower petals, the elegant barouche and its garish decorations, the church bells, the clatter of the nail-studded boots on the road behind the carriage all the way back to Merton House. The public kiss. And the arrival of the guests, whom they had received at the ballroom doors, and the seemingly endless handshakes and kisses on the cheek and smiling good wishes. And the ballroom set up for two hundred guests and so bedecked with flowers that the familiar room somehow looked quite *un*familiar — but gloriously so. And the six-course meal and the toasts and the cake-cutting and the mingling with guests after it was all over. No one was in any hurry to leave.

The first to do so was the Marquess of Claverbrook, who had come without his cane and walked with proud, very upright bearing, though it was obvious to Margaret that he was tired. She took his arm as she and her new husband accompanied him to the door.

"Grandfather," she said, "you must come and see us at Woodbine Park. Oh, please promise you will."

She remembered the child suddenly, but she would not recall her invitation even if she could. There was no reason why everyone should not know about him. They knew about the adultery, after all, and seemed to be in the process of forgiving it. The child was in no way guilty for any of that. And if she was willing to have him in her home and be a mother to him, why should anyone else be offended?

"Hmmph," he said by way of answer. It seemed to be his favorite word. But he did not say no. And he had more to say.

"Sheringford," he said while a footman waited to open the door for him, "I fully expected that you *would* find a bride before it was too late, and I was quite prepared to give my blessing to almost anyone provided she was at least respectable, but I did *not* expect you to find such a sensible bride. Make sure you cherish her."

Lord Sheringford — Duncan — inclined his head. "I intend to do so, sir," he said.

"And remember," the marquess said, "that you have also promised to have a son in your nursery by your thirty-first birthday."

Margaret looked at her husband with raised eyebrows.

"I shall do all in my power to keep that promise, sir," her husband said.

He already *did* have a son there, of course, but that was not what the old gentleman had meant. Margaret smiled and kissed his cheek and the footman opened the door.

"We will come to see you before we leave London tomorrow, Grandfather," she said, "to wish you a happy birthday."

"Hmmph," he said. "Today's toast was not enough?"

"It was not," Duncan said. "We will be there, sir."

And then they returned to the ballroom and the rest of their guests and moved from one group to another, talking until Margaret was feeling almost hoarse but marvelously happy, even when she finally drew a deep breath and approached Crispin. It was not an easy thing to do. She supposed there would always be a corner of her heart that held some residual tenderness for him. He had been her first love — and her first lover. But if she had half expected to feel some panic at the knowledge that she had now set a permanent barrier between herself and him, she was pleased to find that it did not happen.

Crispin *was* weak, and he *was* undependable, and though she no longer hated him for those qualities, she certainly did not want them in the man she married.

Duncan, she believed, was both strong and dependable. And he never made excuses. Quite the contrary.

Crispin bowed over her hand, smiled ruefully as he wished her well, and soon made the excuse that someone was beckoning him from across the room.

Gradually the guests took their leave until by the middle of the evening only her own family was left and her mother-in-law and Sir Graham. They were all in the drawing room, eating cakes and drinking tea.

And gaps began to stretch into the conversation.

"Well," Jasper said at last, getting to his

feet. "I do not know about anyone else, but I have had a busy day and am ready to return home and tumble into bed. Katherine?"

"Oh, absolutely," she said. "I can scarcely keep my eyes open."

"Graham, my love," Lady Carling said, "tomorrow is the day you suggested taking me to buy that pearl-inlaid locket we were admiring last week. You will be cross if I am not ready to go before noon, but you know how impossible that will be if I am not in bed before midnight. Shall we go?"

"I am, as always, at your command, Ethel," he said.

Elliott got to his feet without a word, but he was smiling at Margaret.

"It is time for us to go home too," Vanessa said. "Are you coming with us, Stephen?"

"An earlyish night may be a good idea for me too," he said. "Nessie has warned me that I may be woken in the morning by a couple of children jumping on my bed."

"Having an uncle in the house overnight," Elliott said, "especially here in London, is an irresistible novelty to them, Stephen. You can always jam a chair beneath the doorknob of your room, of course. I would advise it, in fact. Our two are *not* late risers."

Another fifteen minutes passed before everyone had left. There were handshakes and hugs and kisses and tears and a lengthy speech from Lady Carling, which began with an assurance that she would not say much.

It seemed strange to Margaret to wave Stephen on his way from his own house and to find herself alone with the Earl of Sheringford.

A stranger.

Her husband.

Duncan.

"Let's return to the drawing room," he said, offering his arm.

It was a relief. Foolishly, she was not ready yet to go to bed. It seemed that they had had scarcely a moment to exchange a word with each other. And indeed there had been no private moments except in the barouche, which had turned heads all the way home on account of the ribbons and boots.

He crossed to the liquor cabinet when they were back in the drawing room, poured two glasses of wine, and carried them to the love seat.

"Come and sit down," he said, and she realized that she had been standing just inside the door — as if she were suddenly a stranger in her own home.

He sat beside her on the love seat and handed her one of the glasses.

"Did the day continue wonderful?" he asked her.

She searched his face, but it gave nothing away. There was no smile in his eyes, which looked very black in the candlelight. Perhaps a day that had brought her surprising happiness had been nothing to him but a means of keeping his home so that his son could grow up there.

He was indeed still a stranger.

"Did it for you?" she asked, rather than answer his question and be left feeling foolish if he said nothing in return to match it. She would take her cue from him.

"All of it was . . . wonderful," he said, raising his glass. "Down to the last drop."

She noticed the pause, as if he had found it difficult to say the one word. Had he said it only to reassure her? Would he have volunteered the information if she had not asked?

But such anxieties were pointless now. They had married each other for reasons of their own, none of them to do with any tender feelings for each other. And the deed was done. They were married.

Until death did them part.

He sipped his wine, and she did likewise.

"But you did not answer *my* question," he said.

"I suppose," she said, "I have been like every other woman on her wedding day. There is something very special about being a bride, about attracting attention for all the right reasons — for a change. I shamelessly enjoyed every moment of it. I wanted the whole world to look at me and rejoice with me."

Oh, dear. She wished she could eliminate that final sentence. But it had been spoken, and to emphasize the fact, there was a short silence following it.

She looked rather jerkily down into her glass and took another sip.

"I am not in love with you, of course," she said firmly. "But I *am* glad I married you. For some time I have wanted to be a married lady, to have a home of my own, perhaps to have —"

She took a sip of wine that actually turned into a gulp.

"I believe I was twenty," he said, "when I promised my grandfather that I would be married by the time I was thirty and would have a son in the nursery by the time I was thirty-one. I was still young enough then that it seemed safe to promise something for ten years in the future. It was an eternity away. What twenty-year-old can imagine that he will ever be thirty? Or forty? Or eighty? However it was, I have been a little late on the first promise, but there is still time to keep the second. Not that I can guarantee a son, of course. Or any child at all for that matter. But I can try."

Margaret took another gulp from her glass.

"Wine," he said, "makes some people sleepy. I hope that is not true of you, Maggie."

He reached out and took the glass from her hand as she turned her head to look at him. Had he actually just made a *joke?*

And *sleepy?* She had never felt farther from sleep in her life.

"Or of you," she said.

He half smiled as he set down both their glasses beside him, and it struck her as it had once before that a smile transformed him. Had he smiled a great deal in the past — *before?* Lady Carling's description of him as a carefree, somewhat wild young man suggested that he had. Would he smile more in the future?

"I am going to see to it," she said, "that you learn to smile again."

His smile first froze and then faded.

"Are you?" he said. "Have I forgotten how?"

"I think you have," she said, "except on the rare occasion when one takes you by surprise. You are very handsome when you smile."

"And ugly when I do not," he said. "You have your own interests at heart, then, do you, Maggie? You would prefer to look at a handsome husband than an ugly one?"

"I would prefer to look at a happy husband than a brooding one," she said.

"*Am* I unhappy?" he asked her. "Or *brooding?*"

She nodded and lifted a hand to cup his cheek.

"I think," she said, "you have been unhappy for a long time. I am going to change that."

Bold, rash words. He did not love her. She was not even sure he liked her. But she was not talking about love. She was talking about affection and companionship and compassion and . . . well, *love.* But not romantic love. She was going to love him. For her own sake she was going to do it. She had never been able to contemplate living with someone she did not love.

He set his hand over the top of hers and she swallowed.

"Are you?" he said.

She nodded.

Somehow his head had moved closer to hers. She could feel the warmth of his breath on her cheek.

"How?" He was almost whispering. It was hardly surprising. Half the air had suddenly disappeared from the room.

He, *of course,* being a man, had immediately jumped to the conclusion that she was talking about the marriage bed.

"Oh," she said, her voice breathless, "I do not know if I can make you happy in *that* way, Duncan. You may believe I am experienced because of what I told you about my past, but really I am not. It was a long, long time ago, and even then —"

His lips pressed against hers. They were parted, and she instantly tasted warmth and moistness and wine. Her hand trembled against his cheek, and he held it there more firmly. He drew his head back a few inches.

"If I wanted experience, Maggie," he said, "I would go to a brothel."

Which was not at all a nice thing to say. She was not sure she had even heard the word spoken aloud before. But — He was not like *Crispin,* was he?

"Have you often been to one?" she asked, and bit her lip at the same moment as his eyes leapt to life and she was surprised to see laughter in their depths.

He *was* like Crispin. Oh . . . *men!* If she gave him half a chance, he would start babbling on about loneliness and needs, which women were fortunate enough not to feel.

She did not give him a chance to answer her question.

"But you will not go ever again," she said. "I shall cut up very nasty indeed if you even *try* it."

His eyes were still laughing — and they were a warm brown now, the color of a cup of hot, rich chocolate. It was really quite disconcerting, especially when they were only inches from her own.

"I will not need to, will I?" he said. "You have promised to make me happy. And if your lack of experience is making you a little anxious, then we had better see about getting you that experience, had we not? The sooner the better?"

Oh, goodness!

"Yes," she said, and then she cleared her throat and spoke more firmly. "Oh, Duncan, this is very ridiculous. I am *embarrassed.* I am thirty years old and embarrassed. We ought to have gone upstairs as soon as everyone left. By now it would all be over."

The laughter in his eyes, far from fading, actually deepened. He turned his head to plant a kiss on her palm before releasing her hand.

"All over?" he said. "As in *forever and ever, amen?*"

"And now I feel stupid as well as embarrassed," she said, "and I do not like the feeling one bit. I am going to bed whether you are ready or not."

She got firmly to her feet and shook out the folds of her wedding dress.

"Maggie," he said, getting up to stand before her. He took both her hands in his and set them against his chest, palm in. "You were not ready when our families left. Neither of us was, actually. We needed some wine and some conversation. We have had both, and now I believe it is time for sex."

Oh, she *wished* he would not use that word. Did he not know that it was not an everyday part of a lady's vocabulary? She could feel her cheeks grow hot. Her inner thighs were aching, and something was pulsing deep inside her.

And it was all the fault of *that word.*

"Yes," she said coolly. "Yes, it is."

And she lifted her face and kissed him on the lips. Open-mouthed and none too swiftly. She darted the tip of her tongue across his lips.

The pulsing became a throbbing.

"Come, then," he said, and he offered her his arm.

It seemed strange — oh, very strange indeed — to walk upstairs with him, to stop outside her private apartment and have him open the door into her dressing room — her inner sanctum, her private world. No longer private, though. There would *be* no private space for her ever again. Even her body would no longer be her private sanctuary.

Her wedding day had turned into her wedding night.

"I shall return in fifteen minutes," he said, stepping back to allow her to enter the room and then closing the door behind her.

Stephen had given him the use of a guest dressing room. His bags had been taken there earlier.

Her apartment already seemed different, Margaret thought as she undressed and her maid unpinned her hair and brushed it out — though nothing in it had changed. There were, of course, her trunks and bags, almost completely packed and standing against the far wall.

This was the last night Merton House would be her home. Yet even tonight her rooms were not her own.

She was waiting for her bridegroom.

For the consummation of their marriage.

For *sex,* to use his disturbingly graphic word.

She dismissed her maid with a few of her fifteen minutes left and went into her bedchamber. Two candles burned on the side tables. The curtains had been drawn across the window — usually she left them open. The bedcovers had been turned back — on both sides.

Margaret clasped both hands about one of the bedposts at the foot of the bed and rested a cheek against it.

She was a married lady. She was Margaret Pennethorne, Countess of Sheringford. It was quite irrevocable now.

This one day, which had seemed quite wonderful as she lived through it, had changed her life for all time.

Oh, *let* her have done the right thing.

There was a light tap on the bedchamber door and it opened.

18

A wonderful day!

Had it been?

It had certainly had its high points, Duncan conceded. If it had not restored him to complete favor with the *ton,* at least it had allowed him back into the fold. No one could attend his wedding today and then refuse to receive him tomorrow, after all.

It had certainly delighted his mother. He could not remember seeing her as genuinely happy as she had been today. It had restored the belief he had taken for granted as a boy, before his father died, that she loved him totally and unconditionally. Perhaps he had been right then and wrong more recently to think her merely vain and shallow.

And today had brought his grandfather out of Claverbrook House. He had looked quite his old self too — older, it was true, and just as fierce as he had ever been, but with that indefinable look in his eyes that was almost, but not quite, a twinkle. He had never used to be a recluse. Duncan wondered suddenly if his running off with Laura and abandoning Caroline had had anything to do with making him into a hermit. Perhaps he had done more than disappoint his grandfather on that occasion — perhaps he had crushed his spirit. Perhaps his grandfather loved him after all.

Perhaps tomorrow morning, his grandfather's birthday, he should tell him at least as much about that elopement as he had told Maggie. Perhaps he should tell his mother too. A promise made to Laura was one thing. His family — and their bruised love for him — was another.

Make sure you cherish her, his grandfather had said when he was leaving.

. . . cherish . . .

And that brought him back to the original thought — *a wonderful day.* He had not married her in order to cherish her. And of course he felt guilty about that even though he had been almost completely frank with her about his motives. What he had *not* told her — what he had deliberately withheld — did not really matter.

Even so, he felt guilty, for there *was* more to tell. And she was his wife.

I wanted the whole world to look at me and

rejoice with me.

Those words had given him a nasty jolt.

And now he was jolted again when Smith cleared his throat.

"Do you want a nightshirt, then, m'lord?" he asked. "Or just your dressing gown?"

Duncan gave him a hard look. He supposed he possessed a nightshirt or Smith would not have offered it. But when had his valet ever known him to wear one?

"The dressing gown," he said.

"The new one, m'lord?" Smith asked.

"Of course the new one," Duncan said, getting to his feet and checking his jawline to make sure his face was smooth — not that Smith ever left any stubble behind when he shaved him. "Do you think I bought it just to sit in a wardrobe until the moths get at it?"

He was feeling irritable, he realized as he pushed his arms into the sleeves and then slipped out of his breeches and drawers. Irritable and lusty. Irritable *because* he was lusty. It did not seem right somehow. One ought to feel more than just lust for one's bride.

Did he? He searched hopefully in his mind for some tender feelings and discovered with something bordering on relief that indeed there was *something* there. He had grown to rather like her as well as admire her. He could perhaps grow fond of her if he tried — and try he must and would.

If the truth were told, he had felt something like a lump in his throat when she had spoken those words earlier — *I wanted the whole world to look at me and rejoice with me.* He had wanted to gather her up into his arms — rather as he always did whenever Toby, during his insecure moments between play and mayhem, tugged at his breeches and asked him if he really, *really* loved him.

"I'll see you in the morning," he told his valet, his voice abrupt and still sounding irritable as he left the dressing room and made his way back along the corridor to Maggie's bedchamber.

He was certainly feeling lusty. Guilt had not affected him there. She was delicious even when she did not taste of wine. But when she did — as she had in the drawing room a short while ago — she was quite intoxicating. He did not suppose she realized how close she had come to being tumbled on the drawing room carpet when *she* had kissed *him* and traced the seam of his lips with her tongue.

He had not been expecting it. He had always found her rather inhibited, even prudish, sexually. The typical and perfect lady, in fact. But she had kissed him down-stairs, and it had been a definite invitation.

Dash it all, he hoped she would not live to regret this marriage.

He was going to have to see to it that she did not, was he not? He owed her that much. And even apart from that, he could not really contemplate a marriage that he made no effort at all to make into a decent one. He had not wanted to marry, it was true, but he had done it and now he must live accordingly.

He was still feeling that curious mingling of irritability and lust as he tapped on her door and let himself in — it would be mildly absurd, he thought, to wait for her to answer his knock.

She was standing at the foot of the bed, hugging the bedpost. She was wearing a white nightgown, which shimmered in the light from two candles and looked somehow more gorgeous than the most elaborate of ball gowns. And — oh, Lord! — her hair was loose down her back, and it reached almost to her bottom. It was dark and thick and shining. And that gorgeous nightgown, though perfectly decent, did absolutely nothing to hide her even more gorgeous curves.

He fought the advent of an early arousal.

"The canopy will not stay up without your assistance?" he asked.

She gazed blankly at him for a moment, looked at the bedpost to which she clung, glanced up at the canopy over the bed, and smiled as she dropped her arms to her sides. Then she laughed and looked more vibrantly beautiful than ever.

"I daresay it will," she said. "Perhaps it was I who could not stay upright without the bedpost's assistance. I *did* drink that glass of wine."

"I thought," he said, "that perhaps you would be fast asleep from its effects."

"Oh." She laughed again. "No."

"I am delighted," he said.

"Are you?"

He was delighted that she was awake so that he could bed her, though he had not really expected she would be asleep. Was he also delighted to be here with his wife? With the woman who would be his companion for the rest of their lives? Was he delighted that tomorrow morning, his lust sated, he would not simply walk away from her and forget her but would take her with him to Woodbine and into the future?

Would he ever be able to forget her even if he were free to do so? Now *that* was an interesting question.

"What is it?" she asked, and he realized that he had been standing there staring at her for several silent moments.

"You are almost too beautiful to touch," he said.

She raised her eyebrows. "But not quite, I hope."

"Do you hope so?" he said, and he walked closer to her and set his hands on her shoulders, holding her at arms' length while his eyes roamed over her. "But you *are* beautiful, Maggie. I am a fortunate man."

He lowered his head and kissed her at the base of her throat.

She tipped back her head and sighed softly.

"I am not embarrassed any longer," she said. "It is so foolish to be, is it not? This is the most natural thing imaginable. I want it, Duncan. I want it more than anything else in the world, in fact."

He wondered what the words had cost her in courage. Though he could tell from the heat radiating off her body that she did mean them.

He slipped his thumbs beneath the shoulders of her nightgown and moved them partway down her arms. He kissed one bare shoulder and moved his mouth over the swell of her breast, lowering the nightgown further as he reached the nipple and took it lightly into his mouth. He touched it with the tip of his tongue and felt her shiver. With heat.

He stood back a little and released his hold on the nightgown. She was pressing it against her stomach with both hands and could have kept it there if she had chosen. Instead, she let her arms fall to her sides and let the flimsy garment slither and slide downward to pool at her feet.

Her cheeks flamed and her eyes held his — until he looked away to see all of her.

Full breasts with rosy tips, small waist, curvaceous hips, long, slim, shapely legs — if there was any imperfection in her, he could not see it. She was every man's sexual dream come true.

Then one of her arms lifted from her side and pulled on the sash of his dressing gown until it came loose. The garment fell open and she pushed it off his shoulders so that it too fell to the floor.

He was surprised — at her nakedness, at his own. He had been prepared to be far more . . . what? Decorous? Considerate? Gentle? She was not a virgin, it was true, but if his guess was correct — and he would wager on it — she was as close to being a virgin as it was possible to be without actually being one.

"More beautiful than ever," he murmured.

"Duncan." She set her hands on his shoulders and moved them down his arms, looking him over frankly as she did so. "You are beautiful too. Is that an inappropriate word? I am sorry if it is. But it fits. You *are* beautiful."

He took her hands in his and wrapped them about his waist, bringing her full against him as he did so.

God in heaven!

He touched his lips to hers, opening her mouth with them as he did so and thrusting his tongue deep inside. She moaned and arched in harder against him. His erection pressed against her belly.

So much for gentle discretion.

"May we lie down?" she asked against his lips when he withdrew his tongue. "I don't think my legs will hold me up much longer."

He bent and picked her up and carried her the short distance to the bed. He lay her down on the bottom sheet and kissed her openmouthed again. She still tasted of wine. She smelled of lavender soap. Siren and lady all rolled into one.

"Do you wish me to blow out the candles?" he asked her. "I would prefer to leave them burning — I want to watch what we do. But it will be as you wish."

Watching them have sex by candlelight had not been part of his original plan either, by Jove.

Her eyes opened and widened.

"Oh," she said. "Leave them burning by all means, then."

He lay down beside her, slid one arm beneath her back, and moved the other hand over her body in a light caress, tracing her curves, feeling the soft heat of her skin, breathing in lavender and wine. He really must *slow down.* His hand roamed over her breasts and lifted one in his palm, feeling the soft, firm, magnificent weight of it as he rubbed the nipple with the pad of his thumb and lowered his head to take it into his mouth again. This time he sucked firmly.

She inhaled slowly and audibly, and her fingers twined tightly in his hair.

"Oh, please," she said, but did not elaborate.

He moved on top of her and pressed his knees between her thighs, pushing them wide until he could kneel between them. He gazed down at her with half-closed eyes. She was gazing back at him, her hair a riot of dark glory over her shoulders and breasts.

Candlelight flickered over her face.

She lifted her arms and spread her hands

over his chest before moving them in slow circles there, her fingers bent back, smoothing the light hairs with her palms in one direction and ruffling them again in the other. She looked back into his face and smiled.

He could feel the soft smoothness of her inner thighs against the outsides of his legs. He could see the heavy fullness of her breasts. He could smell lavender and wine and woman.

And his erection was so taut that if he did not bury it inside her soon, something very embarrassing was going to happen.

"Forgive me," he said, lowering his head and kissing her lips, "I cannot wait any longer."

"Good," she said, still smiling. "Neither can I."

He could have stretched out on top of her then and taken her with swift, urgent strokes. He would feel that whole lovely, curvaceous body beneath his, and the feeling would further ignite the fire in his loins.

She had said she was ready.

But to her their wedding day had been wonderful. This, the consummation, was the culmination of the wedding day. He would not let it be a disappointment to her.

It was the least he could do.

He spread his knees, lifting her legs over them until she twined them about his. And he slid his hands beneath her buttocks, lifted her and held her firm, positioned himself at her entrance, and pressed firmly inside.

He both watched and listened to her inhale slowly, her eyes fluttering closed until he was deeply embedded in her. He held still.

Lord God, she was all wet heat and soft sheath and clenching muscles. And he —

He clamped his teeth together for a few moments. He would *not,* by Jove, give in to pure instinct.

She opened her eyes and looked up at him. He slid his hands from beneath her, moved them up her sides, pressed them beneath her breasts, and brushed his thumbs over her nipples.

"Oh, no," she said. "Oh, no, it is too much, Duncan. It is too much."

"Is it?" He settled his hands on her hips and withdrew from her and pressed in again and withdrew and thrust, beginning a deep and steady rhythm, gritting his teeth against too early an ejaculation.

He looked down to watch what he did. And he glanced up to see that she watched too, with heavy-lidded eyes and parted lips — until her eyes drifted closed and her hands, spread on the bed on either side of her, pressed into the mattress and her head tipped back against the pillow and her inner muscles clenched hard about him and she breathed in labored gasps.

He took her hands in his and raised them above her head, straightening his legs and bringing his whole weight down on top of her as he did so. He quickened and deepened the rhythm, pumping hard into her until she cried out, shuddered convulsively against him, and fell limp and relaxed beneath him.

Her hands were hot and slick with sweat. So was the rest of her body.

The blood pulsed through him, hammering in his ears, thundering in his chest, making his erection an agony. He worked her swiftly until the climax came, and then he sighed against the side of her face and relaxed.

He listened to his heartbeat return to normal, perhaps drifted off into a sort of sleep while it did so, and marveled at the feel of her beneath him — and at the realization that she was a woman of great passion.

"Duncan," she whispered, "are you awake?"

"Mmm? No," he said. "Am I heavy?"

"Yes," she said, "but you need not move

yet. It was lovely. Thank you."

The prim lady again — lying naked and sweaty beneath him and all twined about him.

He propped himself on one elbow and looked down at her.

"It was," he said, "and thank *you,* Maggie. But it might grow a little tedious if we feel we must thank each other every time."

She cupped the free side of his face with one hand.

"I am not sorry," she said. "That I married you, I mean. I am really not."

As if she had thought she might be.

Because of Dew? It had been a little disconcerting to see the man at their wedding breakfast — to see her talking with him, to see him take her hand.

He opened his mouth to say something, but changed his mind.

"I am not sorry either," he said. "However, if there is to be any more to this wedding night, Maggie, I am going to have to get some sleep, I'm afraid."

"Oh," she said — and smiled.

He disengaged from her body, rolled to one side of her, and lifted the bedcovers up over them. He looked across at her and realized that, just like that, she was asleep.

He lay beside her, looking at her for a

while until sleep overtook him too.

Tomorrow they would be on their way to Woodbine and the rest of their lives. Within a few days Toby would join them. He was to live with them, just as if he were a normal, regular child — as he was, of course.

He would, Duncan thought, forever be grateful to her for that.

His heart ached with longing.

Daylight was making a bright square of the window behind the curtains when Margaret woke up. She stretched tentatively, remembering instantly — how could she forget? — and was aware of her unfamiliar nakedness between the sheets.

She felt wicked and wonderful — and amused by the former.

She turned her head, smiling. The bed was empty beside her, the covers thrown back.

She had slept through his getting up and leaving the room? She could scarcely believe it. She had always been a light sleeper and an early riser. Of course, it *had* been a busy night.

They intended making an earlyish start this morning, though they had promised to wait until her family and his mother came to wave them on their way. And they were to call at Claverbrook House.

It was his grandfather's eightieth birthday.

Oh, goodness, what if everyone was already downstairs waiting for her to wake up and dress and make herself look respectable? Whatever would they *think* of her? What sort of a wedding night would they imagine she had just spent?

Would they guess the truth? But *of course* they would.

Oh, dear, she would die of mortification.

She was about to throw back the covers when the door opened.

"If I were a proper lady's maid," Duncan said, stepping inside the room, carrying a tray, "I suppose I would have anticipated the exact moment of your waking and would have had your chocolate steaming beside your bed and your curtains drawn back so that you could see it when you opened your eyes. I am not a proper lady's maid."

He set down the tray on the table beside her bed. It held two cups of chocolate and four sweet biscuits on a plate.

"I would hire you anyway," she said, drawing the covers up to her chin, "but Ellen would be out of employment and I would miss her. I daresay you cannot dress hair as well as she does, anyway."

He sat down on the side of the bed. He was dressed, but only partially — in pantaloons and a shirt that was open far enough to reveal the light dusting of hair on his chest. His hair was damp. He was freshly shaved. He was looking solemn and black-eyed — but he had joked with her. And she had joked back. And he had brought her chocolate and biscuits.

They were such little things, but they warmed her heart on this, the first day of her marriage. The wedding day was over. So was the wedding night.

"I feared I had slept half the morning away," she said.

"Which," he said, "would have been a marvelous compliment to my skills. But instead, you are awake and it is still early."

Oh, he was still joking with her. It felt so very strange to have a man in this room, into which even Stephen had scarcely ever set foot.

Her husband. It had a new reality today. Yesterday he had been her bridegroom and she had viewed him through all the euphoria of the nuptial celebrations.

Today he was simply her husband.

They had had relations three separate times during the night. The second time must have lasted an hour or more. She had

had no idea that the female human body had so many places that could be aroused almost to madness. She had had no idea that the marriage act could consist of more than just preliminary kisses and the entry and the swift ride to release — to the man's release, that was.

She had had no idea that a woman could find release too — a total and mindless abandonment to . . . Well, to pleasure. There were actually no words to describe the experience.

"A penny for them," he said.

"For my thoughts? Oh, nothing," she said, but her cheeks were hot, and she knew she was blushing. Perhaps within the next few days she could become very blasé about all this.

"If you are going to lie there," he said, "with the covers clutched to your chin, you are not going to be able to drink your chocolate, Maggie. That would be a shame. It smells delicious. You are shy this morning?"

"No, of course not," she said.

But he looked at her and cocked one eyebrow, and she really had no choice now but to prove it by lowering the covers to the tops of her breasts. But if she sat up . . .

And then he did what he had done in the

drawing room last night. He laughed deep in his eyes while his face remained perfectly serious.

She lowered the covers to her waist and turned her head to look at the tray. The chocolate really *did* smell good.

"This is most unfair," she said. "You have had time to dress."

"You had an equal opportunity," he said. "But you did not take it. Do you want me to wander into your dressing room in search of a dressing robe? They are probably all packed. Or shall I remove my shirt?"

Oh, this was a very different Duncan this morning. This was — perhaps this was the intimacy of marriage. Perhaps things would always remain like this between them. Perhaps . . .

"And your pantaloons too," she said.

He pulled his shirt off over his head and dropped it to the floor beside the bed. He stood up and moved his hands to the buttons at his waist.

"Only if those covers get pushed the rest of the way down," he said.

She threw them off, and he dropped his pantaloons and then his drawers.

Oh, goodness.

Oh, goodness!

"Are we supposed to drink our chocolate

now?" she asked.

He raised both eyebrows.

"What if Stephen comes home?" she asked. "Or Nessie and Elliott? Or your mother?"

"It is seven in the morning, Maggie," he said. "And even if any of them should take it into their heads to come here at such an ungodly hour, I seriously doubt any of them are going to come bursting into your bed-chamber."

She opened her arms to him.

It was all breathtakingly swift and deep and fierce after that — and every bit as satisfying as any of the more lengthy sessions during the night.

She was sore, she realized when they were finished. She had been sore even before they started, but that fact had not diminished her pleasure one little bit.

"I will wager," he said against her ear, "that that chocolate is still warm. I believe we were running a race that time. Shall we try it and see?"

And so they sat side by side, naked in her bed, propped against the banked pillows, and ate sweet biscuits and drank chocolate that was still a little bit better than luke-warm.

"I think, Maggie," he said, "I am going to

tell my mother this morning what I told you before our wedding. Will she keep the secret, do you think?"

"If you ask it of her," she said, "I am quite perfectly sure she will, Duncan. She loves you."

"And I am going to tell my grandfather," he said. "I owed my loyalty to Laura while she lived, but I think I owe something to my family now. Would you not agree?"

"I *would* agree," she said. "Your grandfather loves you too, you know."

"Yes," he said. "I believe he does. But that love will be put to the test again."

She took his free hand in hers and curled her fingers about it. Oh, *this* part of marriage felt very good indeed. This talking and confiding in each other, this asking for advice of each other.

"I think love is always being put to the test," she said. "It bends, but it never breaks. Not if it is real. Your grandfather and your mother really love you."

And perhaps, she thought, she would too. Perhaps soon.

"I think," she said, "I ought to go and get dressed."

"A pity," he said. "I like what you are wearing now."

She turned her head and laughed at him.

19

They were traveling in a new carriage, a wedding gift from the Marquess of Claverbrook. Nothing, it was true, could quite make English roads seem smooth and an unalloyed pleasure to travel, but nevertheless there was a marvelous feeling of luxury about being inside a well-sprung conveyance with soft, new upholstery and the smell of new leather.

It was the afternoon of the second day. They would be arriving at Woodbine Park soon.

Margaret was trying to decide whether women were more or less fortunate than men when they married. They moved to a different home and sometimes — as in this case — one they had never seen before and one that was far from where they had grown up. Everything was new and strange and different, and there was nothing they could do to prevent it. It was always the wife who moved to her husband's home, never the other way around. It was as though she lost part of her identity. Even her name was forfeited on her marriage.

On the other hand, there was something marvelously stimulating about starting a wholly new life. One could not literally become a different person, of course, but with a new name, a new home, a new part of the world in which to live, there was the opportunity to start again, to make life better in every imaginable way than it had been before. To make it happier.

Not that she had been unhappy in her old life. But she had been . . . Well, she had not been quite happy either. There had been the sense that somehow life had passed her by. Last winter had been the worst. Thirty had been a dreary age to be. Now it seemed the very best age. She was no longer painfully young and vulnerable. But she was still young enough to —

"I once thought the world began and ended here," her husband said beside her. "I thought it was ruled by two people who loved me and would always keep me safe."

She turned her head to look at him. He was gazing out of the window on his side of the carriage.

All children — if they were fortunate —

felt that way, she thought. Even when they did not live among wealth or plenty.

"Your childhood was a happy one?" she asked.

"Entirely," he said, turning to her, "though I was not always consciously aware of the fact, especially on those occasions when I had to avoid sitting down for a while because of a stinging bottom. Or on those other occasions when I was suffering from a scraped knee or a bruised elbow or, once, a broken arm. But children grow into boys who cannot wait to be men, and security and love mean little to them. They cannot wait to get out into the wide world, to seek adventure and an elusive happily-ever-after. They go off in search of what they already have, and in the process they lose it."

"*Were* you unhappy after you left home?" she asked him.

"No," he said. "I was too busy enjoying myself to be unhappy."

She smiled.

"Do all children imagine," he asked, "that when they grow up they will be free at last and able to do just whatever they wish?"

"I suppose most *boy* children imagine it," she said.

"But not girls?" he asked. He answered his own question. "No, I suppose not. There is nothing much for them to dream of, is there?"

"Of course there is," she said, smiling. "There is the perfect marriage to dream of, and the perfect husband — handsome, rich, charming, attentive, gentle, tender, considerate, passionate . . . What have I missed? Oh, and *doting*. Girls dream of love and romance, I suppose, because there is no real point in dreaming of much else. But it can be a pleasant dream for any girl as she waits for her prince to come riding along."

She had never particularly thought about that most basic of all contrasts between men and women. Was it only the pointlessness of dreaming of freedom and adventure that made most women romantics, dreaming instead of home and a warm lover for a husband and children to bear and nurture? Or was it a nesting instinct built into the very fabric of the female being to ensure the preservation of the human race?

"And for you that prince was Dew?" he asked.

Her smile faded, and she looked down at her hands clasped loosely in her lap. Lush green countryside moved past the carriage windows.

"That is the trouble with dreams," she said, "as you discovered after you had left home. They do not always translate well into reality. But new dreams always come along to take their place. We are, on the whole, an endlessly hopeful species."

She certainly had new dreams, even if they were not wildly romantic. Their marriage had not made a bad beginning, all things considered. And there was hope . . .

"Poor Maggie," he said, reaching across the space between them to set a hand over both hers. "This is hardly the perfect marriage of your dreams, is it?"

"And this is not the perfect life of adventure and freedom of *your* dreams," she said. "But you are on the way home again, where you were happy as a child, and I am married to a man I can respect and admire. We have not done badly. It is up to us to make something special of the future."

He was looking broodingly at her when she turned her head again.

"*Are* we a hopeful species?" he asked her. "Or is it just a few of us — or of *you* rather? Have you always been an optimist?"

"Always," she said. "Well, almost always, anyway. Sometimes something happens that is so catastrophic it is impossible for a while — or even for a long time — to see beyond the darkness, even to believe that there *is* anything beyond it. But there always is.

Even, perhaps, at the moment of death. Especially then, in fact."

He did not answer her, and she turned away to watch the scenery. They must be almost there now. He had said there were two hours still to go when they had stopped to change horses and eat luncheon, and surely they had been traveling for almost two hours since then.

"When were you last home?" she asked him.

"Six years ago," he said. "Even when I planned to marry Caroline and bring her here, I was aware that it had been a whole year. And even then it seemed a lifetime. I longed to be back here."

"You must have known when you fled with Mrs. Turner," she said, "that you might never come here again."

"Yes," he said.

She tried to imagine that decision, that realization of all he would sacrifice if he took her away from an abusive marriage that had become intolerable to her. Had they found comfort together? To a certain degree they must have done if they had had a son together — though he had told her he had never loved Mrs. Turner. What had his life been like during those five years? They had moved about a great deal from place to place, he had also told her. But had he found a measure of contentment, even happiness? Had she? He had said she had fallen into a depression after Tobias's birth. Had it been endless? Or just occasional?

How difficult her moods must have made his life!

Had her death devastated him? Or had there been some sense of release? But she had been his son's *mother*. She had died only four months or so ago — very recently. Perhaps he was still grief-stricken.

She could not ask him about those years. Not yet. Perhaps never. She did not believe she would ever be ready to talk with him about Crispin. Some things belonged to one's own heart.

"But I *am* coming home again, after all," he said. "You are right, it seems, Maggie. There always is something beyond the darkness."

"When will your son arrive?" she asked him.

"Tomorrow," he said, "if there are no unexpected delays."

She turned one of her hands beneath his and clasped it.

"There is the prospect of plenty more light to come, then," she said.

"Yes."

She had not told her family about the child. She had noticed that he did not mention him to his mother or grandfather either, though she had been present when he explained to them exactly why he had run off with Mrs. Turner the night before his wedding to the present Mrs. Pennethorne.

His mother had hugged him hard and shed copious tears. She had assured him that she would not say a word to anyone since Graham was seated beside her now and therefore already knew — although it was going to be *extremely* difficult not to give Randolph Turner a very large piece of her mind the next time she saw him and not to say a thing or two to Caroline Pennethorne the next time she saw *her*.

His grandfather, when they had called upon him later, had frowned fiercely and pursed his lips and harrumphed and told Duncan he was a damned fool. But Margaret had not been deceived for one moment. His eyes beneath the shaggy white brows had been suspiciously bright.

"The village," Duncan said quietly now from beside her — his hand had tightened about hers.

She could see through the window on his side that the road curved around a wide bend, following the line of a river, and that around the bend there was a cluster of red-brick cottages and a church spire rising from among them. Trees had been planted on either side of the river.

And then the carriage followed the curve, and they lost sight of the buildings for a few minutes until they were among the cottages and approaching a village green. They drove along one side of it.

They passed the church and, next to it, a thatched and whitewashed public house and inn. The publican, wearing a long white apron, was standing outside brushing off the step with a broom. He raised a hand in greeting after peering curiously into the carriage and seeing who was within. Three children at play on the green stopped to gawk and then went streaking off in three different directions, presumably to tell their mothers that a grand carriage was passing through the village.

And then the carriage turned between two high wrought-iron gates, which stood open, and onto a tree-shaded driveway. Almost immediately the wheels rumbled over a bridge as it crossed the river.

Margaret turned to look at Duncan.

He was looking back, his eyes dark, his face inscrutable.

He had not been here for six years. When he had planned during the past four months to return here, he had not intended to bring a wife. But he was not the only one whose plans had gone awry during the past three weeks.

Oh, goodness, three weeks ago they had not even met each other. Three weeks ago she had been planning to accept an offer from the Marquess of Allingham.

"Take comfort," she said, "from the thought that it took Odysseus something like twenty-eight years to get home to Ithaca after the Trojan War."

"A sobering thought," he said. And there was that smile lurking deep in his eyes as it had on a few previous occasions. "Look out *your* window."

At first there were only the tall trunks of ancient trees to look at and thick undergrowth between. And then, as the carriage moved out of the woods, she saw a wide, tree-dotted lawn sloping upward to a house on the crest of the hill — a large mansion of mellow red stone and long windows and a gabled roof with a pillared portico and what looked like marble steps leading up to double doors. And a stable block to one side, a little farther down the slope, and a flower garden at the other side — a riot of color flowing down the slope to the river, which looped around behind the hill and the house.

It was, Margaret thought, one of the prettiest houses and parks she had ever seen.

And it was home.

She was home. *They* were.

Duncan's clasp on her hand was almost painful.

Neither of them spoke.

If he had come alone, as he had intended, Duncan thought, he would have prowled about the house, looking for what was familiar, what was not, trying to recapture the presence of his father in the library, of his mother in the morning room and drawing room, standing at the window of his old bedchamber, looking down the steep slope behind the house to the river and across it to the wide, straight, laburnum-shaded grass avenue, which ended with the summer house and views of fields and meadows and woods in every direction. He would perhaps have strolled along the portrait gallery, viewing the old family portraits through adult eyes. He would have spent the evening slouched in a chair, perhaps in the drawing room, more probably in the library, reading a book.

Reveling in the feeling of being home where he belonged.

At last.

It had been a long, weary exile — much of it self-imposed. He had gone away to sow some wild oats, and he had stayed away because he had stepped past the invisible but nonetheless real boundary between wild oats and that barren land that stretched beyond the pale. For five years he had yearned to be here with a gnawing ache of longing.

Oh, he might have paid a visit now and then, he supposed. But there had been no leaving Laura, even with the Harrises, whom she knew and trusted. A few times he had gone away for a night or two just because he had needed some time to himself, some semblance of a life of his own. But each time he had been sorry when he returned. Not that she had railed at him. She had never done that. She had always . . . loved him. Yes, that *was* the correct word, though it had not, of course, been a romantic love. And she had needed him. Oh, how she had needed him!

It should have felt good to be needed.

It had not.

Poor Laura.

He had loved her too. *Not* with a romantic

or sexual love.

He had not come here alone now, alas. He had brought a wife with him.

He showed her the house after their arrival and marveled at how little it had changed in six years. Why had he expected that it would have done? Any orders for change would have had to come from him — or from his grandfather.

He could not dislike Maggie, he found, even though he had half expected to. She was sensitive and compassionate. Good Lord, she had insisted upon having Toby in their home as if he were a legitimate son of the house. It was not just that, though.

It was . . . Well, he did not know what it was.

"You have not seen the gallery yet," he told her as they sat together at a late dinner, one at the head and one at the foot of the dining room table, from which the butler had had the forethought to remove all the extra leaves so that they were not a great distance apart. "It is best seen in the daylight. I will show it to you tomorrow, if you wish."

"Are all your family portraits there?" she asked.

"It is an interesting gallery," he said. "All the main family portraits are at Wychen

Abbey, my grandfather's country home. But all the marquesses for the past seven generations grew up here, just as I did, and so the portraits of them as children and young men are here, as well as portraits of all their other family members, of course. It is a cheerful place. I was an only child and did not always have the company of other children, though my cousins were forever coming for extended stays. I spent a great deal of time in the gallery, especially in wet weather. My pictured ancestors were my playmates. I weaved stories about them and me."

She was smiling.

"It must be lovely," she said, "to have an ancestral home, to have that connection with your own roots and with those who went before you."

"It is," he said. "There is a wonderful portrait of my grandfather when he was fifteen or sixteen, astride a horse and bending down to scoop up a shaggy little dog. And another of him as a young man with my grandmother, my father an infant on her knee."

She smiled along the length of the table at him.

"I shall so enjoy looking at those particular paintings," she said. "Oh, Duncan, he loves you very dearly. I am going to persuade him to come here before the winter."

"He has not been here," he said, "since my father died — fifteen years ago."

"Then it is time he came again," she said. "We will see to it that he replaces those sad memories with happier ones."

We will be happy, then? he almost said aloud.

"If you can persuade him," he said, "you will be a miracle worker."

"Watch me," she said, laughing. "Shall I leave you alone to your port?"

It would have seemed mildly eccentric of him when they had no company. Besides, he did not want to sit alone — strange, really, when he had been dreaming of returning here by himself.

"We will retire to the drawing room," he said, getting to his feet and going to draw back her chair, "and have tea brought there. Or coffee?"

"Tea, please," she said, and he looked at the butler and raised his eyebrows.

"And that," he said as he led her toward the drawing room, her arm drawn through his, "was gauche of me, Maggie. I should have left the ordering of the tea tray to you. You are not a guest in my home, are you? You are my wife."

"How improper it would be," she said, laughing again, "if I were only a guest. I *will* pour the tea, however."

Which she proceeded to do as soon as the tray arrived in the drawing room. He watched her, poised and elegant and beautiful. Still a stranger. Was it inevitable in any new marriage? Was it possible to know any woman in advance of living in intimacy under the same roof with her? He had courted Caroline for several months before offering her marriage, and they had been betrothed for several more months. And yet he had not known her at all until very close to the wedding. And even then, he supposed, he had not completely known her — only one fact about her that had repelled him.

Perhaps it did not matter that he had known Maggie for less than three weeks.

"It *is* awkward, is it not?" she said into a rather lengthy silence as they sipped their tea.

"The silence?" he said.

"I could keep talking," she said. "So could you. But not forever. What *do* we talk about, Duncan?"

"What do you talk to your brother about?" he asked her. "And your sisters?"

She was looking directly at him.

"I am not really sure," she said. "With strangers and even acquaintances I can keep a conversation going indefinitely. It is a part of being polite, is it not? With my family I do not have to make conversation. They talk, I talk — we do not have to make any effort to find topics. They just happen."

"And are you ever silent with your family?" he asked.

She thought.

"Yes, often," she said. "Silence can be companionable. It can be that even with close friends."

"I am neither family nor a close friend, then?" he asked her.

She stared back at him.

"You *are* the one and must be both," she said. "But can friendship be forced, Duncan? Or the *ease* of friendship?"

He was feeling a little shaken, if the truth were known. He had not been finding the silence uncomfortable. If he had been, he would have filled it with some form of conversation. He had spoken a great deal about his home and family and childhood, for example, since their arrival. But he had not asked her anything about her own life. Those details would have filled the rest of the evening.

Of course, he realized suddenly, *he* was at

home. She was not — not in a place that had had a chance to *feel* like home yet, anyway. Woodbine Park was a strange place to her. It was understandable that she was a little uncomfortable.

"We are not enemies," he said.

"No."

"Are we not therefore friends?" he asked. She smiled.

"We are *lovers,*" he said.

"Yes."

"But not friends?"

"I think," she said, setting down her cup and saucer, "I am just tired."

"And a little depressed?" he asked softly.

"No," she said. And she laughed suddenly. "That would be disconcerting after I told you earlier that I am always an optimist. I am just tired and forgot for a moment that marriage is a journey, just as life is. I must not expect it to be perfect from the start. If it were, we would have nowhere to go with it, would we?"

"Our marriage is not perfect?" he asked her.

"No, of course it is not," she said, still smiling. "We married for imperfect reasons, and we have been married for only a few days. I want contentment, happiness with husband, home, and family. You want . . .

well, you want simply not to regret your marriage as deeply as you fear you might. They are not impossible dreams, are they? For either of us?"

He had been struck by her honesty from the start of their acquaintance. She was being honest now. Her expectations were not impossibly high. Neither were her demands of him.

"I do not regret it," he said.

It struck him that if he were here alone now, he might also be feeling lonely — even though Toby was coming tomorrow. He was not feeling lonely now. A trifle irritated, perhaps, but not lonely. And not unhappy.

"Thank you," she said. "One day you will say it with more conviction, I promise."

"And you will tell me one day," he said, getting to his feet, "that you are not only contented with our marriage, but happy. I promise."

He reached out a hand for hers and drew her to her feet.

"And one day," he said, "we will be able to sit a whole hour together in silence without you feeling awkward."

She laughed again.

And then she drew her hand from his, wrapped both arms about his neck, and leaned in to him, pressing one cheek against his. His arms closed about her.

"Oh, how I have *longed,*" she said, and paused for such a long time that he thought she would not continue. But she did. "How I have longed all my life for just this — a home of my own, a husband I can like and respect, intimacy, togetherness, the promise of happiness within grasping distance. Duncan, I *really* am not depressed. I am . . ."

She drew back her head to look into his face. She did not complete the thought.

"Lusty?" he suggested.

"Oh, you horrid man!" she cried. "You know words like that are not in a lady's vocabulary."

He gazed back at her and said nothing.

"Yes," she said softly. "*Lusty.* What a deliciously wicked word."

Women were complex creatures, he thought as he kissed her — and *that* was surely the original thought of the century. Lust for them was not the simple need for a thorough good bedding. It was all mixed up in their minds with marriage and home and liking and respect and romance and love.

And for men? For *him?*

He deepened the kiss, opening both their mouths and thrusting his tongue deep, spreading his hands over her buttocks and snuggling her in against his growing hardness.

He too had longed . . .

For a woman in his arms and in his bed and in his —

Life?

Heart?

He did not know and would not puzzle now over the answer. But he *had* longed.

Yearned.

"Maggie," he murmured into her ear. "Come to bed."

"Mmm," she said on a long sigh. "Yes. That is a *good* part of our marriage, is it not?"

"Shall we not analyze it?" he suggested, settling her hand on his arm. "Shall we just *do* it? And *enjoy* it?"

Her lips curved into a smile and her eyes brightened with merriment.

"Yes," she said. "To both. I think you are making a wanton of me."

"Good," he said.

20

The morning after her arrival at Woodbine Park, Margaret was ashamed of the way she had allowed herself to be overwhelmed the evening before by the newness and unfamiliarity of everything in her life.

She had found herself during that lengthy silence in the drawing room missing her family, Merton House, Warren Hall, the familiar round of her daily life. And knowing that everything was changed forever with no chance — ever — of going back.

Which had all been quite absurd. Why should she wish to go back? And it was not as if she had lost her family forever. She had merely got what she had longed for all of last winter.

In the morning everything looked brighter — even literally. The sun shone from a clear blue sky beyond the windows of the bedchamber she shared with Duncan, and she could see the view out over the park at the front of the house. And a lovely view it was too with the house situated as it was on the crest of the hill. Beyond the inner lawns she could see the trees that circled the park, the river to one side, the roofs of some of the houses in the village, the church spire, and farmland stretching like a giant patchwork quilt to a distant horizon.

She was filled with energy despite last night's lovemaking. Or perhaps partly because of it. That aspect of her new life was wonderful indeed and far surpassed any of her expectations. She had expected, and hoped, that it might be pleasant. It was . . . Well, it was much better than that.

Duncan was a skilled, patient, thorough, and passionate lover. And she had discovered an answering passion in herself. Perhaps it was unladylike to enjoy the marriage bed quite so much. But if it was, then she was content to be no lady — at least during the nights and in the privacy of their own bedchamber.

She intended to spend at least a part of the morning in consultation with the housekeeper and perhaps the cook too. There was much to learn, much to organize, if she was to establish herself as mistress of Woodbine. She would find it easier this time. When she had moved to Warren Hall with Stephen and Kate, she had gone from managing a small village cottage to running a grand country mansion. The two tasks had had very few similarities. It had taken her a great deal of effort and determination.

Duncan arrived in her dressing room before Ellen had quite finished styling her hair. He had been gone from bed when she woke up earlier. He was wearing riding clothes and looked as if he had been out already.

"I thought," he said, meeting her eyes in the mirror, "that perhaps you would get lost between here and the breakfast parlor and would wander aimlessly about the house all day before someone found you and rescued you."

"And so you came to escort me?" She smiled at his image. He looked as full of energy as she. He looked younger somehow, more carefree, more handsome. It struck her that he was probably far more at home in the country than he was in the city.

"I did."

He sat down on a chair by the door to wait for her and crossed one booted ankle over the other knee. Oh, yes, and he looked very virile too. Very attractive.

"I must spend the morning with the housekeeper," she said when they were on their way downstairs for breakfast. "Mrs. Dowling, that is. There will be a great deal to learn, and I am eager to begin."

"But not today," he said.

"You must need to spend time with your steward after such a long absence," she said.

"But not today," he said again. "Today we will start with the gallery, though we will not spend a great deal of time there when the weather is so good. We will go outside, and I will show you the park."

A day of pleasure instead of duty? How irresponsible! And how irresistible!

"Is that an order?" she asked him, turning her head to smile at him as they reached the bottom of the staircase and turned in the direction of the breakfast parlor.

He stopped walking rather abruptly, and he was not smiling when he looked back into her eyes.

"It was *not* an order," he said. "You will never hear one of those from me, Maggie."

"It will be a holiday because we both wish for it, then," she said, tipping her head to one side, still smiling. "A sort of honeymoon."

He raised his eyebrows.

"Yes," he said. "Precisely. Though I am not sure I have heard that word more than once or twice in my life."

"It is a holiday," she explained, "in celebration of a new marriage."

"Oh, yes," he said, "I know what it *is*. It is a span of time in which a newly married couple can give, ah, vigorous attention to their new relationship."

"Yes," she said. "Precisely."

Oh, she felt very wicked, very carefree, very . . . *happy?*

So after breakfast they proceeded to the portrait gallery, which ran the whole width of the top floor of the house on the east side and was filled with light from windows on three sides.

The portraits were youthful and cheerful, as Duncan had indicated last evening. And he knew who every painted figure was and could recount numerous anecdotes about them.

It surprised Margaret to see how much he resembled his grandfather as a young man.

"Oh," she said, "what a very handsome man he was. And you look just like him, Duncan."

"Is that a compliment?" he asked. "I seem to remember your saying that I am not handsome or in any way good-looking."

Had she really said that? But she seemed to remember that she had.

"I was wrong," she said. "It was because

414

you looked bleak, almost morose. People are always better-looking when they are happy."

"I am happy, then?" he asked.

Oh, why did he keep asking questions like that?

She turned to him, stepped closer, and reached up to cup one side of his face with her hand.

"I don't know," she said. "I can only guess at all you have suffered in the last five years, Duncan. I can only guess at how you must have longed for some solitude after your bereavement in order to deal with your grief and recover from your loss and enjoy the company of your son. But you *are* happier than you were when I first met you. I do not know if returning home here has done that for you or if I have had a hand in it."

"And you," he said, setting a hand over hers. "Are *you* happier, Maggie?"

"Than I was when I met you?" she said, and smiled. "I was fleeing Crispin and the Marquess of Allingham at the time, and the realization that all the dreaming and planning I had done over the winter had come to naught. And then I met you. Yes, I am happier. Oh, and I did correct my first impression of your looks on our wedding day. I told you you were beautiful, if you remember."

The smile began deep in his eyes and ended by curving his lips upward at the corners and lighting up his whole face.

"I was naked," he said. "Perhaps my body is prettier than my face."

"But your face is part of your body," she protested, and they both laughed.

Oh, it felt very good, she thought as she rested her free hand on his shoulder, to laugh together over something so absurd. The sun, slanting in through the south window, bathed them in light and warmth.

She moved away from him to look out through the window, and he followed her. The view was very similar to the one they had from their bedchamber. When they moved to one of the east windows they could look down upon the flower garden. It had been built over a series of low stone walls, which were almost like steps in the hillside. There were roses growing there and pansies, marigolds, hyacinths, sweet peas, daisies — oh, almost every flower Margaret could think of, all rioting together in a glorious mix of color and height and size and texture, and all apparently spilling downward to the river.

Someone had wanted both wildness and cultivation in that garden and had succeeded wonderfully well. There were a few wrought iron seats set among the flowers, she could see.

"Was that your mother's creation?" she asked.

"My grandmother's when she lived here as a young wife," he said. "I have always thought it lovelier than any carefully regimented formal gardens I have seen."

They strolled on to look out the north window. There was a cobbled terrace directly below the house and then a steep bank ending at the river. There were a few low trees on the slope and masses of wildflowers. There was a boathouse and a short jetty off to the left.

And beyond the river was a long avenue, whose grass surface had been shaved so close that it might almost have been used as a bowling green. There was a stone structure in the distance, at the end of it. Trees lined it on either side, like soldiers.

"This is all very, very beautiful," she said.

He took her hand in his and laced his fingers with hers. "Shall we go outside?"

They did not go far from the house, though they remained outside for several hours. They did not even return for luncheon. There was so much to see, so much sunshine to be soaked up, so many flowers

417

to be smelled and touched, so many different vistas to be admired. So much talking to do. So many short silences to enjoy, filled with birdsong and the croaking of unseen insects.

They ended up strolling along beside the river behind the house, watching fish dart beneath the surface, watching the slight breeze rippling over it.

The air was warm without being oppressively hot.

"There used to be a private little nook down here," he said, "not far from the boathouse. I used to sit there dreaming when I wanted to be alone or inventing some darkly secret club with my cousins. Ah, yes, here it is."

It was a small inlet in the bank, grassy and overhung by coarse grasses and shaded by a cluster of bushy trees. It was a place to sit unobserved from the house above.

They settled there side by side. Margaret clasped her knees and gazed out at the light dancing off the river.

"This homecoming has been all me, me, me, has it not?" he said after a few minutes of silence. "*My* home, *my* park, *my* ancestors, *my* memories."

She smiled. "But it is my home now too," she said. "I want to learn all I can about it and about you."

"But what about you?" he said. "Who are *you,* Maggie? What childhood experiences shaped you into the person you are now?"

"It was a very ordinary childhood," she said. "We grew up at the rectory in Throckbridge. It was a smallish house in a small village. We were neither rich nor abjectly poor. At least, I believe we *were* rather poor, but we were sheltered from the knowledge by a mother who was an excellent manager and a father who preached, and believed, that happiness was something that had little to do with money or possessions."

"You were happy, then," he said.

"And we had good neighbors," she told him, "including the Dews at Rundle Park. There were a number of children of all ages both there and in the village. We all played together."

"And then," he said, "your parents died."

"There was some time between the two events," she said. "Our mother died first. It was a terrible blow to all of us. But our lives did not change a great deal — though I suppose our father's did. He was a sadder, quieter man afterward."

"How old were you when he died?" he asked her.

"Seventeen."

"And you promised him," he said, "that you would hold the family together until all of you were grown up and settled."

"Yes," she said.

"If your father had not died," he said after a while, "you would have married Dew."

"Yes," she said. "It is strange, is it not? All these years I have believed that if only that could have happened I would have lived happily ever after. It was all I ever wanted, all I ever dreamed of."

"But now you have changed your mind?" he asked.

"I can never know how my life would have turned out," she said. "But I think perhaps I would not have been very happy. Even if he had remained devoted to me — and I suppose he might have done if I had been with him all the time — I would have been an officer's wife. I would have followed the drum, and I would have had no settled home all these years, or on into the future."

"You would not have enjoyed that?" he asked.

"It seemed glamorous at the time," she said. "It has always seemed glamorous since — until recently. But I am not an adventurous person, you know. When I remained home with my brother and sisters, I thought I did so out of necessity. And that was indeed part of the reason — maybe even most of it. But home is where I belong. I do not mean necessarily one particular house and neighborhood. I have never had that attachment as you have. But *home.* Somewhere — some fixed place — that is my own with people who are my own and neighbors I can like and trust and with whom I can socialize. Somewhere to make into a home not just for myself but for those who are close to me. I do not believe I could bear to be a nomad."

The silence stretched for a long time. It was not at all uncomfortable. Margaret was absorbing what she had just said. It was absolutely the truth. If she had married Crispin at the age of seventeen and gone off with him to the wars, perhaps she would have adapted to the life she would have been forced to live, but she did not think so.

She was a home maker.

She had always been happy making a home for her sisters and Stephen. The only thing missing had been someone to share the heart of the home with her.

She had always thought he was Crispin.

But Crispin, she knew now, could never have filled that role.

And she would not have been entirely happy.

. . . someone to share the heart of the home with her.

She rested her forehead on her knees and tightened her arms about her legs.

Would she ever find that someone? Had she found him? If she had not, she never would, would she? She was married.

After a few moments his hand came to rest warmly against the back of her neck.

"Maggie," he asked softly, "what is it?"

"Nothing," she said, but her voice was thin and high pitched, and before she could clear her throat and say something in a more normal tone, he had unclasped her hands and drawn her down to lie on her side on the grass. He lay close to her, one arm beneath her head.

He dried her eyes with his handkerchief.

She had not realized that she was crying.

She felt very foolish. For so many years she had guarded her emotions. Now her control seemed to be slipping.

"What is it?" he murmured again.

I have been so lonely, she almost blurted aloud. *So very, very lonely. I am so lonely.*

It was all very well to be cheerful and practical, to make plans for a workable marriage and a home that would be comfortable and welcoming and not unhappy.

But it was impossible to fool the heart all

422

the time.

I am so lonely.

It was abject. It was selfish. It was despicable.

It was not like her.

"Nothing," she said again.

"Maggie," he said, "I wish there had been time to court you as you deserved to be courted. Time to win your love. Time to fall in love. Time to do everything properly. I wish there had. But since there was not —"

She set two fingers across his lips.

"There never would have been time," she said. "If we had not both been desperate for different reasons when we collided, we would not have stopped for anything more than a hasty, embarrassed apology. The only time is *now.* Now is the only time there ever is."

"Then I will court you now," he said, and his eyes were very deep, very dark. "I will make you fall in love with me. And I will fall in love with you."

"Oh," she said, "you need not make such promises just because I have been shedding tears, Duncan. I do not even know why I have been doing so."

"You are lonely," he said just as if she had spoken her thoughts out loud, "and have been for a long while. So am I — and have been for a long while. It is foolish to be lonely when we have each other."

"I am not lonely," she protested.

"Liar," he said, and kissed her.

She kissed him back with a sudden, desperate ardor. She had everything. If she were to write a list, it would be a long one indeed, and it would include almost every imaginable dream any woman could possibly want or need to make her happy. Except something at the core of her being. Something for which she searched blindly in the kiss and knew she would not find there.

Could one make a conscious decision to fall in love? Could two people?

"I do love you, you know," she said, drawing back from him.

"Yes," he said, "I *do* know. But it is what you do in life, Maggie. It is what you have always done. You have always selflessly loved others and given of yourself for them. It is not enough."

She looked at him, stricken.

"But you have been a giver too," she said. "You gave up everything in order to shelter Mrs. Turner from harm — your family, your friends, your home, your good name. You are no stranger to love. That is what love does when it must."

"It is not enough," he said again. "We have to fall in love, Maggie, and falling in love is different from simply loving. It calls for the willingness to receive as well as to give, and you and I are probably better at giving."

She stared back at him. Was he right?

"Opening ourselves to love is to make ourselves vulnerable," he said. "We might get hurt — again. We might lose the little of ourselves that we have left or that we have pieced back together. But unless we can open ourselves to receive as well as to give, we can never be truly happy. Shall we take the risk? Or shall we decide to be content with contentment? I think we can learn to be content with each other."

She still could not find words.

He tipped his head back and shut his eyes. The arm beneath her head was tense. She guessed that he had spoken from impulse, that he had not known what he was going to say until he said it.

He had already made himself vulnerable.

He was afraid to love. No, not that. He was afraid to *be loved.*

Was she? Oh, surely not. But she thought of how she had always hidden her emotions even from her own family — *especially* from them — so that she would always appear strong and dependable. Of how she had cultivated a cheerful placidity during the years when the absence of Crispin had been a constant pain gnawing at her heart. Of how she had hidden from them her intense grief when she heard of his marriage, though they had guessed at it. Of how she had planned to make this marriage work in the same way as she had made her family life work — by being placidly cheerful, or cheerfully placid.

She did love him. She would not be able to live a lifetime with him if she did not. But could she let him love her? What if the love he had to offer turned out to be not strong enough or deep enough or devoted enough or passionate enough? What if he could never be heart of her heart?

It would be better to guard her heart instead.

Or not.

"How is it to be done?" she asked him. "How are we to do it?"

But before he could answer they both became aware of the clopping of horses' hooves and the crunching of wheels over gravel in the distance on the other side of the house.

It was the reason they had not gone far from the house all day, Margaret realized, though neither of them had put it into words. They had wanted to be within earshot of any approaching carriage.

He tensed again, listening. So did she. But they had not mistaken.

"A carriage," he said.

"Yes."

They scrambled to their feet and half ran up the steep bank to the terrace and around the west side of the house, Duncan slightly ahead of her.

A heavy traveling carriage had just drawn up before the portico, and the coachman was opening the door and reaching inside even before he set down the steps. Someone was shrieking in a high treble voice, and the coachman swung him out and set him down on the ground — a slight little boy with a mop of blond curls, Margaret saw as she stopped running and walked forward more slowly.

The child must have seen Duncan at the side of the house. He came running as soon as his feet touched firm earth, still shrieking, his arms stretched out to the sides.

"Papa!" he cried as he came. "Papa!"

He did not have far to run. Duncan had not slackened his pace. He bent down and swung the child into his arms, spun him in a circle, and held him tight. The boy's arms were wrapped about his neck.

Margaret stopped some distance away.

"Papa," the child was saying over and over again into the side of his neck.

Duncan turned his head and kissed him.

"I thought we would *never* get here," the boy said in his high, piping voice. "I was a trial to Mrs. Harris — she told me so. Mr. Harris slept most of the way. He was *snoring.* I thought you would not be here. Mrs. Harris said you might not be. She said we might race you home. I thought maybe you would never come and I would never see you again and I would not have a papa. But you *are* here. And now Mrs. Harris will tell you all the bad things I have been doing, and you will frown and tell me that I have been unkind, and I will be sad. Don't be cross, Papa. Please don't."

And he lifted his head, spread his little hands over Duncan's cheeks, and kissed him on the lips.

"I won't ever be bad again," he said, all wide, innocent eyes and wheedling tone, "now that I am home and now that I am with you again."

"I daresay," Duncan said, "you have been driving poor Mrs. Harris to distraction with all your prattling, have you, imp?"

"Yes, I have," the child admitted, and patted Duncan's cheeks before wriggling to be set down. His eyes alit upon Margaret. "Who are you?"

"Not a very polite question, Tobe," Duncan said, taking his hand. "I would have told you if you had waited a moment. This is Lady Sheringford, my new wife. Your new mama."

"No," the child said, shrinking against Duncan's side, trying to hide behind one of his legs. "*Not* my mama. I don't *want* a mama. We don't need her, Papa. Send her away. Now."

Margaret made a slight hand gesture when Duncan would have spoken, his brows knitting together.

"Of course I am not your mama, Toby," she said. "I am your papa's wife, that is all. You fell out of a tree a little while ago and bumped your forehead, did you not? Your papa told me. Do you still have the mark there?"

He leaned against Duncan's leg and circled one finger about his forehead.

"I think it's gone," he said. "But it was the size of an egg. *Two* eggs."

"I wish I could have seen it," she said. "My brother fell off a horse once when he was about your age or a little older, but the lump on his head was certainly no bigger than one egg. He used to get cuts and bruises all over too — and scabs."

"I have a scab on *my* knee," Toby said. "Do you want to see?"

"I am sure —" Duncan began.

"Oh, yes, please," Margaret said, stepping closer. "How did you get it?"

"I was *trying* to catch Mrs. Lennox's cat," he said, bending to pull up his breeches and roll down his stocking to expose one knee. "She *never* lets him out, and when he does escape, he will not let anyone pet him because he is not used to people. I had my hands on him, and then she stuck out her broom and I tripped over it."

"Nasty," Margaret said, and bent closer to look at the dried scab that covered his kneecap. "Did you bleed?"

"All over my breeches," he said, "and they were not even *old* ones. Mrs. Harris had to scrub them for an hour to get it all out. And then she had to mend the hole. She said Papa would have paddled my bottom if he had been there."

"It sounds to me," Margaret said, stepping back as the boy bent to roll up his stocking again, "as if perhaps it was Mrs. Lennox who deserved to have her bottom paddled."

He shrieked with surprised laughter and reached for Duncan's hand again.

"Is this *really* home, Papa?" he asked. "Forever and ever? No more moving?"

"This is really home, Tobe," Duncan assured him.

"And you are not going away *ever* again?"

"Ever is a long time," Duncan told him. "But we are going to live together here, you and I and —" He glanced at Margaret but did not complete the thought. "Come and see your room. And I expect you are hungry. Cook, I hear, has been baking some special cakes just for you."

Toby climbed the steps at his father's side, his hand clasped in his. But he stopped before they reached the top and looked back at Margaret.

"You can be my *friend* if you want," he said.

"Can I?" Margaret asked. "I'll think about it and give you my answer tomorrow or the day after."

"All right," the child said, and disappeared through the door.

Blond delicacy beside dark strength.

A garrulous, active, mischievous child, who was quite innocent of all the ugliness that had surrounded his birth and early years.

Now he was home.

They all were.

She could be his *friend,* Margaret thought as she entered the house more slowly. He had already disappeared upstairs with Duncan.

She smiled. It was better than nothing.

And she and Duncan were going to fall in love.

Would they succeed?

21

Duncan spent the rest of the day with Toby. He had tea with him, showed him the schoolroom, which was part of the nursery, and the toys and books that had been there from his own childhood, and he took him outside to show him the river and the wide lawns to the west of the house, where they would play cricket and other games that needed wide open spaces. He took him to the stable block to see the horses and the puppies in the far stall, jealously guarded by their mother, a border collie. And no, Toby might *not* take one of them into the house — though Duncan did not doubt he would be coaxed and wheedled until he consented to allow one to be adopted, once the animal could be taken from its mother without crying all night in the nursery and keeping everyone awake.

He had dinner in the nursery and suggested that they invite Toby's new friend to join them there.

"But she is not my friend yet," Toby pointed out. "She said she would let me know tomorrow or the next day. Perhaps she does not like me. Do you think she does, Papa?"

"I think," Duncan said, "she will like you a little bit more if you invite her to dinner. We gentlemen have to be crafty where ladies are concerned, Tobe. If we are always polite and considerate and include them in our various activities, they will usually be our friends."

"What does *considerate* mean?" Toby asked. When Duncan told him, he nodded and agreed that Maggie really ought to be invited to dinner.

After the meal, Duncan spent an hour listening to Toby's much-embellished accounts of the adventures he had narrowly survived in Harrogate before telling him a few stories and tucking him into bed for the night.

"Sleep tight," he said, kissing the child on the forehead. "Tomorrow we will play again."

"You will be here, Papa?" Toby asked. "Promise?"

"I promise." Duncan smoothed a hand over his soft fair curls.

"And we can stay here, Papa? For always? Promise?"

"Maybe not for all the rest of our lives, Tobe, unless we want to," Duncan said. "But for a long, long time. This is home, a place to play and grow up in, a place to come back to whenever we go somewhere else for a little while. A place to belong."

"Together," Toby said. His eyelids were growing heavy. "Just you and me, Papa."

"Yes," Duncan said. "You and me. And perhaps my wife, your new friend — *if* she decides to be your friend, that is. I think she might, though. She was pleased to be invited to dinner, was she not?"

"It was kind of us to ask her. We will do it again," Toby said, yawning hugely and closing his eyes. "Am I safe now, Papa? Nobody will come and take me away, as Mama always used to say?"

"You are as safe as safe can be," Duncan assured him, and sat where he was until he was sure the child was asleep.

He hoped he had spoken the truth. Devil take it, but he hoped so. Perhaps after all he should have kept Toby's identity a carefully guarded secret. But no, Maggie was right. The time for secrecy was over. Except that there were still secrets — heavy ones, which perhaps he ought to have divulged with the others. But Laura had always been adamant that for Toby's sake, and hers, the truth must never be told. And he had promised her over and over again . . .

Did a promise extend even beyond the grave?

Should loyalty to a new spouse supersede all else?

His life had been defined for five interminable years by secrets and the certain disaster that would result if they were uncovered. It was not easy to shake himself free of those years. It was not always easy to know what was the right thing to do — or the wrong.

Especially as it was an innocent child who would suffer if he were to make the wrong decision.

Had he already made it?

What would happen if he went downstairs now and told the whole truth to Maggie? But he feared he knew the answer. She would persuade him that it was in everyone's best interest that the truth be told openly at last, that nothing good ever came from secrecy and subterfuge.

The very idea that she might talk him into agreeing with her made his stomach churn uncomfortably. There was far too much risk involved.

He sighed and stood up, touching his fingers to Toby's hand before tucking it beneath the covers.

He had not forgotten the strange conversation he had had with Maggie down by the river just before Toby arrived with the Harrises. In fact, it had been very much on his mind ever since.

He had no idea where the words had come from. Or the idea behind them. Falling in love was as much about receiving as it was giving, was it? It seemed selfish. It was not, though. It was the opposite. Keeping oneself from being loved was to refuse the ultimate gift.

He had thought himself done with romantic love. He had thought himself an incurable cynic.

He was not, though.

He was only someone whose heart and mind, and very soul, had been battered and bruised. It was still — and always — safe to give since there was a certain deal of control to be exerted over giving. Taking, or allowing oneself to receive, was an altogether more risky business.

For receiving meant opening up the heart again.

Perhaps to rejection.

Or disillusionment.

Or pain.

Or even heartbreak.

It was all terribly risky.

And all terribly necessary.

And of course, there was the whole issue of trust . . .

He found her in the drawing room, working at an embroidery frame, something he had not seen her do before. She looked up and smiled when he entered the room.

"Is he asleep?" she asked.

He nodded.

"Maggie," he said, "I am sorry he was so rude when he arrived."

"You must not be," she said. "He was not deliberately ill-mannered, only honest in the way of young children — and very frightened. He saw me as someone who could take you away from him. I was touched when he told me I could be his friend."

"It was inspired," he said, "to tell him you needed to consider the matter and would give him your answer another time."

She laughed.

"He is a sweetheart," she said.

"And a little devil," he said. "He almost toppled into the river looking for fish when he had been here scarcely two hours — after I had told him not to lean out beyond the edge of the bank."

She laughed.

"But I did not come here to talk about Toby," he said.

She rested her hand holding the needle on her embroidery and looked up at him. Her eyes were wide and somehow fathomless in the candlelight.

"Didn't you?" she said.

"I will spend time with him each day," he said, "because I must and because I wish to. And of course I must spend time about estate business just as you will go about the business of the house. There will be visitors soon, I do not doubt, and calls to return. But there must be time for you and me."

She looked down at her work and with the forefinger of her free hand traced the silk petal of one embroidered flower.

"To fall in love," he said.

She looked up at him.

"Can it be done so deliberately?" she asked.

"How else are we to do it?" he asked in return. "Let us not call it falling in love. Let us call it courtship instead. There was no time for it before we married, but it is not too late for it now. Is it?"

"But courtship is a one-way thing," she said. "A man courts a woman."

"Let us be rebels, then," he said. "Court me too, Maggie, as I will court you. Make me fall in love with you. I will make you fall in love with me. There will be magic."

Her eyes filled with tears suddenly, and she bent her head to thread her needle into the cloth and set it aside.

"Oh," she said, and her voice sounded a little shaky, "that is it, is it not? The grand dream. There will be magic." She looked up at him again. "Will there be?"

"The moon is almost full," he said, "and the sky is clear. The stars are a million lamps. Let me fetch you a shawl and take you outside. What setting could be more conducive to romance?"

"What indeed?" she said, laughing softly. "Go and fetch a shawl, then."

Ten minutes later they were at the bottom of the flower garden and stepping onto the humpbacked wooden bridge that crossed the river. They stopped halfway across it to gaze down into the water, which gleamed in the moonlight. She held the ends of her shawl with both hands, and he had his hands clasped at his back.

He was thirty. So was she. The first flush of youth had passed them both by, ending abruptly for him just before his twenty-fifth birthday, leached gradually out of her after the death of her father and the departure of her lover and his ultimate faithlessness.

They had both given up on romance.

There was no scene more romantic than this. The evening air was cool but not by any means cold. He could smell the flowers and hear the water gurgling beneath the bridge. And he was in company with a beautiful woman who was his lover as well as his life's companion.

"Turn your face to me," he said.

She did so, and they gazed into each other's eyes for a while until they both smiled.

He bent forward and rubbed his nose against hers before kissing her softly on the lips.

"I think," he said, "it is possible to start again, don't you? Life, I mean. It cannot possibly be intended that we simply acquire experience upon experience like a lot of excess baggage to carry about with us until we stagger into middle age and old age beneath the impossible weight of it all. We must, as we grow older and wiser, be able to allow all the . . . all the pain to seep out of our bones and our souls so that we can start again. Do you think?"

"I thought it was a matter of will and discipline," she said. "I thought the past was gone — off my shoulders, out of my life, until I had a letter from Lady Dew a few months ago telling me that Crispin was a widower and that he was back in England with his daughter and asking about me and wanting to see me again. I have used my will again since then, and discipline."

"But to no avail?" he asked.

"I married you," she said. "I did it for a number of reasons, none of them consciously to do with Crispin. But he was one of the reasons. I wanted to forget once and for all. I wanted to stop loving him — or rather, I wanted to stop fearing that I would love him again. I don't want to. I want the pain to go away. I want to start again. I want to love you. Oh, Duncan, I already do. But I want . . ."

"The magic," he said.

"Yes."

He took one of her hands in his, laced his fingers with hers, and crossed to the other side of the bridge with her. They strolled along the avenue in silence, and it seemed to Duncan that she did not feel the awkwardness she had felt last evening. He felt that together they were allowing the cool quiet of the night, the moonlight and the shadows, to pour into their souls and heal them.

After a few minutes he released her hand and wrapped one arm about her waist. A moment later she wrapped her arm about his. Inevitably, her head came to rest on his shoulder.

Desire for her hummed pleasantly in his veins.

He was at peace, he realized.

"Duncan," she said without raising her head, "I have just realized that I am happier than I have been in years."

"Are you?" he said.

"I am here in this lovely place," she said, "and it is where I belong. And I am with a man I like and admire and with whom I have . . . pleasure. A man with whom I am embarking upon a courtship, a romance."

"There is a summer house at the end of the avenue," he said.

"Yes," she said. "I can see it."

"Be prepared," he told her. "I intend to kiss you silly when we reach it."

She laughed and lifted her head to look into his face, her eyes shining with merriment.

"I would think the less of you if you did not," she said. "But be warned. I intend to give as good as I get."

And he laughed too, throwing his head back, and felt more carefree than he remembered feeling in years.

They released their hold on each other and joined hands, their fingers laced.

He had intended lighting the lamp that he hoped was still kept ready in the summer house as it had always used to be. But there was enough moonlight streaming through the windows on all five sides of the structure that artificial light was unnecessary.

There was a leather sofa there as well as two upholstered chairs and a round table in the center. They sat together in one of the chairs, she on his lap, her arms about his neck, his about her waist.

"This is what every girl dreams of," she said, "being taken somewhere lovely and moonlit and quite private by a handsome gentleman."

"Girls dream such wicked dreams?" he said, rubbing his nose across hers.

"Oh, not wicked," she said. "*Romantic.* Girls dream of kisses to make their hearts beat faster and their toes curl up inside their slippers. They dream of heaven blossoming like a perfect rose in the center of their world."

She laughed softly.

"Do they?" he said, nibbling on her bottom lip.

"Yes." She pressed her lips softly to his. "I

am still a girl at heart, Duncan. And I still dream."

"I am a handsome gentleman, then?" he asked her.

She laughed again, the sound coming from somewhere deep in her throat.

"I think you must be," she said. "Certainly my heart is all aflutter, and my toes are curling up in my slippers. Now there is only that certain heaven to travel to, Duncan."

"May I come too?" he whispered against her lips, and deepened the kiss.

"Mmm," she said on a long sigh.

Duncan was not sure he did not respond with an answering sigh.

They kissed long and deep, murmuring to each other when they came up for air, returning over and over again to the feast. And yet they kissed without any urgent sexual passion. That would come later, when they returned home to their bed. This was not about sex. It was about romance. It was about falling in love.

It was all very strange — and it was all strangely enticing.

Romance more enticing than sex?

He was not even sure he could not smell a perfect rose.

Margaret spent almost the whole of the following morning with Mrs. Dowling. She inspected the china and glassware and silverware and linen and sat poring over the account books and the order books with her. She was taken belowstairs to inspect the kitchen and pantries and storehouses, and stayed to drink a cup of tea and sample some sweet biscuits fresh out of the oven while she discussed menus and meal times with Mrs. Kettering, the cook.

She met a number of the servants and thoroughly enjoyed the morning. She was very aware, as she had never been at Warren Hall, that this was *her* home, that these were *her* servants.

She felt consciously happy. And though she remembered the night with pleasure — they had made love twice, once when they went to bed and once before Duncan got up for an early morning ride — it was last evening she remembered with a warm glow about the heart.

They had kissed each other out in the summer house with a deepening affection and a promise of passion when they went home — but with something that went beyond affection or passion. They had talked between kisses and had even been silent for a longish spell, her head on his shoulder, his fingers playing lightly with her hair. And they had laughed.

Their shared laughter had caused her to slide closer to falling in love with him. She had not heard him laugh often, and almost never with total lightheartedness at some silliness that was probably not really funny at all. And she could not remember laughing herself in quite so carefree a manner for a long time.

There was mutual trust in shared laughter.

She trusted his unexpected commitment to making a love match of their union. He had been open and frank with her. She had to trust him. She *needed* to.

Duncan was busy too. He had taken breakfast with Toby in the nursery, but he was spending the rest of the morning with Mr. Lamb, his steward. They had gone out on horseback just after breakfast, probably to tour the home farm.

Honeymoons were wonderful things, Margaret decided, but it felt equally good to be settling to what would be the routine of daily life whenever they were in the country. And that, she supposed, would be most of the time, at least for the next several years, with Toby so young. And perhaps soon there would be another infant in the nursery.

Oh, she *hoped* so.

Duncan was to spend the afternoon with

Toby. Margaret told herself that she did not mind. He had said from the start that the child must come first with him, and he had arrived here just yesterday. He needed to spend time with his father.

However, just before luncheon, when Margaret was in her dressing room changing her clothes, there was a knock at the door. Ellen opened it.

Toby was standing there, Duncan behind him.

"There you are," the child said to Margaret. "We looked in the big room downstairs, but you were not there. You are to tell me today if you will be my friend."

"Oh," Margaret said, looking briefly up at Duncan and finding that for some reason her knees felt suddenly weak, "I have been busy and have not given the matter a great deal of thought. But I think I might like to be your friend, Toby. Indeed, I am certain I would be. Shall we shake on it?"

She stepped closer to the door and held out a hand for his.

He pumped her hand up and down.

"Good," he said. "We are going out after I have eaten. We are going to play cricket. Papa is going to bowl to me and I am going to hit the ball. You can catch it. If you want to, that is. I'll let you bat some of the time."

"That is kind of you," she said.

"And then," he said, "we are going to the lake, and Papa is going to let me swim if I have been a good boy."

"*Is* there a lake?" She looked at Duncan with raised eyebrows.

"At the foot of the west lawn," he said. "It is out of sight from the house behind the trees."

"Splendid," she said, looking at Toby.

"What shall I call you?" he asked her. "I won't call you Mama."

"That would be absurd anyway," she said, "since I am *not* your mother. Let me see. Papa calls me Maggie. Everyone else in my family calls me Meg. How about Aunt Meg, even though I am not really your aunt either?"

"Aunt Meg," he said. "You had better be ready after luncheon or Papa will go without you. He said so."

"I was talking to *you,* imp," Duncan said. "Off you go now. Mrs. Harris is waiting for you in the nursery. Can you find your own way?"

"I can," the child said, darting off. "Of course I can. I am four years old."

"Going on forty," Duncan said when he was out of earshot. He stepped inside the dressing room — Ellen had already left. "I

449

am sorry about this, Maggie. Playing cricket with a child who has not yet learned to swing his bat on a collision course with the ball is probably not your idea of an enjoyable way to spend a sunny afternoon."

"On the contrary," she said. "I always did find fielding the ball the most dreary part of playing cricket. Now I can claim a different role and teach Toby how to hit a ball. If he will grant me the favor, that is, as his newest friend."

They both laughed — and locked eyes.

"This evening," he said, "will be just for us. And for romance."

"Yes." She reached up and cupped his face with both hands. She kissed him lightly and briefly on the lips.

"I really do not know," he said, "how I could have imagined even for a moment that I would be able to find a bride, marry her in haste, and then settle her somewhere on the outer periphery of my life."

"You have accomplished two out of the three," she said, "and that is not a bad average. However, you must have imagined all that before you met me or got to know me at all well. I do not function at all well when balanced on peripheries."

He laughed and returned her kiss just as briefly.

"If we do not go down and eat immediately," he said, "I daresay Toby will go without us and we will be doomed to an afternoon with nothing to do but entertain each other."

"Oh goodness," she said, "whatever would we find to do?"

She laughed when he merely waggled his eyebrows.

She had done the right thing, she thought as she took his arm. Oh, she had done the right thing in marrying him. That collision in the Tindell ballroom *was* something that had been meant to be.

She was happy already.

They were going to fall in love.

And perhaps their determination to fall meant that they had already fallen — at least a part of the way.

22

Duncan found that his days were busy with varied activities — so different from most of the past five years, when time had often hung heavily on his hands. Now there often seemed to be not enough time.

He set about reacquainting himself with the estate and the home farm after six years of absenteeism. The work took up all his mornings and often cut into his afternoons. He spent as much of those as he could with Toby, for whom he would find a governess or tutor once the summer was over, though he would always give the child a few hours of his company each day. There were also neighbors to receive when they called — and they all did over time. Some came out of genuine cordiality, others probably out of mere curiosity. It did not matter. He received them all with courtesy while Maggie always showed genuine warmth. And she always spoke openly about Toby. Whether anyone was scandalized was unclear, but the Murdochs invited the child to attend the birthday party of their youngest son, and the day after their whole brood of four youngsters came to play.

The calls had to be returned. And Maggie was already promising both him and their neighbors dinners and a garden party and perhaps a Christmas ball when the time came — with an afternoon party for all the children.

In the evenings, after he had told Toby a bedtime story and tucked him into bed and kissed him good night, there was a courtship to pursue. They strolled outside most evenings, their hands joined, their fingers laced. On the one wet day they danced in the gallery — to music they supplied themselves with breathless, not particularly musical voices and a great deal of laughter.

Always they ended up kissing and holding each other with a curiously chaste lack of sexual passion considering what always happened later in their bedchamber. It was amazing that they were not both hollow-eyed and haggard from lack of sleep, in fact.

But the evenings were as intoxicating in their own way as were the nights.

He was falling in love, Duncan realized.

He liked and respected her and enjoyed her company and conversation. His physical hunger for her was insatiable. But somewhere between liking and lust there was — well, he was beginning to trust her and her affection for him and Toby. He was in love with her, though he tried not to verbalize the fact in his mind — and never put it into words. Perhaps he did not trust enough yet. He brought her flowers from the garden every day, and she always pinned one of the roses to her gown.

She was good with Toby. She never pressed her company on him or her attention, but she was ready with both when he asked for them. She was content to be his friend while they all played cricket or dodge-the-ball or hide-and-seek or one of any number of other games. She was prepared to be his audience when he swam in the lake or climbed trees or thrust captured frogs or butterflies close to her face for her inspection before letting them go. She was always ready with admiration and praise when he called to her to witness how high he had climbed or how many strokes he had swum before sinking. She walked him to the Murdochs' house on the edge of the village and waited through the birthday party to bring him home again — because it was one of the days on which Duncan was busy all afternoon. And she was content to dispense comfort and consolation when he bumped or bruised or scraped himself, as he inevitably did at least once a day. He giggled when she kissed better a thumb he had bent awkwardly backward while catching a ball and then went roaring off to play again, the pain forgotten.

Life fell into a busy but pleasant routine. Only one more thing was needed — from him. The final step into full trust. He dreaded taking it, but told himself that he would — soon. Unfortunately, he waited a little too long, but there was no real warning of that fact the evening before it happened. Though *happened* was perhaps the wrong word.

It had been a particularly hot day. It was still warm — one of those nights that never did fully cool off.

She came half running down the stairs to meet him in the hall, just a light shawl about her shoulders.

"Toby is sleeping?" she asked as she came.

"Yes."

And then she stopped abruptly, her eyes on what he held rolled up beneath one arm.

"What is that?" she asked, though the answer was quite obvious.

"Towels," he said. "We are going swimming."

"Swimming?" She looked up into his eyes and laughed.

"Swimming," he repeated. "I went in with Toby this afternoon and a few days ago, leaving you sitting on the bank, looking decorative. And, I noticed this afternoon, wistful."

"I did not," she protested.

"Liar," he said, grinning at her. "You were itching to dive in there with us."

"I was not," she said.

"Can you swim?" he asked her.

"I used to as a girl," she said. "I have not even tried for years. It would be quite indecorous to submerge myself in the lake, Duncan."

He grinned and said nothing.

"But oh, dear," she said, "it would be so much fun."

"*Will* be," he promised, "not would be."

She took his free arm without further argument, and they stepped out of the house and began the longish walk across the west lawn and through the trees to the lake. The sun had already disappeared below the horizon when they got there, but the sky still glowed orange and purple — and so did the water of the lake.

"Oh," she said, "it is all so very beautiful, Duncan. Perhaps we should just sit here on the bank and drink in the loveliness of it all."

"I think," he said, "you are a coward."

"I will ruin my dress," she said.

"Which you will, of course, remove before you jump in," he said.

"My shift, then."

"That too."

"Duncan!" She looked at him, shocked. "I cannot go in —"

"Naked?" he said. "Why not?"

She looked about, as if she expected to see a whole army of interested onlookers march by.

"I see you naked every night," he reminded her.

"But this is different," she said.

He loved her occasional primness. It contrasted so deliciously with her ardor and passion at night.

"I could promise not to look," he said, "until you are submerged to the chin."

She laughed and so did he.

"Perhaps I will not remember how to swim," she said. "Perhaps I will sink like a stone."

He waggled his eyebrows at her.

"Then I will have an opportunity to play

the hero," he said, "and dive in to rescue you."

"Oh, Duncan." She tipped her head to one side. "Our evenings are supposed to be for courtship and romance and falling in love, not for —"

He tipped his head in the same direction as hers.

She sighed and turned her back on him.

"You had better unbutton me," she said as she discarded her shawl. "I suppose it might be fun after all."

He dropped the towels to the grass.

"It will," he promised, setting his lips to the back of her neck after opening the top two buttons of her dress. He slid his hands around to cup her breasts through her shift after opening her dress to the hips. He did not keep them there, though. This was about romance.

He knelt and rolled down her silk stockings and drew them over her feet after she had kicked off her shoes. He grasped the hem of her shift and drew it off over her lifted arms as he stood up again. She drew the pins from her hair.

He kept his drawers on when he swam in the daytime with Toby. Tonight he did not.

She shook her head, and her hair cascaded down her back.

He turned and dived into the water, came up and shook the drops from his face, and reached out his hands for her.

"It is best to jump in boldly," he said, "rather than do it one toe at a time."

"I remember that much," she said. "Stand back."

And she came running and jumped in, feet first, causing a mighty splash. She came up sputtering, her eyes tightly closed, her mouth open on a gasp.

"Oh," she said, clearing her face with her hands and then smoothing them over her hair, "you did not warn me that the water is cold."

"Only for the first moment," he said.

She was standing close to the bank, where the water was only chest deep. He trod water, spreading his hands over its surface and looking at her.

He had never seen her with wet hair. It was dark and sleek over her head. She looked younger, more carefree, though he was seeing her only through a heavy dusk, of course. The light on the water had been fractured by their entry.

"Come," he said, and began to swim away from the bank in a lazy crawl.

He looked back after a while. She was coming after him, her feet splashing up behind her, her head up out of the water, her arm movements awkward. But her strokes became smoother even as he watched, and she dipped her face into the water and turned her head to catch breaths. Her body was dark and sleek amid purple and gold and silver ripples.

He stayed where he was until she drew abreast of him and saw him and raised her head.

"Oh," she said breathlessly. "There are some things one never forgets. If I tried to put my feet down, there would be nothing under them but water, would there?"

He had brought them to the deep end of the lake. There was a shallow end, where they always went with Toby, but it was some distance away.

"You are tired?" he asked.

"Only breathless," she said, and he saw the flash of her teeth in the gathering darkness. "I am out of practice. Oh, this is like being a girl again, Duncan."

"Turn onto your back and float," he suggested.

She did so, spreading her arms across the water, laying back her head and closing her eyes. He moved behind her and under her, slid his arms beneath her to support her, and swam backward with her.

She opened her eyes, tipped back her head to look at him, and smiled. She kicked her feet slightly to propel them along.

The sunset gradually faded, leaving darkness and moonlight and starlight and the lapping of water in their wake and the smell of sap from the trees.

They swam for an hour or more, sometimes together, sometimes side by side. Sometimes they merely floated on their backs, watching the stars, trying to identify them, agreeing finally that stars had no real names anyway, only what had been attached to them by humans.

"Of course," he said, "the same would apply to trees and flowers, would it not?"

"And birds and animals," she said.

"And humans," he said. "Perhaps none of us have real names at all — only what our parents chose for us."

"And a good thing too," she said, "or the only way we would have of attracting one another's attention would be a 'Hey, you.' There would be thousands of *hey, you*s all over the world."

"Millions," he said, "and in many different languages."

"A mite confusing," she said, and they both laughed.

It seemed to be years since he had allowed

himself to indulge in nonsense talk and laughter.

It *was* years.

Finally they left the water and dried themselves off with two of the towels — he had brought three so that they would have something dry to use afterward. They sat on it, her back to him as he toweled off her hair. They had not dressed.

"I thought days like these were long over," she said, hugging her knees. "Swimming in a lake, sitting on its bank in the middle of the evening, laughing . . ."

"You have not laughed since you were a girl?" he asked.

"Oh, I have," she protested. "Of course I have. My life has not been a sad one — far from it. But I have not felt for a long time such . . . Oh, I do not even know the word."

"Joy?" he suggested.

"Carefreeness," she said. "There is no such word, though, is there? And oh, yes, joy. That is the perfect word. A carefree joy."

He tossed the towel aside and combed his fingers through her hair, teasing them through tangles.

"It is an impossible task without a comb," she said, turning to him and then lying back on the towel to gaze at the stars again. "It does not matter. I will brush it out later."

He lay down beside her and took her hand in his. He laced his fingers with hers.

Joy.

Yes, life still had it to offer. And in the most unexpected place of all — in his own home, with his own wife.

He felt quite consciously happy.

He raised himself on one elbow and leaned over her. Her eyes changed focus and looked back into his. She touched the fingers of one hand to his cheek.

He dipped his head and kissed her, and she pressed her lips warmly back against his.

"I want to make love to you," he said.

"What?" Her eyes widened. "Out here?"

"Out here," he said.

She inhaled deeply and exhaled slowly.

"I want it too," she said. "There could be no more romantic setting, could there?"

Though she might find the ground rather harder and more unyielding against her back than the mattress of their bed.

He lifted her over him and she kneeled astride his hips, hugging them with her thighs as his hands roamed over her, and hers over him. They smiled into each other's eyes as he settled his hands over her hips, guided her onto his erection, and brought her down onto it until he was fully embed-ded.

"Mmm," she said.

"I could not have said it better myself," he said, and she braced her hands on his shoulders, lifted herself half off him and proceeded to ride him, rotating her hips at the same time in a slow, almost lazy rhythm that brought a delicious mingling of pleasure and pain until he joined the dance, thrust-ing and withdrawing until they burst to-gether into climax and beyond it into a relaxation that was so total it felt like —

Joy.

They lay side by side for a long time afterward, their hands linked, their fingers laced again.

He almost said it aloud — *I love you, I am in love with you* — but he did not.

One day later it struck him that he had broken the rules of courtship by making love to her when he ought to have been content with kisses and romance until they got home to their bed.

But perhaps that would have made no dif-ference.

Perhaps fate took no notice of such things.

Anyway, perhaps it ought to have been something other than just *I love you.* Some-thing like *I have not been quite frank with you. I have not quite trusted you. Even now I am afraid . . . Ah, just afraid.*

How could one love and not trust? Perhaps he did not love her after all. Except that the possibility brought the ache of tears to the back of his throat.

After another half hour of idle star-gazing and dozing, they got dressed, rolled up the towels, and strolled back to the house, hand in hand.

"What a lovely evening this has been," she said.

"The very best," he said — though all the evenings of their courtship had seemed the best at the time.

"The absolute best," she said. "*Not* that I am trying to have the last word."

"In that case," he said, "I'll have it. It was the very absolute, perfect best."

They both laughed at the silliness as he set one arm about her shoulders and she wrapped one about his waist.

And tomorrow, he thought confidently, would be even better. Perhaps tomorrow he would tell her the full story at last. It was strange how true that old cliché was — the one about molehills developing into mountains if one were not careful. Except that the story he had to tell bore no possible resemblance to a molehill.

He bent his head to kiss her lips, and she kissed him warmly in return.

It was possible to walk among trees about three sides of the park south of the house without ever emerging into open ground except to cross the main driveway.

It was a child's paradise.

On the afternoon after their swim at the lake, they tiptoed through the woods with Toby. They were explorers in the jungle, watching out for all sorts of ferocious, man-eating beasts and fierce, spear-hurling tribesmen.

Half of Margaret's mind was on a scheme she had concocted a few days ago and shared with Duncan the same evening to make a wilderness walk out of part of the woods. It must enhance the beauty of the natural surroundings rather than damage it with too much artificiality, of course. But it would be a lovely place in which to stroll and sit on hot days, a lovely place to bring visitors. It would be her contribution to the beauty of the park, as the flower garden had been Duncan's grandmother's.

The other half of her mind was upon Toby, whose energy and imagination were boundless, and upon Duncan, who was almost unrecognizable as the man with whom she had collided at a ball not so very long ago. Gone was the dark, brooding, almost morose gentleman he had seemed then. He looked relaxed now, cheerful, contented.

Oh, and she was contented too. More than that, she was happy. She loved, and she was allowing herself to be loved in return. Nothing had been spoken in words yet, but words were unnecessary. Or perhaps they *were* necessary. Perhaps an unwillingness to speak them aloud showed that they still did not quite trust each other.

Perhaps soon she would speak the words and trust that he would say them back to her.

Soon.

Perhaps this evening.

Toby was scrambling up a tree to avoid the clutches of a ravenous lion — and Duncan, it seemed, was the lion, his fingers curled into claws as he snarled and roared.

Toby shrieked.

"And you are a friendly tribeswoman, Aunt Meg," he called, orchestrating his own fate, "and come to my rescue with your spear and drive off the lion. You do not kill him, though, because he is only looking for food for his cubs while the lioness stays with them. He is just being himself."

He shrieked again as Duncan lunged with one set of claws, and Margaret looked up at his flushed, excited face, as she had done so many times during the past week, trying to see something of Duncan in him. Sometimes she thought she did, some fleeting recognition when he turned his head at a certain angle or assumed a certain expression. But it was always gone before she could grasp it, and he was again a small and delicate little blond boy with the heart of a warrior and the conscience of his father.

He is just being himself.

She crept forward with exaggerated stealth as Duncan lunged again and Toby shrieked and laughed. And then she tapped Duncan on the back with her imaginary spear and drove him off with a blood-curdling yell when he turned to her in exaggerated surprise and terror.

"Come," she said, reaching up her arms to lift the child down. "You can pet him now. He realizes that you are a cub just like his own except that you are human. He will not harm you."

Duncan snarled and then purred.

Toby giggled.

A few minutes later they were all reclining on the ground, Margaret with her back against a tree trunk, Duncan cross-legged,

Toby on his stomach, his chin propped on his hands, his feet waving in the air.

"Tobe," Duncan said, reaching out a hand to ruffle his hair, "I am getting too old for this. Once the summer is over, we are going to have to find a governess for you."

"Oh," Margaret said, "is he not a little young for that yet? He is only four."

"I am four and a half," Toby said with some indignation. "I'll be five just after Christmas. Will she teach me to read, Papa? Then I can read a story to *you* when I go to bed."

"And put me to sleep?" he said. "Would there be room in your bed for me, do you think?"

"I'll move over," Toby said. "And will she teach me to do sums? I can do two and two. It is four. I can do three and three too, and four and four and right up to ten and ten. Do you want to hear, Aunt Meg?"

"I certainly do," she said. "Is ten and ten twenty-one?"

"Twenty," he said.

"Ah," she said, "silly me."

Four and a half. At first she was simply amused by the preciseness of a child not wanting to appear younger than he was.

Just after Christmas.

The Christmas after Mrs. Turner left her

husband and ran off with Duncan. And that had happened during the Season, just before she herself had arrived in London for the first time with Stephen and her sisters.

Mrs. Turner had been with child when she ran away.

That must mean she had been Duncan's mistress before then.

It was a fact that surely changed everything.

Everything.

He had lied to her.

To make himself look better. To appear the big hero. And she had passed on the lie to her family, and he had repeated it to his mother and grandfather after the wedding.

So that they would all admire him and forgive him and deem him a worthy husband for Margaret.

Or . . .

Oh, dear God, there was an alternative explanation too.

But it was one so horrifying that she dared not contemplate it.

If the first explanation changed everything, then this one . . .

Oh, God. Oh, dear God.

The unwilling thoughts hammered through her brain as she somehow managed to listen to Toby's prattling and even answered him when he spoke directly to her. She smiled at him with wooden lips. She felt as if the blood had drained from her head.

"You look tired," Duncan said after a while.

"I am a little," she said.

He rumpled Toby's hair again.

"We have worn Aunt Meg out," he said. "We will go back to the house and let her rest, and perhaps I can take you for that ride I have been promising you."

"Y-e-e-e-s-s-s!" Toby cried, jumping to his feet. "May I hold the reins, Papa?"

"Probably not," Duncan said. "I will be getting you a pony soon, and then you can learn to ride."

Toby jumped up and down with excitement and then dashed off ahead through the trees.

"Take my arm," Duncan said, offering it. "I must have kept you awake too long last night."

He was grinning at her.

"I do not need assistance, thank you," she said, and was aware of his grin fading even though she was not looking at him.

"What is it?" he asked.

She swallowed.

"Nothing," she said. Coward that she was, she wanted to obliterate the last few minutes, to go back beyond those words of Toby's — *I am four and a half.* What the mind did not know . . .

"You make *nothing* sound like a whole lot of something," he said, his face turned to look closely at her.

She opened her mouth to speak. Closed it again, the words unspoken.

There could be no happy answer to her question once it was asked, could there? Either way, everything would be changed. And if her worst fears were realized, everything *must* change.

Oh, dear God, no, not that. *Please* not that.

"Maggie," he said, his voice soft and even trembling with some emotion, "I need to —"

"Duncan," she began at the same moment. "Tell me the tr —"

But even as they both stopped to allow the other to finish first, Toby was dashing back toward them, yelling as he came.

"Come *on,* Papa," he cried. "I want to go riding."

And he inserted himself between them, took a hand of each, and half trotted along what remained of the path, pulling them along with him and prattling excitedly.

Despicably, Margaret was relieved. She did not want to know. She needed to demand the truth, and she would do it. She *must* do it. But, ah, God forgive her, she *did not want to know.*

For the truth, whatever it was, was going to change things. Was going to lower him in her opinion. Was going to call for some action. Was going to create some conflict. She did not want things to change. She liked everything as it was — and as it was becoming.

She was falling . . .

Oh, never mind.

Why could she not have let Toby's protest about his age pass her by without noticing its significance?

She feared that the courtship might be over.

How could it possibly continue if . . .

Had she really married a liar? And possibly worse than that?

Perhaps the marriage would be over too, for all intents and purposes.

She was going to have to insist upon hearing the truth — at last.

Margaret swallowed panic.

23

She had not missed it, then. If Toby was four and a half years old, if he had been born just after Christmas, then he must have been conceived during the previous spring — before Laura left London.

It was inevitable that she discover the truth sooner or later, of course. It was foolish of him to have delayed, to have waited until his hand was forced, until she was upset and bewildered and had undoubtedly jumped to all sorts of seemingly obvious conclusions.

She was still subdued when he went down to the drawing room after tucking Toby into bed for the night. She had avoided his company until now, and he half expected to find the room empty. Perhaps he had half *hoped* to find it empty. Would he have gone in search of her or put off the confrontation until tomorrow? It did not matter. She was sitting beside the empty fireplace, bent over her embroidery.

She did not look up or stop stitching.

She did not look like a woman waiting for the daily hours of courtship. He knew beyond all doubt that he had not misunderstood this afternoon.

"Were you lovers before you ran away together?" she asked, drawing her needle out of the cloth, trailing green silk behind.

"No," he said. "Maggie —"

"It was his child she was bearing, then," she said. She attempted another stitch, but her hand was shaking. She rested it on the cloth, the needle pointed upward. "Randolph Turner's."

"No," he said. "Maggie —"

She looked up then and her eyes were swimming in tears.

"It has to be one or the other, Duncan," she said. "It cannot be both, but it cannot be neither. It is *one or the other.* Either you were lovers and fled when she discovered she was with child. Or she fled with you, taking her husband's unborn child with her — in which case you have withheld a legitimate child from his father all this time. Which is it, Duncan?"

He stared at her, grim-faced.

"Neither," he said.

She moved her embroidery frame to one

side and stood up. Her hands closed into fists at her sides, and she took one step toward him, her face pale.

"You cannot tell the truth even when you are cornered, can you?" she said. "I try to tell myself that at least there is a noble motive behind your lies — that you love Toby and cannot bear the thought of relinquishing him to his real father. But there is no real excuse. I wish it were the other — that you and she were lovers and ran off together and then concocted the story of violence and abuse to excuse yourselves. It would still be despicable, but God help me, I wish it were that. Which *is* it?"

He had brought this upon himself. He understood that. Even so, he could feel the stirrings of anger in himself. Her face was only inches from his own.

"It is *neither,*" he said curtly.

"I suppose," she said, "she had another lover and *he* would not run off with her. How very noble of you! And the dead cannot defend themselves, can they?"

"Let me explain," he said.

But she was angry herself now and horribly upset — that was quite clear to him. She clapped both hands over her ears in quite un-Maggie-like fashion.

"I am *sick* of your explanations," she said.

476

"I am *sick* of your lies. I will not listen to any more. And I *hate* you for one thing more than all else, Duncan. You brought me here without telling me the truth, and now I have grown to love Toby too. And I too feel the temptation to hide the truth forever so that he can remain part of our *happy* family. I will never forgive you for that."

And, without removing her hands from over her ears except to use one to open the door when she reached it, she hurried out of the room.

God damn it, he thought.

God damn it!

She would not listen to him, and he could hardly blame her. But if *she* would not listen, would the rest of the world? Had he always been right to fear as much as Laura ever had that it would not?

And what would Maggie do now? Keep her mouth shut? Speak out?

Should he *force* her to listen?

They had been falling in love — or so he had thought. They had been learning to trust life again, to trust love again, to trust each other.

But her trust in him had been jolted because he had not been frank with her. And he had only himself to blame for that. He had been afraid to tell her everything, afraid of what she would advise, what she would perhaps try to force upon him, what he knew in his heart he must do.

He sighed deeply and left the room. But rather than follow his wife upstairs, where he assumed she had gone, he headed outdoors and strode in the direction of the stables. He was going for a ride.

For the next week Margaret kept herself busy, learning more about the running of the house, making tentative plans for dinners and parties to which to invite the neighbors, making calls upon the laborers' wives, bearing baked goods with her, exploring the park on foot, often taking Toby with her in the mornings while Duncan was busy, writing letters to family and friends, working on her embroidery.

She did nothing about the new knowledge she had acquired. Actually, it was only *suspicions* that she had acquired, and it was unwise to act upon suspicion alone. Or so she told herself. He had refused to answer her question, but he had wanted to *explain* to her — the eternal plea of the guilty. Perhaps she should have listened anyway.

Oh, *undoubtedly* she ought to have listened. She had asked questions and answered them herself, because it had seemed to her — and still did — that they could be answered in only one of two ways. Neither of them pleasant.

Was there another explanation?

She did not believe it was possible. But surely she ought to listen. She had always prided herself upon being a reasonable being, upon giving everyone the benefit of any doubt there might be of guilt.

But it was incredibly difficult to raise the matter again now that they had quarreled. She procrastinated. Which, she admitted to herself sometimes, was a kind way of saying she had become a coward. It was almost as if she believed that by keeping herself busy and by avoiding any private conversation with Duncan, the world could be kept from exploding into a billion pieces.

He in the meantime had become cold and distant, almost arrogant in manner — except when he was with Toby. He slept in a bedchamber next to the suite they had shared for a week.

There was no more courtship or romance.

Or marital relations.

Margaret's love for Toby, recent though it was, became something of an agony. He was careless, and carefree, in his affection for her much of the time, but sometimes he made her heart ache more than ever. One morning, for example, she was sitting on the riverbank while Toby darted about, playing some solitary game in which he did not need her participation. After a while he came skipping toward her, a posy of daisies and buttercups and clover clutched in one hand.

"For you, Aunt Meg," he said, thrusting them at her and pecking her cheek with puckered lips.

And he went skipping off back to play before she could thank him properly.

There was something else that weighed heavily on her mind. She had been married for almost a month, and she had not had her courses since her wedding. She was three days late. *Only* three days, it was true. But she was usually very regular indeed.

She did not know if she hoped or dreaded that her lateness had some significance.

And then, in the middle of an afternoon eight days after her quarrel with Duncan, Margaret was coming up from the flower garden, her arms laden with flowers that she had cut for the drawing room. Duncan, she could see, was walking up from the stables with Toby, who was holding his hand and prattling on about something. They had been out riding. Margaret turned to go into the house without waiting for them.

She turned, though, when her foot was still on the bottom step, and looked down the driveway. Duncan too had stopped and was doing the same. A horse and horseman were approaching, though the man was still too far distant to identify.

And then more horses appeared behind him — four of them pulling an elegant traveling carriage, which Margaret recognized despite the distance.

It was Elliott's.

Elliott and Vanessa were coming here? And Stephen? She recognized the horseman suddenly.

"Look, Aunt Meg," Toby cried, flying up beside her, his arm pointing. "Some people are coming. Who can they be? Papa says it is no one from near here."

"My brother," she said, smiling. "And my sister and brother-in-law, I believe."

Oh, she *hoped* Nessie was in that carriage. And the children too. She ignored the absurd urge to race down the driveway toward them. She stood clutching her flowers instead and glanced briefly at Duncan when he came to stand beside her.

"It is Stephen," she said, unnecessarily, as he was close enough to recognize. "And Elliott's carriage."

"Stephen," she cried as his horse's hooves

clattered onto the terrace. She set the flowers down on a step and held up her arms to him, smiling and tearing up at the same time.

He dismounted in one fluid motion and wrapped her in his arms. He held her tightly and wordlessly.

"Meg," he murmured as he released her, and they both stepped aside to allow the carriage to come up and stop at the foot of the steps.

And then in no time at all Margaret was hugging her sister joyfully and turning to hug Elliott too.

And only gradually noticing something.

Nobody was smiling. Nobody was talking either except to say her name.

Something was wrong.

Kate! One of the children. The children were not with Nessie and Elliott. They never went anywhere without the children.

Margaret stepped back and looked fearfully from one to the other of them. She could feel the color draining from her face.

"We had to come as fast as we could to warn you," Stephen said, looking from her to Duncan. "Tur —"

"Stephen!" Vanessa said sharply. "The child!"

"Oh," Margaret said, looking down at

Toby, who was clinging to one of Duncan's legs, half hidden behind it. Oh, of course. She had not told them about him. Although Duncan had reluctantly agreed to let their neighbors know who he was, he had not wanted the rest of the world to know — including their families.

"This is Tobias," she said, smiling at him. "Toby. He is . . . He is Duncan's son."

"Hello, Toby," Vanessa said, smiling at him. "I am very pleased to meet you."

Toby stayed half hidden.

"I think," Duncan said, his hand on the child's head, "we had better step into the house. Maggie will take you all up to the drawing room while rooms are being prepared for you. I will join you after I have settled Toby in the nursery."

He looked grim.

They all looked grim.

Margaret gathered up her flowers again and led the way up the steps. She handed them to a footman in the hall and led the way up to the drawing room. And incredibly, when they were there, they all conversed politely for ten minutes, until Duncan came to join them. Margaret asked about the children and Vanessa answered. Margaret asked about the journey and Elliott answered. She asked about Stephen's plans for the summer and he answered.

Just as if they were not all perfectly well aware that disaster loomed. It was not about Kate, Margaret realized, or about any of the children. They would have told her immediately.

She was pouring the tea when Duncan came into the drawing room and the door closed quietly behind him.

Margaret set down the teapot though she still had one more cup to pour. Nobody got up to hand around the cups that had already been poured.

"We came to warn you," Stephen said after a few moments of silence. "Fortunately we three were still in London, though Monty and Kate had already gone back to the country. Word is going around, Sheringford, that you are harboring a child here."

"My son is living with me here, yes," Duncan said, advancing a little farther into the room, though he did not sit down. None of the men were sitting, in fact. Elliott was standing by the sideboard, Stephen by the window. "Maggie knew about him before we married and refused to allow him to be hidden away somewhere."

"I love him," Margaret said, "as if he were my own."

There was a slight buzzing in her ears.

"Oh, Meg," Vanessa said in a rush, "it is being said that Toby is not Duncan's child but Randolph Turner's. And indeed he seems to be the right age, and he does have the look of Mr. Turner."

"Laura was blond and delicate," Duncan said, his voice curiously flat.

"I never knew her," Vanessa said. "But of course you are right. You would not have run off with another man's son. I know you would not, Duncan. But —"

"But Turner himself believes that the child is his," Elliott said, one hand playing with the brandy decanter though he did not pour himself a glass. "So does Mrs. Pennethorne. Norman Pennethorne is beside himself with fury. It is being said that they are all coming here, Sheringford. To take the child away."

"Toby is mine," Duncan said. "No one is taking him anywhere."

"Perhaps he *is* yours, Sheringford," Stephen said. "I would not call you a liar, and I cannot think why you would want to keep the child if indeed he were not yours. Not now that the mother is dead, anyway."

"Oh, Stephen," Vanessa cried, "you know nothing about parental feelings. Just you wait."

"That is all beside the point, Vanessa," Elliott said. "The point is that the child,

485

whoever his father actually is, was born to Turner's wife — within nine months of her elopement with Sheringford. The boy is legally his. No court of law in England would rule against him."

"No one," Duncan said again, "is taking Toby away from this house. I invite anyone to try."

Margaret sat mute, her hands cupped in her lap.

It had happened, then. It was happening. She had no decision to make. It had been taken out of her hands. Toby was going to be taken away from them. As was only right.

She thought for a moment that she was going to faint. Or vomit.

She understood something suddenly — something that perhaps her mind had deliberately blocked during the past week. She understood those elusive flashes of recognition she had felt sometimes when looking at Toby. It had not been a likeness to Duncan she had been seeing, but a likeness to Randolph Turner.

His father.

Her question was answered now. There could be no more doubt.

Toby was a legitimate child. He was the only son — and heir — of a wealthy, prominent member of the *ton.* Who had very possibly never beaten his wife in his life. Who had possibly loved her and been cruelly cuckolded.

Duncan had robbed a man of his son for almost five years.

He had robbed — or tried to rob — Toby of his birthright.

Why he had eloped with Laura Turner she did not know. Perhaps there *had* been some abuse. But it all did not matter now. Toby was Randolph Turner's.

"Excuse me," she said, and she got to her feet, pushing the tea tray back as she did so, and hurried from the room and down the stairs and out of the house. She was halfway along the avenue to the summer house before she slowed her steps. No one was coming after her.

Her family must know that for the moment there was no comfort they could offer.

And Duncan would not come.

She did not want him to come.

She never wanted to see him again.

That child. Oh, that poor child.

Duncan would have wasted considerable time going to the lake, but fortunately he had the presence of mind to ask a groom, who was in the stable yard rubbing down

Merton's horse, if Lady Sheringford had passed that way.

She had not.

Duncan's second guess was the summer house, and he saw as he approached it along the avenue that he was right. She was sitting inside, not watching his approach, though she must have been aware of it.

He had not wanted to come. He wanted to be at the house, his arms tight about Toby. He had asked the three members of Maggie's family to protect him — should all the forces of the law arrive on his doorstep while he was gone, he supposed.

"Of course we will," the duchess had said, tears swimming in her eyes.

"Yes, of course," Merton and Moreland had said, almost in unison.

"Go to Meg," the duchess had added.

He did not even want to be doing this, he thought as he neared the summer house. He had been angry with her all week — and more hurt than he had been willing to admit. He had thought she was coming to love him. Yet she had not trusted him enough even to listen to what he had to say in answer to her questions, which she had answered herself.

Of course, the fault was at least half his. He ought not to have waited so long before telling her something she had every right to know.

He stepped inside the summer house and leaned back against the doorjamb. She did not look up at him.

"It makes me feel sick to be in the same room as you," she said, her voice toneless.

"And it makes me angry to be in the same room as you," he said. "You always have all the questions, Maggie, do you not? And all the answers too. How comfortable for you!"

She looked up at him then, with eyes that were very direct and very hostile.

"You are right," she said. "I might have saved my breath on questions to which the answers were so glaringly obvious."

He folded his arms across his chest.

"I have been very guilty as far as you are concerned," he said, "believing perhaps that my solemn promise to a dead woman was more binding than my duty to my own wife. Or perhaps just procrastinating out of fear of where telling the truth would all lead. Everything I have told you in the past, Maggie, is the truth. Unfortunately, I told you only a part of it, and that was very wrong of me. You had a right to know it all before agreeing to marry me."

"Yes, I did," she said. "I was a fool."

She leaned further back in her chair and

turned her head to look out through the window.

"And so," she said, "Mrs. Turner was an abused wife — if indeed you told the truth. If you also knew when you took her away that she was with child, you did very wrong to take her. If you discovered the truth later, you did very wrong to keep her. And if you really felt her life or her sanity were at risk and kept her away anyway, you did very wrong to allow her to keep the existence of his son from Mr. Turner. And even if you did so to appease her, you were very wrong to keep Toby from his real father after her death."

"Good God, Maggie," he said, angry again. "Toby is not Turner's son."

She turned her cold gaze back on him.

"Liar!" she said. "I have *seen* the likeness. I refused to understand it until I heard what my family had to say this afternoon. But then I did. Toby looks like Mr. Turner."

He laughed, though amusement was the very furthest emotion from his mind.

"You see?" she said. "You cannot deny it when the truth is staring the world in the face. You are going to have to return Toby to his father — and it will damage that child immeasurably. May God have mercy on your soul, Duncan."

"Still," he said, "you have all the answers, Maggie. I lived in a fool's paradise for almost two weeks after our wedding. I thought you were a loving person."

Anger flared in her eyes, her cheeks, her thinned lips.

"I cannot love someone," she said, "who would steal a child from his father and deny him his legitimacy and his birthright. I cannot love someone who has perhaps destroyed that child's life for all time even after he has been taken back where he belongs. He loves you. He thinks you perfect. He does not know you are the devil incarnate. He is just an innocent child."

She was sobbing and not even trying to hide her tears.

He stood against the doorjamb, his arms crossed, his eyes also filling with tears.

Punishment, it seemed, was indeed never ending when one had transgressed society's laws. He had thought there was peace to be had at last. And even happiness. But no, he had not. He had known Pandora's box to be open. He had known this would all happen.

She was swiping at her eyes with the heels of her hands and glaring at him — and then looking closer at him, perhaps seeing his tears.

"Last week," she said, "I refused to listen to you when you wanted to explain. It seemed to me that there *was* no explanation except lies. But perhaps I ought to have listened anyway. Tell me now what you were going to say then. But tell me the truth. All of it. Don't try to cover it up or make it look pretty. I already know the worst. Pardon me, I already believe the worst. Tell me the truth."

"Randolph Turner has a brother," he said.

"Oh, please," she cried sharply. "Don't insult my intelligence, Duncan. Tell me the truth!"

He stared dully at her until she folded her arms.

"I will not say another word," she said. "Tell your story."

"Turner," he said, "has no title, but he is enormously wealthy, probably one of the wealthiest men in England. The family money was made, it is rumored, in the slave trade and has been converted into property and rock-solid investments. Like many men, he wishes to pass on his inheritance to a son of his own. It was his reason for marrying Laura."

She was looking at the hands in her lap. But he believed she was listening to him. He inhaled slowly.

"I think," he said, "it is altogether possible Turner prefers men to women."

She looked up sharply and then down again.

"Or perhaps," he said, "the problem is something else. However it is, he was . . . impotent with Laura. Whenever he tried, for the first year or so of their marriage, he would leave her bed in frustration and not go near her for some time. But after that first year or so, his frustrations were acted out far more violently. He blamed her for his impotence. He started to beat her."

Her hands, he noticed, were clenched tightly in her lap. They were white-knuckled.

"And then," he said, "after a couple of years he got rid of his valet and employed another — a man who looked so much like him that they might have been twins. I know — I saw him once, an insolent fellow with a knowing smile. He was an illegitimate brother of Turner's and caused considerable amusement in the household, though Turner did not display him a great deal to public view."

Maggie's hands had crept up to cover her mouth and she was looking at him with horrified eyes.

"You are not going to tell me," she said, "that Mrs. Turner had an affair with him?"

"It was far more ghastly than that," he said. "The man had been brought to the house to impregnate Laura. I suppose he was being paid a small fortune. It went on for almost six months altogether. Turner supervised — he watched. And he always beat her afterward and called her a slut and accused her of enjoying it. And every time her monthly cycle came to an end and she was not with child, he beat her even more viciously. The man is insane, Maggie."

Her hands covered her mouth and her eyes now.

"And then, finally, she *was* with child," he said, "and hid it for the first month, taking the beating rather than confess the truth. At the end of the second month she came to me — it was the night before my wedding to Caroline. She had confessed to the beatings before then. She did not tell me the rest until that night. I did not doubt for a moment — I had *seen* the fellow. I took her away and hid both her and the child — Toby — after he was born. I hid them until after her death. I would have hidden him and passed him off as the Harrises' orphaned grandson for the rest of his boyhood if you had not insisted otherwise. Though I concurred with you on that. A child cannot be hidden forever. I am Toby's papa, Maggie

— and he is my boy. That is the way it is and the way it will remain. There, you have it now — the whole sordid, nasty truth."

She was rocking back and forth in the chair, her hands still spread over her face.

"Toby," she whispered at last. "Oh, poor Toby. But Stephen was right. Legally he is that man's. He did not divorce her. And even if he had, it would not matter. Toby was conceived while she was still with him. He can come and take Toby anytime he wishes."

"Over my dead body," Duncan said softly.

She lowered her hands and looked up at him. There was no vestige of color in her face. Even her lips were white.

"Duncan," she said, "forgive me. Oh, but how glib such a request is. How *can* you forgive me? I would not even listen to your side of the story. I did not trust you."

"With perfectly good reason," he said. "The fault is mostly mine, Maggie. I would not trust you with the truth, because I had promised Laura that no one would ever know the ugliness that had been her life with Turner. And because I was afraid."

"That I would not love Toby," she said.

"Not that," he said. "I feared you would try to persuade me to bring the whole story into the open. But who would believe it?

495

Who *will* believe it? It will be Turner's word against mine. And she *was* married to him right up to her death. Even if the truth is believed, Toby is still legally his."

She said nothing.

"Maggie —" he said. He rested his head against the doorjamb and closed his eyes.

She was on her feet then and taking his hands in hers and lifting them to her cheeks.

"We are going to have to *think,*" she said. "We are going to have to find a way of saving Toby and keeping him here. Oh, good heavens, of course we must. You are his father, and I am his . . . Well, his Aunt Meg. Aunts can be formidable creatures."

He withdrew his hands from hers, wrapped them about her, and drew her close. He lowered his forehead to her shoulder and surprised and embarrassed himself horribly by weeping.

24

There was a whole day when nothing dreadful happened and it seemed that nothing would.

Surely Randolph Turner would not dare to come, Margaret thought. And yet the stakes were high for him. The son he had wanted and schemed so desperately and fiendishly to get was actually in existence. The child had been born to his legal wife less than nine months after she left him. And it might seem unlikely to him that he would have any other children, unless he used the same method as before.

Margaret knew he would come.

They all knew it.

Duncan had told the whole story to Stephen and Elliott. Margaret had told Vanessa. The time for secrecy, for the keeping of a promise of secrecy, was long gone.

On the second day they took a picnic tea down to a secluded stretch of the river, which was nevertheless within sight of the front of the house. Elliott fished with Toby for a while, and then Stephen galloped about with the child on his back. Duncan swung him in circles until they were both dizzy, and Vanessa told him about her own children, whom she was missing dreadfully.

"Your cousins," she said, ruffling his hair. "They are going to enjoy playing with you."

Margaret fed him a meat pasty before it was officially teatime when he claimed to be starving.

"He is going to be a horribly spoiled child," she commented to Vanessa when Toby had run back to demand more attention from the men.

"Oh, don't, Meg," Vanessa said, patting her on the back. "Loving and paying attention to a child is not spoiling him but just the opposite. All will be well. You will see."

Margaret wiped away her tears, which seemed to flow so easily these days.

"Yes," she said, and smiled. "It will, Nessie." And then, abruptly, "I am several days late."

"Oh, Meg." Vanessa looked sharply at her. "Does Duncan know?"

"No," Margaret said. "There is really nothing to know yet. Nothing at all certain, anyway. Perhaps it is nothing at all."

Her sister continued to pat her back.

Margaret was feeling cautiously cheerful as she and Duncan packed up the picnic basket later and they all prepared to stroll back to the house. Perhaps the alarm had been sounded for no good reason — except that it had brought some of her family on an unexpected visit. They would probably stay for a few more days, and then she and Duncan and Toby would be alone together again and life would return to normal.

Or would it?

Could it?

And was she really feeling cheerful? How could she when her stomach was knotted with dread? *Something* was going to happen.

Toby went skipping and dashing off ahead as he usually did. The men walked together ahead of the ladies, the picnic basket tucked under Stephen's arm.

And then they all became aware of a large traveling carriage approaching up the driveway.

"Toby," Duncan called sharply.

But the child either did not hear him or was too excited to stop to see what his papa wanted of him. He went running off in the direction of the terrace, and Duncan went after him.

They all increased their pace.

Toby reached the terrace before Duncan caught up to him. So did the carriage. The door opened and someone vaulted out without waiting for the steps to be set down. He grabbed Toby, but the child wriggled free and came dashing back to Duncan, who bent briefly to say something to him and then strode onward to meet his visitors.

Toby came dashing back to the others, his feet pumping beneath him, his arms outstretched, sheer terror on his face.

Elliott would have scooped him up, but he dashed past, wailing in panic.

"Mama," he cried. "Mama, Mama."

Margaret bent down, gathered him into her arms, and stood again.

He wrapped his arms about her neck tightly enough to half choke her, and pressed himself to her as if he would have climbed right inside her if he could.

"Mama," he said. "A bad man. A bad man has come to take me away."

He was radiating fear and heat.

"Shh," she said, rocking him. "Shh, love. No one is going to take you anywhere. Papa is here, and so is Mama. No one is going to hurt you."

Pray God she spoke the truth.

"He is a bad man," he said, his chest heaving, his face pressed to her neck.

"But Papa and Uncle Elliott and Uncle Stephen are *good* men," she said. "And Aunt Nessie and I are good ladies. We are not going to let anyone hurt you or take you anywhere."

Oh, dear God, let it be the truth.

His body gradually relaxed against hers and he stopped wailing, though he still clung tightly to her.

Elliott and Stephen had kept going and were on the terrace with Duncan.

It was Norman Pennethorne who had vaulted out of the carriage, Margaret could see now. He was handing down his wife from the carriage, and Randolph Turner was coming behind her.

Strangely, it was almost a relief to see them. This matter needed to be settled, and now perhaps it would be.

She kissed Toby's damp curls before moving onward.

"*There* he is," Caroline Pennethorne cried, pointing toward Margaret as she stepped onto the terrace. "Oh, look at him, Randolph. He is a boy already, and you have been deprived of him all this time. It is criminal. You will surely swing for this, Lord Sheringford, and I will be delighted to come and watch and cheer with the rest of the mob. The kidnapping of a child carries the death penalty, does it not, Norman?"

Toby had tightened his grip again and was moaning, his face pressed to Margaret's neck. His whole body trembled convulsively.

"You will indeed suffer for this, Sheringford," Mr. Pennethorne said. "You —"

"Might I suggest," Duncan said in biting tones, "that we conduct this discussion in civilized fashion in the drawing room, away from the ears of servants — and children?"

Randolph Turner was standing at the foot of the carriage steps, silent and pale, his eyes riveted on Toby.

"We will not set foot inside Woodbine while you are master here, Sheringford," Mr. Pennethorne declared. "Which will not be for much longer, I am delighted to inform you."

"Then we will talk outside," Duncan said. "On the avenue behind the house." He gestured in the direction of the bridge. "Will you be so good as to take Toby up to the nursery, Maggie, and have Mrs. Harris remain with him there?"

Toby wailed and tightened his grip.

"We are not going to allow that child out of our sight," Mr. Pennethorne said, "only to have him spirited away by the time we return for him."

"Then Mrs. Pennethorne must remain and risk sullying her person by stepping inside the house with us," Margaret said, suddenly coldly angry. "I will stay with Toby in the nursery, Duncan. He needs me. I daresay Nessie will too."

She hated to miss what was about to happen. Waiting to hear about it would be a mortal agony. But Toby was not going to be left in the care of servants, even if Mrs. Harris had had the care of him all his life. He was the important one in all this, after all. And he had just called her Mama.

"I am not setting foot inside that house," Mrs. Pennethorne said. "The devil's lair. I am coming with you, Norman. And with Randolph."

There was no further argument.

Margaret climbed the steps to the house, Vanessa beside her, and she carried Toby up to the nursery, where she sat in a deep chair, cradling him on her lap.

Vanessa disappeared for a few moments and returned with a large woolly blanket, which she tucked about Toby even though it was a warm day and his body was still radiating heat.

In no time at all he was fast asleep.

Duncan strode off in the direction of the

bridge and the grassy avenue beyond it. Merton and Moreland were just behind him. He did not look back to see if the others were following. He did not stop until he was far enough down the avenue that they were quite out of earshot from the house or stables.

Norman spoke first.

"You deserve to be horsewhipped, Sheringford," he said. "And it would give me the greatest pleasure to be the one doing the whipping. Unfortunately, you may escape with nothing worse than transportation or a hanging. I did not believe even you capable of such villainy. Caroline has been inconsolable since she learned the truth, and Randolph has been —"

"Norm." Duncan held up one hand. "Before you launch further into your speech, may I ask if Turner has lost his tongue since I last saw him at my aunt's soiree? I would have thought this was *his* speech to deliver."

Turner had not uttered a word since his arrival. But everyone looked at him expectantly now.

He cleared his throat.

"You aided and abetted my wife in keeping my son from me, Sheringford," he said. "And then you continued to keep him from me after her death. I am not as hot-headed as Norman. I am of a more forgiving nature. I have come for my son, and I will take him with me when I leave. I am prepared to leave you to your conscience."

"Randolph!" Norman exclaimed, puffed up with outrage. "You cannot possibly —"

Duncan held up his hand again.

"Yes," he said, "it is what I expected you would be prepared to do, Turner. Is my guess correct? Is Norm the only one in this group who does not know the whole story?"

Turner blanched more if that were possible.

"I know —" Norman began.

"Oh, hold your tongue," Turner said sharply, and Norman was left with his mouth hanging open, unutterable surprise on his face.

"My brothers-in-law know the truth," Duncan said. "My wife knows it. So does my sister-in-law. The other members of our immediate family will know it soon as the time for secrecy is over. The truth can no longer hurt poor Laura. My wife's family are people of some influence, Turner. So are my grandfather and my mother and stepfather. All are people whose word is trusted. And all are people who can keep their own counsel when it is asked of them.

It is up to you now to decide how many other people outside my family circle will know the story surrounding Toby's conception — no one or everyone. It must be one or the other."

Turner attempted to bluster.

"I do not know what you think you know, Sheringford," he said. "I do not know what lies my wife told you — she was not much given to truth-telling, God knows. The child is *mine*."

"He even *looks* like you, Randolph," Caroline said. "When he came running up to the carriage, it was like seeing you as a child again. No one, seeing him, can possibly dispute the fact that he is yours."

"He also," Merton said, his voice perfectly amiable, "resembles your half brother, ma'am. Or so I have been told. I have not met the man in person. Though I will if I ever need to. It would be a pleasure, in fact."

"Gareth?" Caroline said.

"If that is his name, ma'am," Merton said, inclining his head. "I understand he was your brother's valet five years or so ago — a pleasant arrangement for you all, I am sure. You must be fond of him."

"Caroline, my love, what —" Norman began.

"You cannot prove a thing, Sheringford,"

Turner said, his face flushing with color suddenly, his hands opening and closing at his sides, his face contorted with fury. "Of all the filthy things to suggest. Is *that* what she told you? I —"

Duncan raised his eyebrows when he stopped abruptly.

"You will punch me senseless for provoking you, Turner?" he asked. "I doubt it. I would punch back, you see, and might knock *you* senseless. You would not like that, would you? Let us be rational and sensible instead. I have a proposal to make to you."

"Now, see here, Sheringford," Norman said. "You are not in any position —"

"Oh, *do* be quiet," Caroline said.

Norman shut his mouth with a clacking of teeth.

"This is it," Duncan said. "You return to London, be quite open and frank with anyone who will listen — and everyone will — about where you have been and why you came here, and then declare that you were quite mistaken, that you are convinced beyond a shadow of a doubt that Toby is *not* yours, that he was conceived in sin while Laura and I were lovers before we ran away together. You will publicly repudiate him and refuse to accept him as your son or to take any responsibility for him. Then you may carry on with your life in any manner you please."

"This is *preposterous,* Randolph," Norman cried. "He is in no —"

"You would be well advised to button your lips, Pennethorne," Moreland said.

"How can I repudiate my own son?" Turner asked, licking his lips. "He is *mine,* Sheringford. I —"

"You *what,* Turner?" Duncan asked him. "You watched him being conceived?"

Caroline clapped both hands to her mouth.

Norman gaped.

Turner blanched again.

"There will be some snickering behind your back, I do not doubt," Duncan said, "over the fact that I was cuckolding you even before I ran off with Laura. But it will be no more than most people already believe. And you will get off lightly, Turner. The ladies will weep over you. You may even put it about, if you wish, that you blackened both my eyes while you were here. I will not contradict you, and I daresay my brothers-in-law will not either."

Turner continued to stare at him.

"Take it or leave it," Duncan said. "If you leave it, Turner, the entire *ton* will know the whole truth. Doubtless most of them will believe the story even if it comes only from my mouth — people like to believe the worst of others, as you may have noticed. But when other, well-respected voices are joined to mine — the Duke of Moreland's, the Earl of Merton's, Baron Montford's, the Marquess of Claverbrook's, Sir Graham Carling's, not to mention their wives, I doubt you will be able to find a corner of England in which to hide from the scorn and scandal that will be the inevitable result. The law and the church may give you Toby, but your life will be worthless. The choice is yours."

"I *wish* someone would tell me," Norman said, "what this is all about. You do not have a leg to stand on, Sheringford. You are a child kidnapper and a rogue. You have hidden the very existence of a child from his lawful and loving father for almost five years."

Everyone ignored him.

Turner licked his lips again.

"He is my *son*," he said, his voice almost a whisper.

"But he is not, is he?" Duncan said. "Not in any way at all. In all ways that matter he is mine. He even has my name. He was christened Tobias Duncan Pennethorne — my natural son, who will be loved all his life as dearly as if he were as legitimate as my other children will be."

"And whom his new mother and uncles and aunts love dearly and have welcomed into my family too," Merton added.

"Randolph," Norman said, "would you —"

But Turner had turned on his heel and was striding back in the direction of the house.

"Caroline," Norman said, "would you —"

"Oh, be *quiet!*" she cried, turning on him, her eyes flashing. "Cannot you see that he is blackmailing Randolph and that Randolph has no choice but to allow it? You do not believe Laura would have run away from him if the child had really been his, do you? And he is not Lord Sheringford's either — he was besotted with *me* at the time. Oh, I wish in my heart I had never suggested that Randolph bring Gareth to London. I might have *known* he would be too jealous to make the idea work and that Laura would be too squeamish. And I might have *known* that she would run to Lord Sheringford and that he would take her away and abandon me to *you.* Oh, do stop gaping in that ridiculous way, Norman, and come along, or Randolph will leave without us."

And she went hurrying back along the

avenue, all delicate, feminine little steps and flouncing muslin.

For once Norman was speechless. He looked at Duncan, his lips working soundlessly, and then went scurrying off after his wife.

"*Dash* it all," Merton said when he was out of earshot. "Neither one of them gave me enough excuse to break his nose. My knuckles will itch with frustration for a week."

"A woman's way of doing things is never quite satisfactory to a man's way of thinking," Moreland said with a sigh. "I still prefer your original plan of pounding Turner to a bloody pulp, Sheringford, while Stephen and I tossed the dice over who would have the pleasure of breaking Pennethorne's nose. But Margaret's plan really was the better one. Turner has been thoroughly and permanently vanquished, and not a drop of blood shed. *Damnation!* Why could he not at least have taken a swing at you?"

"At one point," Duncan said, "I really thought he was going to. Alas, he remembered his true nature in time. Maggie has made Toby safe, but I *wish* her plan could have included just a small degree of violence. Or, even better, a whole lot of it."

Moreland clapped a hand on his shoulder.

"And talking of Margaret," he said, "I daresay she and Vanessa are having a very bad time of it, waiting to hear what happened out here."

"Yes," Duncan said, closing his eyes briefly.

Was it really all over? As easily as this?

Could he now return to Maggie and to Toby and assure them that their life together as a family was secure at last?

Where were they? In the nursery?

He hurried off in the direction of home without even stopping to thank his brothers-in-law for offering such formidable moral support.

He was running by the time he had crossed the bridge.

The carriage, he could see when he reached the terrace, was already disappearing down the driveway.

He took the steps up to the front doors two at a time.

Margaret had not moved from the chair in the nursery where she sat with Toby. Vanessa was standing at the window looking out, but there was nothing of any significance to see. The nursery was in the west wing with a view over the stables and the west lawn.

Margaret imposed deliberate relaxation on her body so that her anxiety would not convey itself to Toby, even in sleep. But, oh, it was so difficult to wait.

Bullies were usually cowards. Perhaps extreme bullies were extreme cowards. She fervently hoped so. She had based her whole plan on the theory. She had talked Duncan and her brother and brother-in-law into following her plan — Nessie had needed no persuading.

What if she was wrong?

She *hoped* the encounter would not turn violent. Men always found it easier to use their fists than to be rational. Perhaps it was as well that Caroline Pennethorne was with them. Perhaps her presence would force them all into talking rather than using their fists.

Her rational mind told her that Toby was safe, that her suggested plan of action was bound to work. But it was hard to trust cold reason when so much was at stake. Randolph Turner had the legal right to take Toby no matter who his real father was. And he had wanted a son desperately enough to concoct that ghastly scheme. Perhaps he did not care what people thought of him. Perhaps . . .

The nursery door opened quietly. Even

so, Toby stirred. He rubbed an eye with one fist, burrowed closer for a moment, and then turned his head to watch with sleepy eyes as Duncan approached.

It was hard to read his expression.

Vanessa turned from the window.

"Papa," Toby said, "has the bad man gone?"

Duncan's eyes met Margaret's briefly before he bent forward slightly and set a hand on the boy's head.

"He is not really a bad man, Tobe," he said. "Just a rather annoying one. He is a cousin of mine and used to annoy me dreadfully when we were lads. He still does, but he is harmless. Yes, he has gone. I sent him away along with the two people who were with him. They will not be back — they will never be invited. You are perfectly safe here with Papa and Aunt Meg to look after you."

"Not Aunt Meg," Toby said. "She is not my aunt. She is Mama. Where is Uncle Stephen? I want to ride on his shoulders, not just on his back. Do you think he will let me?"

He threw back the blanket and climbed down off Margaret's lap, eager to resume his day.

Margaret swallowed a lump in her throat

514

and looked across the room to see Vanessa smiling at her. She was officially *Mama,* it seemed.

"I suppose," Duncan said, holding out a hand for Toby's, "we can go and ask. But why Uncle Stephen and not Papa?"

"Because he is taller than you are, silly," Toby said, ignoring his hand and dashing for the door.

"Ah, yes, quite so," Duncan said as Margaret got to her feet. "Silly of me to ask."

He turned to Margaret, took one step toward her so that his body collided with hers, and kissed her hard on the lips.

"*Nessie* is here," she said, her face flushing.

He turned his head and grinned at Vanessa.

"Turner chooses reputation over the acquisition of a son and heir," he said.

"I *knew* he would," Margaret cried. "And once he has publicly repudiated Toby and declared him to be your son, he cannot change his mind. Not that he ever would. He knows that Stephen and Elliott know and that soon Jasper and your grandfather will know. He knows that none of them would scruple to tell the truth if he should prove troublesome."

"If only," he said, "Turner were one

smidgen less of a coward than he is. He actually flexed his fists and looked belligerent for all of two seconds. I *willed* him to throw a punch. Alas, he did not."

"I daresay Elliott and Stephen were disappointed too," Vanessa said. "And I must confess that even I am — a little."

"You could not have fought," Margaret said, "with Caroline Turner there."

"Oh, Maggie," he said, "it was all her idea."

"*What* was?" she asked.

"Using the half brother to get Turner his heir," he said. "It was *her* idea."

She wrapped her arms about his waist regardless of the presence of her sister in the room.

"We might have guessed it," Vanessa said. "It is too clever and fiendish a scheme for a man to have dreamed up. I shall go and tell Elliott so merely for the pleasure of listening to his retort."

She whisked herself out of the room, laughing.

"And to think that you might have married that woman," Margaret said.

Duncan grinned. "Never in a million years," he said. "I was always quite safe from her, Maggie. Fate was saving me for a certain flying missile in a certain doorway in a certain ballroom."

She kissed him on the lips.

"We had better go down," she said, "and rescue my poor brother."

But when they arrived at the head of the staircase, they could hear sounds of commotion coming from the hall below. Margaret's stomach turned over. Duncan released her arm and went charging downward ahead of her.

Had they returned?

Were they going to try to take Toby after all?

She came to an abrupt halt when she was still a few stairs above the hall. Duncan was down there already. So were Vanessa and Elliott and Stephen — with Toby astride his shoulders.

And so were Sir Graham and Lady Carling and the Marquess of Claverbrook.

"Duncan, my love," Lady Carling was saying, "whatever has been happening? Is *this* the child? He is perfectly adorable. Oh, just look at those curls, Graham! You utterly provoking man, Duncan, to have said nothing about him to your own mother. Graham has said that *of course* you said nothing under the circumstances, but that is nonsense. I am his *grandmother*. There is the most dreadful gossip making the rounds in London, though, and Randolph Turner must have listened to it and even believed it, or he would not have come here to see for himself. And he *did* come. We passed his carriage just the other side of the village, but he would not stop it when I waved to him or even look at us. Though he could not possibly have missed seeing us. How could he? He had other people with him too. I daresay it was Caroline and Norman, but they would not look at us either, and really they were quite pointed about it, were they not, Graham? They were not on their way to fetch a magistrate, were they? Oh, do tell me all, Duncan. No one ever tells me anything. It is most provoking."

And she burst into tears.

Margaret hurried downward, but Sir Graham had already taken his wife in his arms, looking pained.

"If you would just let Sheringford *talk,* Ethel," he suggested, "perhaps you would be put out of your suspense a little sooner."

Toby, Margaret could see, was clutching fistfuls of Stephen's hair and was trying to duck down behind his head. His eyes were frightened again.

"They were going back to London, I assume, Mama," Duncan said, "or to the devil for all I care. Meet Toby — Tobias Duncan

Pennethorne, my son and Maggie's. I will tell you the whole story later, after you have rested and had some refreshments."

"Grandpapa," Margaret said to the marquess, "let me take your arm."

He was leaning heavily on his cane. He was looking fierce, but his complexion was gray-tinged with fatigue.

"Hmmph," he said, and he looked at Toby with a ferocious frown.

Toby was making small wailing sounds, and Stephen's hands had gone up to hold him protectively by the waist.

The Marquess of Claverbook was feeling about in the pocket of his coat with his free hand.

"What the deuce is this poking into my ribs and rubbing them raw?" he asked of no one in particular.

Toby's eyes were riveted upon him.

He pulled something out of the pocket and held it up between his thumb and forefinger.

"A shilling," he said. "Deuced uncomfortable thing. Here, boy, you had better take it from me. Spend it wisely on some sweets."

And he took a few steps closer and held it up to Toby, who hesitated for only a moment before releasing his hold on one clump of Stephen's hair and closing his hand about the coin.

"Tobe?" Duncan said softly.

"Thank you, sir," Toby said. "Can I buy sweets, Papa?"

"Tomorrow," Duncan said.

Margaret took the old gentleman's arm and turned him in the direction of the stairs.

"Come up to the drawing room," she said, including Sir Graham and Lady Carling in her invitation. "You will be ready for a drink before going to your rooms to change for dinner. Oh, how *very* pleased I am that you came. I do hope you will stay for a good long while."

"Hmmph," the marquess said.

"I would give my kingdom for a cup of tea," Lady Carling said. "Not that I have a kingdom to give, of course, but I am parched. Oh, Margaret, do let the child come to the drawing room too. I do not care what Graham says about how inappropriate my raptures over him are. I am quite determined to know him and to love him and spoil him quite atrociously."

"In all fairness, Ethel," Sir Graham said, "you must admit that I have not said a great deal on the subject yet. I have not been given the opportunity."

Margaret glanced at Duncan, and they smiled at each other.

"How many sweets will I be able to buy, Uncle Elliott?" Toby was asking.

"Enough," he said, "to tempt your mama and your nurse to insist that they be kept on a very high shelf and doled out in small amounts over the next month or two. And we all know that *that* is no way to enjoy sweets. If I were you, I would hide them away in a secret hiding place before they can get their hands on them, and pick away at them whenever you please."

"Oh, Elliott!" Vanessa protested. "Meg will be forbidding us the house."

Toby was shrieking with helpless giggles. His terror was forgotten, though it would, Margaret supposed, reappear in his nightmares for some time to come. They would deal with it, she and Duncan. Just as they would deal with the fact that he would forever be illegitimate and different from any brothers and sisters he might have.

And eventually he would learn to deal with life himself.

Life was never perfect.

Only love was.

25

Some days were so uneventful that a week later one could not recall a single thing that had happened. Other days were crammed so full of events that it was impossible to believe that so much living could be packed into twenty-four hours.

Today, Duncan reflected at the end of it, had been the latter sort of day.

He was feeling drained, both physically and emotionally, by the time everyone had retired for the night. So was Maggie. She had looked quite exhausted all evening, in fact. Both her sister and his mother had tried — without success — to persuade her to have an early night.

And even now, when it was close to midnight, she was not in bed. Neither was he. In fact, they were not even inside their home. They were seated on the riverbank, where they had picnicked earlier before all the excitement and activity began.

They sat with their backs to a thick tree trunk. The water rippled darkly past them and lapped against the bank. The leaves overhead rustled in the cool breeze, which was welcome after the heat of the day. A night owl hooted some distance away.

Duncan felt relaxation seep into his bones. At the moment it meant as much as sleep.

Toby was safe. They were all safe. His family and Maggie's knew the whole truth, and incredibly none of them were scandalized at the presence of the child in his nursery — even though Tobe was not in reality his son at all but the product of incredible ugliness. Duncan's mother was quite determined, despite those facts, that she would be his grandmama. And his grandfather had somehow managed to fish a shilling out of his coat pocket.

Duncan had felt embarrassingly close to tears when that had happened.

"I wish," Maggie said, reaching for his hand in the darkness of the night and clasping it in hers, "you did not have to appear the villain in all this yet again, Duncan. I wish everyone did not have to believe that you and Mrs. Turner were lovers even before you ran away together."

"But it must be what people have always believed," he said. "Why would we have eloped if we were *not* lovers, after all? Nothing has changed. And it is very old news. The recent discovery that there was a child of our illicit union has doubtless titillated a few fancies, especially when it seemed he might have been Turner's. But Turner's repudiation of him will soon put an end to that speculation. All will be forgotten again soon enough."

"I just wish," she said, "you might have been vindicated in the end. I wish people might know the truth."

"About Toby?" he asked, turning his head to look at her.

She was silent for a while.

"About you," she said. "But one could not be known without the other, could it?"

"Life is not perfect," he said. "It is one thing one learns in thirty years of living, Maggie."

He watched her smile.

"No," she said. "Life is *not* perfect. Will you shield Toby from the truth all his life, Duncan?"

He sighed.

"No," he said. "He would surely find out. Too many people know the truth, after all, and someone would be sure to think it a fine thing to tell him. I will let him know about his birth when he is old enough to deal with the knowledge, and when he is secure enough in my love and yours not to have his sense of self destroyed by it. We can love him and love him, Maggie, but only he can live his life. Just as only we can live ours."

"There is no happily-ever-after, is there?" she said.

"Would you want there to be?" he asked her. "Would not life be horribly dull? I would rather aim for happiness."

"Happiness?" she asked, turning her face to look back at him. "When everyone will think the worst of you?"

"Oh, not everyone," he protested. "All those who are nearest and dearest to me know why I did what I did — both five years ago and this year after Laura died. Sacrifices must sometimes be made, Maggie. And sometimes they bring with them blessings that far outweigh the suffering they caused. If I had not run off with Laura and scandalized the *ton,* I would not have known and loved Toby. And I would not have met you. Or if I had, it would have been too late — I would have been married to Caroline."

"Would that have been so dreadful?" she asked him, her voice soft and surely wistful. "Not meeting me, I mean?"

"Yes," he said. "It would have been the

most dreadful thing of all. I would have missed the whole point of my life. I would have missed the reason for my existence. I would have missed the love of my life. I might have known what it is to love, for there are people in my life whom I *do* love and always will. But I would never have been *in* love. There would never have been that magic — or that missing part of myself to make me whole."

"Oh," she said.

"Just *oh?*" He lifted one hand to set the backs of his fingers lightly against her cheek.

"You *love* me?" she asked him. "Truly love *me?* Love betrayed me once, Duncan, and then life and youth passed me by. I have wanted so desperately to gather the dregs of life and love to myself so that I could give contentment to someone else and draw contentment to myself. Have I found love instead? A love that makes the other one pale in comparison?"

"I cannot answer that," he said, feathering his lips across hers and discovering that her face was wet with tears. "*Have* you?"

"I tell myself," she said, "that I love you because I admire the courage with which you have lived your life. And I tell myself I love you because you love a poor helpless child totally and unconditionally. And I *do* love you for those things. But Duncan, I love you most because you live *here.*" She patted one hand over her heart. "Because I know I was meant all my life to meet you and discover the joy for which I was created."

"Ah," he said.

"Just *ah?*" She attempted a soft laugh and hiccupped instead.

He kissed her, and when she pressed her lips back against his, he wrapped her in his arms and deepened the kiss as he turned her to lay her down on the grass beside the tree.

They made love at half past midnight on ground that was none too soft surrounded by air that was none too warm — and when they were both almost light-headed with exhaustion.

Life was not perfect.

Except when it was.

"Duncan," she said when they were finished and she lay cradled in his arms while moonlight danced in patterns of light and shade over them as the branches of the tree swayed in the breeze. "I must tell you something, though I did not mean to do so until I could be more sure. It is not a day for secrets, though, is it? Or am I talking about yesterday? Today is not for secrets either. There is a chance — the merest chance — that I am with child."

He pressed his face to her hair and inhaled slowly. Already? He had been a father for four and a half years, but was he now to be — a *father?*

"I am only a few days late," she said softly. "Perhaps it is nothing."

"I promised my grandfather when I was twenty," he said, "that I would be married by the time I was thirty and would have a child in the nursery by the time I was thirty-one. A son and heir. Is it to happen after all? Or could this be a daughter? Oh, good Lord, Maggie, a daughter! Could life offer a greater miracle?"

"I cannot even be sure yet," she said, "that there will be a child at all, Duncan. But perhaps there will. A son or a daughter. Oh, perhaps it is true. I am never late."

He drew her more snugly into his arms. He breathed in the warm woman's scent of her and closed his eyes.

"No matter," he said. "We will have an excuse to try even harder if this is a false hope. I love you and you love me and we are married and living at Woodbine, and we have our families and Toby. All that is quite happiness enough for now, Maggie. We will hope there is a child but not be too disappointed if there is not. Agreed?"

"Life is not perfect," she said, and laughed softly.

"It feels pretty close at the moment," he said.

"Except," she said, "that I have a tree root or something digging into my hip and my feet are like blocks of ice."

They walked homeward with their arms about each other's waists.

"Are you as tired as I am?" he asked.

"At least twice as tired," she said. "Shall we persuade your grandfather to stay with us for a good long while? Perhaps even to make his home with us if he wishes? And shall we invite some of our neighbors to dine before Nessie and Elliott leave? Shall we —"

He bent his head to kiss her as they stepped onto the terrace before the house.

"We certainly shall, my love," he said. "But tomorrow. Or later today. Much later. Shall we go to bed now? And sleep?"

"Sleep?" she said. "Oh, that does sound wonderful, Duncan. I could sleep for a week — but only if your arms are about me."

"Where else would they be?" he asked her, his one arm closing more tightly about her waist as he led her up the steps to the house.

"Nowhere, I suppose," she said.

"Precisely."

She yawned and tipped her head sideways to rest on his shoulder.

Being in love, he thought, was the most wonderful thing.

The best thing in the world, in fact.

ABOUT THE AUTHOR

Mary Balogh is the *New York Times* best-selling author of the acclaimed Slightly novels: *Slightly Married, Slightly Wicked, Slightly Scandalous, Slightly Tempted, Slightly Sinful,* and *Slightly Dangerous,* as well as the romances *No Man's Mistress, More Than a Mistress,* and *One Night for Love.* She is also the author of *Simply Perfect, Simply Magic, Simply Love,* and *Simply Unforgettable,* a dazzling quartet of novels set at Miss Martin's School for Girls. A former teacher herself, she grew up in Wales and now lives in Canada.

Visit our website at www.bantamdell.com.

Cecil County Public Library
Rising Sun Branch Library
410-658-4025
http://www.cecil.ebranch.info

User name: Epps, Martha E

Title: Rose Harbor in Bloom :
Rose Harbor inn series : B
Author: Macomber, Debbie.
Item ID: 31885007652131
Date due: 1/5/2018,23:59

Title: 92 Pacific Boulevard
Author: Macomber, Debbie.
Item ID: 31885005855322
Date due: 1/5/2018,23:59

Title: Reflections of yesterday
[large print]
Author: Macomber, Debbie.
Item ID: 31885007774505
Date due: 1/5/2018,23:59

Title: At last comes love
Author: Balogh, Mary.
Item ID: 31885005768764
Date due: 1/5/2018,23:59